Praise for Vanessa Fewings

"Vanessa Fewings has created an intriguingly sexy and masterful beginning to the ICON series!"
—*New York Times* bestselling author Lisa Renee Jones

"Sultry, heart-pounding romance and a thrilling mystery make this gem by Vanessa Fewings one to chase, grab, and own! You will be clamoring for more!"
—Katy Evans, *New York Times* and *USA TODAY* bestselling author

"A sexy, intriguing romance that will keep you guessing. I can't wait to see what Vanessa has next for us."
—Louise Bay, *USA TODAY* bestselling author

Continue The ICON Trilogy with

THE PRIZE,

coming soon from
Vanessa Fewings
and HQN Books.

The
GAME

VANESSA
FEWINGS

ISBN-13: 978-0-373-80412-2

The Game

Recycling programs
for this product may
not exist in your area.

Printed in U.S.A.

To all creators of art past and present, both professional and personal. This story is for you.

1

This way through The Wilder Museum promised to lead to one of the most significant paintings of French Impressionism, a masterpiece renowned for igniting a sensation in the late nineteenth century for its stunning realism. A work also famed for altering your experience of art irrevocably.

My stilettos carried me across the white marble floor of one of Los Angeles's most distinguished museums, and my heart beat faster as I made my way toward the room showcasing Jean-Jacques Henner's 1879 *Madame Paul Duchesne-Fournet*.

More than this, these sprawling hallways would lead me back to *him*.

Tobias William Wilder, the owner of this grand palace of art, and the reason I'd traveled all the way from London.

I'd flown in to LAX just this morning, arriving on this balmy Monday with my heart heavy with what lay ahead. By the time I'd checked into my hotel in Beverly Hills, I'd rallied my courage to see him again.

Amongst Wilder's many talents, which included running a billion-dollar tech empire and taking the world by storm with his inventions, he was also Icon—history's most notorious art thief. It was this secret that was destroying me.

All I believed about us is a lie.

I hurried onward refocusing on the reason I was here.

I'd worn a deep blue laced dress, the color calming, and the detail of the scalloped lace hemline pretty and nonthreatening. The style made me feel feminine but strong; with the strappy high heels, my height would at least be closer to his. Tucking my Dooney and Bourke pouchette purse behind me, I took a moment to center myself, prepare for what lay ahead.

Taking in a deep, steadying breath, I raised my gaze skyward to the architectural wonder of the multicolored glass ceiling showering shards of radiant light upon me. A vivid display bridging the old world with the new, the complex prisms were quite simply beautiful and provided a rare glimpse into Tobias's nature.

The first curator to greet me had advised that the route I was now taking was the best way to approach the gallery's most treasured piece, generously on loan from the Los Angeles County Museum of Art. The one portrait everyone came to pay homage to.

Along with the imminent visceral experience from viewing such a masterpiece, this moment was filled with a ribbon of emotions unfolding with the complexity they deserved, from seeing the man who I'd thought of as my one true love to the strain of having to persuade Tobias to surrender to Interpol. Or, if it was easier, he could come with me to the police. I'd do everything in my power to make his arrest a little kinder on him.

Tobias had single-handedly shaken the art community to its core by stealing some of its most precious portraits, and all this without leaving a trace.

Right up until that raven had dive-bombed his heist back

in France, leaving a few feathers to mark its uninvited descent into a priceless rotunda in Amboise. Such a chaotic misadventure proved nothing fazed him. Tobias had gotten away with a self-portrait by Titian, no less.

In his own indomitable style he had also incapacitated my world when he'd swept me up into a rapturous love affair that had left me questioning my integrity. I had to know if I'd been merely a means to an end because as a forensic art investigator, I'd seemingly been a pawn to move and manipulate and provide him with insider glimpses into his case. If it were not for me, our private investigation would have otherwise remained secured away on Huntly Pierre's database—the company I worked for and the firm that had tasked me with tracking him down.

I wallowed in guilt that so far I'd done nothing.

Until today.

I'd needed time to analyze the evidence to prove Wilder was our man. Such an accusation could devastate a reputation. There was no room for error or even doubt. It was impossible to deny the raw truth I'd personally witnessed at his home in Oxfordshire, having stood right there in that cold vault and viewed those stolen paintings. My uncanny ability to spot a fake had proven a curse as I'd known I was viewing an authentic Rembrandt, and a Monet. Along with the others I'd viewed, it had added up to irrefutable evidence.

I'd left his home with nothing to corroborate my story. Accusing one of Huntly Pierre's most exclusive clients would see my thin thread of credibility gone, along with my dream job. My future hinged on doing the right thing.

And doing it well.

Yes, Tobias had stolen those paintings to return them to their rightful owners. Having tracked their provenance, I knew these privately owned collections had been robbed before by some faceless thieves for personal profit.

Still, sooner than later Tobias was going to get caught. This beautiful, brilliant man who had shown me how to love deserved so much more than the consequences of his heroic misadventures.

During our last agonizing phone call, a few weeks ago while I was still in London, I'd begged him to give up this life and in typical Tobias fashion he'd teased me with how to find him, giving a clue that only an art lover like me could decipher.

He'd described how alike I was to Madame Duchesne-Fournet, though he'd not spoken her name then. He'd merely mentioned that upon unveiling the painting in the late eighteenth century, she'd brought Paris to a standstill. He'd compared what Madame Duchesne-Fournet had done to France to what I'd done to him.

Brought Tobias to his knees.

How much I wanted to believe he loved me. I needed to know what we'd had was real.

There was no place for weakness.

No time for delusion.

In any other circumstance I would have refused to rush along, simply couldn't imagine not paying any attention to the other paintings like the last frame, *La Promenade*, by Pierre-Auguste Renoir. Glimpsing back at the painting, I felt a wave of melancholy at that 1870 oil on canvas conveying a dashing gentleman with his hand held out to assist his lover up the grassy bank, the flirtatious turn of her head hinting this was a new and thrilling love.

I wanted to go back in time and warn her away from him.

Hurrying onward, I flew around the corner and arrived in the vast showroom displaying a series of masterpieces.

My heels echoed on white marble as they carried me to the center of the large space where I would find her, realizing that part of her allure was Tobias's teasing description of her influence.

Turning, I faced the long stretch of opulent tile stretching beyond and raised my gaze to look at her—the acclaimed Madame Paul Duchesne-Fournet.

Gasping in awe when I saw her…

Madame Duchesne-Fournet was more wondrous than I'd ever imagined, her extraordinary presence emanating out of the frame and leaving me spellbound.

The way her long golden frame hung low on the wall made her appear to be standing right at the end of the gallery.

Waiting for me.

Taking in her natural beauty, those elegant angles of her face, a striking porcelain complexion and pronounced jawline, her refined nose. Most stunning of all was her chestnut gaze that revealed a sharp intelligence and sparked a sense of consciousness. The grandness of her full black gown and plush jacket reflected her status as the wife of a prominent French politician.

As I closed the gap between us, it took all my will not to trace my fingertips along the exquisite canvas—the austere background enhancing her outline and creating realism, her appearance accentuated by the remarkable contrast expertly melding her profile. This was the unmistakable technique of "sfumato," one of the four canonical painting modes often used in Renaissance art. Painting in this mode was a rare skill mastered by Henner and proved his talent at layering colors and tones and shading them into one another to provide boldness and, when needed, a subtlety of form.

A sigh of respect left my lips.

What message had Tobias been trying to tell me by inviting me here to see her? Perhaps he'd wanted me to know he truly understood me and that this painting would somehow endear me to him more because of our mutual admiration for art. Perhaps he wanted me to know our connection was as deep as I believed it to be.

A living, breathing masterpiece.

Reluctantly, I drew my gaze away and glanced at my watch.

I was right on time for my appointment with Mr. Wilder. Three days ago I'd reached out to Maria Perez, his senior curator, and informed her I'd be paying their gallery a visit.

I'd texted Tobias and warned him he better meet me here or there would be consequences. As expected, he'd ghosted me, refusing to reply. Considering this was the phone he'd gifted me and it now served as a tracking device to my whereabouts, I was sure he'd gotten the message.

He was wise enough to turn up.

Back in the lobby, I made polite conversation with the receptionist to prove my credentials and confirm my meeting.

The tall, young steward left her station behind the round desk and guided me briskly along, escorting me back through the foyer and a long hallway to the sprawling office space of the gallery.

We continued all the way down until we paused before a door with his name and title carved into the opaque glass.

She gestured for me to go ahead and with a nod of gratitude I turned the handle and stepped inside—

He wasn't here *yet*.

Shame swept over me that I'd allowed my life to come to this, become so enamored that merely standing here I questioned my moral code. This office, this gallery, represented Tobias, and I hated him because I loved everything about it.

How elegant and modern with that expensive central desk upon which sat the thin computer screen and a sleek keyboard beside it. The shelving behind was stacked neatly with books on art and others on travel; the one on American history had tipped on its side.

His presence lingered like a dark dream that had once owned my soul.

A rush of panic—

No.

Please, no.

There, adorning the far left wall was a familiar painting; a ghost from my past.

All air was gone from the room until nothing remained as I struggled to draw back on my dread, wrapping my arms around myself to hold off this stark chill soaking into my bones.

Lips trembling, I neared the portrait of *St. Joan of Arc.*

My *Joan.*

I reached up, grasping either side of her wooden frame and lifted her off the wire.

I'd grown up with Walter William Ouless's *St. Joan* and couldn't remember a time when her portrait hadn't been part of my father's collection. It broke my heart when I remembered his devastation when he thought she'd been destroyed in that house fire, along with most of the others.

This very portrait had turned up at Christie's auction house weeks ago in London, alighting a family scandal because she wasn't meant to exist anymore.

More recently, *St. Joan*'s disappearance from Christie's had seen her included in the list of art crimes tracked by the police across Europe. And yet here she was placed to taunt me.

Her message clear—

My future in the art world was in *his* hands.

I hugged *St. Joan*, clutching her tight to my chest, sucking in deep breaths of despair that she was no longer mine.

Unless...

To think of rescuing her and walking right through that foyer and out the front door was ridiculous. I'd never get away with it.

No.

Madness.

My life was carved into two parts, before Wilder and after him, with each careful step leading me toward this complex, enigmatic man with the lines of right and wrong blurring. If I truly wanted to succeed, truly wanted to save him after risking so much, I'd have no choice but to push myself beyond anything I'd done before.

Ironically, it was Tobias who'd shown me how to challenge myself and learn how to resist fear.

He's shown me the way.

2

Rising up and dispelling this temporary moment of stupidity, I saw a stocky security guard standing just inside the door and staring me down.

"Miss," he said, louder than needed. "Place the painting on the desk, please."

My breath stuttered. "I was just taking a closer look."

"Desk, please." His fingers clenched around his handgun.

With trembling hands I stepped forward and laid *St. Joan* faceup on the desk. Stepping back, I raised my hands in the air a little. "It's not what it looks like."

Yet it is.

Had there not been cameras, or guards, or any other state-of-the-art security, I'd have taken her away with me without looking back. From that guard's expression he knew it too. With a wave of his hand he warned me to move farther away.

My back met the wall and I froze.

An ice-cold slither of fear spiraling down my spine.

The door opened farther and in stepped a delicate-framed Latino woman, forty or so, those laughter lines now taut with worry. "Ms. Leighton?" Her tone was infused with tension. "I'm Maria Perez."

"We spoke on the phone?" I said.

The awkwardness forced a shameful silence.

She saw the painting and looked horrified.

"I'm so happy to meet you." It sounded silly now, my politeness negated by my suspicious behavior.

"Take a seat," said the guard. "LAPD are on their way."

My feet refused to move. "Who?"

"We've called the police." Maria's gaze rose to the small camera set in the upper right-hand corner.

Its lens trained on me.

Panic-stricken, I stared down at *St. Joan* wondering if Tobias had set a trap. He'd known how beaten up I was about finding her again. He'd witnessed firsthand how incapacitated I'd been when she'd turned up at Christie's. He'd been the one who had embraced me when my knees had buckled with the strain of realizing she'd not been destroyed.

Vulnerable, ice sliding down my spine.

Then he appeared like a suave apparition—

Tobias Wilder entered briskly and paused just inside the door, his expression unreadable. A flash of power in his dark green gaze as he glanced at his desk.

His glare rising to find me.

Igniting a tremble within as I exhaled a slow, nervous breath. *God*, I'd almost forgotten how gorgeous he was, how regal and breathtakingly dashing, the way his dark blond hair framed that handsome face, high cheekbones and that strong jawline. The way he moved demurely and yet with a masculine edge that emanated power. I'd swooned too many times at the way he liked to casually tuck his hands into his trouser pockets like he was doing now in that expensive bespoke suit, no tie, and his collar open to add an arrogant flair.

Few people would know that beneath all that formality his left upper arm was inked seductively with an Aborigine symbol and lower on his well-toned body, along the curve of his groin, were inscribed words in Latin. Both in a suit and out of one he'd once rocked my world. An annoying inconvenience remedied by remembering who I was dealing with—

Icon.

And that curve of his lips proved he was garnering pleasure from my reaction to seeing him again.

I've fallen into his trap.

Of course, I'd underestimated his brilliance, his foresight, his boldness to break all the rules and let the dust fall where it may.

My stare swept from him to Maria, and then sharply to the guard's hand twitching on the gun.

"It's all a big misunderstanding," I pleaded with Tobias. "Can you tell them…*she's mine?*"

"Mr. Byron," Tobias said darkly. "What do we have here?"

The guard pointed to *St. Joan.* "Sir, she tried to steal that one."

Tobias's frown deepened. "I see."

Drowning in the consequences of my actions, my mind swirling—that gun freaking me out.

Tobias stood there quietly, merely emanating his usual charisma.

I stepped forward. "Mr. Wilder, it's wonderful to see you again."

"Likewise, Ms. Leighton," he said with a twinkle of mischief.

My tone turned serious. "Your security is top-notch. After a brief sweep of your gallery I've confirmed your cameras are well positioned—" I pointed to the guard "—your staff are alert and responsive, and your mechanisms are well concealed."

Tobias looked amused.

My heart pounded against my rib cage as I steadied my nerves. "Mr. Wilder?" I arched a persuasive brow.

He walked toward the desk and reached for *St. Joan* and lifted her with ease. He carried the painting across the room and returned her to the wall.

Scraping my teeth across my bottom lip, I willed him to be fair at least, to see reason, to remember we'd shared a passionate love affair. We'd been a couple; *once.*

Seeing him again was destroying me.

When he turned to face me it was with a deliberate authority and I cursed his waft of heady cologne seeping into my senses.

"Mr. Wilder?" Maria asked for confirmation.

He gave a nod. "Maria, may I introduce Ms. Zara Leighton, art investigator extraordinaire." He turned to the guard. "Well done, Anton, keep up the good work."

The guard looked relieved. "So this was a drill, sir?"

Tobias folded his arms across his chest. "Ms. Leighton, how did you find our sensitized marble floor tiles?"

I narrowed my gaze on him. "Looks good to me."

"Invisible lasers?" He smirked.

"Invisible."

If Maria was finding any of this suspicious she had every right to.

"Ceiling entry points?" he asked.

"Next on my agenda." I waved it off.

"Mr. Wilder." Maria looked worried. "Doesn't this painting belong to Christie's?"

He considered her question. "It's very good isn't it. Very convincing."

Her gaze shot to it. "It's a fake?"

"We can't have Ms. Leighton walking out with an original, now can we? Imagine what would happen if I had to tackle her to the ground." He waggled his eyebrows at her. "It's either that or I'm Icon. What do you say, Maria?"

She chuckled. "Silly."

Tobias gave a confident nod. "Thank you, Anton, Maria, I can take Ms. Leighton from here."

A rush of relief came flooding in and I went from ice-cold to flushed at the thought of being left alone with him.

Tobias waited until the door shut behind them.

He turned to face me. "How's the weather in London?"

Wrapping my arms around myself, I ignored his stupid question.

"How are you finding LA?" he added.

"I like the palm trees."

He walked over to me until he was looming dangerously close. "Jade."

Snapping me back to reality as I remembered he had an invisible artificial intelligence that followed him everywhere, his home, car and apparently here at The Wilder.

"Deactivate camera in this office," he ordered.

Had I tipped my chin up I could have pressed my lips to his and felt his mouth upon mine.

"Jade, confirm please." His breath was minty.

An automated sultry female voice perked up, "Camera off." His lips lightly brushed mine.

I stuttered a nervous breath. "She's talking now?"

"An easy tweak."

"That's very clever."

"I like to please."

Oh, God.

Now was a bad time for my nipples to bead because he was pressing his chest against mine and he'd feel them.

It wasn't merely his expression that had softened from moments ago, it was a familiar look of affection in those gorgeous green eyes I'd loved staring into back in London, when we'd shared an unmatched intimacy. Those memories came flooding back, making my body shiver against his as I recalled moving beyond the veil of friendship with this incredible lover. I marveled still at his strength that could control my body just so, fuck me into blissful oblivion from every angle and leave me quivering for more, manipulate me into endless positions of vulnerability, and all for my heightened pleasure. The way his mouth had once glided over my tender flesh as though worshiping every inch of my body, the way his kisses trailed lower still, bestowing an endless array of sensations with his tongue.

My cheeks flushed as my rambling thoughts ran off.

"I'm not going to kiss you," I stuttered.

His eyes closed for a second. "I understand."

Why did he have to say it like that? Why couldn't he just return to the standoffish Tobias I'd first met?

Make this easier.

Because he's Tobias Wilder, came my dark musing, *and he's got you right where he wants you.*

"You came alone?" he said. "Impressive."

"You ignored my calls?"

"I can reassure you I received all your cat GIFs. They did the trick. Forced me out of hiding, as you can see."

I refused to smile. "You know why I'm here."

He broke my gaze and let out a deep sigh.

"You can't continue with this way of life."

"My respect for art?"

"When we last spoke you confessed everything to me."

He looked vague. "Confessed I love you."

"You're Icon."

"To be honest I'm flattered."

"I saw the evidence in your Oxfordshire home."

"Fakes removed from the market."

"Don't."

"Are we still discussing my need to kiss you? Or have we moved on?"

"Listen to me, you're putting yourself in terrible danger. You'll lose all this."

"I've lost you, Zara, that's all I care about."

"Come with me to the police. Admit everything before it's too late."

"Where's the fun in that?"

Shaking my head, I refused to be seduced further. "I'm going to submit my report this afternoon."

"Report?"

"It's ready to email over to Huntly Pierre. It details everything."

He arched a brow seductively. "Everything?"

"Pertaining to my case, yes."

"You and I had nothing to do with any of it," he said, sounding serious. "I need you to believe this."

"I'll never know." I gazed past him. "Jade, turn the camera back on."

"I've reversed your access to her." He smiled. "I love that color on you. Blue brings out your eyes."

"I saw the paintings, Tobias. I know who you are."

He gave a sympathetic smile. "Apparently, while I was away you found a Tibetan singing bowl and returned the stolen item to its rightful owner? Bravo."

"You mean the one you placed on my kitchen table? And

now my fingerprints are all over it. Because you put me in an impossible position."

Those monks living in Bermondsey's Buddhist temple, who I'd unwittingly stumbled upon thanks to Tobias's mischievousness, had more than deserved the return of their sacred singing bowl. Only, for goodness' sake, did it have to be me who'd committed the heroic and yet highly illegal act?

Tobias looked amused. "Free will is a privilege."

I pressed my hand to my heart. "You told me that right before your mom died in that plane crash she asked you to return the painting you were transporting. The one by Annibale Carracci, *Madonna Enthroned with St. Matthew*, to its rightful owner." I reached out and squeezed his forearm. "You were nine years old. Do you see how it's affected you?"

"Let's discuss *St. Joan*. The painting you just stole."

"I was merely taking a closer look. Checking her frame to authenticate her."

"And your findings?"

A lump lodged in my throat and I tried to swallow.

"The original was destroyed in a fire apparently?" he added. "Surely that provides some reassurance."

"Why are you doing this?"

He pressed his firm chest against mine and I rested my hands to hold him at bay, and yet my fingers scrunched his shirt.

Tobias leaned into my ear. "How did it feel when you held her?"

Turning my head to look at *St. Joan*, deciphering if these inner tingles were coming from being this close to her again—

His mouth brushed over my ear. "She belongs to you. Holding her felt right. Your connection is soul deep and worth more than her appraisal could ever be. You want her back."

I cursed myself for looking away.

His last words to me in London hinted there was more to my family history and he knew a secret pertaining to her turning up at Christie's auction house.

I couldn't stir the courage to ask him what he meant.

Not yet.

"I wouldn't have taken her."

"Yes, you would." He stepped back and the loss of him wrenched. "Jade, camera on." He waited for confirmation and then refocused on me. "I hope you've enjoyed your time in LA, Ms. Leighton. We've enjoyed having you here."

"I've only been here a day."

"Pity to cut your visit short. Still, I know they need your certain set of skills back in London." He gestured to the door. "Shall we?"

Following him out, I walked beside him through the foyer and onward out the glass door exit and into the sun.

"Tobias, please." I tried to keep up with him.

He refused to make eye contact and bowed his head, taking long strides as he tucked his hands into his trouser pockets. "How did you like *Madame Paul Duchesne-Fournet*?"

"She's breathtaking."

"Isn't she? I knew you'd like her."

And I wanted desperately to go back in and enjoy her more with him beside me.

The formality felt like a dagger to my heart.

"Tobias, it was wonderful seeing you." And I meant it. "I've missed you."

At the end of the walkway he paused before a Rolls-Royce Ghost idling on the curb and his gaze swept over me. He looked like he was about to speak and then seemed to think better of it, his attention turning to the falling green hills and beyond them to the speeding cars rushing along a busy freeway.

"Say something," I pleaded.

"Marshall will drive you to the airport."

I glanced through the window at his chauffeur, the forty-something, smartly dressed man with graying temples, waiting patiently.

"I'm not leaving."

Tobias strolled to the back of the car and tapped the trunk. Marshall released the trunk and Tobias lifted it the rest of the way. There, lying in the trunk, was my red suitcase.

My jaw dropped at his arrogance.

"I've taken care of your stay at the Four Seasons. Your minibar bill nearly wiped me out." He gave a wry grin until it turned serious. "My jet is fueled and on the runway. It'll land at Heathrow."

"You can't get rid of me."

"*St. Joan of Arc* will be waiting for you in London."

Oh, so this is how it was meant to end.

My heart ached that it had come to this, him blackmailing me with my own painting. More than this, what we'd had now more than ever proved an illusion.

"What will happen if I don't get on your plane?" I searched his face for the answer.

Was he going to expose *St. Joan* to the world if I didn't comply? A sharp stab of fear hit me when I read that in his expression.

He opened the rear door. "It's over, Zara."

My heart shattered into a thousand pieces and I refused to look at him, bowing my head as I climbed into the back seat, throwing my handbag ahead of me onto the soft leather.

His ironclad grip wrapped around my upper arm and he drew me out. Tobias yanked me toward him and cupped my face with his strong hands, crushing his lips to mine, and I surrendered, starved for him, needing his roughness. His mouth forced mine wider, his tongue feverishly lashing mine.

I gasped my relief to be back in his arms, swooning at the sensation of our tongues sweeping together, his mouth raging against mine and then softening to console. His eyes closed as he sighed wantonly into my mouth. When his hand slipped to my lower spine and he yanked me against him, my sex throbbed, making me shudder with femininity, my soul soothed and yet aching with the dread of leaving him.

He drew back. "Forgive me. I don't know any other way."

"I will stop you." My gaze lowered to his mouth.

He ran his thumb over my bottom lip. "Why do you insist on destroying me?"

"Because what you're doing is wrong."

"I meant my heart, Zara."

My body trembled with this cruel need for him, as though my mind and body refused to agree this desire couldn't be more wrong.

"Go." His lips curved into a smile. "Before I change my mind."

"What will happen if I stay?"

He shook his head and nudged me into the car and closed the door to seal me inside.

The Rolls drove me away from him.

I peered out to watch Tobias walk back toward The Wilder, his sadness seemingly as torturous as mine. The way he scraped his fingers through his hair hinted at his confliction.

Being wrenched away so suddenly made my chest tighten and I concentrated on taking slow, deep breaths to calm.

"LAX won't take long, ma'am," Marshall piped up.

"How long will it take to get there?" I forced a polite smile.

"Half an hour. The 405 looks good. Would you like me to turn up the air-conditioning?"

"No, thank you." This dreadful chill was already making me tremble.

I don't want to leave.

There was so much more to see and do and I'd always wanted to visit Rodeo Drive, I painfully mused, pop into Tiffany & Co., and maybe dine in one of the fine restaurants near my hotel, and then of course visit the private art galleries there.

Slumping in my seat I pushed those superficial thoughts away and faced my anguish. I'd failed myself, failed Tobias, and I couldn't bear the thought I'd let him down because I'd not been strong enough to do what had to be done. I'd let my fear of exposure to scandal affect my judgment.

Icon was taking on history itself and his capture was inevitable. This beautiful man who'd watched his parents die in front of him would be tortured for the rest of his life because of this tragedy. Tobias was playing out some kind of retribution as though trying to salvage his past and dull his pain.

He needed a friend. An advocate who cared. Someone who could make him see sense. Or at least find a way to prevent him from ruining himself.

As I ran over my options I came to terms with the fact that whatever was in my suitcase I could live without.

My hand slid toward the door handle.

The door handle wouldn't give.

I was bloody well locked inside this Rolls-Royce.

The luxury leather-and-chrome interior highlighted Tobias's grand lifestyle and in any other circumstances I'd have been thrilled to be taken to the airport in a chauffeur-driven car or have a private jet waiting for me. All I had to do was resign to my fate and I'd be sipping bubbly and heading back to my Notting Hill flat.

Luckily, Marshall hadn't caught my subtle attempt to escape. Staring through the front window I could see we only had one red light left and we'd be on the freeway. Rummaging through my handbag with my fingers tracing over my passport, I shoved it to the bottom of my purse.

"Oh, no." I raised my gaze to look at Marshall in the rearview mirror. "I left my passport in the hotel safe."

"Ma'am, I checked you out of the Beverly Wilshire. Nothing was left behind."

"You packed my stuff?" I hated the thought of this stranger handling my underwear.

"The concierge took care of it."

My jaw tightened at the injustice. "It was right in the back of the safe. They missed it. We have to go there."

"Let me have the concierge take care of it. She'll have your passport transported to meet us at the VIP lounge at LAX." He tapped the screen on the dashboard. "Beverly Wilshire."

With a forced smile, I feigned gratitude for his thoughtfulness and listened to him request the staff to retrieve my passport from my room.

"I know where I left it." I sounded chirpier then I felt.

Marshall's eyes met mine in the rearview.

I gestured my relief. "UCLA. I was showing an old professor of mine how different they look now. This issue with the EU had us changing them." I waved it off as though it was boring. "Would you mind taking me there?"

"The university?"

"Yes, the campus." I pulled out my phone. "I'll text him."

It wasn't too much of a lie, though. I'd not had the time yet to visit Gabe Anderson—one of my favorite professors at my old alma mater, The Courtauld Institute of Art. Two months ago he'd returned to California to teach Asian art history, a subject he was obsessed with. I didn't think I'd be taking up Gabe's invitation to visit him so soon and neither would he.

After Tobias, Gabe was the only other person I knew here.

Marshall turned left when the light flashed green and navigated us east away from the freeway.

It's going to be okay.

Clothes, that's all I had in my suitcase, oh, and makeup too. I could go without all of it. There were plenty of shopping malls here so I could buy all the essentials later.

This decision had so many consequences—not the least of which was Tobias's lingering threat of ruining my reputation if he exposed *St. Joan* as authentic. He'd gone to so much trouble to steal her from Christie's after an unknown collector had shipped her from Europe to London for final endorsement. Icon had snatched her away before the specialists had gotten to prove she was real. His ulterior motive was now glaring. That painting served as leverage.

Damn him, he knew the effect he had on me.

The ghost of his kiss lingered on my lips and he still had my hands trembling, or perhaps this was merely the tension I'd been holding from the thought of seeing him again. I'd promised myself I wouldn't let him throw me off my reason for being here.

Yet here I sat, thrown.

3

Within twenty minutes we were winding our way along the UCLA campus roads, and my heart rate rocketed from my brilliant plan inspired further by the impressive old brick buildings of this bustling college. Students strolled to and from their classes. I imagined Gabe would be happy here amongst all this prestige and academic camaraderie.

My focus returned to Marshall. He looked like a reasonable man.

Discreetly, I reached into my handbag and pulled out my phone. I hated the idea of being without it, but this was the only way I'd be able to evade him. If he skipped town, there was a chance I could find someone with the skill to reverse engineer the signal and track it to him. I was going to have to stash it somewhere safe for now.

"Right over there, please." I pointed to the Franklin D. Murphy Sculpture Garden.

The car pulled up to the curb.

"I'll let Mr. Wilder know we're running late," said Marshall. "He'll inform his flight crew."

I raised my phone and smiled through my lie. "He told me to take all the time I need."

Marshall narrowed his gaze in the rearview, seemingly unconvinced.

You don't intimidate me, buddy, not even after you broke into my hotel room and violated my privacy.

"Can you open the door, please?"

He hesitated. "Did you text your professor? Does he have it, miss?"

"I hope so." My gaze swept the sculpture garden. "I'll be right back." I grabbed my handbag ready to bolt.

With a click of the lock I was free and my feet hit the curb with a bounce of triumph. I turned to give a wave of thanks and then realized Marshall was getting out.

"I'll be quicker alone." I took off, striding fast through the well-tended garden, passing an array of sculptures, one of them a large golden female torso on a solid granite base. It was beautiful, and I pined to be able to enjoy these modern masterpieces with the attention they deserved and not while running from Tobias's chauffer. A perky tour guide led a long line of prospective students around the campus. I took advantage of the endless line of people and weaved through them and shut off my phone.

Turning left and a sharp right, I saw the Charles E. Young Research Library up ahead and hurried toward it and with one quick glance back I confirmed I wasn't being followed—

The atmosphere was expectedly serene and as I strolled toward the reception desk situated to the right of the glass foyer, I threw a big smile to the librarian, a man in his thirties who was slim and studious looking with his head buried in a book. He frowned his interest when he greeted me.

Within minutes I was heading down the staircase to the rare book reading room after providing a convincing performance as a foreign student. Throwing in some academic jargon that gave me the credibility I needed along with my unusual request to see their out-of-print edition of a collection of paintings by Paul Gauguin from the late 1800s. Gauguin was a famed painter, printmaker and sculptor, and this was the first rare book that came to mind.

I made my way into the air-sealed room, respectful of the other students, and picked up a pair of white gloves out of a wooden box on a corner table and pulled them on. Instead of looking for the book on Gauguin, I pulled a first edition biography on William Shakespeare off the shelf that in any other circumstance would have had my full attention. I pretended to read it.

Tobias might very well hold a press conference to announce the suspicious provenance of my *St. Joan*. Then again, with one phone call from me, the police would turn their attention on him and his days of thievery would be over or at least stilted.

Though I believed Tobias wouldn't hurt me. We were at an impasse.

I needed time to rethink my strategy and if this is what it took, me throwing caution to the wind and trusting my gut, then so be it.

When the room emptied of visitors I returned the first edition to its shelf, pulled off the gloves and returned them to their wooden box. I carried my phone over to the oak book cabinet, knelt and reached around to stash my phone behind it.

There, it was done.

I exited the reading room and headed over to the wall phone. Within a few seconds I was speaking to the campus operator and asking to be put through to Professor Gabe Anderson's office.

"Zara?" Gabe answered with that American brightness.

"Professor Anderson?" There came a wave of comfort at hearing his voice again.

"What a lovely surprise. Where are you?"

"I stopped off at the antiques reading room. You know how I love old books. Are you busy?"

"Never." He gave a sigh. "Are you okay?"

"Yes. Why?"

"Your chauffer was here looking for you."

Oh, no, Marshall had found Gabe's office. He must have called his boss to tell him he'd lost me, and then Tobias had immediately searched The Courtauld's teacher database and cross-referenced it with all the professors at UCLA. How easy it would have been to track down Gabe. Tobias had then directed Marshall to find him on the campus. All in under fifteen minutes.

"Why would I have your passport?" Anderson sounded concerned. "Haven't seen you in three months."

"It's a misunderstanding. Is he still there?"

"He headed off to look for you. He left his number. Shall I call him?"

"No, it's fine." I wondered if Marshall might be trying to follow the GPS in the phone I'd just stashed, the same one Tobias had conveniently gifted me.

"Is now an okay time?" I asked.

"Of course. I'm in Boelter Hall, office 112."

"I'll be right there."

After asking the librarian for directions I headed out of the library, weaving my way along the college lanes.

There came a rush of relief when I saw Professor Anderson waiting for me outside his office door. I hurried toward him and gave him a big hug. He gestured for me to follow him into his office but I hesitated for a second, wondering if Marshall might come back. Still, if he did I could handle him. It wasn't like he'd be able to force me back into his limo.

I made my way in and shut the door. "It's so wonderful to see you, Professor."

"Call me Gabe. I had no idea you were in LA?" He pointed to one of the two armchairs in the corner for me to sit. "Tea?"

"No, thank you."

His office was an organized chaos with files stacked high on his desk and his impressive collection of Asian history books lined up along the dark wooden shelf. An empty coffee mug. Gabe was wearing his usual tweed jacket and black slacks to offset being in his early thirties, and his raven locks still flopped over his kind eyes.

"Zara, so good to see you. I hear you got hired at Huntly Pierre?"

"Yes, as an art specialist. Sorry I didn't call you to let you know I was visiting LA. I meant to."

"Are you on vacation?"

"Kind of. Mixing work with pleasure." And as I was unofficially in California that version sat well with me.

"Where are you staying?"

"Beverly Wilshire." I cringed inwardly, recalling how Tobias had unceremoniously checked me out of my hotel room.

"Your chauffeur told me you lost your passport?"

"Did he bother you? I'm sorry."

"No, he wanted to help you out." Gabe stood and reached for a Post-it note on his desk. "Here's his number."

I took it from him. "Thank you."

He sat back down. "How long are you here?"

"A week."

"On behalf of Huntly Pierre?"

"Kind of. To be honest I'm going a little rogue. Using my free time to investigate a lead."

He laughed. "My little librarian?"

I deserved that I suppose. I'd been one of his quieter students and only revealed a spark of personality when I handed in my papers that always came back with an A+.

It didn't take us long to catch up and it was lovely to hear how he was now living in Brentwood with his boyfriend, Ned, a technology strategist for a firm in Menlo Park, though Gabe said he worked from home most days.

The last few hours had felt like a whirlwind of emotions and seeing my old professor filled me with happiness; Gabe was the connection to home I'd needed even if he was here now.

Jet lag caught up and I suppressed a yawn. "I need to call a taxi."

"I can drive you."

"I'm fine. But thank you."

He stood and reached for his phone. "Where are you going?"

"Can you recommend a hotel? I need to be closer to the Los Angeles County Museum of Art."

"The Sofitel? It's also near the Beverly Center. It's a big shopping center and is just across the street."

"Perfect."

Gabe made the call and requested the cab park in front of Boelter Hall. With that done he scribbled a number on a piece of paper and handed it to me. "Here's my cell."

"Thank you." I tucked it into my handbag.

"I don't suppose you'd like to join me at a cocktail party tomorrow night?"

"Where?"

"The Broad. One of my students is showcasing his collection as part of a youth program at the gallery."

My attention spiked with the thought of visiting one of

the city's most distinguished museums that was on my list to check out. "I'd love to go."

"Great! I'll pick you up tomorrow at seven. It's black-tie."

"I have just the thing." Ironically a dress that rogue Wilder had bought me back in London.

I gave Gabe a big hug and followed the pathway toward the entrance of Boelter Hall, all the while glancing around for Marshall. When I reached the grassy bank, I saw my taxi idling at the curb. Settling in the back of the car I looked forward to checking into the Sofitel hotel and, just as Gabe suggested, visiting the shopping center. I needed to replace the contents of my suitcase.

Staring out at the passing scenery, the enormity of what I was taking on hit me. I had less than a week to collate data from every single gallery, along with private collections in LA, the kind that might draw the attention of a thief. For now, at least, I had a motive to go on; a broken provenance consistently occurring with each painting stolen by Icon. A gargantuan task that would quite frankly have been impossible without my access to Huntly Pierre's newly developed software. An ingenious processing program that collated the art collections of international galleries with details including their individual history. This ability was now part of my investigative tool kit.

Why couldn't all this be simple? Why wasn't the enigmatic Tobias who I'd fallen hard for just an ordinary man who I could date without all this drama? Our worlds were clashing and the fallout was going to leave nothing but two broken people if I wasn't careful.

It hurt knowing Tobias was in the same city and I couldn't see him. Being so close to him at The Wilder Museum had reminded me he was dangerously seductive. Recalling the way he'd pressed his body against mine with all that hard muscle and boundless power threatened to make me lose focus.

I'd always wanted to visit The Broad, famed for its avant-garde reputation, and I couldn't wait to explore the endless showrooms.

That's it, think of a vast, frigid gallery instead of Wilder and refocus your brain on why you're here.

After paying for my cab, I climbed out and headed toward the impressive front door of the Sofitel.

"Miss," the taxi driver called after me.

I turned to face him and froze—

He was retrieving a red suitcase out of the trunk of his cab.

Mine.

He handed it over to a young valet who rushed it past me, throwing a welcoming smile.

The blood drained from my face as I realized Marshall had realized the cab was for me and had placed it in there before I'd left Gabe's office.

Tobias is bloody relentless.

4

My reflection in the hotel bedroom mirror was the epit-
ome of a young woman putting on a brave face. This Escada
gown clung like spun gold to my curves and these delicate
fine straps with their diamond beading caught the light; the
back so low it hovered just above my butt to blend glamour
with a sassy chic.

"Why did you even bring this dress?" I whispered to myself, though my eyes answered with a hope for a reconcili-
ation with Tobias. I broke my gaze, focusing instead on my
strappy high heels—the ones Tobias bought me during that
wild weekend when we'd stayed at The Dorchester hotel just
weeks ago.

My stomach muscles tightened with all the uncertainty.

No matter how cozy this room was with its long velvet
drapes or welcoming seating area, it wasn't home. I'd spent
much of the day reading everything I could about Tobias
online. Not one article hinted at any misdemeanors or bad
boy behavior, unless you counted the socialites he flaunted,
hanging off his arm in those glamor shots of him arriving or
leaving exclusive social events.

Of all the possible scenarios of my reunion with him yesterday, being placed on a plane and sent back to London within moments of seeing him wasn't one of them.

Raising my chin high I gave myself a confident nod of approval that I'd handled myself well when he'd tried to push his agenda on me. Turning my thoughts to tonight, I ran my fingers through my auburn locks that I'd styled elegantly to tumble over my shoulders, and I dabbed my soft pink lipstick as I finished applying my makeup.

I couldn't wait to be inside The Broad and it made me smile to know I was going there now. Grabbing my clutch purse and heading out of my room I had a bounce in my step and I even rode the elevator with my newfound confidence, the residue from my phobia of lifts having eased slightly; *because of him.*

Gabe was waiting for me in the hotel foyer and his eyes widened when he saw me. "What's Rita Hayworth doing at the Sofitel?" he called out.

I responded with a confident turn and a flirty flick of my hair.

He looked gorgeous in a snazzy black tuxedo. "Almost didn't recognize you there," he said. "No cardigan?"

I gave him a playful thump. "Left it back in England."

"You look...wow."

"You look amazing yourself."

"Let's go see some art."

The valet brought around Gabe's blue Audi R8 and, with the inspirational music of Sia playing as an atmospheric backdrop, we drove along Beverly Boulevard.

"How are you?" He glanced over to me.

"I'm fine. Looking forward to tonight."

"So what's this case you're on?"

"It's related to a painting my dad once owned." I mulled over what was safe to add. "*St. Joan of Arc* was one of the paintings that was allegedly destroyed in my house fire. A few weeks ago, it turned up at Christie's in London."

"Maybe he sold it? You were very young when all that happened."

"There is that." I preferred to deflect from the fact my father wouldn't have let any of them go.

The passing scenery was fascinating with its modern skyscrapers in between quaint stores, and there was an unsettling sense of the traffic going the wrong way. I tried not to think that somewhere out there Tobias was going on with his life.

Gabe gave a sideways glance. "Anyone special in your life?"

"No." I hated to finally admit this. "There was someone but it didn't work out."

"I'm sorry."

I turned to face him. "You're happy?"

"Ned's easygoing so we're a good fit."

"I'm so happy to hear that."

He reached over and squeezed my hand. "No bad boys, okay? No matter how much we want to jump their bones."

He made me chuckle.

"Any decent man would snap you up in a heartbeat," he added.

Half an hour later we'd arrived on Grand Avenue in downtown LA and were pulling up to the striking honeycombed structure of The Broad. Gabe handed over his car keys to the valet and we headed on in.

Within minutes we were sipping bubbly from tall flutes and sighing with happiness at being back in our natural habitat. With over two thousand paintings and sculptures to view we were in our element. This high-ceilinged space with the remnants of daylight flowing through ornate windows and highlighting all this modern elegance.

A waiter took our empty glasses and we rode the escalator through the second-floor ceiling, the design providing a womb-like feel as we ascended. At the top, we were met by an awe-inspiring sculpture by Jeff Koons, a glorious display of enormous gathered tulips in bright colors including gold, blue, purple and green—all lying upon a thin white base.

Strolling into another room, our attention was captured by a three-dimensional design resting on a high table. At one end was a small body of water that burst from a steel container and morphed into a waterfall, pouring into a cavern which turned a large wheel. Beyond that it ran into a small-scale hallway and within its walls shot out vibrant blue miniature electric rays crisscrossing each other.

"What's this one?" asked Gabe.

I studied the gold plaque on the side. *"Mousetrap for the Inevitable."* I read on, "'Designed to draw out the subject and test its endurance.'"

Gabe stepped forward. "'Where usually form follows function, here American architect E. B.'s design represents form as art reflecting the power of self-regulation.'"

I pointed to the water forcing the wheel around. "It's an ingenious mechanism."

"What happens to the mouse?"

My cringe was my answer as I mused over the kind of person who had invented this. I respected modern art and was thrilled to pass by the striking pieces by Andy Warhol, Cindy Sherman and Barbara Kruger, all of them making my heart soar. We made our way through the well-dressed crowd who'd gathered for the reception. I paused awhile to admire *The Balloon Dog*, an enormous blue balloon-shaped masterpiece by Koons. It was such a fun piece and Gabe joked how he could only afford the miniature one sold in the gift shop.

He pointed out his young student Terrance Hill, who was greeting guests across the showroom. Gabe shared with me how the young man was fatherless and yet his inspiring talent and determination had earned him a scholarship at UCLA.

Gabe stared on proudly. "Terrance excelled in my art history class but found his true calling is modern art. He has my blessing, of course."

The bright young star with neat dreadlocks wore the brightest smile, and I guessed the pretty fortysomething black woman by his side was his proud mom.

We headed on over to them to offer our congratulations. Terrance was enjoying his well-deserved praise as private collectors swarmed him, wanting to meet this gifted young man who'd set the art world alight.

His paintings were featured around the walls. Gabe and I took our time to admire each one and I marveled at Terrance's gift of layering colors and his use of texture. He was being hailed as a young Jackson Pollock and I could see why.

Turning to face the crowd, my breath caught when I saw a vision of pure masculine beauty—Tobias Wilder.

He was here.

Sipping from an amber drink and looking ridiculously sharp in a black tuxedo with his hair predictably ruffled to perfection, so damn gorgeous as he smiled his response to something a middle-aged couple were saying to him. *God*, now he was doing that thing where he arched his brows as he listened with sincerity, seemingly engrossed in conversation, his left hand tucked into his trouser pocket as he leaned forward to engage with them.

A jolt of reality hit me when I saw his ex-girlfriend and powerhouse attorney Logan Arquette standing beside him. She was wearing a pretty green gown and her usual cold glare.

My body froze when Tobias's stare found me in the crowd and his expression reflected intrigue.

"Is that Tobias Wilder?" asked Gabe quietly.

"Yes."

He snapped his head to look at me. "You've met him?"

I managed a subtle nod, though kept my stare on Wilder.

"Where?" Gabe sounded incredulous.

"London. He's a client of Huntly Pierre." A quick glance over at Gabe told me that placated him.

I wondered how Tobias felt about me evading his driver yesterday.

Gabe grabbed my arm. "He's coming this way."

Tobias and Logan strolled toward us, confidently nodding here and there at the other guests who parted respectfully for them.

My back straightened as they neared us and I decided to go with a customary, "Mr. Wilder, nice to see you again."

Gabe flashed me another look of surprise.

Tobias gave a warm smile. "Zara."

A seductive chill spiraled up my spine and I went for my best stony-faced expression to match his amused demeanor.

Wilder wore that dazzling suit as though some artisan had carved it over his muscular physique to highlight his firm chest and broad shoulders, and his grin widened just enough to hide that he was strategizing.

"It's my pleasure to introduce Professor Gabe Anderson, art historian." I gestured to them. "Tobias Wilder and Logan Arquette."

"Nice to see you, Zara." Logan's tone lacked sincerity and she looked triumphant as her arm wrapped through Tobias's in a blatant gesture of possessiveness. Her flirting was being used against me to lessen my resolve.

"Quite the exhibition," said Tobias.

Gabe responded with praise for Tobias's own gallery and he told him how much he loved The Wilder's reputation for its exclusive exhibits they were famed for.

"We have something very special coming to The Wilder." Logan zeroed in on Gabe. "It's something you'll find particularly appealing if you love history."

"Top secret for now," added Tobias, fixing his attention on me.

The full force of his power hit me and his stare held me captive.

A memory flittered through my mind of the way he'd once touched me; a mesmerizing strength and tenderness and there came a stark recollection of the way he made me come so very hard.

Think about something else.

Anything else.

Why did he have to look at me like this? As though we weren't over.

"Please excuse me," I said. "There's a Doug Aitken piece I'm dying to see."

I felt rude for leaving Gabe with them, but I needed to put distance between us. Tobias's glare was burning my back as I walked into the next room. Avoidance was probably the best way to get through tonight.

I willed myself to concentrate on the gold plaque before me. The word *now* had been enlarged to a three-dimensional wall model and was filled with a collage of images.

The last place I wanted to be was in the now.

"Zara." Tobias's voice exuded a deadly seduction.

A jolt of uncertainty trailed up my spine.

He stood a few feet away. "You look beautiful. I love that dress on you. I'm glad you wore it tonight."

I wanted to believe his words were a peace offering but the way his fierce gaze held mine reminded me of our goodbye outside The Wilder. He had that same look now in those green eyes.

I turned to go. "I have to find Gabe."

He reached out and held my wrist. "Dance with me."

He was torturing me with physical contact; his firm touch reminding me what I'd lost, his sensual grip dangerously persuasive.

"I can't."

He arched a brow. "You moved on fast."

"Gabe's a friend."

"I was worried I'd have to challenge him to a duel." He grinned devilishly. "Have you any idea how stunning you look?"

Evidently he knew how gorgeous he looked too, because he was using his magnetism to manipulate me into spending more time with him.

"Boundaries," I said firmly. "What does that word mean to you?"

"In what respect?"

"You broke into my hotel room and stole my suitcase."

He came closer. "I believe it was the concierge."

"Under your orders."

And he'd tracked down Gabe at UCLA. Seriously, did he expect me to forget that?

"Zara, dance with me."

"How did you know I'd be here?"

"I could say the same."

"The artist is one of Gabe's students."

Tobias gave a mischievous smirk. "Don't force me to dance with Professor Anderson."

"I'm sure you'll find someone who'll fall for your charm."

"Yesterday, I should have explained myself better."

I placed my hands on my hips and waited for him to finish his thought.

His frown deepened. "One dance. Or..."

"Or what?"

"Don't tempt me with refusing, Leighton." He arched an amused brow. "Or there will be consequences."

"In what way?"

"I'm still a client of Huntly Pierre. Do it for them. You can always think of England." He winked.

I relented with a nod and when his hand rested on the lower curve of my spine, I resisted the desire to close my eyes and lean into him as though there was no tension between us. Tobias guided me into a cocktail lounge and led me toward the small crowd slow dancing to Nina Simone, her sultry tones setting the scene for romance.

He pulled me into a hug. "It's good to see you."

I let Tobias take the lead as I rested my right hand on his shoulder, my left sliding against his right palm, his fingers closing around mine. The way his body crushed against me felt deceptively good and caused my body to tingle deliciously. My nipples further betrayed me by hardening in response to his provocative cologne.

"I think this might be my all-time favorite gallery," I said.

"What about The Wilder?"

"What about it?"

"I suppose I deserve that."

I dragged my teeth over my bottom lip to tease him and there came a rush of exhilaration when his pupils dilated with arousal revealing I was having the same effect on him. He waltzed me around and we fit together annoyingly well.

Why couldn't this be us? Two lovers enjoying a romantic evening without the looming inevitability of this ending badly.

"Zara, you're intoxicating." He gave a heart-stopping grin.

"Don't!" I wasn't falling for his flattery.

He spun me around and my feet became light as he whisked

me along with a smooth glide. He yanked me against his firm chest and then stilled, his mouth lingering perilously close to mine. Our eyes locked on each other as the world fell away. Those specks of gold in his green irises were hypnotic.

His grip tightened. "How's the Sofitel?"

Adrenaline surged through me. "Lovely."

He nuzzled close to my ear. "I'm glad you came."

I leaned back to see him better. "Tell me how to get through to you?"

He tipped me backward and held me suspended in a scooped pose low in his arms as he leaned forward to whisper, "Tell me you want me."

"Everyone's watching."

"Say it."

"Let me up."

"Say it first."

"Tobias, I'm serious."

"Not until you say it." His mouth brushed mine.

I nipped his lower lip and he let out a moan of pleasure and flipped me up and yanked my body to his again, his hardness digging in to my lower stomach.

He arched an amused brow. "Now we're going to have to dance until my dignity returns. I blame you."

A rush of desire at being in his arms again flooded through me. I was fast becoming drunk with arousal from the way he was holding me so masterfully.

My words spilled out in a flurry. "Mr. Wilder, you misled me—"

"No, Zara."

"If you care about me you'll not taunt me like this."

"Of course I care about you."

"What is this?"

"I'm forgiving you."

"What for?"

He looked surprised. "Your sneak attack on me tonight. I'm completely defenseless against you."

"I have to get back to Gabe."

"Can I take you out to dinner?"

"So you can send me out of the country again?"

"Technically, you never left."

"You're impossible."

"I will have you again," he said with an edge of danger. "I know you want that too."

The room was spinning.

Tobias's glare fixed on me fiercely as though he needed to see I wanted this. These were the words I'd craved to hear but I was past being led astray. I looked over his shoulder so I could access these remnants of strength that were evading me.

"Zara, you misjudged me. Let me prove it to you."

No, and my anguished expression told him that. "Let me go."

And let me go…

He stepped back. "Let's talk at least."

I raised my chin high, pretending he had no effect on me. He went to say something but instead he quickly broke my glare.

"I can find my own way." I rushed from him, needing to put distance between us as my heart shattered. This chill reached my bones and my mind felt dazed from the confliction of seeing him again.

Gabe waved my way to get my attention. "Looks like you've swept one of America's most wanted off his feet."

"Most wanted?"

"Bachelors," he said. "Look at him."

Tobias was standing beneath an archway and he was staring right at me, his expression marred with confusion in a haunting reminder of what could never be.

I spun around to break the intensity of Wilder's confident stance and faced one of Terrance's paintings, focusing on the bright canvas while trying to find my center again and fight this wavering desire to believe there could be an *us*.

The plaque beside Terrance's painting stated this one was called *Unpredictable.*

The young artist had seemingly channeled his emotions onto the large canvas. It spoke in ways I couldn't define. There was freshness to it, a vibrancy and a seeming grasp of pain someone so young shouldn't know.

Perhaps seeing Tobias tonight wasn't a coincidence. *No,* surely he wouldn't hit a gallery with me here? His words of affection had been used to distract me. He'd used his charm and done his worst to send me reeling. I'd almost fallen for him all over again.

I went in search of him, recalling Icon's MO and remembering he always cut the power before a heist. He always zapped the security cameras and he always left no trace. With all these guests milling around, the guards were more easily distracted.

I hurried out of the showroom with my chest tight with tension, on through the expansiveness, scanning the many faces of the guests roaming freely as I weaved my way around them.

There he was—

Sitting alone on a wooden bench and people watching, his intelligent eyes taking everything in. He glanced at his watch and then pushed himself to his feet and strolled eastward down a long hallway.

After turning a corner, I saw him standing at the end, casually leaning against a wall and scrolling through his phone.

I wondered if this was how he deactivated the security system, by using some gadget app he'd invented.

With a confident stride I headed toward him. He showed surprise when he saw me.

"What are you doing?" I said firmly.

He raised his phone. "You didn't answer my text."

"Didn't bring it." Because it's stashed away in a library at UCLA, I mused proudly.

"You should always carry a charged phone."

I folded my arms. "Are you going to hit this place?"

"Don't be ridiculous. Let me get you a drink."

The room to his left was flooded in darkness and yet the rest of the gallery glared beneath fluorescent lights.

I narrowed my eyes. "What are you up to?"

He feigned innocence. "Enjoying the art."

I stepped left to peer into the dark showroom.

His frown deepened. "You can't see that one tonight."

"Really?"

He gestured to the rope cordoning it off. "Out of order."

"That's convenient. I wonder who put that there."

"The staff, I imagine. There's a fault with the sensors."

I moved toward the door and he grabbed my arm.

"Let go, please."

His hand snapped away and his back straightened. "There's a good reason it's cordoned off."

"I'm sure there is." I threw him a look of triumph and climbed over the rope and headed in, pulling the strap of my purse across my chest and easing it behind me.

"Zara," he called after me, "I was standing in front of the sign."

I turned and forced a smile. "Am I ruining your plan?"

"You can't be in here."

Yes, buddy, I've caught you in the act.

Passing the first impressively large portrait on the left of a holographic tornado, I admired its realism. Though with merely digits and codes it wouldn't be worth anything and was impossible to steal. Walking onward there was the footage of a hurricane at sea with rolling waves; a living, breathing masterpiece. Next, an image of the sun shining brightly and I shielded my eyes trying to figure out what would be so appealing in any of these.

My heel caught in the ground and I peered down at the tiny holes in the floor tiles.

Fuck.

"Hurry!" Tobias was inside the rope and frantically gesturing. "This is the rain room!"

I gawped toward the sound of rushing air.

A deluge of rain—drenching me.

When I opened my eyes, I blinked through the blur of water at a horror-stricken Tobias. The rain ceased, though a few droplets still hit my head as my hair squished to my scalp. My dress clung horribly. I'd become the exhibit.

Careful with his footing on the slippery floor, Tobias hurried over and shrugged out of his jacket.

Breathing through these waves of panic... *Oh, no,* I'd ruined this lovely dress. Wiping water out of my eyes, I looked up at him. "It's Escada."

"I love it." He gave a sympathetic smile. "Both versions." He wrapped his jacket around my shoulders.

I welcomed the warmth with a sigh. "I'm so embarrassed."

Tobias cupped my cheeks and leaned in and kissed me, his lips soft and comforting against mine, my mouth tingling, my need for him relighted as I almost forgot this was forbidden.

He broke away and gave a reassuring tug on his jacket to bring it further around my shoulders. "You have a funny way of trying to save me, Zara Leighton."

I gave a shrug of surrender and shivered.

"Oh, sweetheart." He pulled me into a hug.

"You'll get wet." I nudged him away.

"Come on."

Trudging toward the exit behind him, I paused briefly to wring water out of my hem. I couldn't bear the thought of anyone seeing me like this.

How embarrassing.

As I stepped out into the hallway the stark chill made me tremble.

"Let's get you out of here." Tobias rubbed his hand up and down my back.

Gabe walked briskly toward us in a flurry of concern. "What the hell happened to you?"

My teeth chattered. "Bit of an accident."

"Why did you go in there?" He threw a glare at Tobias.

"I've never known it to rain in a gallery." I mean whose idea was this, anyway, and what purpose did it achieve? Where I came from it rained almost every bloody day.

"It's out of service." Tobias gave a look of resignation. "The motion detectors are meant to pick up movement—"

"Stop the water hitting you when they detect you're beneath," added Gabe. "I love this one. When it works."

"Is my makeup smudged?"

"It's a new look for you." Gabe gave a shrug. "Party girl."

Oh, no.

Running my fingertips beneath my eyes I tried to wipe away the mascara.

Gabe reached out and took my purse off me and gave it a shake. "I'll take you back to the hotel."

"Do you have leather seats?" Tobias inflected concern. "This water—" he pointed to me "—will ruin them. What do you drive?"

Gabe frowned. "Audi R8."

Tobias cringed. "Leather seats?"

"I'll get a taxi," I piped up.

"No cab will accept you like this," said Gabe.

"It's settled, then," said Tobias. "I'm taking you." He reached out and grabbed my purse from Gabe. "We'll go out the back to avoid the press."

"Press?" It came out as a screech.

"They're out front ready to get their money shot." Tobias waggled his eyebrows. "Looks like you're it."

Gabe gave me a reassuring smile. "Zara, come to Brentwood and have lunch with me tomorrow. I have the afternoon off."

"I'd love that," I said.

He stepped forward and kissed my cheek. "Call me. Let me know you're okay."

"I'll be fine. I'm so sorry. Please stay and enjoy the evening."

Gabe lit up with an impressed smile. "We so appreciate this, Mr. Wilder."

My glare chastised him for being so enamored.

That's Wilder's superpower, I silently warned Gabe, *he sweeps you up and saves the day and then you go and fall for him.*

All very inconvenient.

When we stepped out the back of the gallery I was at least reassured by the warm climate. One phone call on the way and Tobias had his posh-looking silver Ferrari waiting for us. He tipped the young valet, who was polite enough not to look my way before he hurried off.

"What about your seat?" I peered into his beautiful car.

"It'll be fine."

"But you have leather seats?"

"And?"

"They'll be ruined."

His grin widened.

I fisted my hands and rested them on my hips. "You told Gabe—"

A flash went off.

"Get in!" Tobias snapped. "You drive."

Blinking through the fading glare of a flashbulb, I watched a young man on a skateboard zooming away along the pavement. Tobias leaped over the car door into the passenger seat. Dread spiked my veins as I scurried around to the driver's side and pulled open the door, threw his jacket down to protect the seat and flung myself in.

"Drive," said Tobias. "We can catch him."

Staring at the control panel I panicked when I realized this was an automatic. "I've only driven an automatic once."

"Please hurry. He's getting away."

"I don't know how."

"For God's sake, Zara. Grow a pair."

"You grow a pair."

He looked back at me, amused. "You've already had the pleasure of being acquainted with my—"

"Tobias!"

"Okay, then, Jade, you drive."

"What!"

"Seat belt. Now."

The engine roared to life and I tried to remember to breathe, grappling with my seat belt as the car pulled away from the curb and accelerated along the road.

"What the fuck is going on?" I slammed my hand to my mouth.

Tobias jumped up into a crouching position on his seat and then brought his right foot onto the window ledge as though surfing as he leaned out.

"Careful." I gripped the wheel and then let go when it turned freely.

"Thirty miles an hour, Jade," Tobias snapped. "Make that forty."

Our Ferrari aligned with the skateboarder zipping along and the man gawked when he saw us. Tobias reached out and snatched the camera from him and then flung himself back into his seat. As we sped along he turned the camera screen for me to see.

I stared horrified at the shot of me looking completely naked beneath my wet dress as though I wasn't wearing any underwear. Tobias removed the memory card and tucked it into his pocket.

"Jade," he ordered. "Park."

The Ferrari slowed and then parked curbside. Tobias flung open his door and climbed out. He leaned against the car and waited for the skateboarder to catch up. He threw his camera back to him.

The man looked shaken. "I'll report this," he snarled. "This is harassment."

Tobias gave a confident smile. "Without evidence?" He gestured for me to switch seats and then came around to the driver's side. "Tell your boss 'Hi' from me."

"Fuck you."

"Have a great evening." Tobias snapped a salute.

After sliding over to the passenger seat, and pulling his jacket back over me, I felt grateful to see the man skate off without my naked image on his camera.

Tobias watched him scoot off down the sidewalk. "He's paparazzi."

"Thank you." I reached out to squeeze Tobias's arm.

Once that photo was unleashed on the internet there'd be no turning back. That was the second time he'd saved me tonight. And of course, if anyone had a self-steering car it would be Wilder.

He stared dead ahead with his face scrunched in discomfort. I'd left a wet seat. "I'm sorry."

He pulled the car away from the curb. "You have enough time."

"For what?"

"To come up with an elaborate plan on how you're going to make it up to me." He grinned at his cheekiness. "Let's go home."

A flutter of excitement swirled around my stomach at the thought he was taking me to *his* house.

"Warm enough?" He fiddled with the dial to blow heat over me.

Get a grip, Zara, I warned myself, *remember the mission*. Tonight, I could have access to the kind of evidence that could stop Icon.

I had what it took to save this man.

5

We arrived at Tobias's Malibu home within the hour.

He led me around the side of the impressive house and into the garden. The scenery exuded peacefulness, from the lavish lawn to those towering palm trees and the sun loungers surrounding the infinity swimming pool, all overlooked by his Mediterranean mansion.

I imagined it was just as beautiful in there.

It was easy to become distracted by the awe-inspiring ocean view and the rhythmic sound of lapping waves rising over the bluff.

A few stars twinkled through the cloudy sky and the cool breeze brushed over me, making me grateful for the warmth emanating from the heat lamps he'd turned on.

Tobias eased my wet gown over my hips, and I stepped out of it so happy to be free of the clingy dampness. He laid it on the back of a lounger and neared me again to remove my shoes, his caresses comforting and making my skin tingle beneath his touch. He eased my panties down my legs and threw them toward the dress. I swooned when he stood behind me and unclipped my bra and removed that too. He wrapped a soft towel around me.

He unbuttoned his shirt and tugged it off, undressing, and all the while giving me an endearing smile.

God, all this beauty—

That tattoo on his left shoulder was dazzling with its Aboriginal symbolism and served as a warning this was no ordinary man. And God, I was enraptured by that inked italic writing running along the side of his groin that he'd once translated for me as "Retribution where there is none. He who is about to win salutes you."

This man was wild and dangerously smart and oh so mesmerizing, a vortex of erotic pleasures waiting to be explored. If I allowed myself to surrender, I'd be drawn into the whirlwind of his universe. Still, this wasn't why I was here and, rising from this daze, I questioned the sanity of staying. Yet when he reached out and took my hand in his and interlocked our fingers my doubt lifted.

Tobias led me toward a bubbling Jacuzzi and I freed myself from my towel and made my way in, sighing with contentment because this was the warmth I'd pined for all the way here. Tobias stepped down to join me and settled opposite. He leaned back against the blue tiled wall and closed his eyes to bask in the heat. Steam cloaked around us. I couldn't stop looking at him, couldn't drag my gaze away from his unnerving allure.

He opened his eyes and gave a heart-stopping smile. "I like seeing you happy."

"This place…" I gave a wistful sigh.

"You're the first woman I've brought here."

My breath stuttered at his sincerity and I sunk lower until only my head was above the water. All this grandeur felt overwhelming.

"Feel better?" he asked.

"Yes, much."

"Good."

"Don't blame me for never getting out, though."

He chuckled. "Maybe I'll stay in here with you."

My gaze found that my dripping Escada gown was hanging over the lounger. "I hope no one remembers."

He gave a comforting smile. "Remembers what?"

Scrunching my nose, I replayed the embarrassing scene of the weather room with me in the starring role as water princess.

I turned my focus to his house with its sweeping large windows, that terra-cotta tiled roof and a large central balcony. Tobias had incredible taste and I'd thought his Oxfordshire house was remarkable. This was off-the-charts decadent.

Then there came the memory of those stolen paintings he'd stashed away in his English home.

I rose out of the water. "I should go."

"Stay." He gestured behind him. "I have a guesthouse if you prefer?"

A flash of movement—

I froze in dismay when I saw a floating contraption behind his shoulder. The drone hovered closer and there was a glint of moonlight reflecting off the two champagne glasses it balanced on its surface.

Tobias turned and he reached out to pick them up by the stems. "Thank you, Jade." He handed a glass to me.

Jaw gaping, I accepted the drink. Jade was mobile now?

Surely this isn't a good thing?

I set the delicate glass down and watched the drone making its way back toward the house.

Tobias set his down too, and moved toward me, reaching up to cup my face with his strong hands as he crushed his lips to mine, his tongue tangling, dominating, obliterating my reasons to leave, causing my body to shudder in the wake of his touch. He broke away and dipped slightly to suckle my left nipple, his teeth dragging along the sensitized beading.

A groan of pleasure escaped me as my sex clenched in response and I dug my fingernails into his biceps to hold him there. His arm slipped around my back to pull me firmly against him and this closeness sent me reeling. Wilder's mouth captured my other breast, swirling his tongue around my areola and my head fell back as I swooned.

Soft lips kissed my shoulder. "Your skin feels like silk." His hand disappeared beneath the water and he ran it over my belly and held it there. "Let me touch you."

"Yes."

He slid a fingertip along my sex and my thighs widened for him, and I gasped at the pleasure of his stroking. Reaching out for balance I gripped the edge of the tub. My wrist tapped my glass and it tipped over and broke in two on the tile.

"I'm sorry," I said.

"No problem." He nuzzled into my ear and kissed my neck.

My eyes widened when I saw the drone was back and hovering near us again. It turned on its axis and its metal arms withdrew from its center. It swept up the broken glass.

No bloody way.

With all evidence of my mishap removed, the drone lifted higher and headed back. I marveled at yet another exclusive peek into his techno world.

Tobias slipped into a grin when he realized he'd left me speechless. "Want another glass?"

I shook my head.

He lifted me up and out of the water, laying me back on the edge with my legs dangling. He dragged me toward him and eased my thighs apart. "Like my drone?"

"Bit scary."

"Not when you get to know her."

I raised my head to look at him. "I like getting to know you better."

"I like you being here."

"This is paradise." I let out a long sigh.

"*This*...is paradise." He buried his face between my thighs and my body shivered when his tongue swept along my sex.

"You like that?" he said huskily.

"Yes, it's amazing."

"The last thing you need is me doing this to you for hours."

"Can you be more specific?" I encouraged playfully.

Tobias ran his tongue along me again and feverishly suckled.

"Oh, I see what you mean now." I trembled with pleasure as he flicked away, finding a perfect rhythm of circling.

He plunged his tongue inside, owning my sex as he used a fingertip to circle my clit until I was racing at supersonic speed toward climax, my hips pumping as I rode this endless wave of bliss.

Close...

He ceased suddenly.

And pulled away, leaving me panting wantonly for his mouth to find me again, my orgasm right there waiting for me to reach its pinnacle. Rising onto my elbows, I stared at him questioningly.

Tobias smiled. "Let me show you your room."

Blinking at him, I tried to grasp his reason for revving me right to the edge of an orgasm and then leaving me suspended in a burning desire. Then I realized Tobias was going to take me to bed, which was a good thing with me so jittery with need. I watched him climb out of the Jacuzzi as I pushed myself up, and let him wrap that large white towel around me again.

He grabbed a towel for himself and dipped low for his drink and handed it to me. "Nightcap."

Padding barefoot behind him, my breath stilted from this yearning between my thighs as I followed him toward a guesthouse.

He punched a series of digits into a keypad to the right of the entryway and opened the door for me. "You'll find everything you need in here."

"Where will you be?"

Tobias gestured to the house and leaned forward to kiss my forehead. "See you in the morning."

What was this?

As he headed along the pathway, he scooped up my wet dress and shoes on the way, leaving me standing there with my body about burst into flames with the passion he'd ignited. Even with this supposed rejection I was still tingling all over, and it didn't help to see his sculptured back and his sexy swagger that was hypnotic to watch.

I went in and closed the door behind me and ran through if I'd done something wrong. The guesthouse looked spacious and homey with its open-plan sitting room, a large sofa and a wide screen TV, all of it was inviting. Of all the scenarios I'd imagined, this wasn't one of them. My thoughts spiraled with all the ways he'd made love to me before and the pleasure he'd denied me tonight.

What the hell?

No, you don't bring a woman to your beautiful home after tricking her to come with you, strip her naked and pop her in your Jacuzzi and then push her to the edge of pleasure until she's a writhing mess of bliss—and then amble off.

I have more self-respect.

I set the glass on the entryway table and headed out of there ready to challenge Tobias about his teasing. After circling the property and finding all the doors locked and the windows secured I stomped back to the guesthouse.

Cheeky bastard.

He'd locked me out.

The touch of his kiss still lingering between my thighs made it challenging to come down from this erotic roller coaster. I went back in for the champagne flute and made my way outside the front door.

Oops.

The glass slipped from my fingers—shattering shards on the tile.

I waited…

Tobias had told me he'd not brought anyone else here. My heart skipped a beat wanting to believe this. Maybe, just maybe the proof was in there. A jolt of adrenaline hit me when I saw a flash of movement—the drone coming toward me.

I wasn't letting him off the hook after bringing me all the way out here. I ran through what motives he had for his actions.

Wait.

Unless he was planning on hitting a place tonight, and I'd chipped away at his precious evening with our fun time in the tub.

The drone lowered and swept up the glass.

Careful of any missed pieces I sidestepped the pathway and followed Jade toward the main house; exhilaration rising that this might work. The machine moved toward a low window and the glass frame slid upward. This was clearly a breach in Tobias's security, because I was scrambling after it, over the windowsill and squirming my body around to lower myself in.

My towel fell to the ground and I scrambled to pick it up and wrap it back around myself, tucking in the top to rese-cure it. I was stuck here with no clothes, which meant going after Tobias was going to be a challenge if he left. Still, I rea-soned, he'd probably have something here I could borrow.

Yes, buddy, you're not slowing me down.

I breathed in the floral scent of fresh-cut flowers and pad-ded barefoot along the stone floor down a long hallway. I listened out for Tobias as the drone floated ahead of me. Get-ting one over on Wilder felt so damn good. I turned the cor-ner and saw the wall of water cascading into a blue pool, a soothing showpiece highlighting the open-spaced contem-porary style.

Farther down, an enormous print with the signature style of Mark Rothko adorned a white wall with its glorious gold, pink, orange and a dash of pale blue splendor. I closed in on the vast canvas, admiring the vibrant brushstrokes that were fast and light—

No way.

Tobias had an authentic Mark Rothko hanging in his home. My breath stuttered at the realization this was a multimillion-dollar masterpiece from the renowned Russian Jewish painter who'd been hailed as America's most talented abstract im-pressionist.

My stare roamed over his striking mixture of color with its vibrant tones reminiscent of his earlier days, not his later work that reflected Rothko's painstaking soul-searching. The kind so many artists endure when their star rises and stirs the complexity of art in its purist form versus the financial free-dom it promised. A brilliant man whose tragic suicide sent shock waves throughout the community. More than this,

Rothko left behind his somber paintings from when he'd been at his lowest and on the day he died, they'd arrived at the Tate Gallery in London as though he'd waited for them to find a safe home first.

To honor Mark's wishes, I stood eighteen inches away from the canvas just as he'd instructed us, close enough to experience his brilliance and not impose meaning but welcome its effect on an emotional level. An inner light emanated from the colors that were miraculously merging; my heart and mind drinking in the beauty.

Soul merging and slipping through its center...

This, this was proof art was more than a canvas and paint, but a living, breathing entity, enticing us to see more.

Be more.

I lost track of time.

My gaze rose to the ceiling to look for surveillance cameras. The drone was at eye level and seemed to be watching me. Hurrying up a large staircase, I admired Tobias's decor. There were touches of the Far East, like the exquisitely carved wooden sculpture of the Hindu god Shiva and the Asian chest flush against the wall that gave the place an earthy feel.

Moving from room to room I listened out for him.

I paused inside a room that looked lived in from the half-made bed in the center with a carved headboard. I went in farther and brushed my hand along the soft duvet, imagining him spending time in here. Inside the walk-in wardrobe was an assortment of sharp-looking suits, pristine shirts and more casual wear, and all of them hung neatly. Sitting on an island was a row of polished business shoes and on the shelf below were his expensive-looking sports shoes. I explored his necktie collection which appeared handcrafted and, pulling another drawer open, I saw a selection of expensive watches.

After dropping my towel to the floor, I reached up for one

of his white shirts and tugged it off its hanger. I pulled it on and buttoned it up. I found a pair of his boxer shorts, they were baggy on me but they'd do.

Across the other side of the room was a glass window leading to an expansive balcony and from here I could see how far his property went. There was a tennis court to the left, and to the right was a helicopter parked on a flight pad, and straight ahead was a sandy pathway down to the beach. This place seemed so dreamy.

Inside his bathroom, I found a comb and pulled it through my damp hair, glancing around for any evidence a woman might have left her stuff here. I was relieved not to see any. All the products were for men and all organized perfectly. His shower and bathtub were both enormous. Tobias seemed to love neatness.

On my way out of his bedroom I noticed a portrait-sized package leaning against the wall and it was wrapped in brown paper and tied in twine. I knelt beside it and held a corner ready to rip it a little to take a peek.

There came a sound from the hallway. I went to explore the noise—

Turning the corner, I jolted to a stop when I saw a white kitten wobbling unsteadily on the carpet. It was crying for its mother.

"Hello, little thing." I approached slowly. "What are you doing?"

Bright blue eyes blinked at me and I giggled at its cuteness and went to pick it up.

The kitten morphed larger—

A scream tore from me.

An enormous lion was where the kitten had been and its vivid black eyes were large and wild. His teeth were bared in anger as he shook his thick mane, back muscles flexing and he ran my way.

He lunged at me.

Falling backward onto my bum, my arms up and bracing for the attack, I squeezed my eyes shut to ready for the agony.

Quiet.

Daring to peek, I exhaled a long desperate breath when I saw it was gone.

I am going to bloody well kill him.

"Tobias!" I screeched and scrambled to my feet in a haze of panic-drenched breaths, using the wall to steady myself as I made my way along, realizing he'd used a hologram on me.

The drone hovered at the end of the hallway.

"Jade, take me to Tobias." My voice wavered with fury.

Jade led me down the stairs and through the house and I wondered if Tobias had returned my access to her. She was certainly responding as though he had or maybe this was a safety mechanism in Jade's software to protect him.

My heart was still pounding. I'd been naive to believe this was going to be easy. Halfway down a long corridor I heard a clanging chain and what sounded like thumping.

I pointed a finger at Jade. "If this is a trick I'll rip your arms off."

It hovered, waiting.

Nudging the door open I peered in and my breath caught at the primal beauty of a bare-chested Tobias wearing shorts and boxing gloves. His legs were slightly parted and his gaze was fixed on a large red punching bag that he was pounding with left and right hooks; his chiseled torso rippling as he circled it, perspiration glistening off his body. My jaw tensed at the erotic splendor of the way he controlled each punch.

He stopped suddenly and caught the bag to still it. His green eyes narrowed on me.

I stepped in farther. "Love the house."

"Looks like someone had a run-in with an African lion?" He smiled broadly. "Is that my shirt?"

"Might be."

"We have a thief in our midst."

My glare shifted to the bag and I wondered if he'd chosen this sport to burn off his sexual tension. Right now, I was close to attacking the thing myself. Why did he have to look so damn gorgeous from every angle? So ripped and primed for pleasure.

"Why did you bring me here?" I snapped.

Confusion marred his face. "To spend time with you."

"What made you change your mind?"

"I didn't."

"What you did to me in the Jacuzzi…" I shook my head to say the rest.

He turned and looked across the room as confliction swept over his face.

"Tobias, back at The Broad you begged me to tell you I want you."

"You didn't say it."

"So is this my punishment?"

"Why must you be so captivating?"

"Why must you be so infuriating?"

"I'm not."

"Yes, you are."

Tobias gave another heart-stopping smile as though flaunting his power. He was all well-defined alpha and seductive pose but something told me he wasn't even trying; this was his natural state, fixed in an unwitting stance of seduction.

"Follow me." I gestured to his gloves. "Keep those on."

His arms fell to his sides and his brows rose with curiosity.

I led him over to the seating area where there were two red lounge chairs.

"Sit," I ordered.

He tilted his head in intrigue.

"Now, please." I pointed.

Amused, Tobias sat in an armchair and rested his gloved hands on the armrests.

I neared him and leaned in to ease my fingers beneath the waistband of his boxers. "Up."

He raised his bum off the chair with a smirk. I had his shorts sliding down his hips and his cock bouncing free when I tugged the material over his thighs to pull them off. I threw them onto the other chair. I eased my shorts off and unbuttoned the shirt too and threw them to join his.

"This is getting interesting," he said as he went to remove a glove.

"No," I said. "You won't need your hands for this."

"Really?"

"No."

His frown deepened and he slid into a wry smile.

Maneuvering myself, I climbed onto his lap and positioned my thighs on either side of his. Reaching low for his erection, I eased the tip toward my entrance and then slid onto him and savored this blissful glide downward, my sex adjusting to his girth as he filled me entirely, clenching him with ripples of pleasure. My breath stuttered as the delicious tautness made me tremble. Tobias stuttered a breath of arousal. He felt enormous inside as he grew, his erection twitching and sending incredible sensations into my sex.

He narrowed his gaze. "I need my hands."

"No, no, there won't be any more talking on your part." I rocked my hips. "The rest of you is of no interest to me."

"Jesus, Zara." His jaw clenched with tension. "This is too hot. I'm gonna come."

I tripped up his chin. "You're forbidden. Understand?"

Reaching down, I pressed a fingertip to my clit and luxuriated in my touch. "Oh, that's good." I moaned, rising and falling, setting a delicious pace.

His body felt rock hard beneath me and glimmered with perspiration and he smelled divine, the remnants of expensive body wash mixed with his natural scent that did crazy things to me. I nuzzled into the crook of his neck and kissed him, running my tongue along his hot flesh, sending sparks of arousal surging through my body.

Rising, I let out a long erotic groan as my head fell back and my damp locks cascaded behind me, tweaking my nipples to increase this desire and stealing a glance at Tobias, I felt the rush of victory at his arousal.

"I can never get over how beautiful you are," he said.

My fingertip snapped to his lips. "Let's pretend you're not here."

"Oh, it's like that?"

My mouth lingered close to his. "It's exactly like that." I pulled back when he went to kiss me and it was challenging not to smile.

Reaching up to grab a fistful of his hair I used it for leverage to feverishly ride him, bouncing, as my fingers traced my clit, sending me tumbling over into a blinding orgasm. My hair whipped from side to side, breasts bobbing, as I became wild upon him, drawing out the remnants of my climax, my breaths drawn out.

His gloved hands moved to my waist and I nudged them back to the armrests.

"Oh, yes," I moaned, languishing on him.

A trickle of perspiration ran down my spine.

His frown was etched in frustration, his green gaze ablaze and speckled with gold, eyes wide with passion, jaw tensing as he forced back his desire. "Zara, if you want me to admit I'm obsessed with you—"

"Hush now." Reveling in our connection, I circled my hips wider to savor these lingering sensations.

His breathing was ragged, needful and all arrogance gone.

When I rose off him to let him slide out, my sex felt bereft with him no longer inside. I stepped back to admire the creature that had satisfied my darkest yearnings.

"Well done," I said.

"Get back here." He tugged his left glove.

Laughing, I scooped up the shirt and shorts and dressed in them on the way out. When I got to the door I turned and said, "Thank you, Mr. Wilder."

Down the hallway, I threw a wave goodbye to the drone and continued through the house until I reached the front door. Outside on his front porch I paused for a second realizing I needed to call a cab.

Damn.

I had to go back in and I was also thirsty too. The view was vast and in the distance, dusky rolling hills reminded me we were in the middle of nowhere.

I sensed Tobias.

He stepped forward to stand by my side, those shorts back on and his boxing gloves off, his stare following the horizon as he said, "Someone didn't think this through."

"I'm not staying in the guesthouse."

"Well, there is an alternative." He gave a nod. "But if it's my bed. It's my rules."

"What would those be?" Every part of me fought with this need to reach out and touch that ripped torso again.

He narrowed his stare on me. "I get to fuck you all night long. Hard."

I crossed my arms over my chest. "I'll think about it."

"Yeah, right." He lifted me high in the air and flung me across his right shoulder so I was upside down and my hands rested on his muscular back.

He slapped my bum in triumph.

I shrieked at the shock and laughed at the joy of being in his arms again. My spontaneity was getting me close to breaking down Wilder's wall.

6

Lying on Tobias's bed I realized I'd been right about this being his room.

He'd carried me over his shoulder all the way in here and this was the side of him I adored, his playfulness took a little coaxing but was so worth it.

Tobias dragged me down the bed toward him. "These are mine." He snapped the waistband of the shorts I'd borrowed and then eased them down my thighs. "I'm taking these back."

"What am I going to wear?" I worked on unbuttoning my shirt.

"Not my problem."

"I like it in here." I glanced over to the wrapped frame I'd almost peeked at earlier. Tobias's stare followed mine.

There was something about the way he looked at it, something in the way the twine had been carefully wrapped around it.

Getting his attention back on me before he saw that it had piqued my interest, I said, "Do you have a cowboy hat?" I cringed at how stupid that sounded.

"No." He grinned. "Are you into that? Role play?"

I giggled with embarrassment and covered my eyes.

"Come here." He grabbed my ankles and yanked me toward him.

"Should we wash off this chlorine?" I sniffed my arm but couldn't smell it on me.

"It's a freshwater spa."

"Maybe we should shut the door so Jade doesn't sneak in?"

"You have a lot of demands." Tobias went over to the door and kicked it shut and continued to undress. "You could learn a lot from her."

"Funny. Why didn't you make Jade a he?"

"Easier to control." He smirked at me. "Though when I developed her she had this annoying trait of interrupting me. So I tweaked her circuitry. Took her sassy-arse attitude down a notch."

"Do you realize how cheeky you are?"

"No one's mentioned it."

"Yeah, right."

Tobias leaned toward my sex. "Time to make it up to you."

The jolt of pleasure from his tongue running along my clit made me arch my back. "Oh, yes." I moaned.

He lavished affection with his mouth, sending shudders of electric pulses inside me. Writhing, thighs trembling, my fingers were nudged away from my breasts and he cupped his own hands there. He tweaked my nipples as he thrust his tongue inside me, his fingers lightly pinching with rhythmic tweaks sending me spiraling into oblivion.

He turned me over and raised my arse in the air and thrust into me. "You feel amazing, Zara."

All I could focus on was the bliss he was sending into me as his balls struck my sex with each thrust.

He slowed and ran his hands down my spine. "Everything I do is to protect you. I need you to believe me."

"Locking me outside?"

He pulled out and flipped me onto my back so he could see my face. I scootched closer to him to let him know I didn't want to stop.

Tobias plunged back in and stilled as though making a powerful statement of ownership. "You broke into my home," he said darkly.

My channel tightened around him. "I'm a guest."

He resumed pumping leisurely and his voice softened with arousal. "You strategized your entry point and executed the perfect break-in." He reached low and flicked my clit.

My body shuddered at the erotic shock of his touch. "That's why you teased me in your pool?"

"Jacuzzi."

"So you admit it?"

"If you want something bad enough."

I pushed myself up and slapped his chest playfully.

He gave a smile. "Mission accomplished, Leighton, you got your man. I'm inside you again. Feel this? This is what you wanted. See how ingenious you are. Looks like you have something in common with Icon."

"Not fair."

"Is this fair?" He buried deeper.

My white-knuckled grip tightened on the bedsheet; I was close.

"Need convincing?" He lifted me with ease and I wrapped my legs around him and he carried me across the room. Tobias shoved me against the wall and proceeded banging me hard against it. "How about this?"

This was mind-blowing and the feel of his controlled

pounding sent me into a trance; all I could do was rest my head on his shoulder and let him have me like this.

He carried me over to the armchair and threw me face-first over it so my bum was raised upon the arch of the high back and my hands were gripping the seat. This position left me completely powerless and totally exposed. When his mouth met my sex again, he made me scream through another orgasm.

"I can see you still need convincing." Tobias lifted me up and carried me back to the bed and flung me onto it. "How about this?" He climbed on to join me and rose above my body and yanked my arms over my head and gripped them there, pinning them down. Sinking his cock inside me again, setting off into a startling rhythm and pummeling me into the mattress.

I knew this was Tobias's way of asserting his authority after I'd played with him in his gym.

"I need you to come again." His voice sounded punishing.

"I can't."

"You can and you will." He moved his hips in a circle.

His masterful words sent me reeling and I tipped up my pelvis, my hair falling over my face as I shuddered through another climax. Tobias stilled and became rigid and his heat burst into me, his face buried in the crook of my neck as he rode out his pleasure with continuous leisurely glides.

He held himself up with strong arms either side of my head and looked down at me. "How was that for an apology?"

"Right on point," I managed.

He slipped to my side and pulled me onto him.

With my head nuzzled into the cradle of his neck and my leg draped over his, sated and weak in his arms I fell asleep.

The sound of birdsong stirred me awake and I raised my head off the pillow, realizing I'd been here all night.

"Hi." Tobias reached over and lifted a strand of auburn out of my eyes.

I hoped he'd not snuck out during the night to bloody well steal something. So much for being on guard. Still, he reflected innocence and his hair was its usual mess of perfection.

I stretched languidly. "It's like being on holiday."

And I'd just reminded him the real reason I was here.

He rested his head in his hands and stared up at the ceiling.

I reached out to touch him. "I didn't mean…"

Tobias swept his hand across the room. "My casa is your casa."

Scooting over to him, I planted a kiss on his bicep and he reciprocated my affection with his fingers trailing languidly through my hair, making my scalp tingle.

The uncomfortable silence lingered too long.

"What's it like having homes all over the world?" I broke the quiet.

"Guarantees privacy."

"You have a Rothko, Tobias. An authentic painting by the master himself?"

"Mark gave it to my dad."

Which explained why it was here and not in a gallery. Though this went against Tobias's philosophy of sharing art with the world.

"Did your dad know him?"

"Yes. He was a remarkable man."

"It's beautiful."

"The blue reminds me of you." His eyes crinkled into a smile.

"Do you ever get lonely?"

"I keep busy."

I rested my head in my palm. "You avoided the question."

"I love my work."

"Which? Your business? Your gallery? Inventing? Or…"

"Zara, don't go there."

"What would happen if I did?"

"I told you before. Everything I have done is to protect you."

"From you?"

His eyes held mine and he looked hurt.

"From who, then?"

"Push me at your peril, Leighton."

"What are you hiding?"

"What are *you* hiding?" he mirrored back.

"Me? Nothing."

"Can I ask you something," he said softly.

I shrugged that I'd hear his question at least.

He turned to face me. "How did your dad choose the paintings? The night of the fire?"

"We grabbed what we could."

A flash of fear; disorientation.

"You remember something?"

"It was a long time ago." But I understood the question. It was like asking which child you would save first, because each painting held a precious place in my father's heart.

"Zara?" Tobias whispered.

I loosened my grip from where I'd been digging my fingernails into his bicep. "Dad went back for his favorite."

"You went with him?"

"I couldn't leave him."

He looked horrified. "That was so dangerous."

"He'd removed *Madame Rose Récamier* from my bedroom and placed her in his office weeks before. The frame needed to be refurbished. Otherwise she'd have gone too."

"The smoke could have gotten to you." Tobias rested his head back on the pillow and stared at the ceiling as though working through a difficult thought. "That's where he kept the Michelangelo. That's where he kept all the paintings you saved."

"There were so many. We tried." A familiar guilt that I couldn't manage the Degas.

This drawn-out silence allowed those haunting memories to sweep in. "I should be able to ask you things too."

"Go on, then."

"How do they contact you?"

"Who?"

"Your clients? The ones who hire you to steal their paintings back?"

"Zara, please." His tone insinuated I'd ruin what we'd shared.

I yearned to reach him and now felt so right. I scooted closer and rested my head on his chest and my scalp tingled as he ran his fingers through my hair.

"The thing is," I began softly, "when a painting has been with a family for decades it's hard to come to terms with the fact a family member obtained it illegally years before. The current family bonds with it."

"That doesn't make it right."

"No, but more people suffer."

"When you saw *St. Joan* at Christie's you wanted to take her home. You wanted her back?"

"Yes."

He gave a shrug to indicate he'd made his point.

"You stole her from Christie's for me?" I raised my head to look at him. "Tobias?"

He turned his face away and gave the deepest sigh.

"Toby?"

He slid into a sweet smile, and then his expression shifted to resignation, his gaze sweeping the ceiling.

"There's something you're not telling me?" I whispered.

He turned his head to look at me "This moment could change what we can have. You want that?"

"I need answers."

"Proceed with caution."

A flutter of nerves went berserk in my chest. "I have to know."

His stare bored into my eyes as though gauging I was ready. "Do you remember that first evening we met?"

My eyes brightened with the memory of him half-naked in The Otillie basement. "Of course."

"Later, when we met again in the gallery?"

"You introduced yourself and then left."

He'd suddenly walked out of the gallery as though my name alone had caused his quick exit.

"You'd heard of me?" My voice rasped with emotion.

"I realized you were Bertram Leighton's daughter."

The hairs on my forearms pricked. "Did you know my dad?"

He hesitated. "No."

My heart thundered with all the possibilities of what was coming next.

He blew out a cautious sigh. "I came across information on a painting that appeared to have been stolen. It was *St. Joan of Arc* by Walter Ouless."

"Where?"

He blew out a frustrated sigh of doubt. "I travel."

I reached out and squeezed his arm. "Please."

"I researched the painting's provenance. I didn't like what I saw."

"You realized it was stolen?"

Was he admitting he knew the man's name?

His gaze held mine. "I tracked *St. Joan* to your family."

"I know you stole her back for me." I held my breath, waiting for him to acknowledge this.

Tobias rose and pushed himself off the bed and padded across the room and went straight for that portrait-sized package wrapped in brown paper. The same one I'd caught sight of earlier.

He lifted it off the floor. "This is yours."

I bolted upright, realizing he'd brought it home from The Wilder.

Weeks ago, he'd left me sleeping in my London flat to sneak off to steal *St. Joan* from Christie's. The gallery's footage had not only caught the theft but Tobias's holographic security guard in the vicinity. A trick of the cameras. The actual guard had been recorded eating his lunch in the break room at the same time the heist went down.

Tobias rested the painting on the bed. "I'll arrange to have her discreetly returned to London. Tell no one you have her."

My heart pounded as a chasm seemingly opened again between us.

Lifting the painting off the bed, I delicately tore the brown paper to reveal St. Joan's face beneath. It was her.

Tobias pulled on a T-shirt and grabbed a fresh pair of boxer shorts from a chest of drawers and dressed in silence.

He headed for the door. "Your safety is all I care about."

"I'm not in any danger."

"I'll make coffee—"

"What changed?"

He paused by the door.

"Last night you were whirling me around a dance floor asking me to admit I want you? And last night…it was incredible."

His expression softened. "It was even more than that."

"What's wrong, then?"

"The more you know the more dangerous it becomes for you." The sweep of his hand inferred the rest. "I won't do that to you."

"What are you saying?"

"We're everything we shouldn't be."

My mouth went dry as I realized why he was going cold on me. "You don't want me to ask the name of the man who stole my *St. Joan*?"

Tobias gave a wary nod. "It's a treacherous road."

"So what happens now?"

He headed toward the door. "I'll make breakfast."

A chill washed over me. "Are you sending me back to London?"

Like he'd done outside The Wilder.

All the ground I'd made to get closer to him was lost.

"Look, Zara, knowing *St. Joan* is returned to you is all that matters. Knowing you're safe." He left and closed the door behind him.

Did he have any idea how much he hurt me when he pushed me away like this? I grabbed his shirt from the back of the armchair, glancing at the one beside it—the same chair he'd bent me over and taken me on so deliciously; the kind of passion my body would crave for an eternity. I went back into his wardrobe and searched out a pair of shorts and used one of his belts to keep them up.

Making my way down the stairs I reasoned Tobias had risked so much for me. *My St. Joan* back in my arms was proof of that. More questions needed answers and yet Tobias had closed down so fast I'd had no way of breaking his descent into aloofness.

I went in search of him, following the aroma of fresh brewing coffee. My stomach grumbled and yet my appetite wavered.

Tobias was standing with his back to me before a grill and he looked lost in thought. I needed a few seconds to steady myself at the stark beauty of him standing there working the spatula to flip the batter. The coffeemaker spluttered out fresh brewed grounds into a glass pot.

St. Joan's frame weighed heavy in my hands.

The room looked gorgeous with its sleek modern stainless-steel appliances and it exuded a cozy style. There were badass robotic arms above the stove.

"Hi." He gestured for me to sit at the center island. "Coffee?"

I looked around for Jade but didn't see her. "What is that?"

He followed my gaze toward the two arms above the stove. "My chef. This morning I insisted on cooking." Tobias slipped into a smile as he pointed to the mechanism. "He's a little put out, but still."

I refused to laugh. "Is this your goodbye? It's not as harsh as outside The Wilder but it's just as cruel." I rested the painting on the island.

Tobias's frown deepened. "She's authentic. But you already know that."

"Tell me his name."

"It's over."

My silence resounded louder than words.

He gave a look of understanding. "This isn't an easy decision."

"You know who the man is who scathed my family's reputation. The man who sent my dad to an early grave. The man who stole that—" I pointed to the half-wrapped painting.

"I'm here for you."

My breath stuttered. "He needs to go to prison."

"What was I thinking? You'd prefer tea, right?" He opened a cupboard and rifled through it. "I have it somewhere."

"You really believe I'll let this go?"

He gave up searching and turned to face me, crossing his arms across his chest defensively.

"I'm considered your client now? You gave me my painting back so I'm of no consequence to you?"

"Spending time with you has been…" He gave the kindest smile.

"Cut the bullshit, Tobias. This is important."

"Zara, I believed this would help you see things from my perspective."

"You think I'll change my mind now about persuading you to give it up."

"Give what up?"

"Being Icon."

He raked his hand through his hair. "I'm flattered."

"Are you blackmailing me with my own painting?" My breath stuttered on its inhale.

"Now that would be ingenious." He gestured left. "Would you rather have a bagel? I have salmon."

I turned and stormed through the house past the wall of water in the foyer, all the way to the front door where I saw my high heels. I scooped them up and saw several sets of car keys laying on the entryway table. I grabbed one of them and flew out the door, squinting against the morning sun.

"Zara!" His footfalls closed in on me.

The gravel bit into my soles and I quickly pulled my shoes on. I flicked the key ring and a silver Jaguar's headlights flashed.

Tobias's strong arms wrapped around me. "Zara."

"Let me go."

"We drive on the other side."

"I know, I drove your Ferrari, remember?"

"That was a self-driving car. And I was with you."

"You can't use my own painting to manipulate me."

His front pressed against my back and he held me with a determined strength, his arms holding me in a hug, gripping my arms to my side.

My rib cage ached from his hold. "Why tell me any of this?"

"I believed you'd handle it."

I weakened in his arms and he let me down.

I spun round and glared at him.

"What are you expecting?" He took his keys from my hand. "Relationships are built on a foundation of trust. You're here on behalf of Huntly Pierre—"

"No." Though telling him they weren't aware I was here sent a stab of doubt at my sanity.

"Look—" He stepped forward.

I stepped back so he couldn't touch me.

"You investigate art thefts," he said. "When you catch Icon, it will be case closed. Your career skyrockets."

"Then why haven't I done that?"

"Lack of evidence." He glanced at his home. "You were hoping to find some, no doubt."

A wave of nausea hit me that he really believed that's why I'd stayed.

But I had thought that, hadn't I.

Icon was before me and I was failing the art world. Failing me. All this soul-searching had gone awry because when I was with him everything felt right. Tobias gave the kindest expression of understanding, the kind threatening to render me useless if I didn't brace against it.

He ran his thumb over the key fob. "Unless one of us is willing to relent, we have no future together."

"Being here with you was a mistake."

A dreadful, stupid mistake.

"Don't say that." He looked wounded.

"I have to go."

"Let's go back in and talk this through."

"No."

"Can I get dressed first?"

I gave a nod.

"Wait inside. Come on."

I shook my head, refusing.

"Promise you'll wait."

"Sure."

He gave a reluctant nod and paused in the doorway to glance back. "It's going to be okay."

I feigned a nod of agreement.

"I have some sunglasses you can have." He gave the sweetest smile of reassurance and continued in.

I turned away from the house and looked beyond the garden, out toward the sweeping mountains. I couldn't stay here one more second because my heart would never survive it.

How difficult was driving on the other side of the road, anyway? I mean, I'd driven in France a couple of years ago for goodness' sake. I went back into the foyer, listening out for him. His car keys were back on that entryway table where he'd thrown them.

I grabbed them.

Within seconds I was steering his silver Jaguar out of his driveway and down the path ahead and hoping it would lead me to the main road. His automatic was eerily easy to drive compared to a stick shift, though I was heavy on the break and kept jolting forward.

It is too late to rethink this.

Leaving behind *St. Joan* felt like I was deserting her, and yet taking her with me felt wrong too. Being caught with stolen property wouldn't have been one of my better decisions. Even if the paperwork once pointed to my ownership, provenance could be forged.

My hair blew into my face and I fought with these wayward locks so I could see better.

I steered the car down the tree-lined road, squinting ahead at the mountains rising in the distance—the terrain a strange mixture of green and earth colors, proving we were in a desert climate. At the crossroads, I kept on straight, vaguely remembering we drove along this path last night.

Oh, no.

A Rolls-Royce Ghost was parked ahead and it blocked my way. I shoved the car into Reverse and turned to look out the window to maneuver backward. My car rolled to a stop and the lights on the dashboard went dark. The engine died and I tried to restart it. Resting my forehead on the wheel I realized what had happened and cursed myself for believing I could take on Tobias. Marshall climbed out of the Rolls and removed his sunglasses as he headed toward me. I braced for him scolding me for stealing his boss's car.

He walked up to my driver's side window. "Hello there, Ms. Leighton. I've been asked to drive you wherever you'd like to go."

"If I refuse?" I raised my chin in defiance.

He glanced back at the road. "That was a stop sign. You rolled right past it. You've not driven in the States before, as I understand it?"

I narrowed my gaze on him.

"Here, this is yours." He handed over my phone.

The same one I'd hidden behind a bookcase at UCLA two days ago and my mouth went dry as I tried to swallow the embarrassment that he'd found it.

"I need to restart this car," I said.

"Mr. Wilder's on his way down now."

My head snapped toward the pathway and I knew one smile, one kind word and Wilder would have me doubting all over again. "Can you drive me to the Sofitel, please? I'm in a hurry."

"It'll be my pleasure, miss." Marshall opened my car door. "You don't want to wait for Mr. Wilder?"

"I'll call him from the car." Climbing into the back of the Rolls my thoughts caught up with my miserable musing that Tobias had blindsided me in a brazen move I'd not seen coming.

He'd aimed for my one weakness, art, and even though I'd come to terms with letting *St. Joan* go, I wanted her to find a home in a prestigious gallery worthy of her and one that could ensure her protection.

Clearing her provenance was how I was going to restore my family name.

7

The journey to Brentwood in the back of a taxi was the distraction my soul needed, and I drank in the beauty of the impressive homes tucked away behind tall brass gates and shadowed by sweeping palm trees.

My thoughts drifted back to this morning when I'd fled Tobias's home feeling as though tectonic plates were fracturing beneath me. All I'd carefully schemed over the last few days had come unraveled. I'd not planned on ending up in his bed and being ravished to the point of blinding pleasure—the kind that made forgetting easy.

After Marshall had driven me back to the Sofitel I'd spent the rest of the morning in the hotel, first pampering myself with a hot bubble bath and then grabbing a quick breakfast in Estérel, the cozy restaurant. I even treated myself to a manicure in the luxury spa. My mind replayed every moment I'd spent with Wilder as I tried to decipher his motive; my grit to see this through returning.

Visiting Gabe for lunch was the perfect break from all this intensity. I strolled up the driveway toward his Spanish-styled home, feeling spoiled by this temperate climate that allowed me to wear my Ralph Lauren black sweater dress and boots and go without a coat.

Gabe greeted me in the doorway with a big hug. His blue striped shirt and beige corduroys reminding me he'd just returned from a Wednesday morning spent teaching at UCLA.

He beamed at me. "How was last night?"

"Fine. How was the rest of The Broad?"

"Great. Did you stay at Wilder's?"

"He has a guesthouse." It was a small fib but I wanted to maintain this calm facade. "His house is right on the beach in Malibu. We talked about art, mostly."

"Any fireworks?" He fished for more.

"We're old friends." Playing the disaster down was the best way to protect Gabe, and my words were less likely to come back to haunt me.

I peered in at the open-plan design with its vaulted ceiling overlooking the stylish cream and deep green decor, those plush silk rugs and that designer couch enhancing the lavish space.

"Come in." He gestured for me to follow.

"What a beautiful home," I said.

Standing by the staircase was an attractive older woman who was watching us, her hair elegantly silver, and her chic long knitted cardigan and sweeping skirt highlighted her sophistication.

I walked over to her and shook her hand. "Hello, I'm Zara."

"I've heard such wonderful things about you," she said in a soft American accent. "I'm Sally."

Gabe shut the door. "Sally's my neighbor. I wanted you to meet her. I was telling her you were once my star student back in London."

"I wouldn't say that." I waved off his compliment.

"Modest too." She smiled and it made her look so radiant.

"Sally works at an animal sanctuary," said Gabe. "She's always trying to get us to adopt one of her mutts."

"Oh, that's wonderful." I placed my handbag down on the hall table.

We made our way into the kitchen.

The room was charmingly modern with lemon-and-blue Spanish tiles and low light fixtures all adding an Italian flair. Over in the corner was a cozy seating area with a long couch and comfy armchairs. To the left sat a dining room table with six high-back chairs hinting at Gabe's love for entertaining.

There, lying on the central island was an antique frame and within it held an impressionist painting by Claude Monet. It was breathtaking and I beamed over at Gabe with intrigue. He was busy pouring coffee into three mugs, though when he glanced my way he saw my reaction.

"Gabe told me you're an art specialist now?" Sally rested her hand on her chest with sincerity. "Hope I'm not being presumptuous."

"This is yours?" I asked.

She nodded. "I know there's usually a charge. Gabe insisted I bring it round."

"It's been a mystery for quite some time," Gabe added.

"Of course." With my interest piqued, I stepped closer to the island to better see it, bringing my magnifier from my handbag.

Sally sat on a bar stool at the island and her expression was full of hope as she waited for her appraisal.

This was a Monet, yet...

Confusion marred the moment as I studied the soft blue tones of the still lake and my thoughts carried me into the painting—

A sunny day. A light breeze. The scent of lavender marking the summer. A master at work.

Monet forgetting his own existence as his brushstrokes teased the finely woven fabric, his hand immortalizing a moment in time with each flick of his wrist.

A prelude to his later and far more familiar work of waterlilies resting on a pond.

Someone else was there with Monet. Someone else had painted on this canvas.

Permission had been granted from Monet himself because his strokes came back around to weave through the others to complement them. The clue of another's touch was from my knowledge that Monet rarely used black paint. Yet here on this very canvas were thin brushstrokes of gray and dark morphing into the starkest shade of pitch black that altered the blurring of shades.

"Zara?" Gabe's voice broke the quiet.

Rousing from my trance I mulled over what I saw.

Gabe placed my drink on the end of the island and I lifted the mug and placed it back on the counter in a daze. One tip and history would be forever tainted.

He gave a smile of understanding. "What do you think?"

Sally traced her fingers along the frame. "My husband was devastated when he got it valued. Someone ruined it by painting over the canvas. He signed his name Ren on the back and dated it 1862."

I leaned in and peered through my magnifier and drank in its beauty, recognizing the delicate stroke of another master who'd leant his talent to this. Oh, how he must have been so enamored with the man who'd taught him more.

Sally lifted the frame. "My husband, Clive, refused to believe it wasn't a Monet. I mean, it looks like a Monet to me."

"Your husband had it professionally valued?" I asked.

"A local art dealer. He told him the black paint rules it out as a Monet."

I shook my head ruefully. "Your evaluator didn't recognize 'Ren.'"

"Not all evaluators are created equal," offered Gabe.

I stepped back and lifted my mug and took a sip, tasting the rich beans and cream, savoring this undiscovered Monet. Staring at the beautiful canvas and admiring the brilliance of an artist who had a love for the changing seasons and a respect for how nature transformed a view.

"It's good news and kind-of-good news too," I reassured her. "In its own way."

Sally's face lit up with excitement. "It is a Monet?"

"It's more than that," I said. "There's history here. A profound union. The mark of a great friendship."

"I told you she was good," said Gabe.

Sally beamed with glee.

"Did you know he painted his wife on her deathbed?" I told her.

Sally scrunched up her nose. "That's a bit morbid."

"He loved her very much," I said. "Sadly, she was only thirty-two when she died of uterine cancer. She was seven years his junior. Camille modeled for Monet and she also posed for Renoir and Manet." I rested my hand on the frame. "You have a unique piece—at some point Monet invited another artist to paint alongside his brushstrokes on this very canvas. The darker shades are not his method, but they are the same as those specific to Pierre-Auguste Renoir."

She gasped. "Renoir?"

"Apparently, he was allowed to add his personal touch to this. They were both looking at the same view but interpreted it differently."

"Quite the find," said Gabe.

"It's a unique piece touched by history." I felt a rush of happiness at seeing Sally's face light up with joy.

"I'd never part with it," she said. "No matter how much it's worth. I just wanted to prove my husband right."

"You have."

"Oh, Zara, this means the world to me," she said. "Thank you."

"The time frame fits from this—" I pointed to the date beneath Monet's name. "In 1862, Renoir was studying art under Mark Gabriel Charles Gleyre, an instructor and masterful painter in his own right. It was while at this art school Renoir met fellow artist Claude Monet."

Sally sighed with reverence.

"Monet affectionately called Renoir, Ren. Infrared reflectography will confirm the artists and pinpoint where Monet's work ended and Renoir's began. The use of monochromic lights will ascertain if the paint was applied around the same time and will rule out restoration. This is what I believe threw the evaluator."

Sally looked impressed. "You've made my day, Zara."

Gabe gave me a reassuring smile. "How about a sandwich?"

Sally declined with a wave. "Have yoga, but thank you." She came over and hugged me and the floral scent of Chanel No. 5 drifted; the comforting scent of vanilla. She placed her empty mug near the sink and with a new reverence picked up her Monet and Renoir, and took that grand fragment of the past with her. More than this, she now had a remarkable validation for her late husband's belief he'd invested in something special.

This was the part of my profession I loved so much, seeing the owners leave with their painting knowing they had a unique piece. The financial gain was always going to excite them but the real pleasure was from giving their painting pride of place in their homes.

"Thank you for that," said Gabe. "She lost her husband

several years ago, and she once told me that painting was part of him."

"I'm so glad."

Gabe had prepared a selection of sandwiches and we carried our plates out into the garden, along with our fresh mugs of coffee. We sat at a table overlooking the pool. His garden was sprawling and behind the pool was a tennis court.

It was wonderful to finally find the time to catch up properly and reminisce about The Courtauld. I had only affectionate memories of Gabe's enduring kindness. His passion for art history had infused every lecture he gave with devotion and all of them had been insightful and personalized to relay a greater meaning. In his mind, history served as a dire warning in which to mindfully plan our futures. Spending time with such a Renaissance man lifted my mood.

"Do you have any friends who are good with phones?" I asked. "I'm looking for a geek with special skills."

Gabe looked concerned. "Ned's bound to know someone. What do you have in mind?"

I nudged my empty plate aside. "It's for work."

"It's not illegal, is it?"

I'd already pushed that doubt aside; tracking someone who was tracking me surely canceled each other out. "You know me," I said with a cute smile. "I'm just your friendly girl-next-door librarian."

His eyes widened with wonder. "Well, you were."

"How do you mean?"

"You were whisked off into the night by Tobias Wilder." He looked amused by that hint of scandal.

"I only have my love of art in common with him." I stared at the edge of the garden and its row of trees, their leaves turning a beautiful golden brown.

"No plans to ask Wilder for help? Isn't he a tech genius? He owns TechRule, doesn't he?"

My gaze snapped over to Gabe. "He's far too busy. So, that won't work."

Though, more important, it was Wilder's phone I'd be tracking.

8

Sitting poolside at the Sofitel could easily be considered a small slice of heaven.

I'd left Gabe's home in Brentwood yesterday, feeling invigorated and with a new sense of purpose. Gabe had inspired me with his monologue about how history influenced our decisions. Something told me he was trying to get me to trust again after having my heart savaged by my ex-boyfriend Zach. Wilder had been a promising lover who could do just that; right up to the point of discovering he was Icon.

At nine in the morning the pool was deserted. I'd brought my laptop down from my room and settled on a lounger, wearing my red bikini and sipping sparkling water. I worked with the calming view of the blue water and was surrounded by lush foliage.

With my computer fully charged and my jacked-up phone at the ready, I was prepared to follow Tobias—the small blue blip on my cell phone was an echo from my device back to the phone tracking it in Malibu. As expected it was coming from Tobias's hilltop home.

A sip of Perrier did nothing to lessen my dry mouth. I

was still quietly freaking out at what I'd accomplished—and all at the hands of tech genius Bridget Madsen, who'd reassured me there'd be no trace of my skulduggery. Gabe had come through for me and arranged a meeting with her last night. She'd been kind enough to visit me here at the Sofitel as she lived nearby on Laurel Canyon. He'd told me she was a good friend of Ned's from his specialized world and agreeably discreet.

Bridget had met me in the hotel bar, Riviera 31, and we'd sat tucked away in a corner booth sipping on iced water as she worked her techie magic. She'd been alarmed to locate the tracking device on my phone and was more than happy to install a tracker to ping in reverse. She reassured me it was undetectable. Bridget told me she'd experienced her fair share of crazy boyfriends and accepted my explanation of wanting to keep an eye on my ex too.

My breath caught—the blip on my phone was flashing along the Pacific Coast Highway, proving Wilder was on the move.

Refocusing on my laptop, I slid my mouse across the screen and clicked Start on Huntly Pierre's collating software. I'd set the search so that should any LA gallery list a painting with a broken provenance I'd add them to my list to monitor. The window that appeared alerted me the search was going to take an hour.

There came a rising exhilaration as I increased the size of the blip on my phone to view the location of the signal. Tobias was currently stopped off at a flower shop called Cosentino's in Malibu.

Resting my head back, I stared skyward and let out a sigh of frustration. This was going to be tough because of the glimpse I'd receive into his personal life. I wondered who'd be getting those flowers. A knot tightened in my stomach at the thought of some girl having her world rocked by Wilder and it made me question whether I could push my personal feelings aside.

You're strong enough, I told myself, *stay focused and you'll survive this.*

Survive him.

Tobias knew the name of the man who'd stolen *St. Joan* and I was determined to get it out of him one way or another. With that new information I could clear my family name. I placed my laptop and phone on the glass table beside me and pushed myself to my feet. I threw my sunglasses onto the lounger and headed toward the pool, kneeling first to dip my hand in and sighing with contentment to find it heated.

I dived in.

My mood lifted as I swam breaststrokes along the full length and continued these laps that cleared my mind and made it easier to think. The blip would tell me when Tobias visited an art gallery and that was something to go on at least.

The conference call with my London team loomed. They were eight hours ahead which had given me time to prepare my explanation for why I was supposedly working just outside of London.

Taking in a deep breath, I swam toward the bottom of the pool and along it until my lungs could bear it no more and I pushed off the tile to rise. When I reached the surface, I grabbed the edge and wiped water from my eyes—

Trying to swallow past this panic.

On the glass table, next to my lounger was a tall vase holding a lush bouquet of fresh-cut red roses. A cream card rested against the base. Panic-stricken, I looked around for the person who left it there. I swam to the metal stairs and hurried up, scanning the garden again as I made my way back to my lounger. After drying my hands on the towel, I picked up the card and peeled open the envelope.

Is my princess up for an adventure?
—T.W.

A jolt of excitement, my body quaking with what this meant. I'd doubted I could ever recover from his mercurial nature. I could see he was fighting an invisible force, a conflict revealing he knew more about my dad and maybe that's what this was—a cruel tease he knew I couldn't refuse.

I breathed in the scent of the beautiful roses. As this ache lifted it was replaced with a pining for a man who was forbidden, and that alone sent a thrill pulsing through me. Maybe I'd touched a nerve and made a chink in his steely armor.

Beside the vase rested a Los Angeles County of Modern Art gold-embossed invite. I read the invitation. It was for an exhibition.

Women Who Read: a collection of remarkable paintings.

The invite for the event was tonight at six.

Notes sang out announcing the incoming video conference call on my laptop and Huntly Pierre's logo filled the screen. Twenty minutes ahead of schedule.

Scrambling, I wrapped my towel around myself, threw my phone, laptop and Tobias's note into my beach bag and slipped into my flip-flops. I threw the bag over my shoulder and carried the flowers with me back to my room. I'd be late for the call but at least when I joined them I'd have clothes on and not give away I'd spent time by a pool.

Back in my room I dried myself off quickly and pulled on jeans and a sweater. I brushed my hair and dabbed on some lipstick. After positioning the laptop on the dresser, I sat in front of it and glanced behind to make sure the background wouldn't give away clues to my location.

With a few clicks I was connected to the video call and a blur of a face appeared on the screen.

The luminous smile of Abby Reynolds lit up the frame; the dynamic forty-year-old had a background in law enforcement to round out her uncanny knack for investigating. Her dark complexion exuded a beautiful vitality; her intelligent eyes reflecting the ebullience I adored in her.

Nudging this homesickness away I put my professional face on.

She lifted a mug and took a sip of her drink. "Hey there."

"Am I late?" I glanced past her to see the others.

"Meeting got pushed. How are you?"

"Great. You?"

"We're excited to hear what you're up to. Got a lead?"

"I'm afraid it's a dead end. I thought I'd found a collector who'd received stolen property from Icon."

In truth, the collector I'd met with a few weeks ago—Sarah Louise Ramirez—had already suffered so much and her testimony could wait for the time when we had nothing else. And the last thing I needed was providing them with a direct link to Wilder. It was too soon to blow this entire plan to smithereens.

I continued with enthusiasm. "She's old and a little confused so I think it's best we don't stress her anymore. I'll keep chipping away."

"Okay, write it up and submit your report."

"Got it." I picked up the pen and wrote her request on the notepad, wondering how the hell I was going to avoid doing that—

Two weeks ago, I'd phoned an elderly Sarah Louise

Ramirez to confirm my theory that Tobias had returned her Titian, stolen from her family decades ago when they'd lived in Boginy. At 15, she'd been the only family member to survive her house fire. Sarah Louise had escaped by leaping onto a tree outside her bedroom window to climb to safety, avoiding the flames allegedly set by a member of the Burell family after they'd stolen the Ramirezes' precious Titian.

Weeks ago, there had been a theft at the Burells' home in Amboise in France and I was sure it had been Tobias who'd stolen their Titian with its shaky provenance and then given it back to Sarah Louise. She'd hung up on me when I'd called her and mentioned the painting. That Titian had been conveniently missing from Tobias's Oxfordshire home because he'd already given it to her by then. I was sure of it.

A ringing in my ears—

Pushing aside this doubt, I realized what had happened to Sarah Louise was the same for me. Both of us had endured house fires after an art theft. How had I not seen this before?

Decades have worn away the truth and grief has clouded my view.

I'd suppressed my history in a thwarted attempt to erase it.

"Did you just take a shower?" Abby broke my daydreaming.

Guilt washed over me that my hair was wet from a dip in the pool. I tried to distract her. "You're there late?"

She checked her watch. "I came in late. Where are you?"

My mouth felt dry and I pined for that Perrier. "A little way out of London."

"When are you coming back?"

"Monday." My teeth bit the inside of my cheek. "I've started a search on the galleries in LA."

"I saw you were running that on the software. You think our man's in the States now?"

"Possibly."

"Indicator?"

"I've detected a pattern."

"What kind?"

"Three thefts per country. I believe California is his next job."

"Why Stateside?"

"I'm following a hunch on a high-profile painting with shaky provenance." It was a small lie that I'd dragged *St. Joan* into.

"Could you be more bloody vague?" She leaned into the frame and narrowed her gaze on me. "Looks like we'll have to fly you out there."

Fuck.

I sat back and drew in a steadying breath.

She shook her head. "Your IP address indicates you're in California? How's the weather there?"

I tried to read her reaction. "I've gone out on a limb, Abby."

"Well it's not on Huntly Pierre's dime but it's on their time." She was stern. "What have you found?"

"I've met a connection in the art world who has info that can help us. They want to remain anonymous for now."

"Sounds dangerous."

"It's not."

"What do they have?"

"I'm trying to gain their trust so they give me a name."

Or maybe I didn't need Tobias to tell me who stole my *St. Joan* now because the fog of truth was clearing all by itself.

"Can this person bring us closer to Icon?" she asked.

I went with a nod.

"Fess up and tell Adley you're there. It's best it comes from you."

The thought of having to fess up to our boss back at Huntly Pierre made me tense further.

Her gaze narrowed. "Is Tobias Wilder out there too now?"

Which made things sound even worse. She'd learned about our fling back in London. There was no way around it—I had to give her something.

I gave a shrug of resignation. "As you know, *St. Joan* is connected to all this. There's a lot invested in this for me. Abby, this is personal now."

"My concern is that emotions can get in the way of logic."

"It was a long time ago," I said calmly. "I'm an art specialist. This is what I do."

"I've got your back, Zara, but you need to email me everything you've found so far. You can't do this alone."

"It's complicated."

She set down her mug. "That's the nature of our job."

"Give me more time. I promise to come back with something."

"What can I do?"

"Can you look into the Burells to see if any of the family members have a history of convictions or any suspicious activity?"

She sat back. "It does look like Icon stole their Titian. Same MO."

"And the victims," I strained to call the Burells that. "They're connected to its disappearance in the first place."

"Their profile is unsettling. What with them providing military security in the Middle East, hiring mercenaries and placing them in dangerous regions. Maybe there's something else going on there. Making a profit from war doesn't exactly make them pillars of society."

I leaned in. "My previous report points to a Burell or

someone commissioned by them to steal the Titian from the Ramirez family in the 1950s."

"And then they burned the Ramirez family home."

"Abby, my house was almost burned to the ground too."

"I remember. You think it's connected?"

Ice-cold fear slithered up my spine. "That 1955 newspaper article in *Le Rue Relais* reported the fire at the Ramirezes' home occurred right after their painting was stolen. At the time the Burells' lawyers prevented any further investigation."

"That Titian has a dark past." She held my gaze. "And your *St. Joan* is out there somewhere and might lead us to who stole it. Proceed with caution."

"Of course." I swallowed hard at the suppression of the truth I owed her.

I'd never been so reckless.

"If the Titian's thief is still alive," she added, "he'll be at least eighty now."

"Yes."

She flashed a smile. "I'm almost rooting for Icon."

Stony-faced, I dug my fingernails into my palms.

"I'll see what we can dig up on them. I'll get Danny on it."

I gave a smile of thanks, after all, it had been Danny who'd helped me crack that aspect of the Burell-Ramirez case.

"Message me every day, okay?" she said. "Let me know you're all right."

"I will."

"Be careful." Abby gave a wave. "Don't fuck it up."

She killed the call and Huntly Pierre's logo lingered to haunt my scheming.

I sat back and exhaled in a rush.

No way was I letting the Burells ruin one more life. When I returned to Europe, I'd pay their family a visit in France.

Their lawyers who acted as sinister gatekeepers weren't going to protect them this time.

After closing my laptop, I pushed myself to my feet and made my way over to the wardrobe. A chic dress would be best for my visit to LACMA tonight. My body shivered with the thought of seeing Tobias again and recalling his note burned me up from the inside out: *Is my princess up for an adventure?*

Running my fingertips over my lips I reasoned, *why yes*, I was ready for Wilder, though the question he needed to ask himself was…was he ready for me?

9

François Boucher had always inspired me with the way he reflected a woman's confidence and, standing before his 1756 Rococo portrait, I was reminded of his talent. He'd captured Jeanne Antoinette Poisson, later known as Madame de Pompadour, lounging upon a seat with her lush full green gown billowing around her and a well-loved book loose in her right hand. Her wistfulness mirroring her ruminating upon the words she'd read. Boucher had kept her looking youthful despite the years falling away. Sweeping gold drapes either side framed her elegance and enhanced her position of being the lover of King Louis XV.

I adored Boucher's work for honoring females in all their natural beauty; his daring collection of nudes were flattering and elegantly natural.

Moving along to the next portrait I sighed in wonder at the 1910 *L'Edition de Luxe* by Lilian Westcott Hale, an ethereal painting of a redheaded woman sitting at a table and reading an enormous book as the light streamed through the curtained window and bathed the room with a rosy glow. Rose Zeffler, the model chosen to pose by Lilian, was easily overwhelmed by the room and this perhaps was a suggestion of a woman's quiet strength, and despite the decade it was painted with this brave element to celebrate her intelligence.

I often marveled at our ability to trace fashion through art, from the grandest skirts of the seventeenth century that must have been challenging to walk in to our cosmopolitan clothes that flattered a figure. In honor of the women being showcased in these paintings, I'd worn my black Coco Chanel shift dress. I was grateful for this haute couture that kept the chill of the gallery at bay and these high-heel velvet boots that gave me the height I needed to face off with Wilder. With his nature so bossy he probably drew pleasure from looming over my petite frame.

A glance at my phone showed Tobias's blip in Malibu. This ache deepened in my belly, proving how much I'd wanted to see him. The flowers he'd given me this morning had been a cruel tease to slow me down. I shouldn't be surprised, I reassured myself, as I made my way toward the stairs that would lead me out.

"Ms. Leighton?" a woman called from a few feet away.

I gave a polite smile to the thirtysomething pretty curator who seemed to know me.

"You're here for the private exhibit?" she said.

"Women Who Read." I forced a cheery smile. "It was wonderful."

"You're on my list of guests. It's not open to the public yet."

I blinked my confusion. "I'm sorry?"

"A sneak peek of the white room."

"How do you know me?"

"You used your credentials when you entered."

Of course, the security face-recognition software. With thousands of works of art here every person would be processed by lightning fast technology. One unruly guest could decimate a painting and cause millions of dollars' worth of damage.

"I'm Maggie." She held out her hand to shake mine.

"Zara."

"How long are you in town?"

"A few more days, maybe longer. I'm sorry, why am I being invited to see the room?"

She cupped her hand to whisper. "It's the Wilder exhibit."

Pretending I wasn't surprised by this revelation, I followed her, eager to see which artwork Tobias had loaned to LACMA.

What is this rascal up to?

We chatted about art as we trekked down the long hallways, rounding corners, and this endless journey reminded me just how remarkable LACMA's collection was that spanned history and mixed classic with modern.

Maggie waved hello to a passing colleague and then turned back to me. "Mr. Wilder understands that teenagers need a little coaxing to perceive the worthiness of art."

"His work with kids is so inspiring," I agreed.

One of my fondest memories was when he'd driven me to East London to see a derelict church and he'd shown me the work he was doing within its decaying structure to conserve its Roman history. There had been awe in the faces of the teenagers he'd enlisted to see this project through; a distant look in their eyes proving they knew they were part of something special.

Maggie pressed her thumb against a keypad and then gestured for me to go on ahead. I pushed the heavy door open and stepped inside. The space was enormous—a white-walled empty showroom. I turned back and gave a questioning stare.

"Enjoy." Her expression reflected delight. "We've yet to announce it to the public. No photos and no social media posts. We've not installed security cameras yet but as you're a friend of Mr. Wilder, we know we can trust you." She left and shut the door behind her.

My attention snapped back to the display of nothing. Remembering Tobias's crazy-arse holograms, my back stiffened as I moved farther in. Perhaps he believed we were all too addicted to our gadgets and needed a place to contemplate with no distractions, because there was nothing but white walls and a low flat ceiling and shiny hardwood floors.

Wait.

Hurrying over to the far corner toward the high stand which served as the only object in here, I saw a virtual reality headpiece. A shudder of excitement. Intrigued, I carried the VR gear to the center of the showroom and slid the headset on and peered through the visor.

Wow.

I'd been transported to a room similar in size, only these walls were made of brick and each item in here belonged in the late sixteenth century. This was footage turned into life-like images from a real-world environment that had been filmed elsewhere and digitalized. Someone had visited this room and filmed the natural light flooding in, the low beams running along the ceiling, that beautifully carved antique table, those high-backed chairs and the terra cotta stone floor. Even the large fireplace crackled and sparked with authentic orange flames and I could almost smell the burning logs as my senses filled in the cozy scene.

Recognizing several of the drawings on the table from the genius's own hand, these exquisite renderings proving they were by a master craftsman. I confirmed my suspicion when I looked right and there on a high brass frame lay an open book and upon its page a sketch of a horse—by Leonardo da

Vinci. This place, this setting was a remarkable replication of his home in Florence in the 1600s.

My mind was convincing me all of this was vibrantly real. The sound of a man humming came from around the corner and I raised the goggles to check to see who else was in here.

I was alone.

Reassured I wasn't going to bump into someone, I repositioned the headset and walked forward with my hands out to feel my way. Why did Tobias have to be so annoyingly amazing?

Turning the corner, I froze.

My inhalation caught in my throat when I saw Leonardo and despite his back being turned away from me, I knew it was him. He was humming away and seemingly lost in thought as he ran a brush along a canvas upon which he painted *Mona Lisa*.

Everyone would recognize her as one of the most famous faces in the world and her painting that hung in the Louvre in Paris was one of the most visited and revered in the world.

Tobias had proven his visionary talent for going beyond the canvas of life and blowing my mind all over again.

Leonardo had captured Lisa Gherardini's likeness in 1503 with oil on cottonwood when she had posed for him. That rumor it was a self-portrait of Leonardo had been easily dismissed with science coming through for art again. Mona Lisa wasn't here now but it took nothing away from seeing the master at work.

Moving closer, my hand pressed to my mouth to prevent a gasp at this dazzling sight. I couldn't shake the wonder of this sense of traveling back in time. Leonardo stopped humming and turned sharply to look at me—

I yelped my shock.

My gaze traced over his deep brown eyes and thick wavy

brown-and-gray hair, his simple robe keeping him warm and allowing free movement for that flick of his wrist with a brush. He arched a brow as though recognizing me.

"Leonardo?" I reacted on instinct.

He gave the warmest smile. "There you are." His line of sight focused to someone behind me—

I yanked off the headset and spun round to see Tobias smiling at me. God, if he didn't look gorgeous, with his dark blond hair playfully ruffled and his blue jacket and casual jeans tricking my mind into believing there wasn't danger lurking beneath the surface.

"Turn around." His voice was deep and commanding. "There's more."

"No."

"Humor me."

"You're late."

"She's waiting."

I narrowed my gaze on him. "Who is?"

"I've created something especially for you. No one else will ever see it." His heady cologne wafted as he took the headgear from me.

The blip that placed him in Malibu had been way off—

All I had to do was let go and bask in this genius's presence and something told me this was his intention. Falling for him would be so easy. A mistake I couldn't make.

"Program for Zara Leighton," came the echo of his soft American accent, and he refitted the headgear over my eyes.

He turned me round to face the front and wrapped his arms around my waist, sending shivers through me. My body stiffened in his arms to prove my resistance despite my back fitting annoyingly well to his front.

The visor refocused on a sixteenth-century visage morphing to a shimmering image of light and then...

We were standing in a field of green grass and before us towered an old oak tree, my gaze focusing on the sharp detail and even the leaves looked real as they quivered in a breeze. A young woman sat at its trunk and her porcelain complexion was exaggerated by her flamboyant silver-white wig coiffed three feet high and decorated with feathers and diamonds. She wore a lavish blue gown from the late 1700s. She sniffed at the petals of a single rose. When she smiled at me, I shivered with our connection as though I'd reached through time to find her.

The startling profoundness of a living breathing canvas. This setting and her pose was the same one of Queen Marie Antoinette that had been painted hundreds of years ago by Élisabeth Vigée Le Brun, a female artist commissioned by the queen herself. And later, her majesty had used her influence to get Élisabeth into the *académie*. Élisabeth wasn't here now but this was the exact location in which she had painted Marie Antoinette. Marie seemed happy, entrancing me with her big blue eyes as she reached up and plucked a single feather from her towering wig. She offered it to me.

This is miraculous.

Pushing herself to her feet with her billowing gown around her, she threw the flower and feather toward me and they landed at my feet. Turning on her heels Antoinette gestured for me to follow.

Stepping away from Tobias, I reached out and followed Marie into a dome-shaped building. I'd entered a lavish greenhouse and almost forgot this wasn't real. I hoped Tobias would prevent me from hitting a wall if I walked too briskly. Surrounding me were tall plants, bright lilies, carnations and roses all filling the room with color; a small blue-and-red butterfly fluttered its wings and disappeared amongst the foliage.

I'd once read Marie preferred simplicity to decadence and that her reputation for being pampered wasn't true but made up by those who wanted to influence the French downfall with their propaganda. I didn't want to think of that now. Didn't want to break the spell.

Marie hurried ahead and lifted her skirts as she ran down a glass hallway, turning to look back at me with a playful wonder and laughing as she led me on with her addictive joy. I laughed with her, drawn by Marie's contagious happiness. She entered a small room and I followed and paused in the doorway. Marie turned coquettishly, glancing beneath heavy eyelashes blinking their mischief; a seductive tilt of her head.

The only decor in here were lush plants and in the center a burgundy chaise lounge, and I was fooled into believing that if I ran my hand along it I'd feel smooth velvet. Marie dragged her teeth over her bottom lip as she undressed, tugging her waistband, lips pouty with concentration.

Reaching out for the door frame my hand slipped into nothing to remind me this wasn't real.

Taking her time with undressing, she peered up occasionally to give a flicker of innocence, masterfully working those endless garments beneath, the kind a maid would normally assist with. Her nimble fingers untying her corset and all the while sending flirty glances my way as she let her final undergarment loose and it fell and ballooned around her ankles. She stepped out of it completely naked and bewitchingly erotic.

My breathing was hesitant as Tobias's left hand slid around me again and his right hand rested low on my belly, sending a shiver of desire. I was caught somewhere between reality and a seductive daydream.

Spellbound.

Marie lowered herself onto the chaise and lay along it with her hands above her head in a mesmerizing pose. It was too much—too sensual and, despite wanting to stay, I felt like I'd invaded her privacy. Reaching up to remove the goggles, I felt Tobias's hands find mine, easing the headset back over my eyes in a silent command.

This scene was hypnotically alluring and I sighed in awe at her sublime beauty, the purity of her femininity emanating grace.

Coming from behind us a young man appeared and he looked around twenty in age. He was just as beautiful with his regal features and brown hair in an elegant fop style of aristocracy; his long-tailored jacket, embroiled waistcoat and breeches gave him a decadent air. Whoever he was Marie was enamored. Her lover knelt beside her and plucked one of the feathers from her hair. With an easy smile, he reached low toward her feet and trailed it across the sole of her foot and then began an upward sweep to drag the tip along her calf and higher, pausing over her sex and teasing her there.

Marie arched her back seductively and her nipples hardened when he ran the feather around them, taking his time to tickle the white plume over her breasts, one and then the other in a dance of sensuality. Their shared gazes of affection were mesmerizing.

Tobias lifted my dress and his right hand slipped beneath the hem and his fingers caressed through my panties, and then he slipped them beneath my thong and stroked my sex making me shudder with pleasure. This tantalizing temptation overwhelmed my senses; his seduction impossible to resist.

He removed his hand and I felt the loss too harshly and was only comforted by realizing he was now in front of me, and I sensed from the way he lifted my hem he was kneeling before me as his hand traced up my inner thigh.

Easing up the headgear to look down at him, I blinked my concern.

"It's my code for the door…" He glanced up. "There's no cameras."

"Why are you doing this?"

"Because I know what you need." He gave a sharp nod for me to pull down the headset.

My body thrummed with need but, despite wanting this, my mind demanded I at least try to maintain my power.

"Zara." Wilder's stern tone was hypnotic.

I brought the headset down over my eyes again and returned to the Age of Enlightenment…

Marie parted her thighs a little to invite her lover there, and he lowered the feather until it traced over her belly just where Tobias was kissing me.

The feather hovered along her sex and then his mouth replaced the plume as he kissed her clit, just as Tobias's tongue found mine and flicked; my body trembling against his mouth and my closeness causing my legs to weaken. Tobias grasped my buttocks to keep me against him as he devoured me passionately.

Marie shuddered through her climax.

As I trembled through mine, too swept up in pleasure to reason or even weigh the risk of getting caught or deny myself this blinding pleasure…rising and rising until I let go willingly swept up in this endless orgasm.

Marie was seemingly left in that dreamy state of suspended bliss after being so tenderly adored. I rested the headset on my forehead and filled my gaze with Tobias; his stark beauty was the greatest threat to my resistance.

He rose and pulled me into a hug, and I leaned into him with my cheek resting on his chest, breathing in his heady scent as I tried to calm these rapid breaths and slow my racing heart, my thighs still trembling and my resolve dissipating.

Tobias took the goggles off me and placed them on himself. His head tipped upward. "Jade, delete program for Zara Leighton. Indicate when complete."

"Wait." I squeezed his arm. "It's too beautiful."

He gave a nod as though seeing Jade had followed his command and pulled them off. "I'll make another one for you."

"That was breathtaking," I whispered.

"Zara, you're breathtaking."

My body trembled with the realization of the power he had to entrance me.

His lips pressed my forehead in a long kiss. "You inspire me."

Hold on, I silently willed myself, *don't fall for him. Don't weaken to his brilliant seduction.*

"Zara?" His frown deepened as he searched my face, trying to read me.

I raised my chin to prove my strength. "It's not enough, Tobias."

His expression changed to resignation. "Can I trust you? I mean really?"

"Yes."

He stared off at seemingly nothing and then turned to look at me. "Quid pro quo."

That was his offer, to cave and give me more if I gave him something in return.

"What do you want?" I said.

His green irises shimmered with intrigue. "You."

10

Tobias pulled me behind him along the heavily stacked shelves of antique books and I kept up with him full of anticipation to be in The Last Bookstore, with its decadent scent of leather and these endless mysteries around every corner. Since it closed late on Thursday nights, we were in luck to explore its treasures.

He'd driven us to this eclectic bookstore on Fifth Street and it had taken us less than half an hour to get here from LACMA.

This place was a haven for readers; the lower floor invited guests to wander the vast space enhanced by its tall ceiling and marble pillars. At the front of the store sat a cozy leather couch surrounded by several armchairs. Balconies circled the upper wall, enticing us with more rooms to explore. I'd never seen books so artfully displayed and stacked into creative designs. The decor imbued an aura of freethinkers who presented one-of-a-kind pieces, like the papier-mâché figurine of a woman covered in writing that we moved hastily past.

During the drive, my thoughts had scattered into shards of reason as though some part of me sensed the temporary nature of all of this, the impossibility of a fling with Tobias, and yet I yearned to be with him more than anything. Not that long ago he'd pulled me down the sprawling corridors of Blandford Palace in Oxfordshire and that had been the first time I felt truly alive. The first sparks of realization there was so much more than routines, schedules and strict rules.

With my hand in his, I was led through the twists and turns of the expansive store as we dodged the other visitors.

These tingles in my chest morphed into a thrilling buzz when Tobias turned to glance back at me with that heart-stopping smile. We made our way up the twisting staircase to the upper level and another wave of happiness swept over me. A little way along the empty hallway he paused and nudged me against the wall. I pressed my hands to his chest to keep a little distance between us but he overpowered me, his mouth trailing kisses along my cheek and toward my ear.

"What you do to me." He groaned his frustration and his tongue tangled with mine, his kiss ravishing me.

We continued through the endless labyrinth until we entered a tunnel of books all masterfully stacked to form a curve around us. He pulled me to him and cupped my cheeks to steal another kiss.

Tobias pulled back and reached for my hand and kissed it and then brushed the pad of his thumb over my palm, sending tingles. "From the moment I met you I felt compelled to protect you."

"From what?"

"Everything."

"I need answers, Tobias."

He gave a nod. "You once accused me of seeking you out because you work for Huntly Pierre?"

As uneasiness welled, I glanced through the arched tunnel unsure where this was going.

He brought my attention back on him. "I was at The Otil-lie the night I met you because I had planned on identifying Bertram Leighton's daughter. I wasn't expecting Bertram's daughter to be so captivating."

"At my flat you pretended to know nothing about my dad?"

"I had my reasons. *Joan's* past must be forgotten."

"Why?"

"I know you want answers. Let me tell you what I can."

"No more smoke and mirrors."

Tobias gave a nod of resignation and his voice rose with tension. "There's no room for doubt in what I do."

This was the most dangerous game I'd ever played be-cause it was my heart that was being offered up as collateral for answers.

"You've changed everything, Zara."

"Don't ruin your life. You're too gifted and too important to too many people."

He inhaled a sharp breath. "What I do is important."

"You need to believe your parents' lives had a purpose?"

His eyes were full of pain as he seemed to remember them. That day when he'd opened up to me about them in my Lon-don flat felt so long ago now. He'd told me he'd fulfilled his parents' mission to meet with a woman named Reni and, though he'd only been nine years old and the death of his parents had been days behind him, he'd bravely continued their journey. He'd returned *Madonna Enthroned with St. Mat-thew* by Annibale Carracci to its rightful owner, though her surname was still a mystery.

After he'd witnessed his mother's death, he'd taken her words on as his shield of honor. I wondered if Tobias had held his mom's hand as she'd slipped away, and no doubt he'd comforted her as best he could all alone in that desolate out-back. The threat of death coming for him too.

Stinging tears welled up in my eyes, but I pushed them back.

As the only survivor of that ill-fated journey, Tobias had been sent reeling on a reckless path and all he'd experienced had become the dark inspiration for a lifetime of thievery.

"Icon." I whispered it.

He squeezed his eyes shut.

My breath stilted that he'd admitted it with that one gesture.

"Your father would never want this for you," I said softly. "You know this."

"What have you done to me, Zara?"

I leaned into him. "Think of those children in London who look up to you. All the good you can do."

"If I give you what you are asking—"

"Please." My breath caught at the possibility of a break-through, the reason I was in a foreign land risking everything for a man I hardly knew.

"You understand what I'm asking of you?" he said.

A stab of doubt as I realized. "You're asking me to tell you what Huntly Pierre knows about Icon?"

"I'm meeting you halfway."

What he was asking of me was impossible.

His frown deepened. "You work for the company searching for Icon."

"Why are we here?"

"I'm going to prove you can trust me. And what I need from you is the same level of trust. There will be no compromise. Do you understand?"

I gave a careful nod as my heart jackhammered with the

realization I'd finally gotten to him. "What happens afterward?"

"The more you give me the more I reveal," he said. "The way I see it, you will only understand what I do if I provide you with insight."

"What are you saying?" But I knew, he was suggesting there was more going on within the underworld of art and he was offering me more than a glimpse.

"Are you sure you want to venture down this rabbit hole?" he said. "Once there, you will not be able to return."

Peering up at him I tried to decipher his words. "I've come too far."

"And yet it's not far enough." He cupped my cheeks and crushed his mouth to mine, delivering another kiss, his lips firm, his tongue languishing and battling as though this alone would convey what he wasn't telling me.

"Leave Icon behind," I said. "Promise you will."

He led me down the ramp and along as we headed into a smaller space. A sign indicated this section was for Religious History.

I was teetering on the other side of the art world with whirling emotions warning my heart was close to being irrevocably damaged if I didn't allow myself to stay focused and hold back.

"This is what I am prepared to give you." He looked earnest. "And you will reciprocate in kind." He led me farther along the aisle and stopped before a section on Rome, his fingers trailing over the bindings to search for a book.

There came a shift in the air; the heaviness of dust lifting.

"Zara, give me your word."

"What do you want from me?"

"Loyalty."

Wilder was asking too much but if I pulled back now all would be lost.

His hand ceased searching and he turned to face me. "You're about to see how much I trust you."

I was caught between my need for truth and this confliction at what I was about to vow; my heart pounding against my ribs.

"Are you ready, Zara?"

"Yes."

As though sensing this stab of doubt in me, his palm caressed my spine to comfort me.

I reached for his hand and held it. "Why me?"

"You deserve the truth." He held my gaze. "And for there to be any chance of an *us*, Zara, we need transparency between us."

My gaze swept over the long row of books to show him I was ready.

"There are only a handful of men at the Vatican who know this happened," he began calmly, "and someone who is working for them over at Interpol."

"A secret?"

"Suppressed for centuries. There was a raid on a monastery at the order of Pope Benedict IX, back in the eleventh century, more specifically 1048. There is no documentation of this travesty. There's too much pride involved for a modern papacy to endure the scandal of what these men did to the monks. The kind of bad press the Vatican doesn't want. A crime that is an affront to those of faith."

I glanced behind me to check we were alone.

He pulled a large book off the shelf and it was a compendium of art history. With ease, he flicked through the pages and then stopped, lifting the open book for me to see—showing me a photo of the image of Christ painted on a panel. Jesus was holding a bible in his left hand and in his right he was offering a blessing. A style known as Christian Iconography.

A rush of exhilaration swept over me.

He ran a fingertip over the image. "This is the second oldest Christ Pantocrator encaustic on a panel."

A style of painting depicting Christ as the ruler of the universe and one of the most popular images in the Eastern Orthodox Church.

Its description explained that "this panel is the oldest known of Christ and can be found in Saint Catherine's Monastery in Sinai. An ancient holy sanctuary dated 548 AD."

I'd sat riveted during a lecture back at The Courtauld when a visiting professor from the University of Michigan, Dr. Mark Lyle, had returned from years spent in the East studying their art collections and documenting them. He'd showed us slide after slide in that old-fashioned way of lecturing and impressed us with pictures of historical paintings that interpreted biblical characters and seemed more realistic and unfettered by preconceptions, including the ones that anglicized the Son of God by removing any trace he was born in the Middle East.

"But it says here this is the oldest one?" I pointed to the page. "It's not?"

"No."

"It's the second oldest?"

"Yes."

"How do you know?"

"I stole the oldest panel of Christ in the world."

Stunned, my gaze snapped to the image. "From where?"

"The Vatican. I returned it to Saint Catherine's Monastery." He rested a fingertip on the serene image of Christ. "It's more detailed than this one. His face is mesmerizing."

"Both panels are now at Mount Sinai?"

"Thankfully." He gave a shrug. "The monks told me the image on the panel I returned is the closest interpretation of what Jesus actually looked like. He was a Nazarene, after all."

My gasp resonated at the realization of what he was telling me.

Tobias had stolen the painting to give it back to the people. That precious portrait had been locked away in a Vatican vault for only a select few to see.

The only way you're ever going to trust me. His haunting words sent a tremor through me.

Tobias had given me the key to see his downfall.

He gave a wry smile. "I'd just turned twenty. This was my first job."

I took in a steadying breath. "This is why they call you Icon?"

He arched an amused brow. "Yes."

"Someone at Interpol knows this?"

"Apparently." He closed the book and slid it back amongst the others.

"What did he look like?" I whispered. "Jesus?"

Tobias's eyes softened and specks of gold glinted in his irises reflecting wonder as he searched for the words that never came. Awestruck, my hand slapped to my mouth. I was too stunned to speak and marveled that it had been Tobias who had returned the painting to the people.

Now, though, Wilder expected something from me.

11

I had given a promise I couldn't deliver.

This thought burned up my brain as I tried to relax in his enormous bathroom, soaking in these luxurious bubbles with their rich aroma of jasmine and I peeked over the edge of his tub, musing how this room in his Malibu home was as big as my sitting room. There came a pang of homesickness for London. Two days ago, when I'd fled here in a panic, I could never have imagined returning so soon.

Within the hour, Tobias had run me a hot bath and then headed off to prepare a late supper for us. My stomach grumbled and I realized I'd not eaten since that salad I'd had for lunch back at the Sofitel.

Out the large bay window was the most incredible ocean view, the sunset kissing the horizon and blasting vibrant reds and oranges and golden hues along its seamless edge. The occasional yacht sailed by. In here white marble and sumptuous fixtures were a reminder of his wealth. His complexity was a sweet conundrum to ruminate over; his boyish nature shielded by that alpha charm. His American swagger made my insides quiver. Nothing seemed to faze him.

I had to focus back on my mission to persuade him to leave Icon behind, and well before he did something dangerous.

If I couldn't get through to him the result would be devastating. I'd have no choice but to hand him over to Huntly Pierre.

I'd left The Last Bookstore an hour ago, dazed after hearing him finally admit to being Icon. We'd driven to Malibu in silence with him throwing me the occasional wary glance as though trying to gauge my reaction and probably aware his admission had made me an abettor.

I'd gone quiet in the car, but had Tobias really assumed I'd accept his confession and carry on as normal? There was never going to be applause from me for what he'd done. Even if he had brought joy to the monks on Mount Sinai after stealing back the panel of Christ from the Vatican, or peace to the Buddhists back in London after he'd ensured the safe return of their sacred singing bowl.

Cross-referencing what he'd told me about the theft at the Vatican would be an issue. Researching such an incident would probably alert Rome and bring the kind of attention neither of us wanted. Still, that major clue he'd handed me would be all I needed to make a phone call to Huntly Pierre and alert them to our suspect's location.

He'd risked so much by believing I'd never betray him.

I hugged my knees when I thought about providing him with information from Huntly Pierre.

He was asking too much.

This was not the way I saw my life going, betraying the company I loved working for. I'd settled into being part of the team that did so much good for the art world. We authenticated masterpieces and ensured their deserved care, we dispelled fakes and put their rogue creators under the spotlight, we referred clients to specialists who could restore paintings to their original glory.

Water whooshed as I reached for the sponge and I caressed it along my chest as though that might calm me, trying to clear my thoughts, digging deeper to decipher what would make me happy. Could I betray all I held dear? Taint the memory of my father and let down my beloved professors from The Courtauld, or even my colleagues who had become friends?

The cost was too high.

I had to find some halfway ground between what was right for the world and what was right for me. All I'd asked for in life was to bask in the exquisite eminence of a Rembrandt or Monet or even a Rothko like the one hanging downstairs.

Was Tobias the one for me? Even though he adored art too and owned one of the most prestigious galleries in the world? If only a relationship could be this simple.

After climbing out of the bath I dried myself off with the plush towel and padded out of his bathroom and into his bedroom. Lying on the king-size bed was a matching set of white Coco de Mer bra and panties. It made me smile, remembering how he loved to dress me in this delicate lingerie.

Allowing this melancholy back in, I broke from this spell, realizing this fantasy couldn't last.

Next to the underwear was a white ruffle-front maxi dress and peeking at the label I saw it was designed by Adelyn Rae and was my size. Lifting it up I realized this was a minidress complemented by a long sheer skirt with its hem reaching the floor. In the box beside it was a pair of flat strappy sandals.

I decided not to wear the shoes and a jolt of rebellion rippled through me. Tobias's influence shimmered ever brightly in my show of willpower. I'd go barefoot as though this was the only way the ground beneath my feet would feel steady.

After dressing in the maxi dress, I fixed my hair and used the new makeup he'd bought for me. Dabbing on a pale pink lip gloss and staring at my reflection in the mirror, I noticed an unfamiliar look in my eyes which was a defiance I never knew was there until now. Each day spent with Tobias felt like an awakening, as though he was lifting life's veil for me to see beyond the ordinary.

Heading out and down the stairs I listened out for him.

This tightrope is precariously shaky.

This exhilaration had me inhaling every thrilling second with verve when I saw an endless trail of white lilies scattered in the hallway. I set off following them through the house and out the back door into the balmy evening. The blooms led me around the blue sparkling pool and along a green grassed pathway.

There came the refreshing scent of the ocean and a mesmeric sound of crashing waves; the view of an endless dark blue with the moon's reflection shimmering off the surface. Continuing down the bluff and along the sand I could see a table set for a late-night dinner and two chairs. The romantic setting complete with fiery torches.

Tobias was standing on the edge of the shoreline with his back to me and he looked so ethereal with those small waves rolling dangerously close to his feet. He was dressed casually in blue jeans and a white shirt, and it made me smile when I saw he was barefoot too.

A sleek white yacht was anchored a little way out.

With the wind billowing my hem around my calves and the wind in my hair, I walked toward Tobias, feeling more free-spirited than I deserved.

When he turned and saw me his face brightened. "Are you real?"

I gave a twirl. "It's so pretty."

"You look stunning." He grinned when he saw my feet.

My gaze swept over to the table and the two silver-dome-covered plates. Two glasses of champagne were already poured. There was also a thin square velvet box. Tobias walked over and lifted the two champagne flutes and handed me one.

The crystal glass was cold to the touch and bubbles burst up as I brought it to my lips and tasted the cold, crisp wine.

Tobias was smiling at me. "I have something for you."

"Oh?"

He set his glass down and lifted the velvet box. He neared me and rested his hand on the top of it. "This was my mom's."

"Tobias."

He lifted the lid and there lay a fine gold chain with a beautiful single three-carat emerald—a dazzling green.

He carefully removed it from the box and gestured for me to turn around, and I felt the chain wrap around my throat and the solitaire set against my skin.

Reaching up, caressing the stone as my fingers tingled over its smooth surface. "I'm not sure—"

"I want you to have it."

Turning sharply, I looked at his beautiful face.

"I was waiting for the right time to give it to you." His eyes crinkled soulfully.

I cupped my palm to his face. "I don't know what to say."

He took my hand and led me to the table.

"While you were being a lady of leisure—" he gave a cheeky grin "—I prepared a little something." He swept his hand wide and then lifted the lid of one of the domes. "Ahi tuna tartare on *poppadoms* with Indian curry, Persian cucumber and micro cilantro."

"Don't make me feel guilty."

"I'm joking. I love spoiling you."

"It looks amazing." And it really was so well presented. "You're quite talented."

"Quite?"

"Remarkably so. In every way."

"I was trying to think of a delicious 'pudding' as you call it and I settled on Zara for dessert. With whipped cream."

Smirking, I nodded my thanks when he nudged my chair up.

He lifted locks of my hair away from my nape. "Warm enough?"

"Yes." My skin tingled as he ran his fingers along my scalp.

He kissed my nape. "How was your bath?"

"Relaxing," I said breathlessly, the ghost of his touch causing a shiver as his fingers left my shoulder. This was really happening, I was here with him and the realization made my chest flutter with anticipation.

He rounded the table and sat opposite. "Did you get time to think?"

"A little." I reached for my napkin and spread it out on my lap.

His gaze held mine and then he turned his attention to pouring more champagne, tipping the bottle to top up our glasses.

I picked up mine. "This is quite the setting. It's beautiful here."

He continued to stare as though needing reassurance I was coming round to what he'd asked of me.

"Peaceful too," I added.

"I'm glad you approve. The sunsets are remarkable. When I look out I imagine how Monet might have captured it or Turner. Something tells me I'll become an impressionist painter in my old age."

"Might dabble in it myself too, one day."

"I like having you here."

"Is that yours?" I gestured to the yacht tethered not that far away.

"Yes."

The sleek boat promised endless hours of escape.

"We can go out on it tomorrow if you like?"

Needing to change the subject I asked, "Were you scared?"

"Scared?"

"When you broke into the Vatican?"

"Preparation helped."

I gave a look to punish his avoidance. "How did you know about the painting of Christ?"

"I was on a school trip in the country and heard the story from the monks. It stayed with me."

"Your uncle Fabienne didn't try and dissuade you?"

Surely he'd suspected something? Fabienne had raised Tobias in Reims after his parent's deaths and Tobias had told me they were still close.

"He never knew." Tobias stared at me. "He's innocent in all this. Has nothing to do with any of it."

"What did the monks say?" I ignored his reaction. "When you turned up with their painting?"

"We got drunk to celebrate. They make a mean wine."

"They weren't concerned the Vatican would send someone to get it back?"

He eased tuna onto a *poppadom* and took a bite. "They know the stakes. They're willing to fight for what is rightfully theirs."

I feigned this didn't shake me.

"Use your fork—" He leaned forward and gestured to the tuna. "Put a little on—" He pointed to the crisp Indian bread and lifted his portion with his fingers. "There you go."

The fresh thinly sliced tuna sat easily on the golden crisp.

When I popped it into my mouth, the flavor burst fresh and delicate on my palate. The *poppadom* complemented the flavor with its tangy spices. "Delicious," I managed through chewing.

"Nice and light," he added.

"Goes with the champagne."

"I agree."

"Your gallery is impressive. The paintings at The Wilder are remarkable."

"Jean-Jacques Henner's *Madame Paul Duchesne-Fournet?*"

"I enjoyed her right up until you threw me out."

"I escorted you." He smirked. "There's a difference."

"What made you change your mind about me?" My fingers trailed over the emerald.

"The first time you saw a Rembrandt, how did it make you feel?"

"Mesmerized."

"For me, it stirred a sense of obsession." He held my gaze to insinuate that's how he felt about me.

Holding my breath, I was overcome by this electricity crackling between us, this sense of inevitability.

Waves crashed and sprayed foam; surf rolled dangerously close to our table.

His gaze lingered on my necklace. "It looks beautiful on you."

"Tell me about your mom?"

His eyes lit up in a smile. "She was only twenty-one when she had me. She was a sculptor, so as you can imagine she was a little distracted."

"She was arty?"

"Yes, and talented too. Mom studied the fine arts."

"What did she sculpt?"

"People, I have some of her work on show at The Wilder. I have a few pieces in there." He pointed back to the house.

"I'd like to see them."

"You will," he said tenderly.

"Maybe have an exhibition dedicated to her?"

"I've thought about it."

"She took good care of you?"

"Very loving. We were very happy." He brightened. "Mom took me to this costume party when I was eight. There I was rocking this Spider-Man suit and feeling like I was king of the world. Right up until I arrived."

"What happened?"

"No one else was in costume."

I slapped my hand to my mouth to hide my smile.

"Wrong party." He rolled his eyes. "I think it was a Bar Mitzvah. We're not even Jewish."

I burst out laughing. "Your mom took you to the wrong party?"

"You know what it's like. At that age there's parties every week. She was always spacing out, thinking of her next creation. She was bohemian. That's what my dad loved about her. Her sense of freedom. Her wildness." His eyes lit up as he remembered her.

A shiver of uncertainty ran through me. "What did you do when you realized you were at the wrong party?"

"Refused to remove my mask." He arched a brow. "I was a superhero, after all. Couldn't reveal my identity. I quickly proved my ability to improvise when I mastered the art of eating kosher cake by shoving pieces beneath my mask."

"You're still artful." I arched an amused brow.

"Well I must be doing something right because you're here. Doesn't get any better than this."

"What did your father do for work?"

"Well, you researched me. What did you learn?"

"He was a businessman."

"Dad started The Wilder Corporation. I believe I've seen his vision through, continued his passion for philanthropic work. I kept his charities going and was inspired to create a few of my own."

I'd experienced the importance of his desire to maintain the city's heritage and at the same time inspire teenagers by having them personally interact with history to grasp its importance.

I let out a wistful sigh as I remembered that derelict church he'd taken me to and how those employees working for him had looked upon him in awe. They'd been utterly seduced by the profoundness of what he could achieve. That day he'd guided me into the excavation site in the basement and shown me they were saving a wall depicting Roman soldiers, their faded painted figurines frozen in a fragment of time.

These moments where we comfortably shared the quiet were just as compelling as him speaking so freely now.

"How did your father come across Annibale Carracci's *Madonna Enthroned*?" I reached out and squeezed his forearm. "The one you returned to Reni?"

He sat back and pain flashed over his face, proving I'd touched a nerve. "My parents were returning it as a favor."

"To who?"

He broke my gaze and stared at the ocean.

"I promise everything we discuss will remain private."

"Do you, Zara?"

"Yes."

"You're swimming in dangerous waters."

"Not as dangerous as you," I said firmly. "Your parents were in some way connected to the Burells?"

Tobias looked horrified.

This felt like another piece of the puzzle coming together. "Was this your motive to return Sarah Louise's Titian? And my *St. Joan* to me?"

His eyes widened with surprise. "What are you doing?"

"I know where to look now," I said. "Who to blame for stealing my *St. Joan*."

"Stay away from that family."

"So you admit it?"

"I will tell you this. The Burells take what they want. When they want. How they want. Fuck the circumstances." He looked away. "I'm not sure how much you know but this is a reckless path you're on."

"It was right there. All along."

His jaw muscles tightened. "I deal with this. On your behalf. Understand?"

"Someone in that family burned down my home."

"Trust me when I say they've done worse."

"Worse?"

He waved it off. "Can we not just enjoy the evening?"

"They must be stopped."

"I don't disagree. Now let it go."

I finished my drink. "Give me his name."

"I'm giving you my final warning."

I threw my napkin onto the table. "I'm doing this for my dad."

"Doing what exactly?"

"I'm going to confront the man who ruined my childhood—" I held his gaze. "Destroyed our precious paintings. The man who caused my father to withdraw from me because of the grief."

"I know," he whispered. "Listen to me, there will be no contact with them." He reached for the bottle and poured bubbly into his glass. "More champagne?"

"You can't stop me."

"Actually, I can." He picked up his glass and leaned back. "This discussion is over."

I folded my arms and sat back to prove my stubbornness.

"Zara, we had an agreement. Remember?"

"What do you want to know, then?" My glare answered with *Go on, tell me all the ways in which you want me to betray those who have entrusted me.*

He mulled over his answer. "Let's discuss this later."

"What am I to you?"

He stared out toward the yacht and then fixed his green stare on me. "I want to take you as my lover."

"After everything, you believe we can be with each other like that?"

He wiped his hands on his napkin and threw it aside. "What do you need? Tell me."

"I need…"

"I'd never hurt you." He reached across the table and rested his hand on mine. "What can I say to persuade you how much I care about you?"

"Tell me Icon no longer exists."

He looked down to break my gaze. I yanked my hand away, my thoughts catching up with my instincts and telling me it was a mistake to be here.

Tobias steepled his fingers and brought them to his lips. "I made a promise."

"Who to?"

"I can't tell you that. But believe me when I say this will help mend wounds. Help heal a nation. Fulfill a promise—"

"Tobias?" A shiver slithered up my spine. "You're not done?"

"You have no real idea of what you are asking of me."

I shot to my feet and my chair tipped over onto the sand behind me. "Your uncle?"

"No."

"You promised—"

"When this is over."

"Then you don't get me!" I said sharply.

His jaw flexed with tension. "You ask me to compromise but give me none."

"I'm here, aren't I?"

"I've opened my home to you. Shown you all that I am. And you give me nothing."

"What you do makes me question your integrity."

"None of us is perfect."

"I follow every rule. I do the right thing every time I'm faced with a challenge."

"We all have flaws."

"And what are mine?"

"You are brilliant at what you do."

"How is that a flaw?"

"You lock on. You obsess. It's what helped you find me."

"I don't obsess."

"You do."

"Prove it."

"Zara, please, this is futile."

"Prove it."

He gave a resigned shrug. "You were obsessed with Zach Montgomery once."

"I'm over him."

"You're still affected by him. Zach prevents you from trusting me."

"He wasn't a thief."

"There are many levels of mistrust."

"Between us?"

"You reverse-engineered my tracking device on your phone," he said. "You've been keeping tabs on me. This isn't amateur hour."

Yes, of course, because I was dealing with Icon.

"Listen to me," he said, "we must break down all walls between us. I won't hurt you. All you need to do is believe me."

The night was already ruined because my naivety had led me here into the cruelest trap and I hated myself for being so manipulated again.

Their faces flashed before me.

I didn't want my memory to go back there, and yet I struggled to pull back from the brink of remembering.

I sucked in a shaky breath and whispered, "I also trusted my friend Natalia."

I had no idea when their affair started, but looking back there were so many clues like their glances of affection I'd ignored. During a late study session with just her and me nestled in my flat I'd sworn her to secrecy and shown her the photo of the wedding dress I was going to wear when Zach proposed. I'd pulled out that cutting from *Cosmopolitan*, the one with the auburn-haired model who was wearing a simple cream lace gown. I'd shown Natalia the photo of my mum wearing a similar lace dress on her own wedding day.

"They betrayed me," I muttered with my chest tightening as the stark memory drenched my soul having condemned me to never trust again.

Everyone betrays in the end.

"Isn't there a rule we shouldn't talk about our exes?" He threw in a sweet smile. "Let's stick to talking about us."

Natalie's wedding dress had been woven in fine Italian cream lace; the one from Cosmopolitan.

"We're opening up." He tried to draw my attention back on him. "This is good, right?"

I managed a wary nod, regretting my outburst and vaguely aware of the flickering torches; orange flames dancing in the breeze.

Tobias stepped closer. "Maybe now's a good time to talk about what happened to your mom?"

My breath stuttered with the realization he knew about that. "It was a long time ago," I said hoarsely.

"I've shared with you about my parents' death." He gave a shrug. "Talking with you about it helped me. I owe you the same."

"It was nothing."

"I disagree. I wonder if its significance still affects you today. Have you never talked to anyone about this?"

"What is this?"

"I know what happened," he said softly. "You were in the back of the car strapped into a child safety seat when the drunk driver crashed into your mom's car. You wouldn't remember at two years old but you seem to have a fear of small spaces? Elevators?"

I shook my head, refusing to believe it had anything to do with me hating lifts. My ears were ringing and fatigue was catching up. "I don't remember. And you had no right to snoop around my past. I know what you're doing."

"I want to help you. To get over a fear, you must first face it."

Panic surged and I hated him for manipulating me; after all, I had no memory of the car being forced over the ravine...

I fumbled with the necklace. "Take it off!"

"Zara, careful."

I couldn't breathe. "Get it off." I yanked it from my neck.

The green gem glinted in the sand like a beacon to reality. Tobias crouched and swept up the necklace into his palm and held it to his chest, his eyes filled with confusion.

Don't look at him, don't fall into another trap.

"You've seduced me. Prevented me from doing what I should. Tried to get me to betray all I hold dear."

He stepped forward. "Zara, I know I've asked a lot from you."

It was too much to take in... Icon himself had confessed another theft was looming, and now I was caught between doing the right thing and never breathing again.

I'd given myself over to drown.

I backed away.

He stepped forward. "Take a breath."

That was just it; I didn't want him to know everything about me.

To know me so well, he had the power to destroy me.

I turned on my heels and sprinted fast along the shoreline, glancing up at the dark bluff, looking for other people.

"Zara, please," he called after me.

I spun round. "Stay back."

"You're safe here," he said. "Please, don't worry about the necklace."

Turning sharply, fast on my feet again I pounded along the sand, sprinting away from him into the darkness.

Oh, no.

The cliff edge jutted out and prevented me from going any farther. I could swim round it, but I'd risk unknown currents and turning up on another beach bedraggled and with no phone.

My palms crushed against the cliff and I saw the large alcove. At least it would shield me from the chill and give me time to think and to reason my way through this.

I huddled between two rocks and hugged my knees; I'd followed my heart and ignored my intuition, and goodness knows what was left of my life now. I was about to lose everything.

I should have stayed in London.

Once it came out that I'd slept with the enemy my reputation would be ruined forever, and I'd have to endure those side glances from my colleagues that signaled what they really thought of me. I just wanted to curl up into a ball and hide forever. A little way down the beach I saw the shadowy figure of Tobias nearing.

When he reached the outer alcove, he paused. "I'm so sorry I upset you."

"I won't betray by colleagues," I snapped. "I just won't."

He looked away as though deep in thought. "I asked too much of you."

My gaze fell to his hand to see he was holding a frame. Tobias threw it onto the sand and it rolled closer to my feet. I recognized his parents from the photo from when I'd researched Tobias's life. Within the frame stood a handsome man in his twenties and he was smiling at the camera with his left arm wrapped lovingly around a woman's shoulders. I knew that was Tobias's mom. She was wearing the same necklace I'd pulled from my neck.

Tobias lowered to his knees and looked down at the frame. "She was pregnant with me in this. The necklace was a gift from my dad for creating such a miraculous human being." He waggled his brows playfully.

A dreadful guilt wanted its way in if any of this was true.

He looked at me with compassion. "You're asking me to let them win?"

"The Burells?"

"Let me do what I do best."

Fear slithered up my spine that he was even saying this.

"I hate seeing you like this," he said. "I can't stand to think it's me who hurt you."

I shoved myself up. "You shouldn't have spied on me."

"You've been tracking me." He shrugged. "Following me following you."

"What does that make us?"

"Equally guilty." His smile faded. "Equally obsessed with each other maybe?"

Within the frame his beautiful parents smiled up at me and I knew betraying Tobias meant betraying them too.

He's giving the paintings back, I reasoned, *he's not a bad person. He's returning them all. There's no financial gain and no reward other than seeing justice done.*

The Burells ruined my father and even now his memory was tainted. The only man who'd dared to face up to them and right their wrongs was Tobias. He'd offered to return *St. Joan* to me as proof of that and he had returned the Titian to Sarah Louise Ramirez. As well as all those other victims he'd sought justice for, who I would probably never hear about.

"Zara, this man is ruthless. His family hires mercenaries who don't have a conscience. They kill for money. Don't get on the Burells' radar. That's all I am asking of you."

"Are you on theirs?"

"Not yet."

Still, they probably knew about Icon and that he'd stolen from them.

"They have no right to your life now," he said. "They stole your childhood. Don't let them steal one more second. Our future belongs to us. Promise you won't go after them."

"Tell me you will give up being Icon?"

"I am doing sacred work." He gave a shrug. "On behalf of the gods."

I wiped a stray hair from my face. "Let the gods choose someone else."

"I can't, Zara, they chose me."

I wrapped my arms tighter around myself. "What's so special about this one? That you'd risk so much?"

"It's the way it was stolen," he said softly. "The carnage that came after."

"The Burells?"

"No, they're not the only evil in this world. The man who owns it now uses it as a trophy. It's taken years to find him."

"Can't this family who lost whatever it is just let it go?"

He gave a sympathetic look. "There's too much at stake."

"Promise me you won't go through with this." I stepped forward.

"I refuse to lose you like this."

"Then say it."

He gave the slightest shrug.

I slapped his face hard and he glared at me and moved forward swiftly and pulled me into a kiss, his lips ravishing mine. I moaned my fury into his mouth even though I relented to him, pulled him close and crushed my body to his. My chest thrummed with need as I continued to fight him through my passionate kiss, tongues tangling, my hands scrunching his hair in defiance as I kept him locked to me.

I broke away. "I can't think straight."

"Because you refuse to talk about anything."

My legs weakened and I leaned on the rock.

"Zara, when will you believe me when I say I'm protecting you?"

Looking over at him, I was left with the sense there was so much he wasn't saying.

"You can't be alone tonight." He interlocked his fingers

with mine and pulled me away from the rock. "Come back to the house."

I was too emotionally wrecked to fight anymore and I went willingly with him, feeling as though everything I'd once believed was compromised, but in my heart I knew I was relieved *St. Joan* was no longer in the cruel hands of the man who'd ruined my father. That criminal didn't deserve her. He didn't understand the meaning of what the painting meant or the profoundness of *St. Joan*'s sacrifice. Yet Tobias had proven he did by saving her.

We trekked back along the shoreline with golden sand between our toes, the breeze billowing our clothes.

He led me through the house and up the staircase and pulled me into his bedroom where he undressed me. He yanked the bedsheet back and patted for me to get in.

"Where will you be?" I climbed beneath the duvet.

"Right here watching you sleep." He undressed and climbed in beside me and his warm body spooned behind mine, bringing the comfort I craved.

I turned to look at him. "Was your father flying the plane?"

Tobias kissed my shoulder tenderly. "No."

The sound of waves crashing on the shoreline lulled me and my eyes became heavy.

"I remember the sudden quiet," he whispered. "It all happened fast but looking back that was the first sign something was wrong. The engines failed. My mom was so calm. She was being brave for me. After we crashed she had me rest my head on her lap so that I didn't watch her die. I remember her fingers trailing weakly through my hair and then she became still."

Tears slipped down my cheeks. "I'm so sorry, Tobias."

"I wish you could see inside my heart, Zara. See that all my intentions are good."

It had always been this way. I'd always had to fight for the most precious things in my life, and fighting for Tobias was going to be no different.

Despite resisting this drag of sleep it won out anyway.

12

I looked out beyond the endless dark blueness waiting for the sun to rise from the bow of Tobias's hundred-foot *Sunseeker Predator*, a beautifully crafted yacht with its sleek interior and open-top roof. We'd risen early to make the exhilarating journey out here and had anchored a few miles from his Malibu home.

Tobias had planned on me spending time with him here at some point. I knew this from the brand-new jeans, sweater and thick jacket he had conveniently waiting for me in my size, and with these flat shoes I looked quite at home on his luxury boat.

This week had flashed by so fast. I could hardly believe it was Friday morning already, I'd burned through five days and felt no closer to convincing Tobias to turn away from his reckless ways. Last night he'd shared with me those deeply personal memories of his last moments with his mom and this alone reassured me I was edging closer to reaching him.

I went in search of him, climbing the short way up the steps to the control deck, my hair whipping around my face as I breathed in the fresh sea air. We had both needed to hide out here for a while upon the tame waters; lost from the world on our floating sanctuary where we could be ourselves.

"How's my skipper?" I leaned in and gave him a hug.

"Peaceful," he said, wrapping his arms around me.

We stayed like this for a while in each other's arms, watching the sunrise on the horizon as it burst vibrantly into view and showered the ocean with color.

Tobias led me back down to the lower deck. He lay on a sun lounger and had me join him, and I rested my head on his chest, snug beneath a blanket pulled up over us; snuggling contentedly as the boat swayed gently.

If I had been looking for a moment of perfection, then this was it. Wilder read out loud from his book of poetry by William Wordsworth, his deep voice ideal for the tempo and rhythm of the emotionally filled verse, "The Solitary Reaper." It made my toes curl with the way he spoke the elegant trance-inducing ballad.

Being here with him reminded me of those lazy summer days I'd spent in Hyde Park, languishing on the green while studying and taking a break now and again to indulge in reading poetry.

Never had I imagined I'd be lying on a yacht with a gorgeous American who loved the arts, history and literature as much as me. Sleepy beneath this warm thick blanket, I wanted this dream scape to go on forever.

After a few hours of lounging on the boat we returned to shore and he carried me through the house and into his bedroom and through to his bathroom, where he washed the sand from my feet and then undressed me and finally, he threw me onto his bed like a damsel about to be ravaged.

He left the room.

Intrigued with what he was doing I waited patiently for him to return. When he strolled back in he was naked—other than the cowboy hat he was wearing. I burst into laughter at how ridiculously gorgeous he looked as he folded his arms and posed for me with a triumphant grin.

I sat on his bed and was equally naked beneath this faux fur blanket, unable to tear my gaze from him. His beauty always took my breath away, his tanned sculptured body, those six-pack abs and his muscular biceps and his mischievous green eyes holding mine with amusement.

"As you can see." He flexed a bicep. "I'm a cowboy."

It didn't matter that the question of whether he owned a cowboy hat had been the first thing that had popped into my brain when I'd tried to hide my embarrassment from showing a sneaky interest in his things back when I'd first snuck his home. I was having too much fun to correct him. "Where did you get it?" I asked, amused.

"What are we talking about now?" His hand slid low over his abdomen and he grasped his cock.

"The hat!"

"Every self-respecting American owns a cowboy hat. Who knew!"

"You bought it for me?"

"I know all about your fetish, missy. Ordered it from AmericanHunks.com."

Something told me he knew I'd tried to distract him that night by mentioning a hat that I'd never given a thought to before, and he was purposefully playing along to tease me.

I lifted a pillow and threw it at him.

He caught the pillow and threw it to the end of the bed and came at me fast, yanked off the blanket and scooped me up. "Saddle up, baby."

I let out a gasp of surprise at his strength as he lifted me with ease, his biceps curling when he sat me up and pulled me into a hug.

"Jade, dim the lights," he commanded her.

"Yes, Jade," I blurted, "dim those lights."

"I'm seriously considering returning your access to control her."

"Just think of the things Jade and I will get up to."

"I can only imagine."

I was slipping further into my devotion for him. My own selfish needs were clouding my view and yet I was too drawn to him to resist.

Tobias lay on the bed and pulled me on top of him. "Time to ride, cowgirl." He slapped my butt.

I gasped at the shock—and fell into a fit of giggles.

"Well if I'd have known you'd be this excited I'd have bought the entire store."

I leaned forward and pressed my hands onto his chest and positioned my sex over his. "You're hilarious."

"I have my moments."

My body quivered as I eased his cock inside me, pouting as my body acclimated to his growing size and I stilled, waiting a few seconds for the pleasure to swell.

"Stay with me tonight," he whispered.

Rising and falling onto him. "I can do that."

He sat up and lifted his hat and placed it on my head. My hand rose to adjust the brim so I could see him better. Wearing this made me feel playful and free as all traces of self-consciousness slipped away.

He rested back again with his head on the pillow. "You'll be wearing that each time we fuck from this moment forward."

"Oh, no, what have I set myself up for?"

"Let's just say we need to work on your stamina." He waggled his eyebrows. "Giddyap."

I burst into laughter again, completely seduced by his grin.

He covered his eyes and chuckled and he looked so endearing, so young suddenly, as though he too was letting go of all this tension.

Twisting slightly, I reached behind me and cupped his balls, thrilled to see his eyes close and his jaw slacken as I stroked my thumb and squeezed lightly.

Letting him go, I rode him faster, my thighs quivering as I neared, my thoughts quiet, my breaths stuttering with each downward glide sending shocks of pleasure.

"West meets east," Tobias whispered.

"Isn't that east meets west?"

"Yes, but for our purposes—" He sat up and sucked my left nipple.

"I'm close."

Tobias's hands wrapped around my waist. "Not yet."

Panting my frustration, I stared at him with my heart thundering, waiting for him to let me continue. I felt overwhelmed with this internal ache, this need to come.

He lifted me off him, leaving me feeling vulnerable after having my body so close to reaching bliss; thrumming with heat. I couldn't find the words to tell him how bewildered he made me feel, this rising doubt that he might repeat what he'd done to me before. Let me starve for him.

I needed him inside me.

"No, Zara, this is your way. Time to do it my way."

"Your way?"

"Let me introduce you to tantric."

A shudder of anticipation swirled up my spine.

I'd heard of this ancient method but never indulged in this form of lovemaking, because before now there'd never been anyone like Tobias.

He grabbed the hat and pulled it off my head and flung it across the room. He positioned me to lie faceup on the bed and I raised my hips when he dragged a pillow over and slid it beneath, forcing my pelvis to rise. Gently, he eased my thighs apart until my sex was completely exposed. He pulled apart my labia and his hands were warm and soothing.

"Shush, patience." He gave a crooked smile. "I'll teach you." His right palm rested between my breasts. "Slow your breathing."

"What are you going to do?"

"Everything."

"Everything?" My body trembled with this burst of arousal, causing me to clench in expectancy of his touch.

He cupped my sex. "This is a doorway into the divine."

Resting my head back, feeling the pressure of his hand there, I concentrated on calming, staring at the ceiling and hyperaware of everything.

He climbed off the bed and went over to a side table and opened a drawer. He pulled out a small bottle and removed the lid and held it beneath my nose. The scent of vanilla and cinnamon wafted and stirred a wave of relaxation. My heart skipped a beat when Tobias poured a trickle of fluid along the top of my pubic bone and then twisted the lid back on and set it aside.

He began a slow circling motion over my pelvis with his hands, applying firm pressure and sending ripples of arousal.

My breath stuttered as I realized he was giving me a massage—and it felt amazing. A sigh of wonder, a shiver of contentment, my arousal burning up beneath his touch.

His green gaze twinkled with approval when I lay my arms by my sides and widened my thighs farther apart, realizing this was as much about trust as it was indulgence. Firm fingers caressing my outer folds, he glided a hand in an upward motion and then another in a hypnotic rhythm, barely missing my clit, and this purposeful avoidance made it throb deliciously.

He eased apart my folds and said, "Look how beautiful you are."

I raised my head to see him run a fingertip along me, and let out a wanton moan of pleasure as my back arched when his gentle tugging almost sent me over. I was dripping wet and on fire from his touch; the way he commanded each moment was bewitching.

How beguiling he was, how incredible a lover, and even if right now I learned this was all part of his dark plan to seduce me entirely, I still couldn't pull away, I was too entranced, too enthralled by the way he knew my body, mesmerizing me with each stroke and eclipsing my thoughts.

He blew a cold stream of air over my clit and I had to slap my hand over my eyes to cope with the intensity of sensations. Tobias lulled me back to a dreamy state when he teased me gently with this erogenous awakening, each stroke roaming closer and closer to my sex until I felt that brilliant sweep of his fingers over my clit—and then moving away just as swiftly.

"That's..." I tried to speak, throat tight with welling emotion.

As though he really was unlocking a secret doorway I never knew existed.

"You're soaking wet, baby." He stroked along. "Good girl."

"Oh, please."

He eased my hips back down onto the pillow. "Close your eyes. Surrender to me."

Time dissolved as my thoughts ceased spinning, my focus absorbed by the way he continued to play his thumb over the tip of my clit, deliberately running it along that oversensitive nub and at the same time placing two fingers at my entrance and easing them in and out again and sweeping his hand up to provide an exquisite pressure over my core—keeping a perfect tempo, a deliriously hypnotic loop.

My shuddering thighs gave away how close I was, and my groan was me begging for relief. Tobias ceased moving and punished me by separating my folds and holding them apart to pause the play and let me step back from this precipice. Never had I felt so utterly exposed and so grateful for this bond between us, so free and erotically innocent.

So beautifully feminine.

I was panting now, giving myself away after he slid two fingers deep inside and pressed my G-spot. His mouth engulfed my clit to suckle, sending a jolt of pleasure surging from there and outward, plunging me into a rapturous trance.

Rising and rising and finding my way...

Reaching the pinnacle and yet my erotic master knew just when to pull me away and bring me down again and it was getting easier to slip to and fro after being brought this close to bliss and held on the verge of this crest and then drawn back again.

The sound of the ocean seduced me into a lull.

Let me fall now.

It was as though he was teaching me to trust as much as he was making love to me, showing me he knew what I needed and when, with each stroke, each caress, each gentle suckling of my beaded nipples. He'd tuned into every single shiver of want and was mastering every nuance of my body.

With me weak in his arms, he easily maneuvered me up to sit on his lap and I felt the full length of him pressing against my sex, my hips rocking along him as my slickness aided this leisurely glide.

Finding his gaze, he showed me how to inhale and exhale in unison with him.

His body's heat seared into me, his musculature firm and

uncompromising, and my hands ran over his taut chest and I swooned from his heady scent that reminded me of a scintil-lating blend of ocean breeze fused with his expensive cologne.

Staring into his eyes, I slipped into a trance, soothed by this sense of safety, this connection deeper than anything I'd ever experienced, peering into his soul and seeing him, shar-ing this with him. My hands gripped his biceps as though he was the most sacred lifeline I'd ever known.

When he lifted me to slide inside there came a sense of completeness as I stretched open for him. He crushed his lips to mine, his tongue exploring my mouth entirely until that familiar wave came and I flew higher and higher, my gasps entering his mouth.

So very close...

When I verged on coming he cupped my face with his hands and his eyes commanded me to hold back, warning I must continue to savor every sensual moment, and when I felt my control returning he grabbed my buttocks and pulled me close, thrusting even deeper until I felt his tip nudge my cervix sending a delectable pang.

I obeyed his direction to gently rock, our bodies locked as one, this symbiotic motion alighting every nerve and causing my nipples to press against his chest. Our sex melded together in this sensual dance, my toes curling with this unrelenting erotic tension; like a bird in a cage waiting to fly free.

Pleading with him, I sent a silent message that my heart had opened entirely and was willing him to see I'd let him in.

Given him all of me.

Mind, body and soul.

As though sensing this he gave a nod of approval and his right hand slid down between us and he pressed a fingertip upon my clit and began making languid circles there until the pleasure erupted into endless erotic spasms; my channel clenched him ever more fiercely as we rocked.

"Come for me," he said huskily. "For as long as you can."

I fell against him, resting my forehead on his shoulder, trembling, tumbling into the abyss. There came everything and nothing...

Minutes unfolding into timelessness.

Feeling conquered completely.

Having no idea how much time had fallen away, I felt him grasp my shoulders and ease me back a little.

His eyes steely with passion. "Now do you see what I see?" his voice rasped. "We're so good together."

Resting my head on his shoulder I let out a longing sigh, not wanting to move, I wanted to stay like this forever with him inside me and these internal pangs felt like I'd sipped an opiate.

Too sleepy to stay awake, I slipped into a dream.

13

"Not yet." Tobias placed his hand over my brown paper bag to prevent me from taking a bite from my chocolate croissant.

I frowned at him because my mouth was already watering. That trip out on his boat this morning had left me starving.

"Patience," he said, amused.

We stood outside La Tricia café beneath its awning with a full view of Two Rodeo Drive, the luxury shopping area. I'd finally made it to one of the places I'd hoped to visit. This shopper's paradise was in the heart of Beverly Hills, and we'd stopped off for a midmorning coffee. Tobias had just treated us both to a pastry.

We'd left his Malibu home an hour ago and I was still reeling from watching the beautiful sunrise from his yacht this morning, and afterward being swept up by his erotic mastery; my body was still tingling.

The week had flown by in a whirlwind of passion and intrigue and Friday had arrived all too soon. I felt caught up in a place of wanting this to go on forever and yet fearful of how we'd end.

He peered at me through his sunglasses and I wanted to

see his shielded eyes and work out what he was up to. I almost asked him to take them off but the morning sun was too bright and it wasn't like I didn't have shades on too, and these frames were great for people watching—especially Tobias watching.

He was dressed in jeans, a white shirt and a dark blue necktie; his black jacket threw in a dash of sophistication and that scarf he'd woven artfully around his neck provided a European flair.

I'd matched Tobias with a casual outfit and was in jeans too and a new soft pink cashmere sweater I'd found amongst the clothes he'd bought me. It felt good to let my hair tumble down my shoulders freely.

"I love autumn, don't you?" he said. "This is my favorite time of year."

"Anything but winter," I said and shivered why.

We were mingling with wealthy Angelinos as they laid down some serious cash on the overly priced stores around them.

Careful not to spill my coffee, I leaned forward and with my free hand peeled open his paper bag. I leaned to take a bite out of his pastry and grinned through my mischief; my taste buds did a happy dance.

Tobias rolled his eyes as he took a sip of coffee. "Naughty."

I gave an innocent smile.

"Come on." He led me down the finely cobbled pathway.

In my heart, I knew the wall surrounding Tobias was being chipped away at and when the right moment came I'd approach him again to try to get him to see sense on the subject that made my stomach twist in knots.

We made our way down the center of the luxuriously styled shops of Versace and Gucci and on past Jimmy Choo and Lanvin, and I peered into the windows at the decadent displays all neatly presented as though each handbag, each shoe and each piece of clothing yearned to be hailed as art.

Tobias paused outside a store and turned to face me. "Here we are."

This was the most romantic thing any man had ever done for me. We were having breakfast at Tiffany's. The white marble front with its towering elegance showcased an enormous clock halfway up the frontage.

"You are romantic." My heart fluttered as I realized he understood the whimsical idea of Audrey Hepburn eating a pastry outside a Tiffany's in that 1961 classic film.

Tobias took a big bite out of his pastry and I fell against him, feeling his lips press against my forehead with affection.

"You do realize—" I raised my gaze to meet his "—Audrey's character was an American geisha? I hope you don't think I'm looking for a wealthy man to take care of me?"

"You're too independent," he said. "But you are like Holly Golightly in that you're always searching out for the next adventure."

I stared down at the avenue of stores. "I'm not sure about that."

"What else would you call flying thousands of miles to meet with me?"

A moment of madness that led to this…

"And Holly had the cutest cat," he added.

"A tabby. She named Cat."

He laughed as though it was something I'd do.

Tobias had this way of making every experience magical, as though he'd sprinkled fairy dust over me and with each passing moment I was falling further under his spell.

"You have Audrey's eyes," he whispered. "Full of wonder. You can't hide your emotions."

"I don't think that's necessarily a good thing."

"I love that about you," he said. "Your authenticity."

Blinking at him, I replayed his words and let out the softest sigh.

"Let's go in," he said.

There came the shock of cold from the overly air-conditioned store. Though it was easy to soon forget this chill as we paused inside, admiring the lavish display of fine jewelry presented in long glass cases. A crystal chandelier fell in the center sending out prisms of color. Enthusiastic shop attendants were bringing out selections for shoppers to try on.

"I'm sorry, sir," said the smartly dressed security guard. "You can't eat in the store."

With a wide grin, Tobias replied, "We have an appointment. Adelaide arranged our visit."

"The manager?" he said.

A tall slim woman rushed toward us in an invisible cloud of Chanel. "Mr. Wilder?" She gave a nod to the guard indicating it was fine. "You're here to see the Blue Book Collection?"

Oh, Tobias had planned this down to the last detail; realizing this made my legs wobble with giddiness.

"Yes." He turned toward me. "May I introduce my girlfriend, Zara?"

My heart did a happy dance as I raised my coffee to apologize for not being able to shake Adelaide's hand.

"You don't mind?" Tobias glanced at his cup.

"Of course not, Mr. Wilder." She turned on her razor-sharp heels and led us through the store. "We're thrilled you're visiting us."

From her gushing, Adelaide had to have known who Tobias was. We weaved our way around eager-looking tourists all seemingly enamored with the securely ensconced jewelry. Adelaide guided us up a white marble stairway to another showroom. No one else was in here. Tobias looked over at me and winked.

We were left alone to peer into the glass cabinets and given the time to admire the exquisite collection of diamond-encrusted jewelry. From the white diamond bib necklace to the diamond cuff, all of it was far too self-indulgent, and I couldn't imagine where you'd wear such excessive trinkets. The designs were influenced by the ocean, apparently, and I gave a wry smile at that touch of marketing.

"Pick out something." Tobias turned and leaned back against a cabinet, and he looked endearing with that radiant expression proving he was getting just as much fun out of this as me.

I tucked my sunglasses into my purse.

"Zara?" He raised his glasses to rest on his head.

"No. Thank you, though." There was no event I could think of where it was okay to be drenched in as many diamonds as this. Though, more important, no way could I let him buy me anything that could be later construed as a bribe.

I offered Tobias my cup to hold and peeled back the wrapper of my croissant. It melted deliciously in my mouth along with its chocolate flakes. I was careful not to spill crumbs onto the plush blue carpet.

Tobias and I were such opposites, with me always following the rules and him never caring for them. Or at the very least finding a way around them.

I thanked him for holding my drink and took it back.

He leaned in and gave my cheek a kiss and then turned to wander around the small room, pausing to peer into the cases. That spontaneous show of affection had calmed my spiraling mind. Moving along, I admired the display while savoring my pastry in between sips of coffee.

Tobias nudged up against me. "Sure?"

"Yes."

"Okay," he said playfully. "But you're missing out."

"How?"

"Wearing any one of these would grant you instant access to the Beverly Hills Wives Club. You could stroll right in there and show them who's who."

"Not sure I'd fit in." I lifted a flat shoe to make my point. "I'm awkward at those parties. I'd bore them with my art acumen. They'll be like—" I raised my hand to mimic another woman "—'Excuse me while I go to the loo. Be right back.'"

"I don't believe it."

"No, seriously, I'd start spouting things like how Matisse's best work came after a bout of appendicitis or how Vincent van Gogh was so infatuated with his cousin he held his hand over a flame to prove to her father how much he loved her."

Tobias backed toward the door. "Good to know."

"See."

His fake frown broke into a grin. "Van Gogh's cousin's name was Kee Vos-Stricker, daughter of his mother's eldest sister. She ghosted him."

My face lit up with joy that he knew this and I added, "Kee broke his heart."

"Poor van Gogh."

"Don't mention his ear!"

"Didn't even cross my mind." He shook his head. "Didn't van Gogh deliver his ear to a brothel he used to frequent? Bet they loved that."

I threw him a playful frown. "It doesn't surprise me you know that."

God, Tobias's smile could melt the panties off a nun, I mused, shaking my head and laughing.

He looked so damn handsome silhouetted in the doorway, his eyes glinting playfully as he said, "Stay here."

I went to ask him where he was going but he'd gone.

My gaze returned to the diamond tiara and I assumed it was for a bride, otherwise you'd receive a whole lot of grief for wearing that statement of supremacy.

My body froze, thoughts racing ahead of being able to rationalize what my consciousness was suggesting. Was Tobias about to hit Tiffany's?

No, this was ridiculous; he only ever hit private homes, though he had also robbed Christie's. Oh, no, the Vatican too.

This dreadful chill spiraled up my spine to taunt me. Leaning on the glass case I tried to grasp this rational thought: he only stole from those who'd stolen the item first.

He's Icon.

That's right, began my addled internal rant, *you're hanging out with him like all this is perfectly normal and instead of hiking him down to the police station you're playing tourist. Worse than this even, you're gallivanting around as though you're lovers.* My reflection in the glass counter looked harried.

I threw my empty cup and croissant wrapper in the bin and retraced my steps, using the handrail to descend the staircase as I scanned the showroom for Tobias.

Where the hell was he?

The glint from all that bling was too much so I reached into my handbag and slipped on my sunglasses and headed as calmly as possible toward the front door. Out into the late morning warmth.

Suppressing my tears, I cursed my stupidity for thinking this was going to be easy. I'd fooled myself into believing I'd be able to spend time with Tobias and there'd be no fallout, no consequences for trying to get him to see reason.

"Zara?" Tobias came up behind me.

I spun around and stared into those steely green eyes.

"I was looking for you." He raised a blue box. "We can't leave without one of these." His smile faded. "You okay?"

"Yes, of course." My voice trembled.

"Open it."

A blue ribbon was wrapped around the square box.

Swallowing hard I tried to salvage my pride from this lingering embarrassment.

"I know I'm moving fast," he said softly and his lips curled into the sweetest smile. "You can tell me to take it slower if you want."

My gaze lowered to the box.

Tobias gave the bow a tug and lifted the lid to show me the delicate silver watch. "Do you like it?" His face was full of expectation.

I tried to calm; cheeks still flushed.

"We can switch it out for something else if you want?" he said.

"No, it's lovely."

It really was elegant and glancing in through Tiffany's window display I wondered how much it cost.

"Here." Tucking the box beneath his right arm, Tobias slid the watch around my wrist and fastened it. "Very elegant." His brows rose with kindness. "Do you want the box?"

I leaned in and wrapped my arms around him. "Thank you."

That's all this was, I realized. I was overwhelmed by his affection, him spending precious time with me, and I'd been scared to trust what this was because for the first time in my life everything felt right and that felt foreign to me.

This magnetic pull toward him was impossible to resist. It wasn't just me saving him but him saving me too, I saw this now because all this pain and deceit I'd endured in my past slipped away when I was in his arms.

His frown deepened as he sensed my reticence. "I'm going to take you to meet an old friend of mine. Waya insists he has a painting from an Old Master so you may have to humor him."

"I'd like to meet him." Twisting my wrist to admire one of the most gorgeous gifts anyone had ever given me, I rose out of my melancholy.

I'd been running from fear all my life, which was the cruelest punishment I could have ever dished out on myself. One which I didn't deserve. It wasn't the gift of the watch or even the fact Tobias had brought me here to have breakfast, it was the way he looked into my eyes as he tried to see me amidst this cloud of doubt.

Tobias wasn't a criminal, he was a superhero and he'd promised me he'd leave this life behind soon and perhaps, just perhaps, there could be a future for us. All I had to do was let it happen.

Clearing my thoughts, I drew back from falling further and refused to go against everything I believed to be right.

Don't get lost in his allure.

I peered up at him and took his hand. "Thank you. Not only for the watch, which is beautiful, but bringing me here."

His eyes crinkled with kindness. "I know what's bothering you."

"Oh?"

"You have beauty fatigue." He gave a wry grin.

Falling into his arms, the strength of his hold was comforting and all I wanted in this moment was him.

Let me have a few more seconds like this with him, I begged myself; *let me have this at least.*

We spent the rest of the morning window-shopping, with him threatening to buy me everything and me dancing around his generosity. Eventually he wore me down when he insisted on a new little black dress from Versace and a pair of strappy stilettos to go with the outfit. I thanked him with endless kisses, having given up on this fight to not let him spoil me. Tobias insisted on carrying our shopping bags like a true gentleman.

He chose the Beverly Wilshire hotel for us to have lunch.

I wondered if he'd forgotten this was where I'd stayed the first night I'd arrived in LA, because he didn't seem to register its significance. I flashed wary glances at him but saw no reaction.

Strolling hand in hand into the BLVD Lounge, a lavishly decorated restaurant decked out with a cozy sophistication, and despite its lofty ceiling and large windows it radiated a welcoming atmosphere.

We waited by the concierge desk to be escorted to our table. Tobias interlocked his fingers with mine, and we weaved around the tables and ended up in a semiprivate booth that Tobias had requested.

I'd had breakfast in here the morning before I'd headed off to meet with him at his museum. That stark memory hit me hard as I recalled standing outside The Wilder, with Tobias wearing a casual smile as he pointed to my red suitcase stashed away in the trunk of his Rolls, right before he tried to send me home.

Had he really had such a change of heart? Or was this some brilliant manipulation? His way of winning me over with the knowledge I couldn't stay in the States irrevocably. With only a few days left my time was fast running out.

I sat and looked around the room as that memory returned of me sitting over in the corner just a few days ago, those uncomfortable hours worrying over what I was going to say to him. Yet here I was about to eat lunch with him as though none of that had happened. Tobias was reading the menu seemingly unaware of my spiraling.

The memory of his coldness that day remained vivid. "Tobias," I began, needing him to realize what this place meant to me—what I'd almost lost.

He looked up and gave a nod for me to continue.

"This hotel—"

A twentysomething waiter appeared and flashed us both a warm smile and introduced himself as Lee.

Peering up from the wine menu, Tobias ordered a bottle of Dom Pérignon P2 and decided on a filet mignon as his entrée and I chose the Maine lobster. We continued to swap friendly banter with the waiter before he hurried off.

Tobias held my gaze as he rubbed his jawline, making me wonder if he'd remembered his actions that day. What would have happened had I let his Rolls take me all the way to the airport? My life was changing moment by moment and each decision was sending me farther down the rabbit hole. Though when I looked over at Tobias's beautiful face I knew he was an addiction I'd struggle to break.

I leaned forward and rested my hand on his. "Tobias, we have to talk."

"About?"

I sucked in a tremulous breath. "You know what about. You. Your future—"

Our waiter appeared with a chilled Dom Pérignon, light droplets of condensation dripping, uncorked it and poured a little into a flute. The bottle was sleek and black with a gold embossed label and oozed expensive. Tobias tasted the light golden liquid and then gave a nod of approval. Lee filled our glasses and then lowered the bottle, crunching it into the ice bucket, and then walked away.

"I'm a rebel." Tobias broke the quiet.

I tilted my head in a question.

"I chose white with my steak," he said. "How mutinous. Still, you're predictably in line with tradition at least."

Sipping my champagne and enjoying its zesty freshness, I studied him. "Have you eaten here before?"

"Yes."

"It's a lovely hotel." I narrowed my gaze on him. "You remember I stayed here, right?"

He arched a curious brow; his mocking expression giving away his mischief.

"Let's talk about you, Toby."

He pulled out his phone. "Sorry, it's my London office. Let me shoot them a quick reply."

This momentary distraction was a clear reminder he had an empire to run. He texted away and then set his phone on the table.

"Will you excuse me?" He pushed himself to his feet. "I'm going to the restroom."

I tipped my chin up when he came around to my side of the table to kiss me. A long sigh of happiness escaped me and it made his eyes light up. I admired him from behind as he strolled away, his elegant height was so dashing, the swagger of a man of authority with those broad shoulders emphasizing his fit physique that was undeniable beneath his suave clothes.

There came a glint of pride when I saw the glances from the other diners, women who like me didn't seem to want to let the eye candy out of their sight and some men too, those who probably wanted to know his secret.

My gaze shifted to the silverware, moving over to that trickle of condensation snaking down my champagne glass. I reached out to catch the drop with a fingertip before it fell onto the pristine white tablecloth, and then my eyes landed on Tobias's phone.

The idea of invading his privacy like this tortured me with this level of betrayal.

Everything Tobias had shared with me was under threat and no way was I going to reach out and peek at his private messages because, even though I could see the screen was unlocked, I wouldn't do that to him.

Yet...

I had seconds to decide.

What if he *was* playing me? What if this was merely an elaborate game?

14

Listening to my inner voice, I snatched up his phone and held it hidden beneath the table and went for it—hands trembling as I scrolled through it, searching for any contact with potential Icon clients and looking for dates that might provide a clue to what he was planning next. The last email was from Logan and it seemed innocuous right up until I got to the sign-off in her message: Miss you.

Tobias hadn't answered her yet so I couldn't be sure if he missed her too. I scrolled down to the others from her, looking for any clue that their former relationship had any cinders waiting to respark.

"You're from England?" It was Lee, the young waiter who'd taken our order with enthusiasm.

My fingers tightened around the phone. "Yes."

"I've always wanted to go," he replied.

Usually, I'd have been happy to chat away about all things British, but with time ticking away I was momentarily fazed and went quiet.

"Is he in the industry?" Lee added as he hopped from one foot to the other. "Your friend?"

My fingers hurt from the strain of holding the phone. "Industry?"

"Movie industry? I'm an actor." He looked sheepish. "Well, obviously, a waiter but I moved here from Ohio three weeks ago to launch my career."

"Oh, that's fantastic. No, we're not in the movie business." My jaw dropped when I saw Tobias heading fast toward our table.

Shit.

It was too late to put his phone back. My throat tightened when Tobias reached us.

"Hey, buddy," he greeted Lee. "How's it going?"

Lee looked uneasy. "I was just telling your friend I've moved here from Ohio."

"Wonderful." Tobias pulled back his chair and sat. "Welcome. Don't change. This town can be brutal."

That was all it took for Lee to scurry off.

Tobias cringed. "Did I scare him away?"

"He wants to be an actor." I threw in a smile.

Tobias gestured he expected to hear that and tapped his jacket and then his pockets—feeling for his phone.

Oh, Jesus.

"This dropped on the floor." I placed it on the table and slid it over to him, and then proceeded to look overly interested in the stem of my champagne glass.

His glare went right through me as he sat back down.

Ignoring his death stare as best I could, I feigned innocence. "I wonder if they have chocolate soufflé. You have to order it while you're eating the main course because it takes so long."

"Word of advice," he said darkly, "when you take someone's phone, make sure you return it—" his gaze moved to my handbag "—before they realize it's stolen."

Devastated, I swallowed hard and reached for my bag to

peer in. My own phone was safely resting at the bottom. I'd confessed with that one gesture.

"I trust you, Zara, I don't need to look at your phone to spy on you."

I cringed inwardly as my thoughts searched out something else to fret over and landed swiftly on that email from Logan, the one with her insidious message of "missing him."

This was the woman who'd gotten us an invitation into an orgy at Blandford Palace, proving her own connections to a secret society full of the kind of women who knew how to tantalize a man. A man like Tobias, whose appetite for the erotic was off the charts, whose trust I'd just shattered and who had a beautiful woman waiting in the wings.

"I'll make it up to you," I burst out.

He looked calmer then I deserved.

Nibbling on a fingernail I ran through my options. "I'll be right back."

Hurrying away, my mind swirled so fast it was impossible to gather my thoughts, my cheeks burning at what I'd done. Following the sign for the ladies' room, I hugged my handbag to my chest for comfort. Logan's smug face popped into my head as I worried over her obvious crush, her email proving she'd steal him back if she could. I was competing with a smart lawyer who looked like a supermodel and was a sexy superbitch vixen who'd like nothing more than to get one up on me.

Yes, I was a geek usually, but not today, because I was having lunch with one of the sincerest men I'd ever known who rocked my world in every conceivable way and who brought out my sassy side. I'd allowed my old insecurities to make my decisions for me.

Or had I merely followed a hunch and found nothing?

Either way, I was about to lose the ground I'd painstakingly made getting close to Tobias.

There was only one way to prove I was the kind of woman who could keep up with him, match his passion and be an equal to his Renaissance style. Yet all my doubts were rising to the surface. I'd demanded he prove I could trust him and yet here he was proving he couldn't trust me. I'd ruined our beautiful day which included our trip to Tiffany's, this lovely meal and tainted this morning when we'd gone out on his yacht and then made love.

No, I refused to believe I'd sabotaged the most wonderful thing to ever happen to me—

Tobias William Wilder. I clung to these last remnants of hope for this to be real.

For *him* to be real.

Because if I ever discovered all this was a grand ruse, I knew I'd give up on love forever. If we weren't real, I'd start believing the Old Masters who'd interpreted life upon their canvases as an eternal agony, a continuous outpouring of grief like the work of William-Adolphe Bouguereau, or those breathtaking strokes of Peter Paul Rubens, a Baroque artist who knew how to immortalize movement, color and sensuality. The kind of aliveness I'd not understood until I'd met Icon.

In a dreamy haze, I walked into a bathroom stall and hiked up my skirt and shimmied out of my panties. Within a few seconds my skirt was back down and my blouse straightened. A few moments later I was fluffing my hair in the mirror and allowing the auburn locks to spiral free. A dash of lipstick to add a seductive pout. On the way back toward our table I could see Tobias caressing his brow.

Resting a hand on his shoulder I said, "For you."

He followed my gaze to my hand—the one holding my

panties, and he scooped them out of my palm and tucked them into his jacket pocket. "Sit down, Zara."

I took my seat again.

His stare bored into me and he sent a shiver that unnerved me.

"I'm apologizing," I whispered.

He looked away. "It's over."

My mouth went dry with panic and I searched for the words that could pull us back from the brink of us ending. Nothing, no words worthy of how bad I felt came to me.

Lee reappeared with our meals and we both feigned there was no tension between us. After some polite banter that included the monotony of telling him everything looked fine with our food, he left us alone again.

We ate in silence and I squirmed inwardly that I'd seemingly hurt Tobias with my mistrust. Still, wasn't I here to survey him and get through to his thick skull he was close to ruining his life? My ways might have been construed as heavy-handed but at least I cared enough to try.

"How's the lobster?" he asked with the ease of a man who was never rattled.

"What's over?"

"Our disagreement. How's your food?"

I looked down at my plate and swept up another morsel onto my fork, forcing a taste of the creamy sauce that I wasn't sure I could stomach another bite of. "It's nice. How's yours?"

He reached into his inner jacket pocket and pulled out a business card. He slid it across the table. "Go to this address. You'll see a swimming pool. Get in it."

"I thought our disagreement was over?"

"It is. You may borrow my phone anytime. Look, we shouldn't have secrets. I'll sync your thumbprint for access to my cell. May I have the same privilege for your phone? How about your laptop? May I look at what you've been working on lately?"

Jesus, all I had on there was proof I'd been tracking him. "Yes. Sure. Of course?" It came out as a question and I hoped he'd forget he'd ever asked.

"Good."

"Then why are you sending me to this address?"

"The answer is in my pocket."

I could only assume he was referring to my panties.

"A gauntlet has been thrown." His brows rose playfully.

Searching his face I tried to guess where'd he take this.

"Do not play games with me, Zara. I'm in a completely different league to you when it comes to this kind of sport. As you can see."

I stared down at the card warily and reached for my glass of Dom Pérignon and he shook his head warning me not to drink anymore.

"How long will you be?" I asked.

"Not long." His knife sliced through his steak with ease and he lifted his fork and elegantly placed that piece into his mouth and chewed; washing it down with a sip of champagne.

The booze I could do with right now, but wasn't allowed. "I don't have a swimsuit."

"I'll expect to find you naked."

A thrill rushed up my spine at his sense of daring and my fingernails dug into my palm. "Will there be others there?"

Gold specs glinted in his green gaze. "Marshall will drive you." That tilt of his head told me to go now. "Don't give him a hard time. Or there will be consequences."

I reached for my purse and the Versace bags he'd bought me and pushed myself to my feet and headed away from him, turning briefly to look back with my heart leaping.

"Zara," he called after me.

"Yes?"

"It's waterproof."

"Sorry?"

"Your watch." He narrowed his gaze on me as though challenging me to crumble before him.

With my head held high I strolled through the restaurant. A few minutes later, Marshall swung the Rolls round to the main entrance of the Four Seasons, and I threw him a wave and climbed in the back.

If I asked Marshall to drive me to the Sofitel instead, something told me he wouldn't oblige because he only served one master. The passenger divider rose between us and cut off any chance of communication with him. This was on purpose, I assumed.

Not wearing panties felt so damn naughty; I cursed Tobias for his bossy teasing and sending me out into the world like this—vulnerable and yearning for him.

Do not play games with me, Zara. I'm in a completely different league...

I should hate his alpha-control and yet there came the awareness of how wet those words had made me. How turned on I became when he wielded the power I was meant to be guarded against.

I scrolled through my iTunes, choosing "Breathe Me" by Sia, and popped in my earbuds to allow her haunting lyrics to accompany me on this new Wilder adventure. My body yearned for Tobias, despite the tension of our last interaction. My core burned up for him and I questioned the sanity of continuing this unhealthy obsession. This chase was taking me to dangerous places, territory unknown, and all I had was my will to see this through.

Along the way, I tried not to think about what was ahead and instead admired the architectural wonders of the skyscrapers meshing new with the classic Beaux Arts–style buildings and the other vintage landmarks that lent this city its eclectic air.

Marshall drove us through LA, all the way to where Ninth and Figueroa Street met on a corner. He pointed to a grand entryway of a towering high-rise with shards of sunlight reflecting off the glass windows.

I showed the concierge the address on the business card and he led the way through the marble-and-steel foyer to an elevator. Warily, I stepped inside, those remnants of my phobia causing my hands to tremble as I tried to ignore the seventy buttons. The concierge slipped a silver card into the control panel and a green light indicated its permission for me to ascend. The man stepped back with a nod and the doors slid closed to secure me inside.

With my eyes squeezed shut I ascended fast, and I tried not to think of what Tobias had insinuated, that this fear of lifts had anything to do with the car accident that had taken my mum from me. Wasn't life hard enough already without having subconscious ghosts tempering our days? *Yes*, came my resounding answer, everything mattered no matter how much we wanted to deny the pain that was always one thought away.

Why the hell did it always have to be the highest bloody floor?

When the doors opened, I leaped out into a hallway and went to rest a palm against the glass window to catch my breath after holding it on the way up, though quickly withdrew my hand when I saw the dizzying view. At the end of a long hallway was a single chrome door.

No one answered when I knocked on it. I didn't have a key and cringed at having to go back the way I'd come. I reached inside my handbag for my phone so I could call Tobias.

The door clicked open…

I dropped my phone back into my handbag and stepped inside cautiously, my gaze sweeping across the open-floor loft design. The place was unfurnished.

"Hello?" I called out and placed my purse and the Versace bags by the wall.

This place looked unlived in and for a split second I hoped this wasn't a fuckpad.

"Anyone here?" I went to shut the door but it was already closing and then there came a click of the lock.

That isn't creepy at all.

There was a single lounge chair in what would be considered a sitting room with a chenille throw lying over the back. On its seat rested a sleek laptop. There came the sense that all this had been prepared earlier. It made me wonder if Tobias had placed his cell phone on the table at lunch as a test or a trap.

This felt like another one.

Dead ahead was a long glass wall and as I made my way farther in I saw beyond the end of the building, trying to grasp what seemed like an optical illusion of a swimming pool holding itself up—jutting out with its full length.

Hell no!

The pool and its surrounding walls were transparent and beyond it was a murky view of the street below. Several towels lay on a small table. There was even room along the side for a couple of chairs and overlooking them was a sunshade. I wondered if he liked to read out there. One earthquake and it would be over.

No way am I getting in there.

I went in search of clues to what this place was and how it might fit into Tobias's world. There were five other rooms and all of them equally empty, though one had a king-size bed that was made and it intrigued me with its cozy plush duvet that possibly gave away Wilder's intentions. All the rooms had great views and this entire place looked like it was ready to move into.

Returning to the sitting room I stared at the pool again and resigned myself to never getting in it—ever. I'd placed down the gauntlet as a sexy tease that I was offering myself for his pleasure and yet no way was I up to this erotic game of displaying me naked for all to see. I knew what this was; Tobias was warning me I was out of my depth.

In contrast to the chrome touches in here the blue pool was captivating. I undid the catch, slid the door open a little and walked to the edge of the water and peered into its depths—lying on the bottom was a box. My jaw tightened as my focus fixed on what looked like a mini chest refracting light off its surface. What the hell was in there?

Every cell in my body burned up with the need to know what that was and why Tobias had placed it there. This felt like an impossible command. The kind that delivered dire consequences.

I moved over to the corner of the balcony right before the pool began and brought my legs up and hugged my knees. No matter how much intrigue drew me to fixate on what was in there, this was going to be me sitting here gloriously failing.

There was no way Tobias would have had anything on his phone connecting him to being Icon. He was too smart for that. Perhaps I'd also needed reassurance that what felt so real between us wasn't a grand hoax schemed up by a genius inventor. Keeping your enemies close was the number one rule in war and right now we couldn't have been closer.

The glass door slid farther open and shook me from my daydreaming. Tobias stepped out and strolled down the right side of the pool. No matter the strain of our last interaction, seeing him again made me relax as though his presence alone was enough to calm me.

He kicked off his shoes and peeled off his scarf and laid his jacket on the back of a chair. He unbuttoned his shirt and pulled it off, revealing his sculptured torso as he removed it. Off came his jeans, leaving him stark naked and shamelessly showing off his powerful physique.

Jesus, he'd stripped off in front of everyone who might be lucky enough to look this way and no doubt they'd catch that bad boy tattoo on his left shoulder, the one sparking a dangerous arousal in me now.

Tobias's stare held mine. *That's right, buddy, you can show off your delectable cock to the world, have your image streaming all over social media, but not me, because I won't be seduced by million-dollar penthouses or their flashy pools or mysterious boxes resting on the bottom of fragile glass.*

My gaze shot to it.

He folded his arms across his chest and in a booming voice called over, "Even if it takes a lifetime to earn your trust, I will. I'll undo all the hurt you've experienced and heal your pain and make you forget his name. But you must trust me. Do you think you can do that?"

I want to, really I do, but my heart is warning me against it.

Tobias gave the kindest smile and it looked like resignation— he dived in and water splashed around him. Rising to the surface, his muscular physique sliced through the water with ease, his effortless breaststrokes carrying him the full length of the pool as he swam laps.

Giving me time to think about his promise. Trust was a line I had to cross and yet I couldn't see a way of getting to the other side. Tobias knew this and had probably done all this to force a breakthrough. Or maybe something more sinister was going on here.

He settled at the end of the pool and stretched out his arms either side of the edge. "I heated it for you."

My frown gave my answer and it was a resounding *no*. "Is this my punishment for looking at your phone?"

"No, actually, it's not," he said. "I'll punish you later for that…"

Why did he have to be so devastatingly seductive?

"It's time to wake up." He said it so softly I almost didn't catch it.

"What is this?"

"What do you know about me, Zara?"

I pushed myself up and took a step closer to the water. "You're kind. When you want to be. You like helping people." I gestured the rest.

"I'm a private man."

Exactly, so this didn't make any sense. *Unless.*

My gaze followed the walls. "The glass is one-way?"

"Very good."

My chest heaved with relief. "No one can see us?"

"No."

I wished I'd looked up when I'd entered the building and seen proof of this.

"What is that?" I pointed to the box.

"A piece of the puzzle from your world." He swam toward me and quickly made it to my side and gripped the edge, water trickling off his back as he looked up. "Prove to me you're ready."

"You get it for me."

He shook his head. "Trust the process."

"Why are you doing this? Why is nothing ever simple with you?"

"On the contrary, my life is perfectly streamlined." He

kicked off the wall and swam back to the other side, leaving a wake in his path.

"You like playing with me don't you!" I snapped.

"Take off your clothes."

"You can be a bastard sometimes, you know that."

"Life is about taking risks."

"What will this teach me?"

"You'll prove to yourself you're ready."

"For what?"

"The answer to a question that's haunted you all your life."

All my life?

He was always pushing me too far.

I turned and went inside.

The armchair was comfortable at least. I'd lifted off the laptop and placed it on the floor so I could sit here and wait for him; I brought my legs up and hugged my knees to my chest. When Tobias reappeared, he was standing at the window looking in at me and he was holding the box and resting his forehead on the glass, looking through at me with the kindest smile.

I folded my arms in protest.

He scooped up a towel and wrapped it around his waist and walked in, leaving a trail of droplets behind him on the floor. He swaggered toward me and he was all rippling sun-kissed muscles reminding me of a living, breathing sculpture, chiseled lovingly by the hand of a master. Wilder's body was my weakness and remnants of resistance were scratching their way to the surface.

I felt myself pulling away again.

He neared me. "What I'm about to give you will feel like an abyss has opened beneath your feet. This is not the closure you want, Zara. But it will provide the answers you seek. For obvious reasons, I've kept this from you until now."

"Why that?" I pointed to the pool. "Why make me go in there for it?"

"To prove to yourself you have what it takes to face the truth."

"How would it have proven anything?"

"Only you can answer that."

"But I failed."

"So how you answer this next question is imperative."

I gave a nod that I was ready.

"What have you learned from Icon?"

This rising emotion felt like a tsunami threatening to sweep me away or suck me under into that abyss he was threatening me with. This was him wanting me to see from his perspective and perhaps even find empathy where I should instead find a greater will to stop him.

"Zara?"

"When justice fails and the stakes are too high to let evil continue, you put things right." Or so he believed, I mused, caught up in his mysterious ruse.

He came closer. "Those who have no comprehension of Joan of Arc's sacrifice have no right to her painting."

I agreed with a nod.

Wilder handed me the box and I hugged it to my chest. He knelt before me and worked the latch and with a click it opened. He turned to show me what was inside—a flash drive. I reached inside and removed it. He set the box on the floor. When he placed the computer onto my lap I snapped in the flash drive and my trepidation swelled, causing me to tremble.

I sucked in a nervous breath as I watched him brush a fingertip over the pad to awaken the screen.

He turned the screen to face me. The file was named Zara.

He pushed himself up. "I'm going to take a shower. Give you some space."

My glare shot to his as I silently questioned what he was about to show me.

With a raised brow he said softly, "My beautiful Russian princess."

"What's on this?"

He pulled the green chenille throw off the back of the armchair and wrapped it around my shoulders. "Your provenance."

15

The world fell away as I struggled to understand what Tobias was trying to do to me. Why would he have researched my family history to this extent if not to find information to leverage against me? As I ran my fingertip along the mouse pad I stared in shock at what he'd collated.

There were hundreds of personal documents pertaining to the Romanov family, along with many of my ancestors' personal missives between each other. My chest tightened when I saw an account from my great-aunt of her attempt to escape Russia. I knew that she'd never made it to freedom.

My family tree had been traced with accuracy proving I came from royalty, a fact my father had often told me but the fantastical stories had sounded so exaggerated. Had circumstances been different and Russia not overthrown the Romanovs, there was a big chance I'd be a grand duchess.

Oh, Dad.

Squeezing back tears, I studied my father's personal records and saw the copy of his birth certificate, his marriage certificate and his property deeds to prove we owned my childhood home in Kensington.

There were more documents containing provenance of our art collection and all of them essential to reassure the art community the paintings were once ours. All this felt like a violation of my privacy, and I snapped the lid shut and stared through the glass window at the skyscraper opposite; sunlight reflecting the late afternoon and glinting off its sleek black glass.

What I'd done to Tobias's phone paled in comparison to what was contained here. I wanted to throw his laptop into the swimming pool and demand he tell me why he'd done this. There came the sound of a shower being turned on from one of the rooms. I wondered what he was thinking right now. He was feeling smug, perhaps?

His haunting words returning: *you will feel like an abyss has opened beneath your feet.*

I couldn't swim in that stupid pool, but I was brave enough to search for the answers to why he'd gone to such lengths to rein me in. What exactly did he have on me? It was better to know, I reassured myself as I flipped up the screen and flicked a fingertip over the mouse pad to awaken the truth.

A cruel regime had stripped our family name—our right to the throne—but they couldn't rape our legacy. Somehow, someway, my ancestors had preserved their vast collection of art so the Bolshevik troops hunting them down hadn't destroyed them. Those monsters had murdered the czar and his family but my other descendants had escaped the Bolsheviks' chief executioner and seen to it that some of our masterpieces had survived, though many others were looted and others destroyed in an act of outrage during the Russian Revolution and the rise of the Soviet Union.

For our enemy, our bourgeois art as they'd called it, had no place in their new regime. A few relatives had risked everything to smuggle out what was left of our collection. Still, the house fire had destroyed their best efforts. Four paintings, that's all my dad and I had managed to carry to safety and Tobias had helped me secure three at the National Gallery where they could be enjoyed by so many. I'd personally ensured my beloved painting *Madame Rose* made it to The Otillie.

Every other painting bequeathed to us had been obliterated; all that pain and sacrifice of those who'd gone before us and all for nothing. That's what I saw in my dad's eyes. I'd read the torment of failure, not only grief for the loss of our furnishings, of what had once been our home, but it had been the weight of honoring our legacy and sorrow for the destruction of our collection, including works by Rembrandt van Rijn, Willem Kalf, our beloved van Gogh and the Sandro Botticelli he'd kneel before to pray at night...

Our paintings rivaled some of the greatest private collections and none of them should have hung in a London home but for my father's desire to guard them with his life. And he had sacrificed everything for them.

A sob escaped me when I saw written evidence proving the provenance of the paintings Dad owned. There was even a copy of the paperwork proving his Walter William Ouless's *St. Joan* was indisputably ours. Somehow it had escaped the fire.

I paused on the file marked Top Secret, and my mind scrambled to see the significance of what I was being shown.

And then I saw it.

I felt a sense of suffocating and then tried to focus on the screen as adrenaline surged through my veins, my mind trying to grasp what was surely a twisting of the truth.

A sob burst from me as I scanned the colored photos of each one of our paintings from our collection that should no longer exist—the date marking them as being photographed just months ago.

Impossible…

Moving in a hazy trance, I pushed out of the chair and turned to set the laptop on the seat with the greatest care. Following the trail of water that Tobias had left from his dip in the pool.

I entered the bedroom—

Tobias was sitting on the edge of the bed with his elbows resting on his knees, a fresh towel wrapped around his waist, having left the shower moments ago. His questioning gaze rose to meet mine and that Aboriginal tattoo that marked his shoulder was a stark reminder I was playing with fire.

"Why didn't you tell me?" I said.

"Come here." He held his arms out for me.

I hurried over and knelt on the floor before him, looking up at him as I tried to understand what I'd seen.

Tobias's lips pressed against my forehead and it felt like a confirmation.

"Tell me," I pleaded. "I need to hear you say it."

"They replaced your father's paintings with fakes and afterward they set fire to your house to burn the evidence. They didn't want you to go looking for them."

"The fire started just after we got home from visiting mum's grave in Highgate cemetery."

"They knew your routine."

"They're still out there?" My voice broke with emotion. "My paintings?"

"Yes."

"It doesn't make any sense." I tried to fathom how the ones we'd saved were all confirmed as authentic.

I remembered helping my father carry those four paintings from his office, which was the one room in the house he kept double locked. Whoever had swapped out the paintings hadn't managed to get in there. Perhaps they had no idea that in that room was a masterpiece by Michelangelo himself, and perhaps their ignorance of this was what allowed these paintings to serve as collateral damage. They had no trouble letting what was unseen burn because they'd be getting away with the other priceless paintings.

Maybe that was why my father had told me not to ever mention the ones we'd saved to anyone. Perhaps deep down he'd suspected foul play. Had he filed a police report to investigate this, he would have prevented the insurance agents from paying out on our loss.

My head crashed onto Tobias's lap and I lay there, feeling my scalp tingle as his fingertips brushed through my strands to comfort me. He was giving me time to process this revelation.

I heaved in a deep breath, refusing to cry, refusing to let these men have one more piece of my soul. Within that flash drive was hard evidence proving my father's innocence and Tobias had given it to me. I could return to London with this and begin a campaign to celebrate all my family had done and proudly showcase their sacrifice for the arts. An endeavor that would restore my father's reputation and return his status to the elevation it was once.

"My father had no part in this?" I stared into his eyes to see if he believed me.

"He had no motive, Zara. We can prove this if we have to. This is a heavy burden to carry," Tobias said softly. "To know they're out there."

"How long have you known?"

"We're heading into dangerous territory. But you did ask for transparency. This is my way of giving it to you."

"Tell me you're not lying to me," I burst out. "Please."

"Zara, the photos match your collection. I'm good but I'm not that good. And I've given you everything you need to prove they're yours. Hopefully the time will come one day when such provenance can be used to secure them again."

"Why did you do this?"

He looked away.

Now I was in his debt. Staring down at the hardwood floor, I knew that setting Icon free would place me on a path of self-destruction and that scandal I'd worked so very hard to avoid by working for Huntly Pierre would catch up with me eventually. This was a nowhere land where going back was impossible and yet the price to resolve this wrongdoing was so very high.

Wilder still wanted me to share with him what Huntly Pierre knew about Icon. His goal to extract intelligence from me hadn't gone away, and from the way he was looking at me with such intensity I felt the weight of his demand heavier than ever.

My fingers twisted nervously in his towel and I felt so vulnerable, so confused. "Do you know where they are?"

"Possibly."

"Where?"

"I'm assuming you want me to get them back for you?"

The greatest heist of all—one that would challenge him beyond anything he'd pulled off before and I cringed at the realization I'd be hiring Icon. The very woman tasked with tracking him down.

"Who has them?" I said sharply.

His thumb brushed my cheek to get my attention. "Not yet."

My gaze swept over his face as I tried to read his intention.

He rested a finger beneath my chin and tipped it up. "Now do you see why I walked away from you that first night I met you at The Otillie?"

"Because you knew what I'd endured?" And my father had

died believing he'd failed our ancestors, and Tobias would have known all that suffering we'd gone through, the guilt. With the reappearance of *St. Joan* looming he'd also have known of the scandal about to hit my world again. Perhaps that was why he'd walked away so quickly from me in the gallery, he knew tragedy was swinging back around for me.

Tobias's eyes reflected pain and it was mine, his scorching irises lit up with understanding. He'd risked so much by showing me this, the evidence only Icon could know, and perhaps only he had the skills to restore what was stolen. Perhaps he really had wanted to protect me from this terrible secret but it still hurt that he'd kept it from me.

He rose and reached out for my hand. "Are you okay?"

I pushed myself up and hugged my arms around me.

All I could do was stand here trying to grasp the profoundness of what he'd shown me. "I want them back."

He pulled me into him and kissed me and our tongues swept together, his mouth gliding to my chin with affectionate pecks and down to my throat, tracing along sensitive skin, his hands stroking my shoulders as though knowing this was what I needed more than anything, his touch.

"Please," I pleaded.

That bed was inviting with its softness beckoning and I moved toward it and he pulled me into a hug.

"Tell no one," he said darkly.

I gave a nod I wouldn't.

But then I felt such a sense of panic that I pulled away from him and stepped back from the bed, head swirling with confusion.

"Shush." He lifted my cashmere sweater off me and pulled my jeans off too and I raised my foot for him to tug them off my feet. I fell into his arms, grateful for the reassurance of his hold, too tired to fight.

With a gentle nudge he backed me up and I tumbled onto the bed, aroused by his flash of desire when he ran his fingers over my lace underwear.

"You're so beautiful." He caressed my arm. "I want to make this right for you."

His touch sparked a reaction in my body, firing pulses into every part of me, and when he eased back my panties to allow his tongue to dart along my sex I trembled with waves of pleasure and swallowed back my suspicion. I moaned in rebellion when he pulled away, and then arched my back when his hands slipped behind me to unclip my bra strap and ease it off. He captured my right nipple with his mouth before moving to the other, dragging his teeth and suckling my breast, that pinkness yearning for him as much as he seemed to yearn to never let go, kissing, drawing in as his long groan resonated around it.

"This changes everything," I murmured.

"You change everything."

"I need this…need you…"

"Promise you won't betray me, Zara."

My head lolled to the side when his thumb brushed my sex as he eased my panties down and over my hips.

When I didn't answer, he placed my hand onto his chest and rested his palm over it. "Say it." His expression was a mixture of defiance and intrigue as he repeated his request.

I couldn't answer.

"Answer me," he snapped.

I lowered myself to his groin and lavished adoration along his shaft, letting him know how much I valued what he'd discovered for me. My tongue left his erection to run along those Latin words inked on his groin, these italic letters forming a constant tease, reminding me of the risk of our intimacy.

"Zara." His breathing became ragged and his hands fisted my hair as he held me to him. "This is not a discussion."

I broke away. "I know."

"No going rogue on me, Leighton. Okay?" He gave an uneasy smile.

I scraped my teeth over my bottom lip as I watched him, intrigued with the restlessness in his eyes.

He reached down and grabbed my shoulders and pulled me up to look at him. "I need to hear you say it."

"Say what? That I'd betray all I hold dear? Everything I've worked for?"

"That you're on my side."

My hesitancy caused his pupils to dilate to black and his nostrils to flare with rage, and he flipped me over and pulled my arse upward. There was a jolt of pleasure when his mouth took me from behind, his tongue darting into me, forcing me to let out a long groan and I rocked against his chin shamelessly. My hand clenched the bedsheet when he slid two fingers inside me and he began leisurely gliding them in and out to match the movement of his tongue as though trying to draw back all power.

He turned me over and interlocked his fingers with mine and brought my hands above my head to pin them to the mattress and then captured my mouth with his, bruising my lips with a harshness that brushed close to obsession. As he rode me, the violent power of his hips sent me hurtling toward the edge.

"I'm going to come," I yelled.

"Not yet. Prove your loyalty, Leighton. Then I'll let you come." He drove on with powerful thrusts, his cock as firm as steel and sending a blinding bliss right into the center of my core.

"Please." I tried to inhale.

He'd snatched another breath from me when his lips crashed onto mine. "You feel so tight, Zara. You're so fucking tight and I can feel how close you are, but I will not relent on this. Give me what I'm asking."

I'd already tumbled into the abyss, falling fast and too far into the endlessness and we came together, writhing and grinding as we drove on with our climax, and then he stilled above me, shooting his heat inside me as he glared down at me, both of us fiercely locked together as one, our panting the only noise and our bodies damp and desirously wet with perspiration.

He rolled off me and lay on his back staring at the ceiling.

I couldn't bear being so far away from him, not after we'd fucked so hard, and I rolled over to rest my cheek on his chest and listened to his heartbeat, catching my breath as those raging thoughts came back to settle on my forsaken paintings.

Tobias and I were no closer to finding a resolution between each other and yet we continued to be impossibly drawn, and as he remained laying there, awake and yet quiet, I knew he was thinking that too.

We were the modern equivalent of those timeless stories portrayed over centuries through art—the kind that warned true love never found its way in the dark.

16

While we waited for Tobias's friend to answer his front door, I leaned back in Wilder's arms and felt the reassurance of his firm hug. The tension from earlier was only now lifting after our passionate lovemaking in his sparsely decorated penthouse.

I'd not relented in wanting to stop Tobias. Even after he'd insisted I give him something, I'd tried to come up with a peace offering, something that would placate him and yet not implicate me. The question screaming in my brain was what.

One thing I wouldn't share was my secret plan to expose the Burells. I vowed to spend the rest of my life finding my way back to my paintings.

"This will be fun, I promise," said Tobias, perhaps picking up on my anticipation of leaving his place after such a turbulent afternoon.

The door opened and we were greeted by a handsome middle-aged man with a big smile; Waya had the refined features of a Native American Indian heritage.

"Hey, guys." He gestured for us to come in.

His place had the same floor plan as Tobias's penthouse—

only this was beautifully furnished. The meticulously staged interior reflected great taste. The open floor plan was modern with an Art Deco feel, with its sophisticated metallic accents and homey furniture. The ceiling was gorgeous with an inlaid geometric pattern that provided a sense of space.

Above a fireplace hung a painting of a pretty Native American woman whose likeness to Waya gave away their kinship.

"Wilder?" Waya brought him into a hug.

"How are you, buddy," said Tobias, slapping his back with affection.

Waya shut the door. "Where have you been?"

"London." Tobias glanced over to me. "Brought back a souvenir."

Waya reached out and shook my hand. "We have an escape hatch if you need it."

I laughed and followed them farther into the living room.

"Zara Leighton," Tobias introduced me. "Waya Hunter."

"It's lovely to meet you, Waya." I shook his hand. "I've heard wonderful things about you."

"Can I get you guys a drink?" he offered.

"She's beautiful." I pointed to the portrait of the woman.

"My mom." Waya gave the kind of look that hinted at sadness.

I returned a kind smile to reassure him he needn't say any more, sensing she may have died.

"How's the old man?" asked Tobias.

Waya rolled his eyes. "He'll be happy to see you, though. He's in his room."

"May I?" Tobias gestured toward a door that led off to the west of the suite.

"Sure." Waya paused for a moment. "How is um…"

"Good," said Tobias quickly.

I pretended not to have noticed that exchange.

"Why don't you show Zara your Caravaggio."

"Oh, I'd love that," I said.

"It's my dad's." Waya widened his eyes with humor. "The frame's nice."

Tobias gave me a glance to say this was where I came in with my art acumen and I wondered if this was why he'd brought me there. He headed off through a door and we walked in the opposite direction. Waya gestured for me to follow him down a hallway.

"The painting's a little grim," he said.

"Grim is interesting."

Unfortunately, Caravaggio had been heavily forged even before his death. Though right now I didn't want to share that with Waya.

We stepped into an office—

My eyes fixed on a miracle that felt out of place. On the far wall was a 1601 oil on canvas that could very well have been painted by Michelangelo Merisi da Caravaggio. Stepping forward, my eyes wandered over the scene of St. Thomas, who was leaning forward and inserting a fingertip into Christ's wound, and the saint's expression reflected doubt that he was seeing his dear friend Jesus raised from the dead. They were drenched in a golden hue with exquisite shadows dancing over their faces, a flash of pain in Thomas's eyes in contrast to Christ who emanated an ethereal calmness, and despite its agonizing theme there was serenity there too.

"*The Incredulity of Saint Thomas.*" Waya's voice broke the silence, describing the torment of the apostle doubting the other disciples, what they'd told him was true, and in doing so refusing to believe the Messiah's promise of life eternal until he saw the wounds of Christ himself.

"It's incredible." I marveled at the detail.

"We kept it in the attic at our other place," he said. "We downsized when we moved here and Dad insisted we keep it."

"I can see why he likes it."

"He insists it's real." Waya shrugged. "His sister bought it at a garage sale. When she moved into an assisted living facility she gave it to Dad." He cringed. "I can't make my mind up if I like it or not."

"To me it represents hope. Forgiveness. Grace."

"You like art?"

"Yes, very much."

"That's how you met Tobias?"

"At a gallery in London."

"Are you a curator?"

"Forensic art specialist."

"Wow. Is that your natural hair color?"

"Yes."

"It's pretty."

"Thank you." I ran my fingers through it self-consciously.

Waya had a sincerity about him and it made me smile. I could see why Tobias found him so authentic.

"Tobias is a lucky man," he said.

"We're happy."

Even if our relationship was startlingly new and fraught with peril.

"Dad didn't approve of Wilder's last girlfriend," he said.

A wave of doubt nestled into my chest.

"Sorry, I shouldn't have mentioned her."

"Logan?"

"You know her?"

"Yes, she's very beautiful."

"Dangerously so. Can lure a man in with just a look. My dad called her a scorpion." He frowned. "You're her opposite."

"Are you married?"

He stepped back and leaned against the desk. "Divorced."

"Sorry to hear that."

"My wife had an affair and then left me. Took the kids. Wiped me out financially and started a new life in Philly." He chuckled. "I won in the end. Get to live with my dad."

I smiled at his courage. "What's he like?"

"He only likes one thing, or should I say person. And that's Wilder."

"Really?"

"Yes, says he's the son he never had," he said it with an edge of sarcasm.

"Maybe I could meet him?"

He ran his hand along the edge of the desk. "He's resting. If I didn't tell him Tobias was here I'd be in trouble."

My gaze returned to the painting. "Can I take a closer look?"

"Sure."

I reached into my handbag and rummaged around for my magnifier and raised it close to the canvas, peering through.

"You do like art, don't you?" he said, amused.

"It's an easy obsession."

Just like Tobias.

Oh, my God, I was getting my paintings back. It felt like it only just hit me.

"It is real?" He'd read my reaction.

I didn't want to tell him I'd spaced out after being so inspired by this beautiful piece. "Caravaggio wasn't overly obsessed with color," I said reverently. "He focused on depth by use of light and shadows."

"That explains the darkness."

"The subject matter calls for it."

The profoundness of what he'd created sang with each intuitive sweep, his work protected by that delicate layer of varnish. Fine authentic cracks proved its age. "Caravaggio's brushwork is invisible to the naked eye. That's what I'm looking for."

"Impressive."

"He was considered the father of modern painting."

"I can see why."

"He was gay," I said. "Did you know that?"

"No." He gazed affectionately at the canvas. "He was so talented."

"He was a rebel in every sense of the word. Loved brawling and drinking and gambling."

"You know your stuff." He flinched. "It's not real, is it?"

"It's incredible. Truly, but I'm afraid it wasn't painted by Caravaggio."

"I thought it was too good to be true. Dad will be so disappointed."

"Well, it's not all bad news. This was painted by one of his students. Someone who knew Caravaggio well enough to observe the artist's technique. See this—" I pointed to the right-hand corner. "See these strokes here? Caravaggio's brushstrokes are indefinable. Still, this artist certainly deserves praise."

Waya took the magnifier from me and peered through at the canvas. "I'm going to pretend I know what I'm looking at."

"See how he was taught to use light and shadow on the faces to emphasize who is the most important person in the portrait. The use of extensive space. Look how well he plays with light."

"It's very impressive. But worthless, right?"

"Not to your dad."

"I mean, my aunt found it at a sale." He folded his arms

across his chest and looked at it. "That should have told you everything."

"Not necessarily. *Meleager and Atalanta* by Jacob Jordaens, a seventeeth-century Flemish painter, turned up in a storeroom in Wales. It's worth millions. And there was a multimillion-dollar Old Master discovered behind a sofa in Buffalo painted by Michelangelo himself."

And should Waya poke around the London art scene he'd discover another Michelangelo had turned up at the National Gallery in London; *mine*. After Tobias had persuaded me to pull it out of my bedroom safe and give it a proper home, after discovering my quirkiness to protect a painting and proving eccentricity ran through my blood. We'd soon set the art world alight with excitement on this groundbreaking discovery. Other than the senior National Gallery staff, only one other person knew of my Michelangelo and that was Gabe, who I'd sworn to secrecy after I'd shared my secret over lunch in his garden.

Tobias strolled in and he brightened the room with his presence and his gaze read our faces. "What's the verdict?"

Waya's eyes lit up with amusement. "You just like being right?"

"It's unusual to find an unaccounted for Caravaggio," teased Tobias.

"Not necessarily," said Waya. "*Meleager and Atalanta* by Jacob somebody or other, a seventeenth-century Flemish painter turned up in a storeroom in Wales. Did you know that?" He winked at me.

I smiled, and my gaze returned to roam over the canvas and drink in its beauty.

Tobias slapped Waya's back with affection. "I did offer to have it evaluated at The Wilder—"

"You've done enough," said Waya.

"What's Tobias done now?" I asked.

"It was nothing." Tobias waved it off. "Do you have any coffee? I have nothing in my place. Other than a bed." He flashed me a smile.

"And a stupid pool," I said.

"She refuses to get in it," Tobias added.

"Sensible girl." Waya gave a nod and his gaze fell on him. "I love this man. Seriously, Zara, he's a godsend. When the economy crashed I lost everything. Wife left soon afterward. Even though we could no longer afford to live here, Wilder let us stay rent free for over a year until things picked up again. We own a brewery, you see. It's flourishing again thanks to him. He kept our business afloat."

The realization this entire place was owned by Tobias made my head swim.

Tobias shrugged. "Only helped you out so I'd get free beer."

"You don't drink beer, Wilder," Waya snapped back. "You're a wine man."

"It was nothing."

"It was everything." Waya faced me. "You've got yourself a keeper."

"He's pretty special," I agreed.

"Go on, then," said Tobias, gesturing to the Caravaggio. "Go tell your dad."

He grinned. "You tell him. He likes you."

A ring tone broke the silence and I reached into my handbag and pulled out my phone to silence it. The call was from Huntly Pierre.

My gaze rose to look at Tobias. "I have to get this."

He gave a nod and watched me leave.

Walking fast, I headed back through the living room and

opened the front door and continued a little way down while pressing the phone to my ear. "Hello?"

"Zara?" Abby Reynolds's voice came through clear.

"Hey, Abby," I said. "How are you?"

"More important, how are you?"

"Fine. What time is it there?"

"Late. I can't sleep. Tell me you're not in Arizona?"

"Why would I be in Arizona?"

There was a long pause. "I'm sorry, Zara, I've done everything to watch your back. Adley knows."

"That I'm in LA?"

"Yeah. Sorry. I know what getting to the truth means to you for your *St. Joan*."

"I'm sorry I put you in this position, Abby. You've been so supportive. I just need a bit more time."

"Look, Adley was briefed by an investigator out in LA. The guy works for the west coast Christie's office. Hold on. I'll put you on a secure line—" I heard the phone muffle for a moment. "You still there?"

"Yes."

A click.

"I think that's good," she continued. "Okay, here's the deal, you're right about *St. Joan* being in Cali. Whoever is your contact has good intel."

"That's great." I hoped that sounded convincing. "And the bad news?"

"Adley knows you're spending time with his favorite client."

A jolt of adrenaline made me stand upright. "How?"

"We all respect your privacy back here. It wasn't us. Liam Stark saw you with Wilder in Beverly Hills."

"Who's Liam Stark?"

"He works for Christie's LA office. He's part of the team

trying to get their *St. Joan* back. Damage control and all that. Your bio was in his file because the provenance is in your favor but it's complicated."

And yet Tobias had warned me to keep my connection to Ouless's painting on the down low.

"Where did Liam see me?"

"Some gossip news site snapped you coming out of Tiffany's with America's favorite bachelor."

That had been just this morning.

"He forwarded us the photos. In one of them Wilder was handing you a gift. Very romantic. Liam wasn't as forgiving, he told Adley 'that's how this playboy likes to make a statement. Shows off his current girlfriend by flaunting her.' You know I hate gossip."

My mouth went dry as I wondered if Tobias had posed us outside the store on purpose. Those extra moments giving the photogs time to catch us midflirt.

"Still there?" she said.

"Yes."

"Sorry about this. You're going to have to grow a thick skin if you want to stay in this business."

"I know."

"Hate being the messenger. It's not like Wilder didn't know the paparazzi wouldn't be watching, right? He's always on their radar. Usually wearing sunglasses and making a quick getaway. Unless he wants to show off his latest conquest."

I'd not seen anyone, so the photo had been taken with a long-angled lens.

Abby's voice rose over the ringing in my ears. "Adley doesn't mind this liaison so much. He's happy you're pleasing a client." She chuckled. "Just don't piss off Wilder. He's our biggest account."

I cringed at her insinuation.

"Did Wilder hire you for a job out there? We know how private he can be. He needs to go through Adley, though. He knows the rules."

"Right," seemed the best answer while I gathered my thoughts.

"You never asked me," she said.

"About?"

"Icon."

A shudder slithered up my spine. "That was my next question."

"It's great news, Zara."

"I'm listening."

"No one must know about this, okay?"

"Yes."

"A year ago, Christie's began a security system where they discreetly place a GPS tracker into the frame of each painting upon processing. They attached one to Ouless's *St. Joan of Arc*. Its activation's been problematic. The GPS signal comes and goes. The painting's in LA."

My breath stuttered out the words, "They know where *St. Joan* is?"

"You bet. The retrieval is in process. We just need confirmation on your provenance and it could be yours again. Isn't this great?"

Fucking hell.

The last time I saw *St. Joan* she was wrapped up in brown paper and a twine bow and sitting on Tobias's kitchen table.

Waya's door opened and Tobias strolled out and closed it behind him. He continued toward me with that dark and dangerous swagger.

"Can I call you later?" I said softly.

She let out a sigh of frustration. "Sure. Do you want me to get Accounting to book your flight back?"

"No, I'll do it."

"Be careful," she said.

"Sure." I turned away from Tobias. "What's in Arizona?" She'd hung up.

Tobias neared me and I backed up against the wall when he came closer. He pressed his chest against mine and placed a hand to the right of my head to rest his palm on the wall, trapping me. His heady cologne emitted the scent of sex and scandal and it made my body ache with need, and my nipples responded to the way he was looking at me with pure domination merged with suspicion.

"That was work," I said breathlessly.

"What did they want?" His lips lingered close to mine.

I raised my chin confidently. "Checking in. They want me back in London."

He let out a frustrated sigh. "Call them back. Tell them you're working for me."

"That's what they believe."

"Well, good."

Him scheming wasn't what I needed to hear right now. "Give me a minute, okay."

"What did they say exactly?"

I glanced uneasily at my Tiffany wristwatch.

"Zara?"

When they found *St. Joan* it would be over for him. Every second ticking away put him in jeopardy. My imagination ran rampant with the thought of investigators breaking into his Malibu home and arresting him.

"It's a big leap," I muttered.

He thrust his body against mine and his cock hit my lower abdomen and he made me shudder with his show of power. "I'm here now. I'll help in any way I can."

I reached up and cupped his beautiful face. "I'm okay. Really."

That dark green gaze narrowed. "I know you can handle them." His jaw clenched with tension as he tried to read more from me.

"Tobias." His name sounded like a plea.

"Yes?"

"Waya's dad wasn't too upset about his painting, was he?"

"He's a great guy. Took it well." He reached out and interlocked his fingers with mine. "Ready?"

"For what?"

"To leave."

I took a few moments to say goodbye to Waya and promised to see him again soon, a promise I wasn't sure I could keep.

Walking beside Tobias, I hoped he didn't detect the tremble in my hand as we headed toward the elevator and that familiar dread inched up my spine. He went in first and I followed and faced the wall so I wouldn't have to watch our descent on the scroll.

The doors closed.

Tobias came near and hugged me tight as we descended, and I turned sharply and pressed my cheek against his chest and sighed when his fingers trailed through my locks to calm me. He'd proven time and time again he was a good man and no gossip column or spy for Christie's was going to shatter this bond we'd created. Waya had again reminded me of Tobias's extraordinary generosity.

And that was why I'd flown thousands of miles to persuade Wilder to give up this reckless life. Even now I tried to resist this magnetic pull toward him but my body and soul yearned for him.

The doors slid open to a parking structure.

I grabbed his arm. "Wait."

"Come on." He winked. "I know how much you love elevators."

"Don't…"

He stepped back in and pushed the button to close the door. "Zara?" He pulled me back into a hug. "Hey, it's okay. I can see they rattled you. Do you want to talk about it?"

"I just need a second."

"Whatever you need. Are you hungry? Let's go home and I'll cook for us."

I stared up at him and my voice trembled as I spilled the news, "There's a GPS tracker on *St. Joan*'s frame."

He pushed me against the wall and pressed his lips to mine, ravaging my mouth, claiming my lips passionately, his tongue swirling leisurely, his control so overwhelming it made me swoon.

I nipped his bottom lip to get his attention. "I'm serious."

He caressed my lower lip with his thumb and he let out a groan of need as though wanting to take me again, here, now.

"They're coming for it," I said. "They know where it is."

"Let's hope so." He punched a button and the doors reopened.

"You're not scared?"

"Zara." He squeezed my hand and pulled me out into the parking structure. "I'm always cautious. But never scared."

17

The remnants of his kiss made my lips throb and the ghost of his embrace still rippled through me. We hurried through the subterranean parking lot and he left me speechless when he guided me toward a sleek black Lamborghini.

Tobias held the passenger door open for me, and I slid into the sports car and sank into the luxury. After fixing my seat belt I breathed in the scent of leather and marveled at the glint of high-tech chrome. He climbed in beside me and tapped a button to start the engine and it purred with finesse.

How many freakin' cars does this guy have?

Wilder navigated the Lamborghini out of the building and we made our way onto Ninth Street.

With a crook of my neck I peered up toward his penthouse at that structure jutting out and was reassured to see opaque glass, proving pedestrians couldn't ogle a naked Tobias swimming laps. The memory of his musculature cutting through the water made my insides quiver, those hidden tattoos the only hint of his wayward nature. A bad boy versus superhero, I mused darkly.

Even now Tobias's wealth, including that high-rise and

this car, made my head swim. He moved in a world that was precariously decadent and it seemed nothing was out of his reach if he wanted it.

"You okay?" he asked.

"I hated lying to them."

"Did you?"

"I'm pretending I don't know you're Icon." I turned in my seat and glared at him.

"I've got this. Relax."

Was he insane? "Is *St. Joan* still at your place?"

He didn't even look worried.

"Tobias?"

"Your painting is safe." He glanced over to me. "Whenever you want *St. Joan* back, she's yours."

"You've removed the GPS tracker from her frame already? Or transferred it onto something else?"

He gave a thin smile but kept his eyes on the road, reminding me he was always one step ahead, and yet I was still surprised by his cleverness.

"Tell me about the conversation with your team." He pressed the pedal and sped through an amber light.

"Abby's one of the investigators. Could you slow down?"

He drove faster. "She's a friend?"

"I like her. She's been kind to me."

"Abby Reynolds?"

Of course, as a client of Huntly Pierre he would know of her.

Squeezing my eyes shut for a beat I said, "She's just doing her job."

"She upset you. What did she say?"

I was such an open book to him. "Are you familiar with the name Liam Stark?"

"Is he the man following us in the BMW?"

"What?"

"Don't turn around."

I reached up for the sun visor and pulled it down trying to see the car tailing us. There was a silver BMW close behind and it was weaving to keep up.

"Zara?"

"How would I know?" I glanced up again. "Are you sure?"

"Yes."

"I have nothing to do with this."

He slowed and then stopped at a red light. "I want to believe you."

"All I know is what Abby just told me. Liam works for Christie's LA office and he's been tracking *St. Joan* for the London team." I shot Tobias a look. "Tell me it's not in the back of this car?"

"If it was a federal vehicle there'd be more than one. They rotate as they follow. Usually at least three. Keeps the cars covert. With only one car it's either the press or a private security firm. What do you know about him?"

"Liam? He sent Adley a photo of us outside Tiffany's." My jaw tightened as I waited for him to react.

He focused back on the road and opened up the Lamborghini again.

I shuffled uncomfortably. "They know you and I are seeing each other."

He slid the car into fifth. "Hold on."

We took a corner fast and fishtailed as we went and I reached up and grabbed the handrail.

We dodged a car coming the other way and the driver hit his horn in protest at how close we'd passed him.

Tobias didn't seem to care as he continued to overtake the slower vehicles, weaving ahead through traffic. "But that's not what upset you?" he said.

I gave a frustrated huff. And panicked when he sped through a crossing.

"Zara? Speak to me."

"It was nothing."

"Did they warn you off me?"

"They weren't exactly tactful."

With Liam calling him a playboy and making me out to be his latest conquest, I'd been left with a bitterness in my mouth and it tasted like doubt.

"Remember The Broad?" He reached out and gave my hand a squeeze and then returned it to the wheel. "I had one of the most beautiful women in my car, you, and your dress was soaking wet and clinging to you. I'm not gonna lie, it was fucking transparent. You could see your nipples from space. Not that I was complaining. That's why I gave you my jacket to cover you and why I almost broke my neck getting that photo deleted from that photog's camera. I've always protected you. You're not like the others."

The others, the beautiful women I'd seen draped on his arm as they'd left a party and gotten caught by a photographer and immortalized for someone like me to find when I snooped around on him online.

"Did you set up the shot outside Tiffany's?" I said.

"Is that what they're suggesting?"

"Yes."

"Hell no. Those fuckers are everywhere with their cameras."

"Liam told Adley you're a playboy. What must they think of me?"

"I don't even know this Liam," he snapped. "And he only knows about me from what he's read."

I slammed my hand onto the window. "Tobias, you'll get pulled over by the police."

"I'm hoping he will." He raised his voice. "Jade, call Marshall."

The screen lit up and a series of dots oscillated indicating his AI was doing just this—

"Sir?" came Marshall's voice out of the speaker.

"I have a tail," Tobias sounded eerily composed.

"I'm on it, sir," replied Marshall. "Make and model?"

"Silver BMW." Tobias glanced in the rearview. "Coupe. Six series. Zara's with me. We're on Fifteenth. How does Exposition Park sound?"

"Hermès will be waiting. Anything else?"

"Landing site...make it Brentwood. Get permission for Anderson's."

"Got it."

Tobias hung up.

I hoped he wasn't talking about my Gabe Anderson. "Does this happen to you a lot?" I said.

"Now and again. If I'm releasing a new tech device, that can get the spies excited. They think I'll give away a clue from where I go. It could be one of your friends."

"From Huntly Pierre?"

"Yes."

"Abby asked me to come back to London. She sounded calm. I didn't get that from her."

"You're their responsibility."

"I can look after myself."

"I'm afraid it's a need-to-know basis, Zara. They're keeping something from you, I suspect."

"Why?"

"They have a lead. Evidently."

"On Icon?"

"The GPS tracker got them excited. They know it's Icon who stole *St. Joan* from Christie's. You're connected to it.

They're ramping up the investigation out here. And as your instincts brought you to LA, they're intrigued with what you've discovered so far. What have you told them?"

"Nothing. Where did you put the tracker?"

"I got creative."

"Tell me."

"That's the adrenaline talking."

I snapped him an annoyed glare. "Tobias."

"This has all been an elaborate plan just to hear you tell me you love me." He flashed me a megawatt smile.

"Sometimes you are so bloody annoying!"

"You're welcome." He laughed and pressed the gas. "Hold on. I'm gonna lose him."

We drove the rest of the way in silence.

Hermès turned out to be a helicopter. With the Lamborghini parked in Exposition Park and with Wilder's usual easy arrogance, we took off smoothly and headed into the evening sky of the city.

There came no surprise that Tobias didn't see a problem landing his chopper in Gabe's garden. Once the propellers stopped and he no longer found my annoyed glare boring into him funny, he climbed out and came around to my side.

As I trudged away from the helicopter I realized our landing had sprayed dead leaves all over Gabe's beautifully tended garden and quite a few had tumbled into the pool.

"Tobias," I said. "Who was following us?"

"I'm on it."

"Tell me when you find out."

"Sure." He cupped my cheeks and kissed me, and the way he tipped me slightly to hold me off balance felt so dangerously erotic, he almost made me forget the risk of being with him, almost. Something told me Tobias was planning on leaving me here. I yanked my hand from his in protest.

"This is the best decision," he said. "We'll give them nothing to photograph until this is over."

"They already have a photo of us."

"Christie's team is closing in. I don't want you caught in the cross fire."

"It's time to bring this madness to a stop, Tobias." My chest heaved with emotion and I felt my panic rising.

"Look, we're going to spin this to look like us being seen outside Tiffany's was misconstrued. It was just me thanking you for the great work you've done as an art specialist." He gave a shrug. "I gave you a watch. It's a perfectly safe gift. We'll handle this the way we always do."

His words of denial felt like a noose around my throat ready to tighten.

"Zara, please don't look at me like that."

"You're not listening to anything I say. They're going to catch you. Give this up. At the very least compromise and stop now."

"Too much is at stake."

"Whoever is manipulating you to do this—"

"It doesn't work like that."

"Then help me understand. Because it makes no sense. If anything, you should curtail your plan because you could be under surveillance."

"I'm going to put right a wrong that was so despicable the act of reversal itself will change history. I've let you into my world. I want you to be part of it. You knew this when you fell for me."

"Clearly I'm out of my mind."

"I made a promise, Zara, an oath to someone. It's so much greater than you or me or—"

"I see all the good you do. But how the hell are you going to help anyone from behind bars?"

"Well, if that happens my team can manage my charities."

"Listen to yourself."

Tobias's fury relented. "I'm hosting a charitable event tomorrow at The Wilder. You're invited. As is Gabe and his partner. You will be courteous to me. Professional. The press will observe how we interact. There'll be no affection between us. And that is what they'll report. I'll have a dress delivered to the Sofitel."

I watched him head back to the helicopter. "I'm not going."

He glanced back. "Yes, you are."

"You can't order me to do anything. I'm not an employee."

He spun round and came back toward me. "You're on my payroll. Huntly Pierre will be sent a commission check. It will be waiting for you upon your return. There, problem solved. Your motive for being out here is answered. You're welcome. We're spinning this. This is what I need from you to work with me. I do not tolerate…" He glared the rest.

"I didn't tell them I was here working for you."

"I did."

"You could have contradicted me."

"Did I?"

"I was vague."

"No change there, then."

"You're a bossy bastard, Wilder." This illusion of control was fast fading. "I'm going back to my hotel."

"At least say hello to your friend first."

"I'm putting Gabe in danger."

"Don't be ridiculous."

I turned sharply to head toward the side of the garden.

He swept me up in his arms and carried me past the swimming pool and all the way to Gabe's patio door. I wanted to hate Tobias for the way he lifted me so dominantly and yet protectively, his strong arms carrying me all the way. All I could do was surrender, clinging to him with a terrible dread I was about to lose him and by his own hand, no less.

He set me down and my heels clicked on the porch deck.

"Go have some tea," he said calmly. "I'll call you."

"I'm not going to just stand back and let you ruin your life."

"What's your plan, then, Zara?"

"To make you see sense. To do what I can to put this right."

"I'm handling it."

"Go to the police with the man's name. The person who stole my paintings."

"With what? Evidence I'm not meant to have? Let there be no doubt that justice will be served. And that's what you want too. What you deserve. For your dad's name to be cleared. Your legacy restored. Someone needs to engage their brain first. Notice I'm looking at you."

"I'm willing to let those paintings go if saving them puts you in danger." I sucked in a sob at my own revelation. "Please, Tobias."

"Damn you for making me fall for you." He shook his head. "It's so fucking inconvenient."

"Then leave and never come back."

"You don't mean that."

"You underestimate what I'm capable of." I stood my ground. "It's the Burells who stole my paintings. I just know it is."

He looked furious. "Leave them to me."

"Maybe I'll fly back to London tonight. Go via France to pay them a visit." I glared back at him. "How different is that from what you're doing?"

"Remember that dark secret of a Titian being stolen and suppressed over decades? A young girl climbing out of her bedroom window along a tree branch in the dead of night to escape a house fire set by a member of the Burells after they swiped her family's Titian. A child having to leave her family behind to die. Imagine the kind of guilt she's endured. Not to mention being badly burned."

I shook my head as a wave of terror consumed me, a dread for all Sarah Louise had endured and guilt for all I didn't know.

"Zara, you too ran from your home trying to rescue your paintings. You were ten. What if you hadn't survived? I wouldn't have you now."

My shoulders slumped with this loss of power as time unfolded in slow motion with no ability for me to rein it in. "Don't use my childhood against me."

"I'm trying to make you see sense."

"I hate you right now."

"Really, because if that means you'll be kept safe, then so be it."

"We have nothing in common."

"What are you talking about? We have our love of art?" He let out a frustrated sigh. "It's my fault for preventing you from getting any sleep since you've been here."

"You're impossible."

"I'm impossible?" He pressed a finger to his chest. "You're impossible."

"Why?"

"You want to blow up my life."

"All I've tried to do is to get through to you. Reach out and help you."

He waved his hands in frustration. "You're infuriating."

"How?"

"Okay, time to fess up."

I leaned against the glass door and crossed my arms over my chest as I breathed in an unsteady breath.

"I like cats," he said. "They're cute in their own way if you can get over their death stare and all those fur balls they just love coughing up and their constant aloofness, but dogs are more my thing." He threw his hands up. "I'm a dog person. There."

He was making fun of all the cat GIFs I'd sent him. And for some stupid reason that made me giggle and I couldn't suppress my laughter.

Tobias came nearer. "I adore you. I want to give you everything you've ever desired."

"I just need to know you're safe, Tobias. What if I lose you?"

"You won't." He pressed me against the door and stole another kiss, ironically reminding me of what I might lose: his passion, his kindness and his incomparable presence.

Him.

Melting into Tobias's arms I returned a fierce kiss, trying to change his mind with affectionate sweeps of my tongue to tangle with his. Tobias even took over this embrace, his mouth forcing mine wider, his tongue fucking my mouth to own me.

I nudged him away. "You can't kiss me like this and expect me to agree with you."

His lips trailed over my neck. "Two days. That's all I ask. Then it's you and me back in London and fucking endlessly until you finally admit I'm yours."

Had he just tipped me off with his timeline? "You're incorrigible," I said.

"Maybe I am. Maybe I'm the only one who cares enough to do the right thing. No matter how reckless. But I am in charge." He stepped back and gave a commanding nod. "See you tonight." He headed back toward the helicopter with a determined stride and the way he climbed into it and calmly commandeered the controls made me swoon.

Hugging myself, I couldn't move until he'd lifted off and was out of sight. My hands were still trembling as I tried the handle to Gabe's back door. It was open.

Heading in, I hoped Gabe was going to be okay with my spontaneous visit and I wished I'd gotten the chance to call him first. When I reached the kitchen door I froze—

A tall, slim and starkly beautiful man wearing a silk robe, a fop of brown hair falling over his face, was standing before the fridge with the door open. He reached in and removed a jar of pickles. That eye shield resting on his forehead hinted he'd taken a recent nap or was about to.

He saw me. "Fuck!" He dropped the jar—

It crashed onto the tile and shards of glass went flying amidst rolling green pickles.

I gasped. "I'm so sorry."

"Zara?"

"Ned?"

Relief flashed over his face. "You just scared the shit out of me."

"I'm so sorry. Is Gabe here?"

"He's on his way home from dropping off dry-cleaning. Got caught in traffic."

"Were you sleeping?"

"I was just taking a nap only some rich asshole buzzed my roof with his 'I have a small penis' helicopter."

"That was me. My boyfriend." I cringed. "And he's perfect. His penis size, I mean. Not that you care." Then I remembered. "Maybe you do?"

Oh, Jesus, what just happened to my mouth?

"You're hilarious. Gabe's totally smitten with you. I can see why. You're crazy but so lovable."

"I'm not crazy."

"You Brits kind of are." He closed the fridge. "You kept a Michelangelo in your London flat?"

Gabe had already broken his promise and shared my secret and it made my cheeks burn. "It's now at the National Gallery," I replied in my defense.

"A Michelangelo!" Ned waved his hands in the air. "Got any more priceless pieces hidden away?"

"You mean other than that Rembrandt in my knicker drawer?"

He broke into laughter.

My thoughts flashed over to my father's collection that was out there somewhere and the hairs prickled on my forearms. If retrieved, this discovery would be one of the most significant in the art world. One day those paintings might even hang in The Wilder. If I ever decided to talk with Tobias again.

"You're a woman of mystery." Ned's gaze drifted to the smashed glass. "Strawberries it is, then."

"I'll help you." I rushed forward.

"Mind your feet."

"I'm so embarrassed."

"Don't be. I'm only glad I wasn't naked."

I gave a nervous laugh.

Within minutes we had the small disaster taken care of and I was praising Ned for his tea-making skills. We carried our mugs of Tetley and a bowl of strawberries each into the living room and made ourselves comfy on the couch.

Ned reminded me of someone who'd stepped out of the nineteenth century, his high cheekbones and slender nose reminiscent of an elegant Oscar Wilde character. He looked a few years younger than Gabe and I could understand why they wanted to be together. They were a cute couple.

I accused him playfully, "So you're the man who lured my favorite teacher away from London?"

"My job isn't transferrable to the UK. I need to be in easy reach of Silicon Valley for work. I am guilty as charged for stealing my man back."

"Gabe seems very happy at UCLA. I'm sure his students love him. I know I do."

"I sat in on one of his lectures once. I was smitten all over again. He tells me you're investigating a theft? Is it related to Icon?" He read my reaction. "I saw it on CNN. Some thief is masterfully evading authorities."

I shoved a small strawberry into my mouth.

"Have you got a lead?" he asked.

"Not sure," I replied while chewing; I'd never been good at lying and from Ned's expression I was still crappy at spinning the truth.

Spinning the truth…that's what Tobias wanted to do with our relationship and just the thought of it sent a pang of discomfort into my gut.

"Can't talk about the case?" said Ned. "I get it."

"It's a little confusing."

"In what way?"

"Just want to do the right thing."

"What's stopping you?"

"I'm taking one day at a time right now."

"That's good." He frowned. "Gabe told me Tobias Wilder swept you off your feet at The Broad?"

"Tobias?"

"Do you believe he might be cheating on you?"

The silence felt too heavy to bear. "Why do you say that?" I managed.

"You met with Bridget?"

I suppressed my cringe, remembering it had been Ned

who had helped arrange my meeting with his friend Bridget
Madsen, after I'd asked Gabe for a referral to someone with
techie skills. She'd been the genius who'd enabled my phone
to track Tobias's cute butt around town. Only she'd been up
against an impossible opponent and it shouldn't have surprised
me Wilder discovered my Toby blip.

I had a sudden desire to pull out my phone and see where
the hell Tobias was, though he'd probably disabled the tracker
by now.

"Bridget was lovely," I said. "Really helpful."

Ned looked like he knew more than he was letting on and
despite Bridget's reassurance she'd not discuss my highly illegal request to track a public figure, something told me
Ned knew I was stalking the man who'd just buzzed his
roof. Nothing unhealthy about me tracking his every move,
I painfully mused.

How embarrassing.

"Hey there," said Ned as he pushed himself to his feet.

I turned to see Gabe in the doorway and he was blinking his surprise.

He gave Ned a big hug. "How are you doing? How was
Silicon Valley?"

"Great. We have a visitor." Ned looked my way. "She
landed via a chopper."

"I saw that." Gabe came toward me. "I got an alert from
air traffic control on my cell. I thought it was a joke."

I set my mug on the table and leaped to my feet and met
him halfway, falling into his hug.

"You've blown me away, Zara," he said brightly.

I flashed a nervous glance over at Ned. "Um…really?"

Gabe looked ecstatic. "This is why you're here?" He waved
a cream envelope in the air. "I got it."

"Great," I said. "What did you get?"

"Our invite. To The Wilder tomorrow—" He turned to face Ned, his voice shrill with excitement. "They're showcasing the Qin Terra-Cotta Army. We're on the list, Ned. We've been invited to preview the collection before anyone else."

My jaw dropped that Tobias had pulled off one of the most remarkable exhibitions in the world and all under the veil of secrecy. Even from me.

Now I had to make the quick decision whether to let Ned and Gabe know I was out of the loop on one of America's greatest exhibitions to ever grace its shores.

Burying my pride, my toes curled in anticipation of seeing those dramatic sculptured warriors carved in pottery. Dating back over two thousand years, the figurines were easily one of the most thrilling displays of historical craftsmanship. Though I doubted there'd be the full display of eight thousand soldiers along with their chariots and cavalry horses. Even a few statues from the Qin Shi Huang armies would be spectacular. I mean, this was the kind of event that attracted society's elite. A chance in a lifetime. Maybe he'd wanted to surprise me?

Tobias knew I couldn't resist seeing these rare relics, hailed as the eighth wonder of the world. I'd spent an afternoon fawning over the photos during a lecture taught by Gabe, no less, at The Courtauld back in January when he'd taught how these remarkable artifices had been discovered by accident by peasants digging around in 1974. Some remained in the ground even now.

"I can't believe your man pulled this off," said Gabe. "Did you tell him Eastern history is my specialty?"

"It might have come up." Like the halo of a headache creeping in, I remembered that day Tobias had tracked me to UCLA, all the way to Gabe's office when he'd researched his professorial specialty so Marshall could find him.

All of it is an elaborate plan to make you fall in love with me.
Tobias had wooed me with these words within the hour.

This, this was the mark of a genius who was unrelenting, brilliant, scheming and terrifyingly good. The design of a master thief.

"You don't look too excited?" said Ned, shaking me from my dark daydreaming.

"I am." I forced a pleasant smile. "Tobias can be overwhelming sometimes."

Gabe beamed at Ned. "I can't wait for you to meet him."

Ned's eyes narrowed and his focus returned to me. "Men always pull away when they're falling in love."

"You're not having problems again, are you?" Gabe sounded concerned.

I looked around for a tissue for my nose. "He thinks it's best we pretend we're not that close. To shake off the press."

Ned rested his fists on his hips defensively. "What do you mean?"

"They took a photo of us outside Tiffany's."

"We saw it on TV," said Gabe. "It looked fine. Invasive and totally decimating your privacy but you weren't doing anything embarrassing with Wilder. Why doesn't he want the world to know you're a couple?"

Ned slapped his back. "Let's have the talk."

"What have I done now?" snapped Gabe.

"Not with you," said Ned. "With her. The one about fuckboys."

"He's not like that," I said in Tobias's defense, though cringing with the reality of who I was up against.

What was I thinking to even attempt to pit myself against Icon?

18

Gabe, Ned and I had just entered The Wilder Museum a few minutes ago and we were still gawking in awe at the welcoming exhibit—four life-size terra-cotta horses that were pulling a stone carriage. I'd never seen such a remarkable introduction to a display; it was mesmerizing. A palpable electricity crackled amongst the other visitors who trickled in behind us.

We'd reverently dressed up per the invite with Gabe and Ned looking gorgeous in their black tuxedos and me wearing the dress that had been delivered to the Sofitel, just as Tobias had instructed—a beautiful Alice and Olivia black gown that hugged my curves, and the four-inch heels that had been delivered with it were devastatingly gorgeous and recklessly strappy.

"I want to touch the horse," whispered Gabe.

"Go on, then," I teased.

"Yeah right, get me thrown out," said Gabe, amused at my mischief. "This morning it was like any other Saturday and now I'm here looking at this veritable piece of history carved by the finest artisans. How the hell did Wilder pull this off?"

Ned nudged Gabe's side. "I know you're itching to tell us."

"We're your captive audience," I encouraged.

Gabe drew in a deep breath. "Qin Shi Huang was only thirteen when he took the throne in 246 BC. He's famed for standardizing coins, weights and measures."

"Didn't he build the Great Wall?" I asked.

"Began construction on it," said Gabe.

"See, I was listening in your lecture."

"Yes, you were." Gabe continued to hold us captivated with his impressive knowledge that displayed his passion for the Far East.

We learned from him the emperor's name had been changed from Ying Zheng to Qin Shi Huang, and that shortly after taking the throne Qin ordered the construction of the mausoleum and had hired more than seven-hundred-thousand laborers to create his stone army. It was never finished.

"I could stand here all day and just listen to you," I said dreamily. "You were born to teach."

He shook his head as he marveled at the statue. "I'd love you to teach a class to my students before you fly back to London on Monday."

"What could I teach?" I said.

"Pick an artist you admire."

Ned wrapped his arm around me. "You could always show off that trick you do with art. Sally won't stop talking about it. She's thrilled to own a Monet and Renoir."

"I'm so happy to hear that."

"Guess what," said Gabe. "She wants to loan it to The Wilder for a few months."

"Oh, that's wonderful." My gaze fixed on the stone statue. "Tobias would love that."

"Why don't you tell him?" Gabe's nudge caused me to turn around.

My stomach flipped when I saw Tobias strolling through

the foyer and he looked gorgeous in his black tuxedo, his hair tamer than usual and his expression friendly as he stopped to chat with guests. His gaze caught mine and he held it for a few seconds and it made my stomach flip.

He looked away.

I turned around and feigned that hadn't hurt me and focused on the stone horse, admiring the detail of its sculpted hooves and the way the saddle was finely carved along its mane. Ned caressed my back to comfort me from the awkwardness.

"Ms. Leighton." Tobias was right behind me.

I spun around elegantly on my heels and was greeted by one of Tobias's megawatt smiles. For a moment, I forgot we weren't alone, feeling light-headed from such a visceral connection with Wilder; extraordinarily real and profoundly complex. There was something in the way his eyes glimmered with a burning passion for me, his green-gold irises dilating in wonder and betraying his casual body language.

I gave a flirty flick of a wayward strand of hair, wanting him to know this charade didn't faze me at all. Not in the least. After all, I was sandwiched between two dashing heroes, one of whom could easily spar with Tobias's knowledge of Qin Shi Huang.

"Thank you for the invitation," said Gabe. "This is a groundbreaking exhibit."

"We're pretty psyched," said Tobias, his stare returned to me. "Glad you could come."

This feigning we hardly knew each other caused waves of doubt and I searched for those moments when he'd proven his affection for me, like when he took me to Tiffany's, or when he'd arranged for us to have dinner on his private beach and that endearing way he'd saved me at The Broad. All the memories I cherished and drew on now to get me through this casual act of acquaintance.

A flash went off and Tobias turned to face a photographer, tucking his hands into pockets to add a dash of the ordinary with an easy nod of approval.

Vaguely, rising from this dull ache, I became aware of the introductions being made between Ned, Gabe and Wilder with the shaking of hands and the polite conversation that followed along with Gabe's gushing about his anticipation for seeing the terra-cotta army.

Tobias reached out to shake my hand and his touch sent a shiver up my arm. "Always a pleasure, Ms. Leighton."

"So you're the guy who buzzed my roof with your chopper?" said Ned.

Tobias's eyebrow raised with intrigue. "Thank you for letting me land in your garden, Ned. I appreciate it. Zara and I are grateful. Aren't we Zara?"

I watched Ned go from defiant to appeased with one flash of Tobias's charm.

"There's an open bar," he added. "Feel free to enjoy the rest of the gallery."

When Tobias's intensity burned me up from the insides I had to look away, pretending to rummage around in my clutch purse looking for a nonexistent something—until they fell silent and I peered up to see all eyes on me. "Looking for my phone so I can snap a few shots," I lied.

"No unofficial photographs, Ms. Leighton," Tobias chastised me and broke into another heart-stopping smile. "I'll give you a brochure to take home. How about that?"

"Ooh, lovely." I laid on the sarcasm.

"Gabe." Tobias suppressed another smile. "How would you like a private tour before the hoards enter?"

"That would be fantastic," said Gabe.

"The exhibit is set up in its original excavated state," added Tobias. "You're probably the only man here who really knows what he's looking at."

Gabe gave a nod. "You have friends in high places, Mr. Wilder. This is a remarkable opportunity."

"Call me Tobias, please," he said. "We assured the Chinese government we'd present the terra-cotta soldiers as close to their natural found state. Their generosity has diplomatic implications so we benefit all round. I don't want to ruin the experience but it's as authentic as we could get."

"We can't wait." Gabe took my hand.

Tobias's glare fixed on the way Gabe held me. "I'll have my senior curator, Maria Perez, escort you." His intense gaze shifted back to me. "Ms. Leighton, I want to thank you personally for the great work you've done for The Wilder."

Ned scoffed under his breath. And earned himself a strike to his rib from my elbow.

Tobias didn't flinch. "What would we do without you, Zara?"

"Can we see it, then?" I said.

Maria was called over by Tobias.

She led us away and I felt his stare follow us. At the end of the hallway stood two smartly dressed men guarding an impressive fifteen-foot-high grand doorway, its design was a hint of what was to come. After a brief introduction by Maria we were granted access with strict instructions of no photos and no touching.

The doors opened wide—

I squinted into the dimness until my vision adjusted to the wondrous vision before us.

"The capital of Shaanxi Province." Gabe finished my thought.

Beyond the exhibition was a holographic image of the

surrounding landscape, giving it an authentic appearance of being in a real village. We descended the five steps onto the lower level of the excavation—as though we'd gone back two thousand years and were entering the sacred space of Qin Shi Huang's mausoleum in the Lintong District, Xi'an.

Amongst the terra-cotta soldiers were a few horses here and there beside their masters. We moved on slowly through the center of the statues standing two by two in a row that were lined back at least one hundred feet. Tiny dust fragments floated around us and there came that familiar scent of antiquities; an earthiness mingling with the tang of pottery. The atmosphere was thick with intrigue as though Emperor Qin Shi Huang's ghost haunted these statues.

Gabe gave a nod to let us know he needed a moment alone and even though this evening wasn't without its complications I was happy for him. This was a dream come true for him. Considering that trip to China kept getting delayed, he finally had seen his passion come to him. He disappeared amongst the proud carved officers, and Ned and I continued, swapping awed glances with each other as we weaved through the long line of warriors, marveling at the work of the talented craftsmen who'd chiseled their expressions to reflect pride.

It was always such a strange concept to me that when their emperor died they'd have to go with him to the other side. I'd also learned from Gabe that this myth stretched across cultures and continents, and started with the Egyptians famed for their kings believing their staff went with them when they passed over; though they buried the men and women in their tomb long before their staff were dead. It made me shudder just thinking of it and I turned to share this morbid thought with Ned but couldn't see him.

My gasp echoed—

Standing in the middle of a line of soldiers was Tobias

with his hands tucked into his trouser pockets and his stark gaze fixed on me.

"You certainly know how to woo a girl," I called over.

"Come here."

A chill shot up my spine as I made my way through. "Love what you've done with the place."

"As charming as ever, Leighton."

Fisting my hands, I rested them onto my hips in a show of defiance.

"You look beautiful," he said.

"So we know each other now?"

"I need you closer, Zara." He smirked. "I missed you."

"What happened to playing it cool?"

More like glacial.

He let out a frustrated sigh. "We're throwing off the press."

"I'm not doing this."

"Doing what?"

"Standing by to watch you ruin your life."

"What about your paintings? Are you willing to let them disappear, never to be seen again?"

"Tell me where they are so I can tip off Interpol anonymously."

"If *they* suspect Interpol has any knowledge of where they are keeping them, they will move them."

"They? Does it give you pleasure to have one up on me?"

"You know who I am, Zara." He opened his hands in a gesture of surrender.

I forced myself to look away because it was easier not to look at him and be seduced by the way he wore that black tuxedo like an all-American superhero with that dash of suaveness. He always oozed refinement and it was impossible not to swoon over the way he smiled at me now. And why the hell was his hairstyle going for the postfucked look as though he'd just ran his fingers through it like he did when he was with me?

"I'm grateful your friends are graciously playing along," he said. "How are you finding the exhibit?"

"It's like us, Tobias. Wrong place. Wrong time." I walked away, weaving around the statues with my chest feeling heavy; the air thick with dust. I turned left and made my way along the wall, reaching out to trail my fingers along it.

Tobias cut me off.

He pushed me backward until I hit the wall, and his chest crushed against mine as he lifted my hands above my head and pinned my wrists there to capture me. "Zara, I'm on fire for you. You know that."

My sigh brushed his lips, and the way he was holding me sent a surge of arousal low in my belly. I was growing wet from being held like this with his fierce stare boring into me as though he could read my soul. I wanted to demand he let me go but my sex became so taut with need and the throb so delicious I froze in place as though coming like this was possible.

He thrust against me and his cock felt rock hard. "We're close to the other side. Hang in there, okay." His lips traced along my throat and his teeth grazed my neck before he trailed kisses there. My body was burning up for him and my sex was betraying me and yet I held my determined expression of defiance.

He drew in a sharp breath. "God, I could fuck you right here."

I broke my right wrist from his grasp and reached up to cup a palm to his cheek. "I'm going back to my hotel."

"No, you're not." He grabbed my wrist and again pinned my hands above my head.

I am his willing prisoner, weak and needful for his cock that is pressing my abdomen with a promise of being inside me.

"You will stay," he growled into my ear. "I need to enjoy you from across the room."

My breaths were coming quickly now and my nipples were beaded against his chest and it was impossible to pull back from this erotic brink he'd nudged me over; my eyes burned into his as I begged him to take me.

"Not here," he warned and grabbed my hand and pulled me along the outer edge.

My head snapped back to look at one of the chariots.

"I'll bring you back," he said. "Give you a personal tour."

"Where are we going?"

"My office."

"I have to tell Gabe."

"He'll be in here for hours. Don't ruin his fun."

He swiped his ID to get us through to a hallway and we walked along a route which had us avoiding the crowds, though security could still track our journey through the museum.

When he pulled me into his office the light came on automatically. The last time I'd been in here Tobias had acted aloof and within minutes had sent me away reeling with the threat to fly me back to London. That memory still stung. My gaze slid to where *St. Joan* had hung in that trap he'd set for me to amuse himself.

"Jade." He shrugged out of his jacket and placed it on the back of his swivel chair. "Camera off."

Jade's sultry tone piped up. "Camera off."

He lingered in the shadows with those gorgeous hard edged lines on his face softening as he admired my figure. "I just want to look at you. Time away from you feels like centuries."

My gaze rose to the camera. "Return my access."

He rounded the desk. "You don't need it."

"I want it."

He nudged me until my back met his desk and his lips pressed mine and he savaged my mouth, his tongue tangling with mine, sweeping and exploring, and he moaned as he grabbed a lock of hair and tugged it in a flash of sensual power. That pinch to my scalp made my body tremble with need for him.

I pulled away a little. "Give me access to her."

"Why?"

My pout oozed determination. He bit my lower lip, sending a jolt of pain mixed with a stab of arousal, an exquisite tremor through my clit.

"Jade." He trailed kisses along my shoulder. "Give Zara level one access."

"Full access." I nipped his lip.

"Jade, full command to Zara Leighton. Voice calibration."

"Thank you, Jade."

He tipped up my chin. "Done. Now I get to fuck you."

"Dim the lights, Jade." I snapped my order.

They lowered, making it almost as dark as the corridor outside. Moonlight flooded in through the closed blinds and shimmered over Tobias's face, revealing that dominant expression that softened when he was with me. He lifted me up and sat me on the edge of his desk.

Lying back, I shifted my bum so he could hike up my dress. "I like your office."

"What office?" He crooned as he leaned back and grabbed my right foot. "Your shoes should be illegal." Decadently he licked my toes.

I swooned when his tongue roamed to my inner ankle. "You bought them for me."

"So I did." He kissed my toes.

His erotically charged worshiping of my foot sent me whirling. I glanced at that wall where *St. Joan* had hung and finally resigned to letting him give her back to me. His hands brought my focus back on him as he ran his palm over my belly, tracing slowly toward my sex.

"Jade," I said. "Accept no more orders from Tobias Wilder. All orders to come from me."

He looked amused. "What are you doing?"

"Playing."

"Jade, ignore that," he said.

"Access denied to Tobias W. Wilder," Jade sang out.

Adrenaline rushed through me with the realization it had worked.

Tobias stared up at the camera. "Return all control to Wilder."

Silence.

His gaze zeroed in on me and his frown deepened.

"I'm taking over your empire." I grinned mischievously.

His hands slid up my inner thigh and his fingers tugged my thong. "You win this round, Leighton. Now do as I requested."

"I need you inside me."

He unzipped himself and there came the beautiful view of him fisting his cock and directing it to tap my entrance to wet the tip. He thrust deep, sending a shock of pleasure into me with this thrill of tautness as I clenched him.

"You're so damn tight, Zara." His gaze locked on my sex and he watched himself glide in and out, his eyes darkening with lust, his jaw tensing as he pounded me, his tongue running along his bottom lip as he also devoured me with a look of desire.

My thighs trembled with the intensity of each thrust, and I surrendered to this exhilaration of being taken so elegantly, my skin flushed and overly sensitive to each caress as he ran his hands over me. He was mine again and there was still an *us*. My heart and mind soared after all that had happened over the last few days.

Tobias loosened his bow tie. "Are you close?"

"No." I reached up and grabbed the edge of the desk for leverage and met his strikes, reverse pounding him.

His fingertip went for my clit—

One point to Tobias.

"Don't stop." I groaned.

This proved he'd planned on a quickie—so he could get back to playing host and wowing everyone with his usual charm and sending me back to being merely an acquaintance again. My sex squeezed in rebellion at the thought of him leaving my side.

His thumb circled faster, his glare ablaze with closeness and locked on mine.

"Jade," I called out.

"What do you need?" Tobias sank deeper, his rhythm slowing to a leisurely pace as though realizing what I yearned for, the sound of his pelvis striking against me sending me reeling.

His eyelids were heavy, his breaths shaky with a dangerous urgency. "All I could think of tonight was being inside you."

My head rested on the desk as I held back from falling.

"Pull down your dress," he commanded.

Easing off the material from my shoulders, I lowered it beneath my bra and brought the cups down to reveal my swollen breasts. I reached for them to tweak a nipple, one and then the other, to sensuously squeeze and send a thrill between my thighs. "Fuck me harder."

"How's this?" He went deeper.

"Oh, yes."

He slammed against me.

"Harder." I took everything, my body exalting as he drove fiercely. "Tobias, you feel amazing." I groaned, revving him higher still.

He looked feral, those gold specs darkening to amber. Narrowing my gaze, judging how close he was to coming, I feigned writhing in pleasure. Tobias closed his eyes and focused on his breathing, his tight balls striking my sex as he delivered each delicious smack, sending ripples of bliss into my core. The sound of my wetness teasing our savage fucking.

"Jade, what's Tobias's middle name?" I asked.

"William," Jade replied brightly.

He squinted at me.

"Jade, what's Tobias's favorite color?"

"Eggshell blue," she stated boldly.

"Can we focus, please?" He looked amused.

"Are you close?"

He managed a nod.

"Tell me," I said firmly. "What's Tobias going to steal next?"

19

Jade's words echoed around us. "Searching…"

Tobias's eyes snapped open and he stared at me and pulled out, the loss of him causing me to take a sharp inhale of breath.

Jade is going to tell me.

I bit my lip in anticipation.

Tobias leaned forward and his mouth captured my sex, He began suckling and licking and owning me with each sweep, his head turning from side to side to ravish, devouring with an unmatched passion that made my head swirl.

"Please." I fought against this rapture, my voice trembling against this loss of breath as I listened out. "Jade, tell me what it is?"

Jade spoke with a human inflection. "Mr. Wilder's next conquest?"

Tobias raised his head to look at me and tutted and then resumed flicking; only faster, possessing my clit entirely with sharp sweeps up and down.

"Yes." I jolted when he matched the intense pace of his tongue with his finger.

"Wilder plans to steal Zara Leighton's heart," Jade answered.

My head crashed on the desk and my jaw tightened with frustration when I remembered he was always one step ahead.

His mouth freed my clit, his lips shiny with me upon them. "Good girl for trying at least. Here's your consolation prize." His tongue reclaimed me.

My breaths were impossible to catch. I froze as the pleasure imprisoned me, his hands now upon my breasts and pinching my nipples and that pang resonating all the way to where his tongue flicked with precision, sending me hurtling and coming hard; my moaning was real.

I collapsed, shuddering the rest of my climax.

He threw his head back and laughed. "Jade, lock her out."

I sprang up and punched his chest. "I hate your tests."

He didn't flinch. "I'm going to have to fuck you again, Zara. In way of a punishment for your naughty scheming."

"You're so cruel."

"No, I'm not. I'm looking out for you. I adore everything about you."

I lay back again and widened my thighs in way of an invite.

He smirked at my contradiction and plunged back inside me. "When you fight me like this you make me harder. Just so you know."

That jolt of his cock sliding deeper sent me reeling, and I went rigid as the pleasure rushed through me again.

He took my hands and maneuvered my fingers to ease back my folds for him to see me better. "Hold yourself like this." He played with my clit, tapping it with a meticulous beat, sending me into a trance as sparks of bliss catapulted me into oblivion.

"You like this?" he said with a rough edge.

"Yes." I loved it and needed this pang of pleasure, which

was morphing into an addiction. Peering up at this sensual scene gave me a sense of euphoria. "Don't stop," I begged. With my knees raised and my pelvis arched toward him in a gesture for more, I closed my eyes and took my punishment, exalting in how amazing it felt. Then I heard a long, drawn-out moaning—it was coming from me.

My body stilled as I rode through my orgasm and when his heat flooded my sex I clung to him. Finally, when I opened my eyes again I remembered we were in his office.

"Hey?" Tobias caressed my sex to soothe it and then reached for a tissue from a box at the end of the table and proceeded to clean me—that intimacy was just as sacred.

"Zara." His tone sounded serious.

"Yes?"

As he tucked himself away, his glare stayed on me. His expression reflected disapproval—that tilt of his head serving as chastisement for my flirting with my access with Jade.

"It's only because I care so much about you," I said.

"Don't do it again."

"Can't promise that."

Tobias yanked me toward him and whispered in my ear. "The next time you try something like that, I'll fuck you in the ass."

I arched a brow. "It's pronounced *arse*."

He slid into a smile. "Maybe I won't wait until you make a mistake again."

"Maybe I want that?" My gaze glided to his lips.

"Well at least you're keeping the British end up."

I tapped his bicep playfully.

"Let's go visit Madame Paul Duchesne-Fournet," he said. "She'll talk some sense into you."

I remained on the edge of his desk with my legs dangling while watching him straighten his trousers, reach for his tuxedo jacket and shrug it back on. I took in a cleansing breath and my gaze moved over his large desk and fell upon a stack of papers at the end. Poking out from beneath them was the corner of a yellow Post-it note. With Tobias using the window as a mirror to check his hair, I subtly peeled the top file aside and peeked down at the yellow square. On it were a series of scribbled numbers and I recognized the N. and S. as the latitude and longitude of two rows of six numbers each; these were coordinates.

My heart leaped that I might have glimpsed a clue, and I eased the note off the small pad and snuck it down the top of my dress, resting the sticky side below my breasts to keep it in place.

Tobias rounded the desk back to my side and I feigned innocence as he helped me with my bra and panties, and then he eased up my dress, and all the while I prayed he'd not feel the paper beneath. He smoothed out the material's creases so my dress lay elegantly once more over my body and revealed nothing of our passionate tryst.

"Soon." He swept a stray hair out of my eyes and tucked it behind my ear. "We'll have free rein to make love all day."

My legs wobbled when my heels hit the floor and I willed myself not to look back and give myself away.

We headed out.

He turned briefly. "Camera on, Jade."

With her sultry reassurance, the cameras were reset and his room was secured once more. Hand in hand, we strolled down a quiet hallway as he led me through the museum using a private route again to avoid the crowd. We entered a vast showroom, and I recognized the exquisite eighteenth-century French paintings adorning the walls and a marvelous prelude to the grandest of portraits.

There she was, our beloved *Madame Duchesne-Fournet* and

she was seemingly waiting for us, only this time she stared at us both as though bestowing her blessing.

Resting my head against his arm, I let out a contended sigh. "Isn't she peaceful?"

"Yes. Strong too."

Serene—I wondered what she'd endured in her life to get her to the place of emanating such tranquility despite circumstances having touched her in ways we couldn't imagine.

"She emanates stillness," I whispered. "Wisdom. A timeless beauty."

"Now you see why she reminds me of you." He turned to me and held my hands. "I wish you could see yourself through my eyes. You're bewitching."

Why even try to fight it? I thought to myself, I was gone completely, admit it. Whatever this was or however long it lasted was worth all of it because this feeling may never find me again. There came a panic when I remembered he'd be setting off any moment to go be Icon. My mind ran through what I'd glimpsed in his office.

I had to stop him.

"Tobias?" I swung round to face him.

"We're being monitored, Zara."

I struggled with being shut down again; danger was looming ever closer and my time was running out.

"Thank you for coming tonight," he said with the ease of a guilt-free man.

My mouth twisted to suppress my moan of panic.

His hand rested on the curve of my spine. "You're adorable, Ms. Leighton. Just so you know." His hand swept up and down my back to comfort me.

"Please, Tobias."

"I have to get back." He turned to face me and gave a kind smile. "Will you be okay?"

"I'll find Gabe."

"This way." He led me through the showroom.

We walked along the glass hallway and I leaned on his arm as I peered up at the multicolored stained-glass window above wondering if it was inspired by his love of the Renaissance period. He escorted me into the open bar. The east showroom had been transformed into an elegant Chinese parlor with a pagoda and a central gong and dim lighting to infuse the social meeting place with coziness. Still, I was in no mood to enjoy it.

Tobias got the barman's attention. "Glass of Dom Pérignon, please. Just the one."

We were amongst people again, and went back to pretending to be merely friends. A few other guests sat at the bar and others mingled in the corner so they could talk privately.

"Can I get you anything else?" Tobias handed me a flute of champagne.

"Just reassurance you will seriously consider all we've talked about." The chilled glass sent a shock into my fingers as I took it from him.

"I will." He leaned toward me. "You're not allowed to talk to anyone."

"That won't look strange at all."

He kissed my cheek. "Let that serve as a polite thank-you for your incredible work."

"You are so welcome, Mr. Wilder." I gave a professional smile. "Congratulations on a successful exhibit."

"Why thank you, Ms. Leighton. If you'll excuse me." He walked away with that dashing long stride, nodding here and there at the other guests.

Feeling uneasy, I walked over to the bar and made myself comfortable on a bar stool. I whipped out my phone and texted Gabe. We texted back and forth and he told me he was never leaving The Wilder. He made me smile when he added he was going to marry Tobias if I didn't. He joked that Ned would understand. It was the break in tension I needed. I texted I'd meet him at the bar.

"Can I get you a drink?" The twentysomething man to my left offered it with an East Coast accent.

He looked about twenty-five, his intelligent face was handsome with that dash of Japanese elegance. Honesty, that's what he exuded. His tuxedo appeared a shade too big, hinting he'd borrowed it for the evening.

"No, thank you." I shook his hand. "I already have one. I'm Zara."

"Liam," he said.

I reached for my glass, feigning I was unfamiliar with that name. It wasn't too much of a coincidence for his surname to be Stark. And right on cue he confirmed it by sliding his business card along the bar toward me with the Christie's logo embossed in gold beneath his name and his title of security specialist.

I picked it up and went for honesty. "Abby Reynolds mentioned you. I'm finally getting to meet you."

"She told me you'd talked," he said. "How's it going?"

"Not bad. Abby's a great investigator to work with."

"That's what she told me about you. Apparently, you're on to something? Wanna join forces?" He slid into a lazy smile.

"Who invited you tonight?"

"Came through Christie's. You?"

"Mr. Wilder."

"You're good friends?"

If he'd been looking our way with that same level of scrutiny, he probably caught more than flirting.

"I consult for Mr. Wilder," I told him.

"Wanna collaborate?"

"I'd need Huntly Pierre to approve an alliance."

"I'm sure they would."

Asking him if he was the man following us in that BMW yesterday would be unwise. The last thing Tobias needed was me to alert Liam there was interest in us.

He used his coaster to tap dewy droplets off his glass. "You're not going for that award for capturing Icon, are you?"

"I'll let Interpol do that."

His stare went right through me. "Does your guy know anything?"

"My guy?"

He took a sip. "Your contact?"

Realizing Abby had also shared our conversation sent a stab of betrayal, even if we were on the same side. "Not that I know of." I faced forward and glanced at my phone, willing Gabe and Ned to come save me.

"Could I speak with him?" he asked.

"My lead went cold. I'm returning to London on Monday."

"Anything you can share with Christie's is appreciated. We'd love to get your painting back. Your provenance looks good. Your dad once owned *St. Joan of Arc* by William Ouless, right?"

"Maybe. It's all a little uncertain. I was told it was lost in a fire. My childhood home burned down, you see."

"I read that. Sorry you had to go through that. Well, the good news is if there's no official bill of sale and, if no one comes forward, it could be yours again."

"If it's ever found. And authenticated."

"Which would be great, right? Though I understand it would leave you with a lot of questions."

"Yes. To be honest I doubt it's authentic." I hated lying but there was something in his expression that made me uneasy.

"Christie's believes it's real," he said.

"They didn't have time to authenticate it."

"It went through a rudimentary admission. It was enough to pique their interest."

"Time will tell."

"You don't want to get your hopes up? I get it. Did Abby mention we may have a lead on your painting, Zara?" He gestured to the barman for another drink.

I turned to face Liam. "The GPS pinged to a location?"

"This is 'need to know' only but you've gone out on a limb and I don't wanna send you back empty-handed."

"Oh?"

"We have a significant break on the Icon case."

I unwedged my tongue from the roof of my mouth as that sunk in.

He threw back his drink. "We've located the GPS tracker."

"Where?"

"Offshore. It's coming from a private yacht."

I feigned interest, all the while hoping Tobias hadn't stuck it on his own boat. No, he was too smart for that. "Whose yacht?"

He flashed a sideways glance. "It's registered to Elliot Burell."

I gasped too quickly.

"You've heard of him?"

"His name came up during an investigation in London."

"The feds have been tracking his activity for a while now. All the way to Scottsdale, Arizona."

My forearms prickled as I remembered Abby asking me if I was in that state.

"The Burells have a home out there," he continued. "Elliot Burell is the patriarch and has connections all the way to the White House. He supports the NRA and they support him. He's a legal arms dealer to foreign factions. As you can imagine we're proceeding with caution."

I downed the rest of my drink.

"He also supplies trained mercenaries," he added. "With arms dealing thrown in for good measure. He's also one of the victims of Icon. That's our lead."

"That's right," I said. "He had a Titian stolen from his home in France."

"The Burells have homes all over the world," he said. "One in Arizona, another in France, one in London, a manor in New York, and a place in Switzerland." He slid his finger across his phone and raised his screen to show me an image. "Look at that."

Liam was showing me a vast estate that was at least a forty-thousand-square-foot mansion surrounded by acres of land. "That's what corruption buys," he said.

My stunned reflection looked back in the mirror behind the bar.

Had Tobias removed the tracker from *St. Joan* and placed it on Burell's boat?

"We may have an even bigger find on our hands." He sounded excited. "The FBI went back and analyzed satellite data over the last month and saw several large crates being moved over State lines. They came in through the port in Miami. Why not through LA, right? A much closer port. On the import notice the supply was listed as modern art. When they interviewed the import clerk who signed in the shipment, he reported the paintings looked old."

"As in, by the Old Masters?"

"Apparently."

"The inventory record?"

"Gone. When the clerk returned to his office, the inventory paperwork was missing."

Dizziness welled up in me and morphed into excitement.

"How many?" I managed.

"At least thirty paintings. Far as I can remember. And Christie's would be one of the first auctioneer houses to be alerted to that size of sale. There is no record of Burell ever legally buying that quantity of artwork. It's on the down low. Shady as hell. Elliot Burell gets a hard-on for art. It's his thing. He paid one hundred and fifty million for a Cézanne."

And I'd seen evidence of it in the photo taken in his rotunda in France after the heist. Everything pointed to it being Tobias who'd broken in there. His interest in the Burells had never wavered. "That family doesn't do fakes," I reasoned.

"No effing way."

"Where do you think he got them from?"

"We'd have to see them. As well as their provenance. We don't know what he has, only that he's hoarding paintings of some interest."

It was too much of a coincidence for it not to be my father's collection, and it sounded as though our paintings had been transported to America to get them out of Europe because Burell knew Icon had seen them when he took their Titian.

And there was the risk Icon could come back for the others.

"Do the feds know where Elliot Burell is right now?" The thought of him sent a chill up my spine.

"Yeah, he's in Scottsdale for a family event. An hour's flight away for me if it comes to that."

I borrowed a pen from the barman and wrote down my phone number on a napkin for Liam. "If you find *St. Joan* can you call me?" I said. "I'd love to be kept in the loop with this."

"Sure." He pulled out his phone and entered the number into his contacts.

Using the excuse of wanting to visit the main exhibit again,

I left Liam at the bar with my heartbeat pounding as I made my way into the main foyer, looking out for Tobias. He wasn't here.

I hid behind the terra-cotta horse-drawn carriage and reached beneath the scoop of my dress for the Post-it note. Within a minute, I had my phone out and was entering the coordinates into Google Maps—a location of a wide-open space popped up on my screen and it was Scottsdale.

A shudder spiraled up my spine.

Had Wilder set in motion a plan to retrieve my paintings and not told me? Or, I painfully reasoned, maybe this was his next heist? Perhaps he'd merely given a few of his trophies away to make me believe his motives were pure?

My mind zeroed in on the facts as the obvious answers screeched into my brain.

Wilder had lured me to Los Angeles because he needed to see my reaction to the photos he'd shown me on that laptop. He'd required not only an art expert but the one person who could validate those paintings were indeed from the Romanov collection.

Dear God, I'd willingly authenticated them for Tobias and clearly stated that, yes, each portrait had once belonged to my family. I'd provided proof that taking a risk to steal them would be worth it.

Dazed, I leaned into the stone carriage and placed my phone on the seat to hide it. With unsteady legs, I made my way out of The Wilder Museum.

I had to get to Scottsdale first.

20

I jolted awake to the deep thrum of a plane's engine. Rain spotted the oval window and beyond it was an endless carpet of white clouds. Tobias called this time of year *fall*. The time of year when everything died.

"Miss?" came a female voice.

I turned to look at the flight stewardess who was talking to me. Her uniform was pristine and her expression was kind, and I wondered how she kept that smile.

"Tea, please," my voice cracked with dryness. "With milk."

"Sure." She set about making it on her cart.

I thanked her and pulled my blanket up. "How long before we land?"

"An hour," she said. "Don't let this worry you—" She glanced through the window. "Phoenix's in the nineties when we land."

"Great." I didn't care.

She handed me a cup of tea in a foam cup, and I wrapped my hands around it to warm them and watched her continue down the aisle. I fought the need to check the phone I no longer had after leaving it at The Wilder. There was no doubt he'd find the phone he'd given me in the terra-cotta horse.

I left the museum in a haze of confusion and had taken a taxi back to the Sofitel. I'd phone Gabe once I got back to the hotel and apologize for leaving so briskly. I'd add that my excuse of leaving without saying goodbye was my way of not ruining their night.

A quick search online helped me secure a seat on the last flight out of LAX to Phoenix, the closest airport to Scottsdale. My hand had steadied from its tremble by the time I booked my hotel.

I'd stayed at the Sofitel long enough to change out of my evening gown and into my jeans and a T-shirt. On the way out I'd grabbed my jacket to ward off the impending air-conditioning.

Tobias had always been one step ahead of me. So much so, that I'd even considered the beautiful watch he'd given me could have been purchased before our romantic date to Tiffany's. He could have inserted a tracking device in that too. I'd left it in my room.

The late drive to the airport in a taxi was a blur.

When I'd grabbed that Post-it note in his office, the camera had been off. There was the possibility he'd find it gone and suspect me, but I was already on my way.

I drank the rest of my tea, trying to dislodge the lump in my throat from this continued mistrust of Wilder, and reassured myself that doing this was the only way I could take back my power.

When we landed in Phoenix, I hurried off the plane and followed the sign for the taxi stand. The dry heat of the desert night made it hard to breathe. Getting in a taxi, I asked the driver to take me to the Fairmont Scottsdale Princess Hotel on East Princess Drive.

"They have award-winning chefs," the driver told me.

My fingernails dug into my palms when he'd added I'd love the rooftop pool. *Don't think about that now*, I soothed, *don't think about him.*

Locating Burell and demanding my paintings back was a bad idea, suicidal, probably. I was going to have to secretly discover evidence that would grant a search warrant, and the rest the feds could handle. I needed to get onto his estate and find a clue to my father's legacy.

But tonight, I needed to sleep. I was too fatigued to think straight. It was fast approaching midnight.

The hotel lobby was predictably quiet for this time of night, and I was grateful to hear The Fairmont had reservations. I checked in and headed off to find my room.

It was a pleasant suite on the first floor and if it wasn't for my dread of tomorrow I'd be wallowing in all this Arizona hospitality and wanting to go exploring. Once settled, I found snacks in the minibar and chose a packet of chocolate-covered pretzels.

I settled on the king-size bed and cracked open my laptop. I began searching for more information on Elliot Burell and found his Scottsdale address in a *Wall Street Journal* article, though nothing came up about the inside of the property. Still, I had a location now and it was less than half an hour's taxi ride from here. I started researching his family members and blinked with surprise when I read the *Vanity Fair* article on his granddaughter, socialite and fashionista, Paige Burell.

I blinked at my screen as I read Elliot Burell was playing dutiful grandfather and hosting his granddaughter's wedding tomorrow afternoon at his private estate, which was nestled between the Camelback and Mummy Mountains and hailed as a high-society affair. The article also boasted affluent-sounding names from New York's social scene, along with many of her friends from her time spent studying at Columbia University. I memorized several of her girlfriends' names. Nudging my computer aside, I lay down and pulled the duvet over me and stared at the ceiling. "That's your in," I whispered to myself.

With my energy fading, I readied for bed.

I woke out of a nightmare, realizing I'd slept through to Sunday morning. My body was damp with perspiration and my mind plagued by disorientation until my blurry eyes cleared and I could see the room; my first thoughts turned to…*him*.

I trudged off to the bathroom to take a shower.

Breakfast was a light cheese omelet and several cups of coffee in the hotel's restaurant.

Afterward, I headed back to the lobby and went in search of the concierge to ask for the address of the local shops. I was directed to Scottsdale Fashion Square that was a twenty-minute cab drive away.

At noon the temperature was unbearably hot as I followed the signs for the mall. Here, I shopped in Neiman Marcus, settling on a blue satin strappy dress and complementing the look with a pair of delicate pumps. I found a matching Versace purse that was a subtle touch and roomy enough to hold the disposable phone and camera I'd bought from a nearby drugstore.

I headed back to The Fairmont.

By late afternoon, I was standing in front of my room mirror, giving a pleased nod at my convincing guise of a wedding guest. I looked glamorous enough in my new blue satin dress to get me in and feminine enough to hide me rocking my Joan of Arc side.

I made my way to the lobby and the valet called me a taxi. We drove onward through a wasteland.

This in and out of air-conditioning did nothing for my hair, which I'd allowed to flow freely over my shoulders. I combed my fingers through it to rein in these wayward locks.

London never seemed so far away.

I hated myself for missing Tobias. Yet my body still yearned for him, and I knew getting over him was going to be the hardest thing I'd ever done.

The taxi turned down a tree-lined road that promised to lead to a more inhabitable terrain. I remembered the photo on Liam's iPhone and saw that it hadn't quite captured the immenseness of the Burells' estate, which looked like a palace had been placed in the middle of nowhere. If they were going for intimidation they'd overdelivered. The riffraff was kept out by tall gothic gates.

I paid with cash, having left my ID and credit cards in my room, and braved the climate again, steadying myself against this panoramic statement of power.

Lush, towering palm trees overlooked an enormous blue lagoon stretching out as an expansive body of crystal-blue water. A big fountain added to the opulent spectacle. A kingdom in the sand. How fitting for Burell to live so well surrounded with so much death.

A burly guard stepped out of the small hut just inside the entryway.

"Hi." I forced a smile, though inwardly I cringed as I realized the hike ahead of me looked arduous and even without wearing pumps it was a long walk.

"Ma'am, you better hurry or you'll be late." He gestured for me to come closer. "Do you have your invite?"

"Sure." I peered into my purse and then raised my gaze at the house I was probably never getting into. "Oh, no," I said with a look of annoyance. "Forgot it."

He peered at me through shaded lenses.

"I'm on the list," I said. "Julia Harper-Bastian. Does that help?"

I waited for him to check his clipboard, all the while hoping that *Vanity Fair* article mentioning Julia as one of Paige's guests was accurate.

He held out his hand. "ID, please."

"Why would I need that? I'm virtually family? Paige is going to freak out if I'm not there. And on her wedding day too." I turned to go.

"Ma'am," he called after me. "Says here you're already checked in?"

I swallowed hard. "That doesn't make any sense. Let me give Uncle Elliot a call. I'll tell him there's an issue at the front gate with keeping track of guests. I just hope he's not in one of his moods."

The guard's expression was vexed and I felt horrible.

With a nod of approval I was making my way up the driveway.

I was really doing this.

The road was lined with sublime flowers of every color, and it was challenging not to gawk at all this lush foliage. I elegantly climbed the marble steps toward the two buffed-up men in black tuxedos who were wearing the same sunglasses.

The foyer looked at least half a mile long and was lined with mirrors. Gracing either side of the hallway were female stone statues with their raised crystal light fixtures strewn one after the other all the way along. The floor appeared to be layered delicately in gold leafing. I glimpsed into the rooms as I swept by them and caught the individual color schemes, peering in for a painting I might recognize or even a man of Elliot Burell's age. With no current photographs of this very private man, he was going to be challenging to track down.

Eventually, I made it into the garden and was sprayed by a

refreshing mist swirling around me that took off the edge of the overbearing heat. Beyond sprawled an autumn-themed decor where acres were dedicated to the colors of fall. In the center was a golden-framed canopy with a heavy cream drapery cascading over it and swooping down the center to showcase the bridal party who were yet to arrive.

Above the guests was a structure of lattice interwoven with leaves trailing either sides of the posts. Here too the mist showered over them. The sun was at its brightest for the mid-day sun, glaring its showy burst of oranges, reds and golds as though Elliot Burell himself commanded the sky.

I took a seat at the back.

Sensing all the guests had arrived and had settled into their seats, I left mine and headed back into the house and tucked my sunglasses into my purse.

Oh, no.

At the end of the hallway came a shimmering apparition of a bride who I assumed was Paige, and she was closely followed by her bridesmaids in their golden gowns whooshing toward me in a sea of tulle. After stealing a final glimpse at the bride's pretty face that was frozen with sadness and clearly out of place for her big day, I hurried forward to make my escape through the door dead ahead.

21

This is impossible, I thought as I slumped down on the luxurious velvet sofa and puffed out an exasperated breath; I'd been searching the endless rooms for at least half an hour and found nothing.

This place was too vast and all this endless luxury had an unsettling perfection. Most of the paintings were from artists who'd envisioned themselves as talented and yet mirrored nothing of the spirit of the great masters. Take the 1950 David Canaille hanging above the marble fireplace—an eight-foot-by-six image of a man smoking a cigarette while standing over a naked sleeping woman as though disrespecting her after a night of sex. It made my forearms prickle with the uneasiness it stirred. It was the arrogance in the character's expression; his sense of entitlement. Though I respected the artist's ability to stir such a visceral response in me, his talent unsettled my soul.

This wasn't going to work.

I envied Tobias's ability to access data, the kind I needed right now to find my way around this maze of gold-themed rooms.

The door opened.

In strolled a man in a tailored tuxedo, and from its perfect fit he looked like a wandering guest. His bow tie was undone and dangling from his neck. I was a little taken back by his striking beauty, his dark hair a mass of wayward curls that only the moneyed pull off and his devilish smile was contagious as he grinned my way.

I pushed myself to my feet to greet him. "Hi."

"Hi. Are you hiding?"

I broke into a smile. "I'm coming back now."

His gaze swept the room. "Weddings are a trigger for me too."

"Oh?"

"Pressure to spawn," he said as he came in farther. "You know how it goes." He held out his hand for me to shake. "Elliot."

My throat tightened at the sound of that name and his firm grip made my fingers stiffen with repulsion. "Are you a member of the wedding party?" I asked.

"Bride's side."

Which meant he could very well be a Burell.

"Call me Eli."

"Julia." I prayed he didn't ask for my last name because he'd no doubt know the real Julia Harper-Bastian."

"You're one of Paige's besties?" he asked.

"Yes, we were at Columbia together."

"What a waste of a good business degree." He gave a seductive grin as though untouched by misery because his grand-dad saw to it only the world got fucked over. "Where are you from?" he asked. "Don't want to say London because that's obtuse."

"London."

He held my gaze and then devoured me with it. "Love

that city. Though I'm more partial to Scotland. Great hunting. Do you hunt?"

"No."

"Nothing like stalking a wild stag for hours and then shooting it in the head." Eli carried his confidence with the arrogance of the overly privileged and he worked his bow tie into a neat bow and straightened the jacket of his tuxedo, all while staring at me.

"How do you find Charles?" he asked.

"I like him." I remembered reading he was the groom.

"Crap at golf."

"Paige looks beautiful."

"Please—" He rolled his eyes. "She took bridezilla to the next level."

"It's her special day."

"We're talking Paige, remember? She had this rare silk imported for her headdress."

"It's gorgeous."

"Weaved by spiders." He widened his eyes in response to my cringe. "Yeah, you can't make this shit up. Orb spiders."

"I didn't think that was a thing."

"It's a thing." He shuddered. "She saw it in *Vogue* and had to have it."

"How's your grandfather?"

He narrowed his gaze on me.

"Paige says he's very nice," I said.

"She did?" Eli stared off.

I wondered if I'd pushed my lie too far and yet added, "Is he here?"

"Wouldn't miss his favorite's wedding." He lowered his eyes. "Where's your plus one?"

I hesitated and Eli threw me a devilish smile.

He gestured for me to come closer. "Want to see something special? We have time."

"I should get back."

"They're taking photos. They won't miss us."

"Shouldn't you be in them?"

"Shouldn't you?"

Despite this uneasiness, I left the room and walked beside him down a long hallway.

We descended ten steps into a Victorian-styled parlor. The scent reminded me of magnolias and it clung heavy in the air as though trying to mask another scent; a waft of grass and stale water.

"This was Paige's birthday surprise." He opened a large steel door.

I bit the inside of my cheek when I saw what was behind the enormous glass cage, a large white tiger ripping apart slabs of meat with his powerful jaw.

"His name's Noodle," said Eli. "He's a Bengal tiger."

"Noodle," I repeated his name as though its cuteness lessened the danger.

Moving past me, Eli walked up to the window and placed his palms flat against it and looked down at him. "We wanted Noodle to make Paige happy when she came to visit."

"Your sister?"

He turned and stared at me for the longest time.

The tiger pushed himself to his feet and padded closer to the glass to look up at Eli, and I pretended not to recognize this animal as an endangered species.

Eli turned to face me. "Paige is scared of him."

Noodle tore apart another slab of meat and chewed; blood staining his sharp-edged teeth.

"We don't do fear in this family," he said quietly.

I refused to look at Eli even when he refocused on me.

Within the cage there was just enough space to run a little and there was even a shallow pool to play and wash in.

Coming here was the most reckless decision I'd ever made and yet doing nothing had felt so wrong. Until now—

I swallowed hard and Eli caught it. His eyes sparkled with mischief as though he liked seeing me vulnerable. He oozed a magnetism that was hard to define, the kind of arrogance only money provided to the freewheeling wealthy.

He leaned toward my ear. "What are your thoughts on us having Noodle?"

"I can see he makes you happy."

"That's the meaning of it all. Don't you think?"

"Of life?"

He turned to look back at him. "You're either in the cage or on this side of it."

The lights flickered on and off, and I felt a rush of fear from being so reckless.

Eli stared up and his gaze fixed on the light. "That was a power surge."

"Maybe it's due to all your guests? Let's go back."

We left Noodle's enclosure and I walked beside Eli down another sprawling hallway.

"What do you do?" he asked.

"I work in a bookshop." My eyes stayed on his to carry the lie even though my brain screamed at me I was meant to be a graduate of Columbia and quickly added, "I'm the manager."

He was leading me in the opposite direction of the event. A jolt of fear slithered up my spine.

"Which one?" He moved toward a door and opened it.

"I'm sorry?"

"Which bookstore?"

"Foyles." I peered in. "I'm sure everyone is wondering where we are."

"I'm an architect. I'd love to show you the architectural model that represents what I'm working on now." He went in and called back. "We just completed furnishing my New York high-rise. We secured prime real estate on Park Avenue."

Hesitating, I ran through my options.

"Julia?" He beckoned me.

Nudging the door wider, I entered and looked over at Eli who was standing before a large box with a red bow.

He glanced up from texting. "I need to take my gift to the reception."

I neared the beautifully wrapped wedding present and wondered what he'd bought the bride and groom. My gaze swept the office over the leather sofa and chairs, along the Persian rug upon which sat a large mahogany desk and hanging behind it—

The Storm on the Sea of Galilee, by Rembrandt.

Fuck.

I snapped my gaze back to the wedding gift.

The last time that painting had been seen in public was at the Isabella Stewart Gardner Museum in Boston in 1990, along with other masterpieces from Degas, Vermeer, Manet and a self-portrait of Rembrandt—but all of them had fallen victim to a theft. The men had been let in by the gallery's own security guards who had unwittingly believed the police officers were real.

The red ribbon curled in a bow and it was so pretty; so tight.

Eli texted away.

I stole another glance—I was too far away to judge its authenticity. If this Rembrandt painting was real, there were far-reaching implications, not least because it could put my name on the map and there'd be something of my career to salvage. This was my reason to get the feds in here. All I had to do was take a photo. I could be the one who delivered this Rembrandt back to the people. *This* was the evidence I needed.

Eli tucked his phone into his pocket and strolled through the partition to the other side of the room. "This way."

My feet refused to move as I peered through.

"I'd love to hear your opinion." He crooked his finger to entice me to follow him to the other side.

Stepping through to join him I stared down at the model of a skyscraper on a corner table. "Wow. That's impressive."

He came closer until he towered over me. "Glad you like it."

This side of the room was sparse with only a small window without a curtain, and it looked out of place after the endless labyrinth of decadence. There was a breeze coming from somewhere; the temperature was colder at this end of the house.

My forearms prickled. "This is a striking building. You're very talented."

"I know."

I arched an amused brow. "Humble too."

"Has anyone ever told you how beautiful you are?"

"I'm not your type."

"I disagree." He leaned into my ear. "We have a tradition in my family."

"Oh?"

"If we see something we want, we claim it…" He arched a brow.

"I'm going to head back now. Thank you for showing me your design. It really is amazing."

He grabbed my arm and there was a pinch of discomfort. "Let go."

"That's not how it works, Julia."

Panic rushed in and I tried to pull away. "Eli?"

"Take off your dress—" He let go and stepped back. "Come on, baby."

I went to leave and he yanked me back and shoved me against the wall. It sent a shock of pain up my spine.

"You and I are going to have a little chat. Julia."

"There's been a misunderstanding."

His brow furrowed as something caught his attention and he looked over toward the door.

I followed his gaze—

Tobias was standing in the archway and his black tuxedo was the ideal camouflage for a wandering guest. "There you are, sweetheart," he said calmly.

Eli's brow furrowed further, perhaps trying to place where he'd seen him before.

"What are you up to, darling?" Tobias said, exuding an easy charm as though he'd not just witnessed my rough handling.

I exhaled in a rush. "He was showing me his design."

"Architectural representation," Eli corrected. "My Manhattan high-rise."

"It's in Manhattan," I repeated nervously, still reeling from seeing Tobias and that pain in my arm only now lifting.

Tobias strolled through the partition toward us. "The toasts are imminent." He forced a smile and took my hand. "Let's go back."

"Have we met?" Eli proffered his hand toward him.

Tobias gave it a quick shake. "Great to meet you."

Eli strolled back through the divider and turned sharply to glare at Tobias. "And you are?"

"Boyfriend," he replied.

Eli stepped back. "I'll give you two a moment, then."

Tobias squeezed me into his side protectively, and I resisted the urge to close my eyes and exhale with relief.

"By the way, Julia," said Eli, "if you were a friend of this family, you'd know."

"Know?" My chest constricted as I realized he'd always known I wasn't a guest.

"Elliot Burell." He gave a slow, steady nod. "Is my dad."

Sleek chrome doors shot out from either side of the partition and sealed us off from him. Tobias ran forward and tried to pry them open. I flew toward the small window and peered down at the garden—the guests were gone.

Tobias spun round to glare at me. "What. The. Fuck."

"Nice to see you too," I snapped.

"Just tell me you're okay? Did he hurt you?"

"I'm fine."

He fisted his hands. "I should have punched him when I had the chance."

The partition was our only way out. We were trapped in here and from Wilder's fury he was going to break down the door. I hoped he could.

"I thought Eli was Elliot's grandson?" I blurted.

"He's the bride's uncle. Elliot and his third wife had Eli late in life. Had you asked me for this information..." Tobias glared at me in frustration.

"Can we use the model for leverage?" I watched him examine it.

"The wood's too fine." He snapped the tower to prove it.

"How did you find me?"

He went to the sliding door again, slipping his fingers into the crack and tried to pry them outward. Nothing moved.

"Tobias?"

He turned to face me. "I thought, what would Zara Leighton do?" He gave a thin smile. "She'd make an irrational de-cision and act on it. And here we are."

"I'm here to get my paintings back." *Before you snatch them, mister.*

He blinked at me. "You walked out on me last night?"

"I'm surprised you noticed."

"Oh, I noticed," he said. "Found your phone. That wasn't suspicious at all."

"*I'm* suspicious?"

"Yes, Zara. Your behavior is never without its—" he waved his hand "—incoherency."

"That was a Rembrandt in there." I pointed in its direc-tion. "Or did you miss that?"

"We talked about you not getting on their radar, remem-ber? And yet here you are parading yourself before Burells." He caressed his forehead in frustration. "We were having a perfectly lovely evening. What the hell happened?"

"How did you find me?"

He rolled his eyes.

"Tobias?"

"I tracked your credit card to your hotel. The concierge told me they'd gotten you a taxi here."

"You had no right to invade my privacy like that."

"Well, as you're locked in here!"

I willed myself to calm down and gritted my teeth for courage. "I'm taking things into my own hands."

"Could you be any more exasperating?"

I stepped toward him. "There's a name for men like you."

"You mean reasoned? Logical? Discerning? How about sagacious? Let me know if I'm getting close."

"How about thief—"

A section of floor directly beneath us gave way and we found ourselves plummeting into darkness; arms flailing.

A loud splash sounded as we plunged under the water and were immersed in a stark coldness, stunned by an agonizing chill. My cheeks bulged with precious air as I swam upward with my arms and legs, fighting this drag of resistance, throat tight and burning from lack of oxygen and lungs almost exploding with the pressure. Rising to the surface I sucked in air—

Tobias burst to the surface. "Fuck."

Our desperate breaths echoed loudly in this claustrophobic space. The only light flooding in from above. We were never getting out of here. The trapdoor was at least thirty feet high and there was nothing to grab onto.

"Huh, people still use trapdoors." He swam toward me. "You okay?"

I peered up, unsure how long I was going to be able to tread water. "It was a trap."

"The water's fresh at least."

"What does that mean?"

"Hold on." He went under and water buffered me against the edge. I swam to the center and looked up, trying to think of a way out.

We are going to drown.

My gaze swept the depths searching for him. I willed this not to be happening. How the hell had I been so stupid? It hit me—the Burells probably used face-recognition software or some other form of jacked-up security system. I looked around to see if my purse was floating and reasoned at least my ID wasn't in it and, other than a disposable phone and camera, there was nothing else pertaining to me. I hated myself for the danger I'd put us in. Surely Eli recognized Tobias, after all they had to have moved in the same circles.

Tobias reappeared. "There's a lock." He gestured downward. "I'm gonna try it." He tapped his jacket and then his hands moved beneath the water.

"What's wrong?"

"The necklace." He looked harried. "It was in my pocket."

Oh, no, he'd brought his mom's necklace to give it to me. Tobias dived and disappeared again and I could only assume he was searching for it.

"Wait!" I called to him.

This had been a stupid, miserable decision to come here, and I tried to suppress my dread at our inevitable hypothermia. My body shook. I wanted to find Eli so I could punch that smug look off his face. As Elliot's son, he'd be primed for cruelty and I'd just spent the last twenty minutes with a psycho. That sparse room had tipped me off it was sinister, and yet I'd ignored the glaring danger.

Tobias resurfaced. "It's gone." His face was terrifyingly convincing.

"The necklace? I'll help you look."

"No time." He shook water from his head. "We need to open the lock. The pressure will flush us out with it. Relax your body so you don't hit the floor too hard or, depending on what's on the other side, swim like hell to the surface. That's if I can even open it. We have no idea what's on the other side, so stay calm and stay close to me. Understand?" He gazed up as though reconsidering.

"Are you serious?"

"Unless you have a better idea?"

"I'm trying to remember what I did the last time I was in here," I said glumly.

He swam toward me. "I'm sorry I made you doubt me."

"You're Icon."

"Oh, Zara, I promised you this would all be over soon." His eyes reflected kindness. "I wish you believed me."

"You were planning on hitting this place?"

"Not anytime soon." He shook his head and droplets sprayed. "I was researching Burell but coming here was…"

"Suicide?"

"Let's just say my plan to get you your paintings back needed fine-tuning."

I wanted to believe him, really, I did, but there was so much uncertainty, so many unanswered questions and I still couldn't suppress my discomfort of knowing I'd colluded with a thief.

"Let's focus on getting out, okay?" Tobias reached around to the back of my neck and pulled me toward him, kissing me hard on the lips, firm and passionate, loving and forgiving, his mouth soft and caring against mine, and for a moment, just a moment, I forgot we were in here. Despite this lingering doubt my heart begged me to give him another chance.

He let go and gave a cute smile. "That was for me."

Resting my forehead against his, I drew strength from him, needing him more than ever. "Tell me we'll get out of here."

"Hold on." He plunged again and the water whooshed.

After taking several deep breaths, I dived after him until I saw Tobias floating before a large valve lock. It looked like a hatch. With a wave, Tobias directed me to take the top left side of one of the bars and he took the other side—we shoved—it wouldn't budge.

Letting go, I swam upward until I broke the surface needing to refill my lungs. Braving the depths again I plunged to rejoin him. Tobias's cheeks were puffed out with the strain as he continued to grapple with the wheel. I grabbed my side again and pushed with all my force, my arms aching with this terrible tension, chest tight and fighting this dizziness. The wheel shifted an inch. Tobias twisted aggressively, round and around.

My heart thundered against my chest in a shocking pain, with my need to escape and terror of what came next. The latch shot open—

We were flushed out of the chamber with a gushing torrent of water, tumbling along a hard floor as this endless wave carried us, both of us gasping and spluttering until we landed in a deep pool of water. I raised my head and looked for Tobias.

"Are you hurt?" He pushed himself up and came over.

Bruised and shaken I tried to process his words. "Don't think so. You?"

"Never better." He stretched his back. "We're out of there at least."

"Maybe someone will see all this water?" I accepted his hand and was pulled to my feet, limbs aching and my hair stuck to my head in a wet clump and my dress clung. "Bloody hell," I said. "What was that?"

"The Burells. Sorry you had to learn the hard way." He loosened his necktie. "How did you find out your paintings are here?"

"I met Liam Stark at your exhibition."

"The guy from Christie's?"

"He told me the feds saw a large shipment of paintings come through customs and they tracked them by satellite to here."

"You should have told me." Tobias looked around the large tiled room.

"You were a little busy avoiding me."

"What about what we did in my office?" He gestured his frustration. "That was me reassuring you. Remember?"

I nibbled a fingernail as my brain processed that.

He stared ahead at a hallway. "Did you tell Huntly Pierre you were coming here?"

"No."

"I didn't exactly announce it, either." He held out his hand to me. "Come on."

Trudging after him I slid my palm against his. "Ouch." Pain shot through my sole and coursed into my calf. Lowering to my knees I reached into the puddle—pulling out a delicate chain with a 3-carat emerald. My sigh echoed relief that I'd found it. Tobias closed his eyes for a second and nodded his relief too.

I pushed myself up and cupped this precious find in my palm. "I'm sorry you almost lost it."

"Come here." He took the necklace from me and placed it around my neck and fixed the catch. "It's where it belongs."

My fingertips trailed over the stone and I wanted to be worthy of wearing what had once belonged to his mom; one of his most cherished possessions. I turned and wrapped my arms around him.

"I was going to come here at some point," he said. "You just brought my agenda forward."

"I'm so sorry."

"Just promise me you'll talk to me first about any adventures you're planning." He raised a finger. "Particularly when it pertains to danger."

I crashed my cheek against his chest and hugged him.

"I'm glad you're not facing this alone," he said. "There is that."

Leaning against his arm, strolling beside him as we walked on, gave me the strength I needed to survive what felt like a nightmare. Every time I found my way back to happiness, uncertainty always held me ransom.

We made our way up the central stone stairs.

"If my jacket wasn't soaking wet I'd give it to you." He gave my hand a squeeze.

My eyes widened—blinking toward the impossibly high

hundred-foot waterwheel in the distance. The kind from a mill and designed to convert water into energy.

Impossible.

Tobias stared at me. "Where have I seen that before?"

And then I remembered. "The Broad. They had a display like this but on a smaller scale."

"The gallery, that's right. What the hell is it for?"

"It's called *Mousetrap for the Inevitable.*" I grabbed his forearm. "The creator was E. B. It was designed by Eli Burell. Oh, no."

"Elliot Burell's son."

"This is his design. He's an architect."

The only way to the other side was over that enormous wheel. It sat in a deep cavern and either side of it was a sheer drop hundreds of feet down.

"They look like they're still working on it." I pointed to the woodwork stations.

"Do you remember what comes after this?"

"Oh, God."

"Can you be more specific?"

"Lasers."

"I should have stuck with 'Oh, God.'"

"We're inside a piece of modern art." I turned to face him. He caressed his jaw thoughtfully.

"Which means my paintings are here," I said. "Or else why would they have gone to all this trouble?"

He let out an exasperated sigh. "They knew I'd come."

"It's designed to seal you inside, Tobias."

He turned and yelled as though Eli might hear, "Bravo, you fucked-up psycho."

"We have to go back."

He peered up at the contraption. "There's no way. We have to go over it."

We strolled down the ramp toward the base of the wheel and our gazes rose to take in the structure. No way was I getting on that death trap.

"This gives them time to move the paintings." I cringed at the thought of it.

While we were stuck in here, they probably had men packing up their precious cargo and moving it. We had no choice but to climb and, after all, when we got closer those wooden slats looked doable. I'd hold on and take my time to conquer the height.

"Tear my dress," I said. "Make it shorter."

Tobias knelt and grabbed my hem and tore it to my knees. He rose and pulled off his jacket and threw it down.

A gushing, swishing sound came from beneath us.

I looked over the edge of the cavern, horrified to see it filling up. "That's the water from the tank."

"We have to go." Tobias climbed up the sprawling wheel and reached his hand out for me. "Zara, hurry."

A torrent of water burst against the base of the wheel—the wood croaking and creaking as it turned—and I reached up for Tobias's hand but he was being carried upward.

"Jump on," he called back.

Fucking hell.

With a run and jump, I leaped up and grabbed the wooden panel jutting out and was carried upward, gripping with all my might as I flew around. I was vaguely aware Tobias had landed on the other side. Jumping off was going to catapult me across the room and when I glanced at Tobias, he knew it too.

"Hold on," he shouted.

"What?"

"I'll stop the wheel. Hold on."

He was out of his mind because I had seconds to decide to jump—

They'd gone.

I sucked in a deep breath and was immersed underwater and hanging upside down, dragged along, a roaring in my ears as they filled, my legs wrapped around a rung as I tried to stay on. My eyes popped open when the rotation brought me up again and the resistance lessened.

Too scared to scream.

I sucked oxygen as the wheel carried me to the peak again. Then I felt a jolt beneath me and a violent shaking as the wheel shuddered to a stop. My arms were shaking so badly I had to force myself to continue to hold on as I descended the slick rungs toward Tobias. My foot slipped off and I hung off the edge.

"Zara!"

Through sheer will I brought myself up by swinging a leg round and regaining my footing. Clambering down before it started up again. Tobias's hands gripped my waist and lifted me the rest of the way. I knelt, glancing sideways at the large plank of wood shoved into the wheel's central mechanism.

"I hope the bastard gets eaten by Noodle," I screamed.

Tobias reached for my hand. "Now's a really bad time to have a psychotic break."

"He has a tiger," I said. "He calls him Noodle."

Tobias looked horrified as he grabbed my hand and led us toward the entrance of a shadowy hallway where we sheltered.

He reached up to brush a wet strand out of my face. "There you are."

"Do you hate me?"

"You know how much I love adventure."

I tried to focus on the corridor ahead. Electricity and water didn't mix but there was only one way out of here—through those laser beams, if this really was a replica.

"You fucked-up psycho," I yelled.

"We've already established that." Tobias gestured for us to crawl. "Still, it doesn't hurt to remind him."

The tile was cold against my chest and now and again I glanced up, terrified of being electrocuted. My limbs weakened with exhaustion.

"You're doing great," said Tobias.

My arms ached from the strain of pulling myself along. "I never want to see another piece of modern art." Racking my brain, I tried to recall what came after this from what I'd seen at The Broad.

When we were through, we climbed to our feet and I followed Tobias cautiously into another room. In the middle of the floor was a circle etched into the stone. This design was a replica of the *Vitruvian Man*, a copy of the drawing by Leonardo da Vinci of his interpretation of the human form with another man's image behind it, his arms and legs wider to meet the circle they were framed in. Outside of this in a large circumference were other smaller circles and they looked movable.

"I don't remember this," I said.

Tobias knelt to examine it.

Kneeling beside him, my fingers wrapped around the jutting out circle. "Is it a key?"

He went over to the wall and ran his palms over the rough-looking surface. "Maybe."

"Is this meant to represent man taking control of his destiny?"

"Man at the center of his universe. Or at least Eli believes he is." He reached out for the dial and his fingers fixed into the grooves.

I gave a nod; I was ready for what came next and watched him turn it. A grating noise filled the space and the ground beneath us shifted. We stared at each other as we descended, crouching low as the ceiling rose higher. Tobias wrapped me in his arms and hugged me and I buried my face in the crook of his neck.

We descended into the earth.

"We're getting out of here," he soothed.

I gave a nod and tried to fathom Eli's cruelty. With a jolt we stilled and from here we could see an endless underground pipe probably destined to carry water; but not yet, thank goodness.

"It's not finished," said Tobias.

There, laying on the ground was a thick steel door waiting to be assembled and fitted. We walked the few steps toward a large space where it was yet to be inserted. We went on through. We were standing in an enormous hangar. Here and there were large mounds covered in gray tarp.

"Do you think my paintings are here?" I whispered.

"Let's see."

We headed toward one of the tarps and Tobias lifted the bottom and gave a pull. A few more tugs and he had the cover partially off, revealing a crate. He snapped the lid open. Inside glinted bars of gold.

"Shit," he said.

If all these mountains of tarp contained gold there could be billions here.

"We have to get out of here." He grabbed my hand and pulled me out of the hangar toward the pipe.

"This entire place is the safe." I held his hand tighter. "Had you come here when they'd finished construction—"

"I'd have been trapped in here." He pulled me into him. "Zara, you saved my life."

It was all too much to process. We hurried through the pipe, our breaths echoing, our backs arched as we ran through toward the unknown, with the suffocating heat bearing down on us as we made our way along.

A burst of light shone ahead and we stopped to study the fifty-foot-high shaft that led to a brass drain cover. There was a ladder right at the top but it stopped short ten feet away from the drain, revealing this construction beneath ground was new.

"Should we call for help?" I said.

"We don't want to attract the wrong people."

"Keep going, then?"

"Or." He flashed a smile.

Peering at him through the murkiness I tried to understand what he was insinuating. "I can't climb up there."

He pulled back his sleeve and flashed his watch. "We're going to get pulled up."

"What with?"

"My watch. I'm an inventor, Zara. Surely you remember that?" He stretched his arm out and stared up as though judging the distance. "We'll rise together. Climb onto the ladder and hope the grate moves."

"Why didn't you use it before?"

"It needs to hook through. Otherwise it won't hold. It's designed for air condition vents, that kind of thing."

"Do you have anything else you're going to whip out at a moment's notice?"

He smirked as he unclipped his watch and slid it off his wrist and then gripped it like a handle.

This was insane.

But so freakin' awesome if it works.

He wrapped his arm around my waist and I felt the strong pull of his hold against his chest. I held on tight. Tobias raised his arm and aimed it upward and pressed a small dial on the side with his thumb. An almost invisible filament line shot out of the watch, and there came a clang as it hooked into the metal grooves.

He tested it with several tugs. "Ready?"

"As I'll ever be."

"Here we go." He pressed his thumb to the side of his watch again—

We were reeled upward fast with a whirring from the line rewinding back into his watch. Jaw taut, terrified of falling, I held him tightly with gravity threatening to pull me down. My eyes squeezed shut until we came to a stop and I reached out for the metal rung of a ladder and hoisted myself over. Tobias rose higher and swung to climb onto it above me. He reached up, unhooked the rest of line from the grate and it wound back into his watch. He strapped it back onto his wrist. With a heave, Tobias tried to shove the grate aside but it wouldn't give.

He gave another thrust.

The fixture lifted and dirt fell as he shoved it away from the hole. He hoisted himself through and I climbed the ladder and reached up for his hand. He yanked me up.

We collapsed, exhausted, on a grassy bank, quiet and still and panting our relief. We'd come out in the middle of wide-open greenery and looming in the distance was the mansion. I imagined the wedding reception was still going on inside. Eli had probably returned to rejoin the guests acting all nonchalant that he hadn't just sent two people to their deaths.

Tobias spoke into his watch. "Jade, send Marshall our coordinates and tell him to come get us." And on my frown, he added, "There was no signal down there."

I glanced around nervously.

"God, it's hot," he said.

"I didn't get the proof I came for." I turned to look at him, feeling miserable.

Tobias grinned.

"What did you do?"

"Placed Christie's GPS behind the Rembrandt."

I breathed a sigh of relief and then remembered. "Do you think Eli recognized you?"

He pushed himself to his feet and offered me his hand. "I hacked into their security system and deleted the files. So, we'll see."

They moved in similar circles and Tobias was a public figure so there was such a big chance he'd remember him at some point. I covered my face with my hands when I thought of it.

"Eli is easy to keep track of, Zara. If he comes near either of us I'll know."

"What if he sends someone else?"

The sound of helicopter propellers loomed overhead.

Tobias shielded his eyes from the brightness. "Here's our ride."

22

Warmth from the bathtub finally defrosted my aching limbs and the scent of vanilla rose with the steam to lift that musty trace of stale water. Cupping my face with my hands, I couldn't help reliving the moment I'd emerged on my legs and arms from where I'd rolled out of the tank, and my body still trembled. Only a few hours had passed since our escape and midnight loomed; I was so damn happy to be safe in Tobias's Malibu home.

The dreamy ocean view from the window failed to take my mind off the danger I'd put us in and these terrifying thoughts replayed to remind me how badly it could have gone. All I wanted was for someone to tell me it was over and there'd be no repercussions. If Eli knew who I was and had any suspicion why I was there, my paintings would be moved. He'd probably move them anyway. I'd screwed everything up. Yet Tobias had only exuded kindness.

My fingers grasped the 3-carat emerald that was now mine.

Even though I wanted to believe the Burells didn't know it had been Tobias Wilder they'd captured in their death trap, something had triggered Eli's aggression toward us. He was his father's son.

We'd lifted off their estate in a helicopter, peering down through the window at that sweeping statement of power with a sense this wasn't over. Marshall had flown us to the airport where Tobias's private jet had been fueled and ready.

Snuggling beside him during the flight back to LA, he'd done everything he could to comfort me; *I have resources to protect us*, he'd reassured me.

I found no comfort in his words, I was filled with guilt for what I'd bought on us.

From here I could see Tobias's yacht, and I remembered him reading poetry to me on that luxury boat.

I'd been too scared to trust our relationship then and even after everything there still came a lingering apprehension. A gut feeling not everything was as it seemed; as though a fault line ran in his provenance too.

The door opened—

Tobias strolled in and sat on the edge of the bath. "Feeling better?"

Peering up at his beautiful face, I gave my bravest smile. All I had to do was hold his green gaze and those dark shadows in my mind were pushed away. He looked relaxed in his jeans and T-shirt and it made me smile to see him barefoot.

"Someone wants to say hello." He gestured to the door.

"Hand me a towel."

"Why?"

My stare snapped to the door. In floated the drone carrying two glasses of champagne balanced on top.

He gave a mischievous grin. "Why, thank you, Jade, how thoughtful of you."

The drone hovered low and I reached out and took one of the glasses. "Thank you, Jade."

"She likes you."

"Am I getting my access back, then?"

"Hell no." He reached for the other glass. "That's the last thing we need. Right, Jade?"

The drone hovered in place.

"Stop staring, Jade," he said as he watched it levitate in place. "I know she's beautiful. I'm serious. It's getting kind of weird. Hover along now. Go do whatever it is you do."

I burst out laughing and watched Jade head out of the door.

"Don't forget the laundry." He rolled his eyes.

"Now that would be wonderful."

"How are you feeling?" he said. "I mean really?"

"I'm glad we're home."

He dipped his hand into the water. "I might get in."

"You wouldn't like it in here. It's warm and cozy and I'm completely naked beneath these bubbles."

He scraped his teeth over his bottom lip. "Let's toast to us."

I rested my head back on the edge and took a few sips of champagne and it tasted light and refreshing.

Tobias raised his glass. "To a successful mission."

I sat up and water whooshed around me.

"A search warrant has been granted," he said. "The feds are going in."

"How do you know?"

"I know."

"They're following the tracker to the Rembrandt?"

He nodded. "If your paintings are there they'll find them."

"You don't think they might have moved them?"

"There's no indication of that from the footage recorded by the satellite."

"Did you hack into the FBI's database?"

"There's more than one satellite in the sky, Zara."

I blinked at him, wondering if this was his way of telling me he had a bloody satellite orbiting the earth.

He set his glass down on the edge and leaned over for the sponge. "Lean back." Tobias brushed it over my throat and chest in gentle sweeps. "I'm not like them," he whispered.

"I know."

"That's what I needed to hear."

"And I need to hear you've reconsidered the other heist you're planning."

He broke my gaze.

I shoved the sponge away. "If I lose you—"

"You won't."

"Don't do this to me. Not after everything we've been through."

"I'm going to give you what you're asking. You and me—" His gaze swept up to the window and out across the horizon. "We deserve our happy-ever-after."

But will it be one together?

"Please, Tobias."

He circled the sponge over my breasts, his dark gaze following his hand as he trailed it downward over my belly and settling between my thighs where he caressed my sex, causing ripples of pleasure.

After dropping the sponge into the water, he stepped back and undressed and all the while I sipped my drink and savored the beauty of him.

"You were very brave, Zara." He climbed in behind me and sank into the tub, stretching his legs out either side of mine. "You did what no one else dared to do. You took on one of America's most powerful families."

"Putting us in danger."

He kissed my shoulder. "The consequences of being a hero."

"I can't believe it."

"Now you see what I see. A woman who doesn't compromise."

"I'm glad we're out of that maze."

"Me too."

"Elliot's granddaughter's veil was woven by orb spiders."

"Who told you that?"

"Eli."

"That's fucked up."

"I know. She looked sad too. On her wedding day, I mean. I wanted to rescue her." I turned to look at him. "Thank you for coming to find me. I'm not sure what would have happened... Eli was getting aggressive."

"I'll have to go back and kill him, won't I."

"Don't you dare. I never want to hear that name again."

"I feel the same way."

"I'm glad you stole the Titian from them for Sarah Ramirez."

"Allegedly."

I dug my elbow into his thigh.

"I'm not the only one who likes adventures, apparently." He kissed my shoulder.

"Gabe wants me to give a talk to his class before I leave for London tomorrow." Then I realized it was just after midnight now. "Today. Before I catch my plane out tonight."

Leaving here felt wrong. As though so much was unsaid and, even more than this, so much was still to be resolved.

"That would be wonderful for his students," he said softly.

"What can I possibly teach them?"

"You have a gift, Zara, a unique way of seeing the truth. I hope you told him yes."

"I told him I'd think about it."

"Why don't you stay a little longer? I'll tell Huntly Pierre I have another painting I need you to authenticate."

I slipped into a smile but he couldn't see it.

"Zara?"

I let the suspense linger in a naughty tease staring ahead, knowing he was asking me the impossible but so glad he wanted this too. "My career is important to me."

"I know." He lifted the hair from my nape and kissed me there. "Be happy. That's all that matters."

I turned to look at him. "Will you visit me in London?"

"Maybe I'll fly back with you. Would you like that?"

"I'd love it."

He smiled. "We need more champagne."

"Can we go out on your boat later?"

Alone with him in the middle of the ocean I could deliver my final plea.

He tucked a lose strand of hair behind my ear. "I can't."

A chill washed over me.

"Are you okay?" He'd read my sudden panic.

"It's today isn't it?" Dread settled in my gut. "Your heist?"

He hesitated and slowly, his stare held mine.

"At least tell me where?" I whispered. "I need to know."

"Meet me afterward. In West Hollywood. Perhaps I'll fly back to London with you."

There was his confession that this was really happening. Icon was striking again and here I was with full knowledge of this and yet my heart told me to let it be. I was out of my mind, I mean, I'd come all this way to stop him and yet here I was sipping champagne and soaking in the tub with him and arranging to meet him *afterward*.

When it was done.

"Zara," he whispered. "I'm in love with you."

And I was drunk in love with him—I turned around to face him and water whooshed around us.

Taking him in my mouth, I suckled, lavishing my tongue over his head and lapping the edge of his tip until he thickened against my lips. I continued to shower affection over him with each stroke, each tender kiss. I delighted in his moans and the way his hips edged me on to take more of him.

This was the only way I could reach him and even now with kisses and licks, I pleaded with him to not do this and to see how good we were and see reason.

Even after all this time I was in awe of his raw masculine beauty and the way his chiseled features reflected those hard edges that softened when he looked at me, like he was doing now. His eyes sparkled with lust and love and adoration.

Would I ever be able to reach him? Could we find our way through the chaos and prove to each other we were real?

Tobias's strong arms grabbed my shoulders and he dragged me up toward him and along his chest until our bodies aligned and my thighs spread either side of his as he thrusted deep inside me and broke loose with passion. His lips fought mine for dominance as though possessing me was all that mattered and we were wild and splashing and uncaring as we savaged each other. Water spilled over the edge as we chased after the high of coming. When we fell, it was together, our bodies shuddering out our pleasure.

Lying on his chest and listening to the steady beat of his heart, I whispered, "I am yours completely."

He squeezed his brows together.

I raised my head to look at him. "Toby?"

"I didn't know it could be like this."

"Like this?"

He reached down and played with the emerald hanging

from the delicate chain around my neck. "They would have loved you."

I let out a sigh of wonder that he was talking about his parents.

23

"Art is a doorway to another realm." I flicked the handheld controller to fill the screen behind me and up came a photo of Mark Rothko's *Untitled 1970*, a final piece now hanging in the Municipal Museum in The Hague. A gorgeous bloodred canvas considered a portent to his final days. "Rothko painted this right before he committed suicide," I told them.

Fascination reflected in the eyes of Gabe's students, all of them listening intently as I shared with them the profound talent of this Russian American painter. One by one I'd showcased each of his masterpieces to reveal how his work had evolved over his lifetime.

"Rothko wanted us to know that through art we transcend this world and therefore connect with infinity."

The hushed reverence continued to prove their respect for this genius's craftsmanship and I glanced over toward Gabe who was sitting in the front row, his smile reflecting pride for the way I was captivating them.

His students were soaking in the wonder of Rothko just as I had once done.

This morning, I'd left Tobias at his Malibu home and it

had it been one of the hardest things I'd ever done. Marshall had driven me back to the Sofitel in the Rolls.

I felt so alone.

I'd failed to reach the man I loved and as I stared up at the red canvas of that beautiful painting I found myself relating to Rothko's exultant palette as he'd seemingly faced his fate so bravely. I drew strength from his art.

Back in the Sofitel I'd found the Tiffany watch I'd left behind before leaving for Arizona, and now I circled my fingers around the band drawing strength from this symbol of our closeness.

"Rothko strived to reach us through his work," I continued. "He wanted to provide a clarity that we could connect with, a similar bond that connects us all and a humanness that goes beyond the physical." I turned to face them. "What can art teach us about life? About ourselves? Only you can answer these questions."

I saw that familiar hope I'd once carried like a shield that would ward off life's pain. An illusion that I could survive solely on my own that dissolved with each step I took toward maturity. We needed each other. We needed love.

"Art is not for the few or the privileged or the merely wealthy. It is yours to make your own. It is a lighthouse in the stormy ocean of life and a pathway to free expression of the soul, leading to your birthright of finding your own personal bliss and living the life you were destined for."

I ended with a bright smile and expressed gratitude to them for listening and thanked Gabe for inviting me to UCLA.

"Do you have a favorite painting?" a young student piped up.

"There is one that holds a special place in my heart," I said. "Walter William Ouless's *St. Joan of Arc.* Her faith inspired me when I needed it the most. She serves as a great role model for believing in yourself and going beyond what you think you are capable of."

"Wasn't she burned at the stake?" another student asked.

"Joan dedicated her life for what she believed in. This is the greatest purpose. She lives on in those who fight for justice."

I was that small child tiptoeing past her frame in my old Kensington home and only now do I feel worthy of her.

The Wilder gallery would be her final home.

My gaze swept over the students as they rose to their feet and emptied out of the lecture theater.

At the back of the classroom a familiar face came into view; Abby Reynolds was standing just inside the door. I wondered how long she'd been listening.

What was she doing in LA?

This morning I'd called her cell and reassured her I was flying back to London tonight on the red-eye. Our conversation had been pleasant enough with no mention of her joining me out here. The timeline revealed she'd already been on her way to the States.

"You were wonderful," said Gabe, recapturing my attention as he hugged me.

"Your students are so engaging," I told him, having gotten just as much out of this as they had and it felt invigorating.

"You were always great at inspiring others to see art in a new way," he said.

"Thank you for inviting me."

He stared up toward Abby. "You know her?"

"She's from Huntly Pierre."

"Really?" He threw her a wave.

Abby began the descent down the stairs toward us.

"I have another class," Gabe said. "You and Tobias are invited to our pumpkin-carving party tonight."

"We won't be able to make it. But thank you."

By then it would be all over and we'd have something to celebrate and I'd want Tobias all to myself.

"You're flying out at midnight, right?" he said. "Have a great flight home and we'll see you soon."

"Thank you for all your kindness, Gabe. You've made my visit so special."

"Thank Tobias for inviting me to The Wilder." He pulled me in for a hug. "I'm in awe of your man, Zara."

"Me too, he makes quite the impression, doesn't he."

This was the last time Icon would make history. Or so he'd promised, and I clung to his vow to put his dangerous pursuits behind him. I couldn't wait to be in his arms again and for this to be over. Until I saw him there'd be this unsettling anxiety of knowing his future was in jeopardy.

Gabe headed off to his next class and I felt the drag of uneasiness watching him go. I greeted Abby halfway across the stage and we hugged warmly. She was holding a beige folder secured by a blue band.

"What a surprise." I feigned seeing her wasn't unnerving. "You didn't mention coming here?"

"I'm glad your lecture went well," she said. "Told you it would."

Yes, but I'd not expected her to appear at the end of it.

"You'd make a great teacher, Zara. You're passionate about art."

"You too, Abby. Your perspective is remarkable." My guilt rose that I knew so very much and was holding back the greatest intelligence of all. "What bought you here?"

"Let's sit." She gestured to the front row.

We took our seats and faced each other.

She leaned forward. "We have a new break in the Icon case."

A chill shuddered through me. "Well, that's great."

"Yesterday, the feds raided a home in Scottsdale, Arizona. The residence of Elliot Burell. They found a billion dollars of gold bullion stashed underground." She flicked open the folder and showed me a photo of the giant wheel. The men standing before it provided a sense of its actual size. "What do you make of this?" Her stare rose to meet mine.

"Where was it taken?"

"Burell's home. Have you ever seen this before?"

I caressed my lips; my fingers hid my frown as I shook my head *no*.

"Sure?"

"Why?"

"This was part of an underground mechanism guarding their safe."

"Looks complicated. Kind of whacky, really."

"They had a lot to hide." She reached out and squeezed my hand. "They discovered something extraordinary."

"What led them to search the house?"

"You didn't ask what that thing is."

A chill ran through me at her coldness. "What was it?"

"The GPS tracker that was placed on Walter William Ouless's *St. Joan* was found on another painting."

"Oh?"

"Rembrandt's *The Storm on the Sea of Galilee*."

"That's fantastic." I studied her face carefully. "What an incredible find."

"This is why I need you sitting down."

My mouth went dry with what was coming next.

"Elliot Burell was in possession of thirty Old Masters. We believe this collection once belonged to your father."

My hand slapped to my mouth to suppress a cry of relief.

She gave a warm smile of understanding. "Looks like your

dad's paintings were stolen, switched out for fakes and then your house burned to the ground to hide the fact."

My lips trembled with the realization this was over.

"This is groundbreaking," she said. "The provenance is on record at Christie's and your ownership looks solid. Adley knew your dad and has promised to smooth the transition for you. You have the company at your full disposal to see this through. I wanted to tell you in person."

"I don't know what to say."

"We're thrilled for you. Seriously, everyone at Huntly Pierre couldn't be happier. Some legalese to cut through. You know how it goes."

"You've all been so kind. Supporting me with *St. Joan* miraculously turning up at Christie's."

"It was miraculous, wasn't it?" Her frowned deepened. "I have a question for you."

"Yes."

"What were you doing at Elliot Burell's granddaughter's wedding?"

Steadying my gaze on hers I held my calm focus.

She reached into the folder and removed another photo. It was blurry, but there I was captured sitting at the back of the venue right before I'd disappeared inside the house.

"You weren't on the guest list?" she added.

"Last-minute invite."

"The truth, please." She stared at me for the longest time and then said, "Zara, I know."

Silence served as my response and my heart rate took off; I hoped my pounding carotid wouldn't give away my panic.

"I want the truth about you and Icon," she said.

Blood rushed from my face. "I have no idea what you're talking about. I'm coming back to London—"

She grabbed my wrist. "You hired Icon to find your father's

paintings. Only Icon could pull this off. Only he could get into the Burells' mansion and attach the GPS to the Rembrandt. He led the feds to your father's paintings. There were too many of them for one man to carry out. He got the authorities to do the work. A stroke of genius, wouldn't you agree?"

My brain ran through the appropriate body language to reflect innocence.

"What did you give Icon in return, Zara?" she said. "His freedom?"

"You're wrong, Abby. I went to the Burells' because I believed they had *St. Joan.* I had questions."

"You put yourself in grave danger."

"I know I messed up." My gaze fell onto the photo of me again.

"What did you discover?"

"I left with nothing. No answers. No paintings."

"What aren't you telling me?"

"You know me. You know I would never hire a thief."

"You believe you owe Icon. But you don't. You're right to call him a thief because that's what he is. Now I am going to ask you one more time, how did you find him?"

"Seriously?"

"What's his name? How can we find him?"

"If I found Icon my career would be made."

"Those paintings are awfully important to you."

"They were lost in the Kensington fire. Until now that's what I believed. Every day of my life I've had to live with that." I forced a smile. "What you've just told me is overwhelming. I need time to process it."

"It's too much of a coincidence that you were seen at the Burells' estate and soon afterward there was a groundbreaking discovery in that very home. One that you're connected to, Zara. What is going on?"

"I'm innocent."

"You're scared of them, aren't you?"

"The Burells? Of course I'm wary of that family. They're evil. We discovered this from Sarah Ramirez's case."

"And what connects the cases is Icon, along with the house fires started by someone in the Burell family." She gave a nod. "Icon stole *St. Joan* from Christie's. He knows you exist. Has he been in touch with you?"

None of this was provable. I went with silence.

"It's the same MO," she added. "You see this, right?"

"Whatever you need from me, Abby, just ask. I want this resolved just as much as you."

She let out a frustrated sigh. "What are your plans for the paintings?"

I wanted to say give them to the people but right there I'd be replicating Icon's motivation. Simply, I answered with, "Let's see if they're authentic. I don't want to get my hopes up."

She gave a nod of resignation. "I've always liked you. You're kind. Don't let anyone take advantage of that. Icon cannot be trusted. You know this. These things never end well."

"The old me might have trusted once."

"What changed?"

My thoughts carried me back to Jean-Jacques Henner's 1879 *Madame Paul Duchesne-Fournet*, her strength, her honor and her expression holding a quiet sense of justice. Madame Paul emanated a serenity that leant itself to her eternal secrets never to be revealed.

My gaze turned to where I'd been standing during the lecture. "Art showed me the way."

Abby rose to her feet and gave a comforting smile. "You're in love with him?"

I managed a polite smile. "With who?"

"Before I came here I visited The Wilder Museum."

There came a change in the air; a shift in her demeanor. She gave a nod. "I find it intriguing that Mr. Wilder had Walter William Ouless's *St. Joan* hanging in his office for a while. According to Maria Perez, his senior curator, he was in possession of stolen property and didn't report it. Doesn't that sound strange to you?"

"He asked me to authenticate it." I didn't miss a beat.

"And?"

"A fake. Wasn't worth mentioning. Maria was confused because it looked authentic."

"How did he come to have a fake that he suspected was real?"

"I don't know the details."

"You didn't ask?"

I cringed inwardly at how badly this was going.

"Let's hope your *St. Joan* turns up," she said. "What a tale she'd tell if she could talk." Abby strolled toward the stairs and turned slowly to face me. "Oh, one more thing?"

I pushed myself to my feet. "Yes?"

She held my stare for what felt like a full minute. "What happened to you and your dad, I'm glad it's been righted. Those paintings are quite the find and from what I understand lives were lost trying to protect them back in Russia."

"If they're real."

She tucked the folder beneath her arm and seemed to consider that. "The profile for Icon is compelling. Wouldn't you agree? To me he's enigmatic. That's what I imagine when I think of him."

Those telltale tingles of doubt rushed into my solar plexus.

"He's super smart," she continued, "extremely fit and has the financial means to move around the world with ease. Maybe he owns a private jet. Confident enough to believe he'd get away with it. Someone who loves art and understands its worth. Has the means to move it around the world without too much attention. An art dealer, maybe? Art collector. Super wealthy. Someone with a cross to bear."

"A cross to bear?"

"Terrible thing the Burells did. Don't you think?"

"How do you mean?"

"They're bullies, so they did everything to close the case. Saw the investigation dropped from court. The evidence sealed. But all the evidence was there according to the records. I got to peek at them. Off the record, that is."

"What happened to Sarah Ramirez was dreadful."

"She wasn't the only victim of theirs. Nor were you." Her eyes softened. "Elliot Burell brought down Tobias's parents' plane. Or so his uncle's lawyers accused."

My jaw tensed painfully. "In Australia?"

That dreadful crash only he'd survived.

"You two have never talked about it?" she asked. "Never discussed how they were blamed for sabotaging the fuselage? Wilder was in bad shape when they eventually found him. It's a miracle he even survived."

My body froze, gripped with terror, my expression refusing to show emotion. She gave a knowing nod, the kind that screamed she'd found a motive for Icon.

"During the Christie's theft, Tobias was with me." I gave a thin smile. "If that helps."

"We have nothing on Wilder. Yet."

"I'll see you later, then?"

"Can you stay in town for one more day? We may need you."

"Sure."

"Where are you staying?"

I took a second to reply. "The Sofitel."

"I'm here for you, remember that, Zara." She headed back up the stairs.

I waited until she'd left the lecture hall and then slumped back in a chair. Now it all made sense, Icon was revenging his parents' death. He also felt compelled to right the wrongs of other victims of art thefts. With this final heist he was fulfilling a promise he shouldn't have made; pain clouded his judgment. My heart ached for what he'd been through and all he'd kept from me.

Though now, dread chilled my blood that the spotlight had turned on me.

24

You don't choose love—

Love chooses you. I believed this now with my entire being as I waited for Tobias outside the hotel Sunset Marquis, in West Hollywood. All I wanted and cared about was *him*. How ironic that I'd become one of the victims consoled by Icon himself.

Tobias had silently carried the burden of what the Burells had done to his family and I suspected he'd tried to protect me from this. I felt dreadful guilt that it had been me who'd led him into the center of the Burells' sinister nest. Perhaps the end of their empire would provide some comfort. An overdue solace for those days he'd fought for survival as a nine-year-old in the outback.

Now more than ever I understood what had driven his actions, and I wanted to believe this once reckless path he'd trodden was over. He knew that only with this life behind him could there ever be an *us*. I needed more than mere words of reassurance from him. I needed proof he meant everything he'd promised.

We'd arranged to meet here but as the Halloween parade

surged by, I wondered how I'd ever find him amongst all these people. There were so many men and women and all of them had dressed in costumes, from monsters to movie stars, caricatures of politicians to princesses, and I stood out having merely dressed in my little black dress he'd bought me from Versace and delicate heels.

Abby's words haunted me from our meeting in the lecture hall and I'd called to warn him there was a chance either of us could be followed. Wilder told me it was fine and he wanted to meet anyway.

So here I was searching each face in the crowd and hoping to see him any second, needing to talk this through and beg his forgiveness for the danger I'd put him in, not just now but back in Arizona.

My anxiety grew more intense when I checked my watch for the hundredth time and saw Tobias was ten minutes late. My stomach churned because this was so unlike him. My thoughts circled along with this swirling fear that something had gone wrong. What if this time he didn't make it? What if he was injured? Or caught?

No, don't do this to yourself.

Caressing my chest to ease this dread that was fast becoming unbearable, I hated myself for failing Tobias, not forcing him to explain why this one was so important, why he couldn't just let the victim face their fate and live without whatever it was they wanted him to steal for them. Surely, they knew the danger they were putting him in and the threat to his life.

Despite wanting those paintings from my past returned to me, I would never have placed Tobias in danger to get them back. Art was there to enhance life and not the other way around. How much more did I believe this now after everything.

So much time had been spent self-exploring what would make me happy and my conclusion always came back to a sense of safety that had returned to me for the first time since that dreadful night of the Kensington fire. Tobias had made everything right again. Still, I remained guarded and questioned if my selfish desire to see my artwork returned to me was clouding my judgment. Was the biggest lie here the one I was telling myself? Everything I'd once believed was turned on its head and I'd stood by knowing Wilder was executing a plan that was my job to stop from happening.

Perhaps staying here now was insane, and yet my heart begged me to stay because seeing him again was like finding light in the darkness.

It was the grand Native American Indian chief headdress I saw first with its pure white feathers cascading all the way down his back. Tobias walked leisurely within a sea of people and they respectfully parted for the tall and handsome man strolling through them. He looked ridiculously gorgeous in his costume of hair pipe breastplate, beige trousers and a quilted knife sheath on his hip. His outfit reflected the proud stature of an American Indian chief.

I melted all over again as this vision of masculine beauty strolled toward me with the commanding stride of a man who still intimidated a little with the power he exuded.

He saw me and beamed my way and I smiled back. My look of concern served as a silent question asking him if it was done. He gave a subtle nod to tell me it was and those feathers ruffled in the breeze.

It's over.

He stepped close and he gave me a comforting smile.

Regret for taking such a risk welled. "Tobias, they might have followed us."

"They have nothing." His gaze swept over me. "Yet I have everything."

"Listen to me, Abby..." I became self-conscious others may overhear.

"We'll talk later."

"She's asked me to delay my flight a day."

"Well good, we can revisit The Wilder tomorrow and you can get to see the Qin Terra-Cotta Army again."

I held back on my frustrated sigh, not wanting to ruin his moment. After all, this was a big step for him and was hopefully the end of Icon. The end of an era.

He gestured to his outfit. "What do you think?"

"Very dashing."

"Where's yours?"

I raised my chin high. "I'm dressed as an art specialist. Comfy shoes and all."

He laughed and reached around my back and dipped me, his mouth looming close to mine, and this display of affection mirrored the time he'd held me like this in The Broad, all the way to the time I'd secretly ached for him.

No games. No secrets. Just us.

"Tell me you want me?" His lips brushed mine.

"I want you."

His smile moved over my lips. "Tell me you need me."

"I need you."

"Tell me you—"

"I love you."

"Maybe I wasn't going to ask you that?"

"What were you going to ask me, then?"

"Tell me you're mine."

Joy surged through me and my legs trembled and almost gave way but he was holding me so firmly he'd catch me. He kissed me and his lips were gentle and then fierce, capturing my mouth with his, his tongue swirling mine, dancing in that familiar way that was both comforting and dominating at the same time, loving and protective.

He broke away and lifted me upright. "Want to come with me?" he said. "I know you're intrigued."

I fell against Tobias's side not wanting to part after all I'd endured while waiting for him for so long, hugging him tight and hoping I could somehow soothe the pain he'd hidden from me all this time. Someone was going to experience the peace that came with the righteousness he brought them. I knew that much, even though these conflicted feelings wouldn't leave. He led me back into the crowd and we disappeared amongst them.

A little way along the street he flicked his key fob and a silver Jaguar's rear lights flashed on and off. Standing beside him I watched Tobias carefully place the headdress into a custom-made box and it was seemingly crafted to hold a sacred artifact of this size and shape. Had he just stolen this and blatantly strolled through a crowd wearing it? What about photographs? A record of him in the vicinity? Surely Tobias wasn't that reckless. Seriously, how important was this headdress to whomever had lost it? The reward was never going to match the risk he'd taken.

Tobias opened the passenger door for me and I climbed in and he strolled around to the other side and got in. He drove us out of the town affectionately known as WeHo. After ten minutes I realized we were heading back into the city. Skyscrapers loomed large as the Jaguar weaved in and out of traffic.

Could we be headed to see Waya?

A jolt of adrenaline surged through my veins when I remembered their interaction, a moment when a private conversation had passed between them so discreetly I'd almost missed it.

Tobias blared music by John Legend out of his speakers, and he seemed amazingly relaxed for someone who'd just carried out a heist. He didn't even seem concerned after I'd warned him Abby was in LA and told him what we'd discussed at UCLA.

"She suspects I hired you," I told him.

He reached for my hand and brought it to his lips to kiss my wrist. "A theory that is untrue and therefore could never be proven."

This, this was madness because all they had to do was pull us over and they'd find that stolen item in his boot.

Reaching out, I played with the whispers of his hair at his nape, not quite ready to talk to him about his parents' plane. Not yet, he was too relaxed, and something told me his giving up this life had given him the sense of freedom that he'd possibly chased after.

All we had to do was make it to our destination and drop off the headdress. I mean, only a few days ago, we'd been followed by a BMW. What was to say we weren't being followed now? After easing down my sun visor I used it to scan for cars that might be tailing us.

The Wilder Tower rose into view and there, jutting out from the penthouse at the top of the building, was that crazy swimming pool. Tobias navigated the car into the subterranean parking garage and pulled into his VIP spot. He lifted out the box with the headdress inside and carried it with us to the elevator. He leaned it against the wall and hugged me as we ascended. The lift stopped on the second-to-highest level.

There was only one other suite that took up this entire floor and it belonged to Waya Hunter and his father. My gut feeling had been right. I wondered how they'd react when they saw him dressed up in their native dress. I hope Waya's dad wasn't offended.

Still, it made total sense that the headdress was for them. Tobias had told me what he was stealing would help restore faith that had been lost during a devastating historical event. I couldn't get my head around the fact he'd risked everything for a headdress for one man.

We were expected.

And so was the headdress because Waya accepted the box without batting an eyelid and carried it over to the dining room table. He rested his hand on it and closed his eyes in reverence.

Tobias and I stood back a little and remained quiet, understanding the sacred representation of the pride of a chief of men who'd once worn it. My thoughts swirled with whom Tobias had stolen this from and how they'd react when they found it missing. If a police report was filed and an investigation initiated then perhaps photos of Tobias wearing the thing in a Halloween parade would place him squarely at the scene.

But he always went after stolen property, I silently mused, and he always seemed to think everything through.

Waya turned to face us and took in what Tobias was wearing. "Looks good on you, Wilder."

"I think so too," he said. "Are you going to open it?"

"That should be my father's honor."

"Mr. Wilder," came a commanding voice.

We turned to see Waya's father in a doorway looking back at us, his features similar to Waya's, a little shorter in height maybe and heavier in build. But the eyes were the same, the knowing smile from a life well lived with all its joys and sorrows, those deep etched lines highlighting a handsome man proud of his heritage. He wore a dark suit and it made me wonder if he'd dressed up especially for this.

"How are you?" he asked Tobias.

"I'm well, sir, you?" he replied, and I could see the respect in his eyes. "May I introduce Zara Leighton, my girlfriend. Zara, this is my good friend Delsin."

"Lovely to meet you, Zara," he said. "You've met my son Waya, I believe?"

"Yes, I've had the real pleasure." I recalled Waya telling me Tobias was like a son to his father and now I could see Tobias had found a father in Delsin too.

Delsin looked at Tobias and gave a shrug. "We asked too much of you. Don't be hard on yourself. It was an impossible task. Tea anyone? Coffee? How about something stronger?"

Tobias smiled and turned toward the table and watched Delsin's reaction. Delsin looked astonished and his gaze shot back to Tobias as though for confirmation. He made his way toward the table and eased open the lid and stared down at the headdress before reaching in to sweep his hand over the feathers. Quiet descended on the room as Delsin took a few minutes to ponder. "We're running out of time," he whispered. "The pipeline's protesters are being threatened with legal action. They can't hold out for much longer."

Tobias stepped toward him. "I promised I'd get it for you."

Delsin's expression was filled with hope. "We will owe you a debt we will never be able to pay."

"I don't want anything," said Tobias.

Delsin gestured to the headdress. "We want you to have this."

"I can't." Tobias stepped forward. "But if you want to loan it to The Wilder?" He neared Delsin and rested his hand on his back with affection. "That would be wonderful."

Delsin's gaze settled on me. "My son tells me you're an art specialist?"

"She can spot a fake a mile away," said Tobias.

I wanted to say I was sorry about their painting by Caravaggio but something told me all of this meant more. Much more.

Delsin's gaze held Tobias's as though some unspoken words were passing between them. Tobias slipped his hand behind the breastplate and removed a piece of paper and carefully handed it to him. A crackle of electricity fused between them. It was a look of wonder, that's what I saw in Delsin's expression, a profound relief mixed with awe at what he was holding and he blinked to clear his vision as though doubting what he was seeing. Slowly, he peered up at Tobias.

"Don't ask."

"You're a fox amongst wolves, Wilder," he said, and his face lit up with joy.

I recalled how Toby had once shared how much he loved to paint watercolors of the wild foxes playing in the snow in his English garden. This man was so much more than I'd ever imagined from that first real meeting in his Oxfordshire home, not just a billionaire inventor but someone who was set apart by his sense of justice.

I silently willed his soul to hear my plea: let this be the last one.

Tobias pointed to the piece of paper. "President Ulysses S. Grant's signature. Authentication will be all you need for it to be effective."

"I can see that," agreed Delsin, who swapped a warm smile with his son.

"It was stolen soon after it was signed," Waya told me. "After the entire village was wiped out. What the soldiers had no way of knowing was the chief's son had left earlier that day to go fishing. He carried the memory of this contact."

"One of our ancestors," said Delsin proudly.

And Tobias tracked it down; it sounded like an impossible mission.

"This proves the land is yours," he said. "Present this to Congress and it will stop them from laying the pipeline."

"Who had it?" asked Delsin.

Waya wrapped his arm around his father's shoulders. "We don't ask, Dad. Remember?"

Tobias reached for my hand and winked his reassurance. "Let me know if you need anything else."

"You've done enough." Delsin came over to Tobias and pulled him into a hug. "Son."

I watched Tobias's face in that moment as he became serene; a sense of peace for the man who'd delivered on his promise.

25

It was a conundrum unlike any other.

The world could be a harsh place and yet there was so much goodness too. The profoundness of what Tobias had achieved was remarkable. He'd rectified the devastating actions of history by helping those who'd been wronged by evil men and seen justice for them. Yet society would never see it this way.

We'd left Waya's place a few hours ago, and every moment that unraveled, every word spoken between them, replayed in my mind to reassure me I'd done the right thing in letting it play out.

It was with the heaviest heart I pleaded with Tobias for proof it was over, and he told me he'd give his answer over dinner tonight. First, he had something he wanted to show me, and led me up to the roof of his LA penthouse.

A warm breeze met us when we stepped out and I gasped at the beautiful view of the trailing white lights decorating the entire area. Their illumination fell upon the table in the center with its romantic dinner setting. It looked so pretty with its pristine tablecloth and the neatly presented silverware. Two crystal glasses sat beside a bottle of champagne chilling in a tub of ice.

"We're eating out here?" I was overjoyed.

"Glad you approve." He took my hand and led me farther along.

The view of the surrounding city was spectacular with its modern architecture complementing the older buildings with the thrum of life below.

"This is so beautiful," I said.

"The view is always breathtaking from where I'm standing." He kissed my cheek and turned to enjoy the panorama beside me.

"What must it have been like," I said softly, "to have seen their faces when you returned what they lost."

"There's nothing quite like it," he said.

I turned sharply and peered up at him, realizing the danger.

"It's okay," he said. "I have a sound wall. It blocks surveillance. If they are listening in to our conversation—" he looked out at the surrounding buildings "—their equipment won't pick up a single conversation from the entire tower."

"And that's not suspicious?"

"I'm an inventor and my products are worth billions. I protect my privacy."

I still felt self-conscious at being up here and so exposed. I was going to have to trust Tobias. "I can't get over Delsin's reaction," I said, remembering the reverence.

"The document proves without a doubt that the Dakota land belongs to the tribes. That piece of paper will turn around the construction of what would essentially devastate the earth. Their treaty will be restored. Nature protected."

"That's what you meant by doing the work of the gods?"

"It was a little presumptuous, I suppose."

I looked into his eyes, needing to see he really was ready

to give it up. Even after he'd lived a life believing he did so much good.

He gave a deep sigh. "I had what it took in the way of resources and—"

"Cockiness. Bravery. A splash of arrogance."

"I was just thinking that." He winked at me. "What I can tell you is the view from my perspective was breathtaking. I won't deny it was fun."

I laughed and leaned in for a cuddle. "Tobias?" I whispered.

"I've decided to dedicate more time to art and start tinkering at home. I have a basement ready to be converted into a lab. How would you like to bring me cups of tea while I'm working?"

"I'll be too busy, I'm afraid."

"Oh, no, I fully intend to have you barefoot and ready to service my every need."

"Oh, really?"

"Someone has to keep Jade in check. That drone flies circles around me."

I laughed. "I'm looking forward to getting my access back to her."

"We will see."

"I'm getting used to her."

"I want to whisk you away to a private island. Take a vacation together and forget everything. Just you and me and the ocean?" He turned to look for my answer.

"Yes." I beamed at him.

"We'll plan it, then, for when everything has returned to normal and we are no longer of any interest to anyone."

I squeezed my eyes shut and breathed in all this happiness. "We are moving very fast."

"Do you want me to go slower?" He tipped up my chin. "I can go slower. Wait a week."

"Silly."

"Okay, two."

This was really happening.

Tobias is mine.

"I know what you're thinking," he said.

"What am I thinking?"

"You need proof my adventures are over." He was looking toward a low table tucked in the corner and resting on it
was a pair of three-dimensional glasses.

I smiled. "The answer's there?"

"Yes. Come on." He headed over to it and I followed him
as my gaze swept over the beautiful lights above us and all
around was decorated with a fairy-tale setting.

Tobias's sense of romance was mesmerizing. I loved spending every second with this charismatic man who'd wooed
me so easily. I didn't stand a chance. He'd not really been a
thief, not when he returned the item to its rightful owner,
no, he was a superhero.

I reached up to help him ease the headset over my eyes.
The last time I'd experienced one of his marvelous creations
had been at the LACMA, and I was still reeling from that
daring interactive experience.

The visor cleared—

Inhaling a sharp breath at the view all around us, I absorbed the remarkable image of a multicolored landscape and
it reflected the form of a magical kingdom. Turning slowly,
I took in the peak of the bright green mountain and the village spreading beneath it and there upon a hill was a towering castle.

"It's amazing," I said. "Truly, I've never seen anything
like this."

I heard Tobias step before me into view.

Only, it was a cartoon version of him dressed as a prince

and I slapped my hand to my mouth with the ridiculous charm of it all. He'd dressed his imaginary doppelgänger in blue trousers and a deep black jacket with gold embroidered buttons. Prince Charming gave a low bow and then slid into that familiar adorable smile.

Looking down, I was wearing red slippers and I could see the hem of a billowing blue princess gown and, lifting my arms, I saw long, flowing sleeves.

"Toby." I giggled. "This is so cute."

Prince Toby bowed before me and in his hand he was holding a long black box and he raised it for me to take. I lifted the goggles to see Tobias was standing where the prince was and he had a crazy wide smile, proving how much fun he was having. He was holding the same black box his doppelgänger had presented to me.

Tobias lifted the lid and inside sat a gold plaque with my name inscribed on it. Beneath that was carved the title of Director of The Wilder Museum. He was inviting me to come to LA.

The headset almost fell off and he caught it.

"It's my way of getting to see you every day," he said. "Well?"

I flung my hands around his neck and hugged him, my head fuzzy with happiness at the thought of living here. Tobias kissed me, his lips soft on mine at first and then passionate.

He broke away and looked across the roof. "Hope you got all that?" He was talking to Jade who was hovering a little distance away.

I laughed when I realized Tobias had captured all this on film by having Jade record us.

"We're going to be taking a lot of those, Zara." He strolled over to the dinner table and lifted the dome, revealing a tray of oysters that looked delicious in their half shells.

Still awestruck by this three-dimensional world he'd invented I peeked again and saw the prince was tap dancing now.

"No way." I laughed hysterically.

"Give them here." Tobias reached for the goggles and pulled them over his eyes. "Well that's not embarrassing at all."

"Am I seeing your inner Toby?"

He grinned as he watched through the lenses. "He dances better than me."

With the goggles placed back on their stand and that magical world put on hold, we settled at the table. He pulled his chair next to mine and fed me oysters, and they tasted fresh and salty as though my taste buds had been kissed by the ocean.

"I wouldn't invite you here to LA if I couldn't give you what you want, Zara. You know that, right?"

"It's over?" I said wistfully, "Truly over?"

"I promise." He raised a glass of champagne and tapped it lightly to mine; it clinked.

We also toasted to our future and a life dedicated to the service of others and, most important, we toasted that Icon was now behind him. Reaching out for his hand we sat in silence for a while and stared out at the panoramic view to savor this idyllic setting he'd created.

The evening unfolded with such ease that I lost all track of time, sitting here with Tobias and enjoying his company, his jokes, his charm, and all the while sipping bubbly and secretly thanking God for this man.

My eyes kept falling on that gorgeously engraved gold plaque and Tobias admired it too, smiling every time he saw my reaction to it.

After dinner, I helped him in the kitchen, loading the

plates into the dishwasher and tidying a little. I loved how he enjoyed the normal side of life where he seemed so relaxed.

I made my way over toward the long glass window and looked out at the beautiful sparkling pool and beyond the striking view of the buildings across from his. Sliding the glass door open, I stepped out and breathed in the evening air, gazing upward at the roof where we'd not long ago eaten dinner to celebrate.

The balcony and the pool were bathed in a deep blue florescent light imbuing a sense of serenity. Perhaps it was the champagne I'd finished off an hour ago, or merely the way the pool looked so pretty and inviting, but I could envision me swimming in there now. I was still amazed by the complete privacy provided by the one-way glass surrounding the eclectic design of a jutting-out pool.

Tobias slid the door wider and came out to join me.

"What a day," I said as though we'd been playing house for years.

He kissed my forehead and stepped back, kneeling to dip his hand into the water. "I heated it."

"What makes you think I'm ever getting in?"

"I made a bet with Jade."

I arched a seductive brow and undid the catch on my dress and unzipped it and slid it down over hips, and it pooled around my ankles, leaving me standing before him in black stockings and a sexy garter belt. Tobias looked mesmerized as he drank me in.

I removed my bra and held it out in a seductive pose. "Who bet against me?"

"That would be Jade," he said. "I told her you'd be totally up for it."

"It?"

His beautiful eyes lingering on my breasts and then my sex and then rising to my face. "Making love in the pool."

Those words made my insides quiver with need, and the way he was looking at me with a hard-edged desire was making me wet and my nipples bead with excitement. Teasing him was so much fun.

I slipped out of my shoes and peeled off my stockings. "How much are you hoping to make from Jade?"

"Ten bucks."

"Ten bucks!" I slipped off my thong.

"Okay, twenty."

Laughing, I threw my panties at him and he caught them. I turned to face the pool and dived in and my nakedness felt deliciously naughty. I swam all the way to the bottom and placed my palms on the glass and peered through the murkiness to the vision below.

This was insanity.

Terrifying and scary and oh so brilliant and I couldn't understand why I'd not done this before, looking down at the sheer drop below with adrenaline surging through me.

No, moving to LA was scary, leaving behind everything I'd worked for and all that I'd become. Yet the thought of being apart from Tobias was scarier. Everything about him was addictive and my sex was on fire with need for him. I wanted to drag out every second of my time in his company before I returned to London.

I wanted this moment to last forever.

There was a splash above and I turned to see a naked Tobias swimming toward me. He joined me by my side and mirrored the way I'd looked through the sheer glass. There was something mesmerizing about braving such a view. He flashed a smile through bulging cheeks.

Lungs bursting, I sprang upward all the way to the surface

and within a few breaststrokes I'd made it to the edge and turned around to wait for him. This was remarkable, we were hanging out in midair in nothing but a glass pool.

Tobias burst out of the water and swam closer to sandwich me between his firm body and the tile wall behind me. He flashed one of his megawatt smiles and I melted all over again, reassuring myself I didn't have a chance. This gorgeous man who was looking at me all wide-eyed and carefree was still as beautiful as the first time I saw him. That devastatingly sexy tattoo on his left shoulder promising all kinds of heady passion from a man who knew just how to touch me; setting me alight with kisses and caresses.

I was looking forward to studying the tattoo on his groin again, I silently mused, memorizing each Latin letter that ran along that sensual curve and running my tongue along it too to taste him. All of this was about never forgetting how we began and all that we'd done to get here.

I'd never believed a man like him was possible. A man who had risked his own freedom to right what had happened to my family—

"You're getting your paintings back," he said as though reading my thoughts.

"Thank you for everything."

"Always my pleasure to serve you, Leighton." He gave a devilish smile.

"What other miracles do you have up your sleeve, Mr. Wilder?"

"Just you. You're my number one miracle, Zara Leighton." He leaned forward to whisper in my ear. "You're all I want."

"I've been working on something very special."

"Really?"

"I've invented something."

"I'm assuming you need a test subject?"

"Do you like mermaids?"

He reached out either side of me and gripped the edge. "Who doesn't love a mermaid?"

"It's a complex underwater experiment," I said. "Perhaps it's better for me to demonstrate?"

He brushed his lips over mine. "I fully support your research."

After taking the biggest breath, I used his body to leverage myself downward and held on to his thighs to keep me at his groin, my mouth opening over his cock and suckling, feeling his hardness growing against my lips as I moved my head to draw him in and out along my tongue. Through the water his moan reached me and his body stiffened.

I came up and breathed in gulps of oxygen and dived again, and again and again, until he captured me above the surface and kissed me, his mouth firm against mine, his teeth nipping my lower lip as his cock pressed into my belly.

I tapped the side of the pool to tell him to pull himself up there and he did with biceps curling as he easily lifted to sit on the edge with his legs dangling over in the water and, leaning forward, he played with strands of my hair.

I moved to position myself between his thighs. "That was a huge success."

"I'm on board with getting a patent on your technique."

"How about this one." I ran my tongue along his shaft and lapped around his head with verve. "As you can see the experiment has been extended."

Spreading his thighs apart when I gave him gentle encouragement, I moved in closer and took his balls in my mouth and suckled, glancing up to see his jaw slackening and his hand around his erection fisting himself. It was thrilling to see how much I mesmerized him.

I peeled his hand away and wrapped mine where his had been. "This is mine."

"Are you claiming my cock?"

"Yes, I am. This is where we ascertain how hard you can come."

"Zara, hearing you talk dirty is going to kill me... Oh, Jesus, that's good."

"I'm so wet for you right now." I took him in my mouth again, sex throbbing deliciously as I licked around the head and he felt like iron wrapped in silk as I lapped at the marbled skin; his erection twitched.

He grabbed my hair at the nape and held me there, his firm hand coaxing my movement to go faster and controlling the pace as I took him all the way to the back of my throat, continuing this sensual pace, my body using the water for leverage.

"I'll come if you don't stop," he growled.

Picking up the pace, I worked him powerfully with my mouth and hand in unison to bring him to a blinding climax, tasting his pre-cum and wanting more. That was just it, I always needed more of him, more time in his company, a closeness with this remarkable man, more promised that we had a future together. Perhaps, just perhaps, I'd been the one destined to save him all along.

He threw his head back and yelled his orgasm as his thighs trembled through the pleasure and his body went rigid. He shot his heat down my throat. I exulted at how forcefully he came; his hips pumping and rising off the tile to give me all of him. He collapsed and lay back with his hand over his eyes.

He slid into an easy smile. "Now it's your turn."

"What do you have in mind?"

"I have scuba gear in Malibu. I say we go home and mask up."

26

Tobias's Rothko reigned brilliantly upon the crisp white wall.

I sat before this masterpiece, drawing the kind of calm that reminded me of Wilder himself. This beautiful Rothko of gold, pink, orange and pale blue was one of my favorites of all this artist's work and I bathed in the vibrant brushstrokes that were fast and light. This was the painting Tobias had inherited from his father and it was here, hanging in The Wilder Museum amongst three other canvases of Rothko's, and each had been given their very own wall to adorn. I was sure Rothko himself would have approved.

It meant everything that Tobias had finally felt ready to let his father's painting leave his Malibu home and have it presented here for the public to enjoy. Art was an extension of both artist and owner and sharing such a piece expressed the greatest respect for what his work conveyed.

There was so much pleasure in spending time here and the architecture alone was beautiful to visit. My thoughts carried me back to yesterday's events. Yes, I quietly mused now, I could see me spending my days strolling the hallways, lingering in the showrooms and spending more time with *Madame Paul Duchesne-Fournet*.

More time with him.

A flash of movement distracted me from my swooning and I smiled when I saw Tobias walking toward me. I pushed to my feet and met him halfway, falling into a big hug.

He looked dashing in his dark blue suit and white shirt, his hair a little neater, though with no time to shave this morning he had a five o'clock shadow which scratched my face when he kissed me, sending shivers of arousal. I'd worn my blue laced dress with the scalloped hemline because I had chosen this very outfit when I first came to The Wilder, and for some reason I found it cathartic. This belief I'd carried with me a week ago, that I could change destiny, had since been realized. I believed with all my heart that it was.

"I knew I'd find you in here," he said softly.

"I'm in love with this one." I pointed to his Rothko. "I'm proud of you."

"Dad would have wanted it here. With the others. It would have made Mark happy too."

"The positioning is marvelous, look—" I pointed to other Rothko with its deep blue and green canvas and then to the one on the other wall with its softer orange tones "—they complement each other. I know that's how Rothko envisioned them all to be together in the same room like this."

Tobias rubbed his chin thoughtfully as though only now realizing it. "It's relaxing in here."

"So very safe."

"I suppose we need to talk about the elephant in the room," he said.

"I didn't think we had anything like that between us?"

He smiled. "We have to work out a way of getting your *St. Joan* out of hiding. Without raising suspicion."

"I'd like her to be here." I caressed my brow. "Abby's fascinated with her provenance."

"How did your call go with her this morning?"

"She was vague. I have a feeling she's keeping me at arm's length for now because of her suspicion I might have been in contact with...you know who. I told her I'm catching a flight out tonight. I'd see her back at Huntly Pierre."

"I'll have the jet ready."

I turned to face him. "Fancy coming out for dinner for some fish and chips in London?"

"You've gone for my soft spot. Can't say no to a trip to the UK now. Of course I'm coming with you. It will be good to check in at Wilder Tower in the Wharf. See what those crazy kids over there are up to." He looked at his father's painting again and he gave a nod of approval; a flash of readiness in his expression to prove he could let go.

I knew what this moment felt like from having left my Jacque Momar's *Madame Rose* at The Otillie, and later when Tobias had arranged for my Vermeer, da Vinci, and that grand Michelangelo to find a good home at the National Gallery in London.

"Want to come and see what could very well be your office?" He gave me a playful nudge.

"I'd love to."

We headed out and through the gallery.

"Later, I'm going to personally escort you around the Emperor Qin Shi Huang's exhibit. No peeking for an hour. I want to watch you walk around and see everything."

"I'd love that." Of course, I'd glimpsed inside there with Ned and Gabe but had spent so little time enjoying it because Tobias had whisked me away for some luscious frolicking.

"I've booked you into my schedule." He grinned as he said it in his gruff, sexy tone, melting my panties off.

"How far is my office going to be from yours?" I asked.

"The only room available was next door to mine."

"That's very convenient."

"That was my thought exactly."

"We can enjoy our coffee breaks together."

"That's what I thought too." He smiled to himself.

"No funny business, mister. I'll be at work."

He frowned. "You'll be too busy doing the accounting."

"I'm not doing accounting."

"Talk to your boss like that again and see what happens."

I elbowed him and he laughed as we walked past his office. Tobias gestured for me to go on ahead. I stepped into the remarkably large space. There was a shelf at the back, like the ones in Tobias's office next door. The desk was beautifully crafted in oak and the swivel chair looked comfortable.

"I thought you might like to decorate it," he said. "I know it's months away but knowing it's waiting for you…"

Upon the desk was a sleek desktop computer and a thin keyboard and mouse. Further along the desk sat a silver tray with a teapot on it and two mugs with a milk jar. Next to it was a box of Cadbury chocolate biscuits. It made me smile.

"That's from Maria and the staff," he said. "They wanted to make sure you say yes to my job offer."

"Now they've gone for my soft spot," I said.

He rounded the desk and lifted a painting that had been facing the wall. He laid it on the desk—it was Walter William Ouless's *St. Joan of Arc.*

There came a flash of joy at seeing her again and then an uneasiness settled deep in my belly and my smiled slipped away. "Tobias, we shouldn't have this here."

"Look closer."

Moving forward I clutched my belly nervously at the risk he was taking.

Wait.

Something was off with the brushstrokes; a questionable signature, those small cracks to the left of the frame where the painting had aged unnaturally exposed its garish attempt to persuade.

I stared at him, confused. "It's fake?"

"Abby is coming back, Zara. Sooner then we'd like to think. She'll have more questions."

"She'll ask to see it?" I realized.

"I imagine she would, yes."

"Who painted this?"

He gave a shrug.

"I don't want this anywhere near me."

"We'll find a storeroom for it."

"Abby didn't warn me she'd be turning up at UCLA. Her focus is on me now."

"We must be prepared."

Yes, and I'd underestimated the chance of her ever suspecting me in all this.

"You okay?" he said.

"Can you shut the door, please?"

"Sure."

I busied myself lifting the silver urn and pouring tea into two mugs and then added a splash of milk in both.

"It must be serious if we're having tea," he said.

I handed him a mug. "It kind of is."

"Oh?"

"Abby mentioned something when I saw her at UCLA."

He wrapped his hands around the mug and blew a cold stream of air onto the surface of his tea. "Go on."

"I understand why you didn't tell me. I just wished I'd not heard it from her."

His frown deepened and then his expression softened and he dropped his gaze to the floor.

"I'm so sorry, Tobias, for what the Burells did to your family. What they did to your plane?"

He stared at his drink as though searching for answers, and there came a fleeting glimpse of that vulnerable boy who'd endured so very much. And then it was gone.

"Toby?"

"I have some work to do," he said softly. "A conference call to prepare for with Asia."

"You'll be next door?" I was torn between wanting to wrap my arms around him and letting him have a moment to process what I knew.

Seeing him like this now seemed so cruel to have returned him to the memories of the worst days he'd ever endured in his life.

"Do you want to talk about it?" I said gently.

He placed his mug on the tray and made his way to the door. "I'll see you later."

"Do you want a biscuit to take with you?"

He paused in the doorway and looked back with confusion. "Sorry, what did you say?"

"Something to eat?"

He shook his head and left to head back down the hallway.

Closing my eyes to shut out the world, I questioned why I'd chosen now of all times to talk about this. This was the rawest, cruelest, memory for him and I'd been the one to ruin this moment. Caressing my brow, I felt a headache looming.

I pulled out my phone and scrolled through to find the best GIF I could and chose one with a Boston terrier puppy wearing glasses and turning his head slowly toward the camera with cute comedic timing. He was adorable. Let me take you out to lunch? I added in the text.

A blip on my screen revealed Tobias was replying and the suspense felt endless as I waited for his message to appear.

I should have gone after him.

He stopped typing as though he'd deleted the message, after all. Sadness settled in my heart and I regretted my decision. A GIF flashed on my phone and it was a baby panda asleep on his feet and then falling over. He had the cutest tummy. I brushed my thumb over the image Tobias had sent and sighed with relief he knew this gesture would comfort me. He just needed a little time, that's all, and I needed to give him space to process our conversation.

I tried to distract myself by sitting in the swivel chair that would be mine if I accepted Tobias's offer. It was super comfy and as I ran my hand over the desk I felt the smoothness of expensive oak. The flat screen computer looked expensive too. Every touch in this museum had been well thought out and decorated lovingly. There was no question this would be a great place to be part of.

It's no use; until Tobias was feeling better I was going to feel like crap. I let out a sigh of frustration. Even if things were getting easier for us, we had a long way to go before either of us completely trusted each other. Too much had happened for us to surrender so easily. He'd promised his extracurricular activity was over and his future was brighter than ever. All I needed to see was consistent proof of this.

A phone rang from somewhere down the hallway.

It amazed me The Wilder could be my permanent place of work and I marveled how quickly everything could change. I'd never imagined living in America until now. I loved England so much but there was beauty here too and the palm trees were exotic and I'd be able to enjoy the sunny climate and even swim every day. The sun made everything feel a little brighter.

Wilder, made everything brighter.

Although I loved being part of an investigative team, being director of a gallery and using my skills had a nice ring to it and I'd be a great fit. I'd be on the side of the art lovers wandering the rooms and admiring the beauty created by some of the greatest masters in history. Tobias had promised to take me all over Europe with him as a museum diplomat on business, and the thought of officially traveling to visit art galleries and explore different cultures sounded exhilarating.

Right now, I needed my art fix.

I rose from the chair and headed for the heart of the museum. It was time to pay another visit to Jean-Jacques Henner's 1879 *Madame Duchesne-Fournet*. She'd easily become one of my favorite paintings of the French Impressionist period and as I strolled down the multicolored glass ceilinged hallway toward her, I marveled at her reputation for having ignited a sensation because she was so very real.

Just like Tobias, and that was why this ceiling reminded me of him. He was every color from above, every complex prism of beautiful light, and instead of using his gift for greed he'd dedicated himself to people. Perhaps that was where his subconscious desire came from to see art made accessible to the world.

There were so many questions for him about this place and I couldn't wait to tour properly and chat about the choices he'd made. I was excited to go back into the terra-cotta exhibit that was thrilling to immerse in. I'd not imagined in my wildest dreams Tobias could have pulled off that exhibit under such secrecy.

It had been inspiring to see the joy it bought Gabe too. I was going to miss him but I'd be able to visit him and Ned as much as I liked when I came out here. I'd need a work permit and was sure Tobias would help me arrange one.

A shift in the air.

I felt a sense of dread when I saw them behind me and, forcing myself to remain calm, I paused briefly to shoot off a quick text to Tobias, telling him Abby was here. My hands trembled as I typed into my phone.

I made a concerted effort to remember to say as little as possible. I knew I'd have to face Abby at some point only why did it have to come so soon? This was my last day in LA and I'd wanted it to be drama free. Instead, it felt like a tidal wave was fast approaching. I breathed in a steadying breath and turned to face them—

Abby strolled toward me down the long hallway and beside her walked two men in smart suits. They wore their expressions with the formality of the FBI, their faces reflecting an intense scrutiny I wasn't ready for.

"Abby," I greeted her confidently.

"Zara Leighton," she said.

For their benefit, I assumed, trying not to swallow my dismay, I turned to throw a polite smile at the men and act casual. I hated not being able to see their eyes through their dark lenses. Abby's formality had screamed the truth of why she was here.

"I'm so glad I got to see you before I leave," I said. "My flight's at ten tonight. When are you heading back, Abby?"

"Soon," she said. "This is a great place. I'm not surprised you like it." Her expression changed to confliction.

It sent a pang of panic. "Are you going to introduce me to your friends?" I gave a pleasant wave.

"This is Special Agent Pearson, he's in charge over at the Wilshire Boulevard office." She gestured to the other man. "Agent Hale. They're both in the loop on all things Icon."

"Great to meet you," I said. "We're glad we got a break in Arizona. Thank you for all you're doing out there."

"We came to speak with Mr. Wilder?" said Agent Pearson.

"I'll see if he's free," I said. "He had an appointment. He'll come chat, though."

"That's not what his receptionist just told us," said Abby flatly. "Mr. Wilder went home for the day, apparently?"

I pretended to not be fazed by this. "Would you like me to get the fake painting of *St. Joan* for you?"

"Later," she said. "That would be great."

"Sorry you missed him. Why don't you visit the Chinese exhibit?" I feigned nonchalance. "It's quite something."

Abby stepped toward me. "Zara, it's best we get straight to the point."

It wasn't only the way she looked at me, it was also her tone, her troubled expression every time she held my gaze. Sympathy, that's what I saw now and it felt as though time slowed as my roiling thoughts settled on the facts and came to a devastating conclusion. Tobias wasn't here to face them, I was, and if he had left and not told me…

He had the technology to place the spotlight on someone other than himself, someone vulnerable who he'd outsmarted and outpaced at every turn. Had he used my obsession for him against me?

That footage Jade had captured of us on the roof of his penthouse of him handing me that gold plaque was evidence I'd received something in return. *But for what exactly?*

In a blur, I became aware of Maria Perez heading down the hallway toward us and she offered Abby and the men a welcoming nod as she made her way around them.

She approached me. "Ms. Leighton—" She handed me a Post-it note.

"Thank you." I felt too uncomfortable to unravel it in front of them and instead squeezed it into my palm.

"May we see that?" Abby pointed to the note.

"Why?" My fingers ached from the strain.

Abby waited for Maria to head back down the hallway. "Zara, we know."

"I'm sorry?" It was too late to not swallow nervously.

"It took us a while," she continued, "but we gathered the facts. It was right there. You were right there."

My mouth went dry. "How do you mean?"

"You were hired at Huntly Pierre right before we got the Icon account from Interpol. Your painting by Walter William Ouless turned up at Christie's and the next day it went missing right after you visited the auction house."

"The theft was during the night," I corrected. "If you're referring to *St. Joan.* Which hasn't been authenticated."

"Because it's conveniently lost."

"Abby, what is this?"

"And now you're in Los Angeles and there's been another theft. A Native American headdress and a sacred antique document." She raised her phone to show me a photo on the screen. "And here is Mr. Wilder snapped by the press wearing traditional Native American Indian attire yesterday by the paparazzi. Oh, look, that's you hanging out with him."

"It's a coincidence," I said. "Mr. Wilder wore that because he loves American history. It's one of his passions. He was at a Halloween parade. Everyone was dressed up."

A fact his attorney could use if needed and maybe that was why he'd worn it. A brilliant ruse on his part. He'd allowed for a dash of reasonable doubt and after all, what thief would parade in the costume he'd stolen? A crazy, wild one, I mused darkly.

And here I was defending him…

Throwing myself before them instead of him.

"We know you're in touch with Icon, Zara. We know who he is."

I shook my head as terror slithered up my spine. "What are you talking about?"

"We need you to come with us to the Wilshire office for questioning," she said. "I would say I'm sorry but—" She shrugged the rest.

"Abby, you know me."

"Don't make a scene." She tilted her head to make her point.

"You have your man, Elliot Burell," I snapped. "And while you're at it check out his son Eli. Focus on them."

"Mr. Elliot Burell's out on bail, Zara." She glanced over at the men and gave a look of resignation. "We've been asked to take a step back from the family for now."

"You mean their attorneys repeated what they did with Sarah Louise? How can you stand back and allow this?"

"Let's go and talk it over," said Pearson. "Let's not make a scene here."

I ignored him. "What about my paintings they found in Arizona at his home?"

"Tied up for now until we can process his provenance to them," he replied. "Looks like we're going to be offering Mr. Burell an apology."

"No." Tears stung my eyes.

"You know how these things go," said Abby. "The world isn't perfect."

"You're wrong. He stole them. You caught him red-handed with the artwork."

"You should never have gone to Arizona," she said. "That's where you screwed up. That's the third time you've turned up at a location of a heist. First Christie's, then Arizona and now West Hollywood during the Halloween parade. The house hit was just down the road from there. Was Wilder wearing the Native American Indian outfit your idea? Are you setting him up?"

"Abby, you've got it wrong."

"Are you trying to implicate Tobias Wilder?"

"Those thefts go way back." I sucked in a breath as I realized I shouldn't know that. Tobias had warned it was Intel contained by an inner circle at Interpol. The same people who were connected to the Vatican. An insidious link so deep those at its center were protected.

"You are looking in the wrong place," I reasoned.

Or perhaps, just perhaps, they were meant to be looking at me all along. Tobias knew my feelings for him would cloud my judgment and make betraying the man I loved impossible. "I'm innocent," I muttered to myself as the ground beneath me felt shaky and was threatening to open and suck me into hell.

"We'll let a jury decide, shall we?" Abby stared past me and she squinted down the hallway behind me as though trying to make out something she saw. "What is that?"

My mind fractured with the insanity of her accusation. *Tobias? Please no, don't betray me like this, not like this, leaving me stranded to face them.*

"Mrs. Perez," Abby shouted back down the hallway to her. "Mrs. Perez! You have a cat in here. You need to come see this." She turned to the men. "Shall we catch it?"

Turning, I stared at the small white kitten at the end of the hallway trying to remember where I'd seen that little pet before with its bright blue eyes and fluffy white fur, its tiny paws tottering along...it disappeared around the corner.

No way.

A flash of moment—

As a roaring lion tore around the same corner shaking his mane, his jagged teeth bared and angry eyes fixed on us as saliva dripped from his gaping mouth, his large body pounding toward us, big paws padding along marble floor with his muscles rippling across his powerful back as he neared fast.

Someone screamed—

The sound of footsteps running away. The sound of panic. Yelling.

Standing my ground and facing the inevitable, holding my breath and repeating my silent mantra, *It's a hologram, it's a hologram, it's a hologram*, as the large beast closed in and my stomach clenched in terror as he rushed me—moving through my body.

Trembling violently, I spun round to see the lion continuing down the hallway toward the foyer. The sprawling space now empty of people.

Unraveling the note, I recognized Tobias's handwriting.

Get to the roof.

I bolted forward down the hallway and rounded the corner fast and burst through the fire exit, taking two steps at a time, round and around with my heart crashing in my rib cage, my breathing ragged as the realization hit me—I was running from the FBI. Running from Abby.

Running from the life I'd known because surely going back to Huntly Pierre was lost to me now?

Stop running. You've done nothing wrong. Go back. You have nothing to hide.

In a blinding panic, I crashed through the roof door and ran toward the helicopter with its loud, whirling propellers and bent over to avoid the strike of air with my dress billowing, locks of hair in my eyes and my hands shielding my face from the heat of the engine that sucked my breath from me. Tobias was in the pilot seat of the Hermès. I scrambled in and he twisted to help me secure the seat belt.

He threw me a comforting look. "You okay?"

"No. We have to go back!"

He shook his head *no* and gave what was meant to serve as a reassuring smile as we lifted off, rising and rising and turning north and heading over the museum and away. We flew across a freeway and rose above the green-and-brown-tinged mountains. Clutching my arms to my chest to comfort myself, I felt each stab of each second that fell away, glancing over to Tobias who was focused on flying us away from the city.

This, this was a nightmare of my own making. I couldn't think straight and refused to believe this was happening. I was always the one who followed the rules. The one who carefully mulled over every plan, every undertaking, and yet now my life was spiraling out of control.

And Tobias was too calm, too serene, too distant.

When we landed, it was at an airport and as we walked away from the helicopter, Tobias greeted Marshall warmly. As they talked with each other, I realized another plan had been hatched and was being flawlessly implemented.

"You're good to go," said Marshall to him, glancing back at the jet fifty feet away.

"I'll call you later," said Tobias, and he grabbed my hand and led me toward the plane.

In a blur, we headed up the metal staircase and I knew this was his private jet, though instead of boarding happily to return to London, to my ordinary life, chaos was unleashed and there was too much uncertainty swirling around us. Surely leaving like this shone a spotlight of guilt upon us?

Or maybe, just maybe, this was the point and I was so caught up in this web of deceit I was still being pulled along farther into its dark web.

Tobias guided me to a cream leather seat and settled me in
and then headed off to chat with the pilot. There was a blanket resting on the seat beside mine and I pulled it over and
snuggled beneath it. Goodness knows what Abby thought of
me now after accusing me of being connected to Icon, and
what hurt most was her saying I'd set up Tobias.

Or had Tobias set me up?

I was surrounded by chrome and cream leather and I
wanted to turn back time and go back to a place where such
luxury could be enjoyed and my life was magical again. I
only had myself to blame. I'd set my mind on coming out
here and had inserted myself into this storyline. Right into
the drama of Icon.

Staring out my window, I saw that it was pouring now,
with heavy droplets soaking the tarmac and leaving large
shiny puddles upon it. I broke my gaze from the runway and
breathed in a panic-drenched breath.

I had to get off this plane.

I pushed myself up and hurried back down the aisle. There
was a jolt beneath my feet and as I peered out an oval window, I realized we were about to take off. Nearing the escape
door and gazing out at my freedom slipping away, my hand
rested upon the escape hatch handle.

"Zara." Tobias's voice came from behind me.

Slowly, I turned to face him.

"Come sit down. You need to put your seat belt on," he
said.

"I thought it never rained in LA?" I whispered.

"We have drinks on the way." He reached out and interlocked his fingers through mine and led me back to my seat.
He took the one next to mine.

"What have we got to celebrate?" I sucked in a nervous
breath. "What have we done?"

He rested a hand on my knee and gave a comforting smile. "Remember who I am."

Who he was; Icon.

"You promised me all that was over?" My throat burned with the truth.

"Yes, but now we need my resourcefulness more than ever."

The plane glided along the runway and it turned to face the long strip ahead.

"Seat belt, Zara," he said and turned to help me with mine and he clicked it into place.

He secured his own, and then crossed a long leg over another and peered out at the view from his window. "We needed rain."

I let out a nervous laugh because he was talking about the weather. No mention of the fact we were fugitives. That our lives were over.

A young, pretty steward appeared with a tray carrying two champagne glasses balanced on top and she offered me one. *No*, this wasn't a time to be drinking and yet I accepted it anyway, bringing the champagne flute to my lips and sipping the delicate bubbly; my hands trembled.

The pilot's voice announced takeoff was imminent.

Tobias took several sips of his drink. "We're getting your paintings back, Zara. While we're able to travel freely we can make that a reality."

There came the pull of gravity as my body was pressed into my seat as the plane sped along the runway, lifting off and rising higher and higher and then banking left, revealing the vast cityscape of houses, buildings, land and ocean spreading out below.

I stared at my delicate Tiffany watch that Tobias had bought me to look at the time. "How long before we land in London?" Though I still counted the hours myself.

"We're not going to London."

My gaze snapped to him. "Where are we going?"

"Somewhere safe."

"I've lost everything," I whispered to myself.

Tobias turned to face me. "Come here." He leaned sideways in his seat toward me and his lips met mine and he kissed me leisurely, drawing me to him again, forcing my surrender with his masterful affection, his hand gripping me against him possessively.

I broke away and stared out the oval window as the jet shuddered with turbulence. It continued to climb, entering a thick layer of storm clouds.

Dear God, what have I done?

★ ★ ★ ★ ★

What happens when Zara Leighton finds herself branded as a fugitive and hunted by her ex-investigative team from London? Be sure to watch what happens when Zara and Tobias escape to New York and risk their lives for one final heist that could very well tear them apart forever. Don't miss the dramatic conclusion of the ICON series, THE PRIZE, as love itself is the ultimate expression of art, coming only to HQN Books in December.

And now for a sneak peek, please turn the page.

1

I shouldn't be here.

My life felt unrecognizable. I was standing in a New York drawing room, and all its decadence seemed a mere extension of the grand wealth and endless secrets I'd been exposed to ever since meeting *him*.

Tobias William Wilder, the man who I'd unwittingly fallen for and the reason I was here. A man seemingly wiser than his thirty years, dangerously charismatic and a captivating inventor and CEO of the leading software company TechRule. He also owned the renowned Wilder Museum in Los Angeles. It felt as though fate itself had shot an arrow into my heart to strike my greatest weakness—my devotion to art.

Above me swept a dramatic ornate plaster ceiling and below my strappy Louboutin heels lay a brightly patterned Persian rug encompassing the entire room. The surrounding paintings from centuries past completed this grandeur within this Upper East Side mansion. The heat from the pine logs in the hearth spat orange sparks and brought a warmth that still couldn't lift the chill from my bones.

No, I wasn't meant to be here at all.

Nor should I have been draped in a precocious shimmering Dior gown to attend a prestigious social event.

I'd left behind my dream job at Britain's distinguished art investigation firm Huntly Pierre, as a forensic art specialist, and now my world swirled in turmoil. A disarray I couldn't see how to pull back from.

Yesterday, we'd both fled LA on Wilder's private jet and evaded the FBI. Just over a week ago, I'd made the journey stateside to persuade Tobias to give up his secretive pursuit of stealing artwork and apparently returning it to its rightful owners. Even if his intensions were heroic, they were daringly illegal. His misadventures had earned him the title of Icon and the reputation for impressively evading the authorities. That was until he'd met me because I was the one who'd caught him.

And he was the one who'd caught me.

Never had a love affair been so forbidden.

Just the thought of him sent a quake through me as evocative as I imagined opium would feel surging through my veins. Though Wilder was a deadlier addiction...

I could leave.

This was the lie I'd told myself so I wouldn't fall apart, but in reality I was a wanted woman. Exhaling an uncertain breath, the same one I'd held since leaving the West Coast, or so it felt, I steadied myself for another wave of panic and concentrated on the self-portrait by Peter Paul Rubens hanging dead ahead. Though now the artist's rendition mocked me with his hawkish brown eyes—even though I'd done nothing wrong, *not really*.

Wilder's deep, even tone rose from beyond the door in his usual masterful cadence as he carried on a conversation in French, and it made me wonder if he was on the phone with his uncle. Maybe he was telling him all that had happened to us. Maybe he was asking for help. Either way, Tobias sounded just as collected as that first evening I'd met him in The Otillie Gallery in London.

The day everything changed.

My body tightened with a yearning that was taboo now as I watched the door open and him enter. My feelings were as complex as the man who strolled toward me with that long, elegant stride exuding confidence, and his stark beauty left me breathless; his three-day stubble highlighted his dangerous edge that was perilously beguiling. He was dressed in a black tuxedo, and he always stunned with his short, ruffled golden blond hair and sharp chiseled features that were ridiculously gorgeous. A timeless masculine beauty inspiring the same wonder of a Greek sculpture by Praxiteles himself, a living, breathing Hermes. Wilder had the greenest eyes that sparkled with intelligence and kindness too, a mischievousness that was the catalyst for my falling for him.

His scrutiny fixed on me and sent shivers into my core. It hurt too deeply that I could never let him touch me again the way he once had. Our lovemaking threatened to woo me into compliance and addle my thoughts and right now I needed to remain razor-sharp. The tension between us was ever more palpable.

He came closer. "Let me go alone. It'll be safer."

"You need me for this to work." I broke his gaze; it was easier that way. "Besides, this is my life we're talking about." I refused to descend into powerlessness.

He stepped back into my line of sight. "I get that, Zara. This is my fault. All of it—"

"I put the spotlight on you—"

"That was your job. To investigate." He shrugged. "To find me."

"Still, I understand why you did what you believed was

right." Even if his deeds had been misguided. Though perhaps his grand ruse continued and my fate was yet to be realized; the thought of this possible betrayal caused ice to slither up my spine.

My legacy was within reach and owning my father's paintings was my birthright. I owed that at least to my father and his beloved memory.

And only Tobias could lead me back to them.

"We'll find them." He'd sensed my thoughts were on them again. "We'll put this right."

Was I naive to believe him?

"Zara, have you thought anymore about my suggestion?"

It was out of the question for me to surrender and let the blame fall on him. He'd been willing to throw himself onto his sword; he'd stated as much when he'd seen how torn up I was on the plane.

At least I'd gotten to a place where I could talk with him again. I wrapped my arms around myself. "I wish it was possible to let them go." Yet my agony was real when I thought of allowing my dad's art collection to fade into the past.

"Zara, this is more than us recovering them. This is getting justice for Burell destroying your home and inflicting pain on your father. On you. He believes he's won."

My gaze locked with his as I conveyed the silent message: *revenge for you too, Tobias, for Burell bringing down your plane and murdering your family.*

He answered with a nod. "I want my life back too."

My stare caught the portrait of Rubens again and his eerie focus. "Is it even possible?"

"We proceed toward the life we want. The future we deserve." His hand rested on the lower arch of my spine. "Do you remember the plan?"

His plan was insanity.

This evening's event had fed his obsession with danger.

"Give me the chance to prove I can solve this." His tone had a husky allure.

Maybe he was right, maybe he could. "More smoke and mirrors?"

"If necessary."

I ran my fingers over my blond wig.

"You make a stunning blonde." He reached up and ran a strand through his fingers. "Very convincing."

I marveled it had come to me wearing a disguise and joining forces with Icon.

I'd lost my way.

"Ready?" He gestured to the door.

We made our way out and through the grand foyer and Tobias helped me with my long black coat. He grabbed his masquerade mask off the foyer table and we stepped out into the crisp autumn air; the sting of a November night made its way into my lungs. I glanced left and then right down 69th Street, grateful it seemed quieter now.

We walked toward the blue Aston Martin parked out front and Tobias pressed his thumb to the passenger door to open it for me. I climbed in and sank into the luxury leather seat of his stylish Vanquish S. He rounded the car and got in beside me, starting the engine by using his thumb on the ignition pad. He steered the car away from the curb and into traffic.

"Whose house are we staying in?" I'd already asked him this but Wilder had avoided the question. "Tobias, who are you protecting?"

"It was my grandmother's." He didn't break his stare from the road. "The artwork will make its way to a new gallery I'm opening in The Bronx. Well, it was before all this."

"You didn't tell me you were opening a new gallery?"

His shrug showed that his guard was back up. He had the same wariness of me that I had of him.

"Your grandmother doesn't mind us staying there?"

"She's dead."

"I'm sorry."

"Me too—she'd have liked you very much." He threw me a smile.

I sensed there might be a chance to enter through that chink in Wilder's armor if I let him open up naturally without me prying.

He parked a little way down from 432 Park Avenue, and the impressive mirrored skyscraper that loomed was impossibly high. Peering up at its sheer height brought a wave of vertigo.

Tobias killed the engine. "It's certainly impressive."

Which was his way of saying we'd be taking the elevator whether I liked it or not.

We watched the decadently dressed guests arriving in their luxurious chauffeur-driven cars, then exiting and strolling elegantly toward the door. They were already masked and it infused an eeriness into the evening. The concierge greeted guests in the doorway and checked them in before they could proceed any further.

"You're in Scotland right now." Tobias unclipped his seat belt.

I unclipped mine and turned to face him. "That's where my phone signal is?"

"I placed you in Dalkeith Palace."

There was no surprise that my imaginary self was having more fun and was tucked safely away in the Highlands.

"It's bloody cold in Scotland," he said. "You went shopping for warmer clothes."

"You placed it on my credit card?"

"Yes. The FBI will track every email you send. Every purchase. Every call. Every move indicated by your phone's signal. They'll catch on soon but we only need a week."

Wilder's techno genius would keep the authorities busy for a while as they continued to hunt us. Our plane had taken off yesterday in LA and landed on a private airstrip off the East Coast with no record of us on the flight or arriving in New York. What must they think of me back at Huntly Pierre, I thought painfully and caressed my belly to ease the guilt for letting them down.

"I had to split us up." Tobias gave a thin smile. "I'm currently in Rome and enjoying an expresso at a little café called Giolette. They serve delicious pastries. I bought one."

The realization we were about to see Elliot Burell, patriarch of the infamous family and CEO of Burell Industries, sent a wave of terror cycling up my spine.

We had to pull this off. And then get the hell out of there. Alive, preferably.

"One step at a time, Zara." Tobias scrolled through his phone.

A quick glance down and I saw he was tracking a blip on his screen. "Is Burell here?"

He dipped his head and looked through the window. "He's in the penthouse."

Tobias pried the masquerade mask from out of my hands. "Turn around."

Wilder gently brought the mask to my face and I held it there as he secured the ribbon behind my head and then trailed his fingers through my blond bob to smooth it out. It made my scalp tingle.

I faced him again and reached out to press my hand against his chest, needing his affection. He caught my hand before it reached him and he gave it a comforting squeeze and nudged it away. That one gesture proved he'd come to terms with us being over. It shouldn't have come as a surprise—I mean, there'd been an underlying tension since I'd boarded his plane.

Wilder provided our fake names to the concierge, who stood beside a tuxedo-wearing security guard with an earpiece. The concierge threw Tobias a big smile when she found our names on her list, though had she known he'd hacked into her system a few hours ago to add them and they weren't even real, she wouldn't be smiling at all.

We were granted access and made a beeline for the elevators at the back.

Once inside the elevator the steel doors slid closed and we ascended fast. I tried to remember how to exhale. I hated small spaces. Lifts, mostly. And it was only an inconvenience to the person with me who equally hated taking the stairs. We didn't have the time to pander to my foibles now.

"Almost there," Tobias said with an edge that anchored me.

The doors opened to a cacophony of laughter and clinking wineglasses: a sea of beautiful people within a sprawling modern penthouse with pink marble floors and walls that reflected the same gaudy decor in Burell's Arizona estate. The potent presence of heavy gold trimming and the Louis XIV–style ivory couches and chairs and classical ceiling murals were all seemingly designed to suffocate his adversaries with opulence.

Tobias led me into the thrall of beautiful masked men and women who held themselves with the stature of the social elite. Their luxury perfumes and custom-made colognes drenched the air in a plume of extravagance. The ebullient mood was lifted further by the hypnotic music of a solo violinist, whose notes threatened to lull the unassuming.

After giving my hand a reassuring squeeze, Tobias gave me a firm glance to let me know he'd just seen Elliot Burell.

He was really here.

Drawing in a deep, steadying breath, my gaze followed Tobias's and fell upon our enemy, sending a jolt of terror into my core. Burell's sharp chestnut eyes peered through his black mask to survey his guests with a suspicious glare. He was taller than I imagined, and even with his face partially covered with his mask I could see the hard lines of a worn and yet handsome face. His black tuxedo fit him flawlessly and I was unnerved to see such an athletic-looking man of eighty.

This masquerade mask may have concealed my expression but my eyes failed to hide my disgust.

A waiter hurried over to Burell carrying a single tumbler on a tray and offered the amber-colored liquor to him. Burell accepted the glass without even acknowledging the man's presence.

"Will you be okay?" asked Tobias softly.

I gave a nod. There was no room for second-guessing.

We were inside the lion's den now.